COME WINTER

DOUGLAS C. JONES

COME WINTER

A Donald Hutter Book

HENRY HOLT and COMPANY / NEW YORK

Copyright © 1989 by Kemm, Incorporated
All rights reserved, including the right to reproduce
this book or portions thereof in any form.
Published by Henry Holt and Company, Inc.,
115 West 18th Street, New York, New York 10011.
Published in Canada by Fitzhenry & Whiteside Limited,
195 Allstate Parkway, Markham, Ontario L3R 4T8.

Library of Congress Cataloging-in-Publication Data
Jones, Douglas C.
Come winter / Douglas C. Jones. —1st ed.
p. cm.
ISBN 0-8050-0944-2
I. Title.
PS3560.O478C6   1989
813'.54—dc19   89-1760
CIP

Henry Holt books are available at special discounts
for bulk purchases for sales promotions, premiums,
fund-raising, or educational use. Special editions
or book excerpts can also be created to specification.

For details contact:

Special Sales Director
Henry Holt and Company, Inc.
115 West 18th Street
New York, New York 10011

First Edition

Designed by Katy Riegel
Printed in the United States of America
1 3 5 7 9 10 8 6 4 2

CONTENTS

AUTHOR'S NOTE

Come Winter is not about real people or real places. It is all fictional, except for an occasional president or general who doesn't matter anyway.

So it will be futile for anyone to see if they can find their great-aunt Maud or cousin Hershal in these pages.

However, it was designed to be the truth concerning person-alities and environs of its time, so even though Great-aunt Maud and Cousin Hershal might not be here, they would have recognized the folk and situations and dusty roads described.

Therefore, everything following is dedicated to all those Great-aunt Mauds and Cousin Hershals who didn't make it into the story. Because without them, there wouldn't have been any basis for the story in the first place.

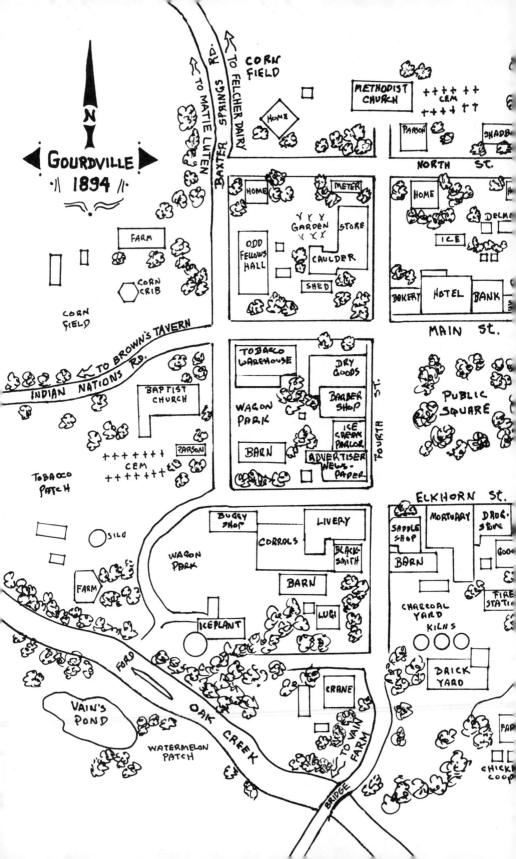

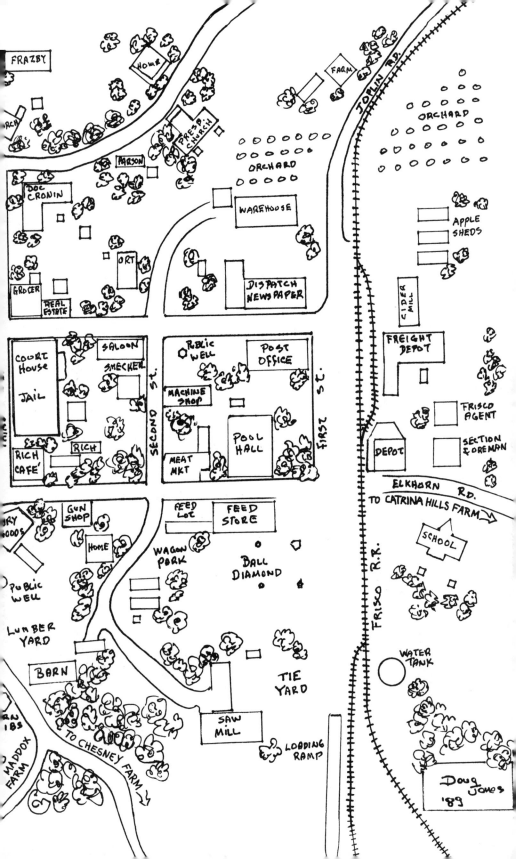

PROLOGUE

The House on the Knoll

Winter and Dylan Price came at the same time. It hadn't been planned that way. It just happened.

There was a wind along the railroad tracks blowing from the north, out of Missouri, when he stepped from an empty boxcar. Not jumped, but stepped, as though he were alighting from a coach on a passenger train.

This was no bum or hobo. Anyone who looked into the clear gray eyes could see that they never wavered with shame or humility. He carried himself erect, his head back, as a soldier might, and indeed he had been a soldier most of his life.

For those citizens of Gourdville who saw him that first day and all the days afterward, the question of his age confounded. He wasn't old, or young either, but somewhere in between. His face was long and hard, much exposed to the sun and other elements. And perhaps too many times in some canteen where there was beer and stronger beverages. His hair, what little there was of it, defied description. It was the kind of hair people argued about: its color, how much of it there was, what its texture was, what kind of brain it might cover in the dome of his Welsh head.

Dylan Price was not clothed for cold weather. From bottom to top there were lace-up brogans, the soles of which had not yet separated from the uppers; blue woolen trousers held in place by suspenders; a rather frayed gray cotton shirt; a duck jacket showing some signs of wear at the elbows; and a hat with a wide brim looking suspiciously like United States Army issue except that it was so stained and used that it really did not lend itself to any classification. In one hand he carried a canvas knapsack that appeared to be mostly empty.

Once off the freight train, Dylan Price surveyed the small northwest Arkansas hill town. What he saw was not reassuring. But at least, just a few steps from the tracks, was a sign on the front of a frame building that proclaimed its use:

TORTEN'S BILLIARD PARLOR.
COLD BEER. LADIES WELCOME.

In the latter years of his military service, Dylan Price had come into the habit of talking to himself, and now seeing the sign, he said aloud, "Ladies, is it? Very unlikely. But a cold beer on this cold day, likely as sin."

It was the usual late-nineteenth-century kind of beer palace. There were two domino tables along one wall, and farther back in the long room were three pool tables. Not for billiards, but with pockets. At one domino table a group of older, bearded men was playing a game, and at the pool tables groups of younger men were shooting Nine Ball or Rotation or Death on the Eight, with ten-cent bets on each contest and much shouting and swearing and stamping of pool cues against the floor, as is always a part of such games.

At the front of the place was a small bar, beer kegs underneath, and on top a glass case displaying cigars and cans of snuff and piles of plug tobacco and a jar with multicolored sour balls. On the wall behind the bar was a crudely printed sign: VOTE DEMOCRAT! Beneath it, and leaning on the bar, was a small man with small eyes and mouth and hands. His name was Glen Torten, and he owned and operated this place.

When Dylan Price walked in, everything stopped. The pool players stopped. The domino players stopped. Glen Torten stopped whatever mental gymnastics were required for him to read the newspaper spread on the counter before him. All eyes went to Dylan Price, eyes sharp and sensitive like the eyes of foxes in a wire cage when a hound walks past. Or maybe the other way around. The only sound was a cue ball already set rolling before Dylan Price entered, going its course along the green felt table under kerosene lamps, kissing other ivory balls with little clicks.

It was the kind of charged atmosphere that any old soldier understands, as when a trooper walks into the club of another regiment and everyone there is saying to himself and to his comrades, "What the hell is that bastard doing here?" So Dylan Price understood the feeling. But he did not yet know the reason for such hostility.

"From your sign," he said, "I supposed I might have a glass of beer."

Dylan Price placed his hands on the bar and looked only at Glen Torten, making a special effort not to allow his eyes to touch the gaze of all the immobile pool shooters or domino players, because he knew, also from his army experience, that such visual contact could be very dangerous, for no reason at all, and he with no weapon except his fists. Which, as he had proved on many occasions, were not inconsiderable. But at the same time, one must count odds.

Glen Torten drew the beer, which was mostly foam, and Dylan Price consumed it with one lifting and indicated another, which Torten drew. No one had moved. No one had made any sound. Every eye remained on Dylan Price.

Then Torten spoke. "That'll be a nickel apiece. Dime total."

Dylan Price tossed a dime onto the counter and it made the hard little ring of real silver on hardwood. Then he turned his head and looked at each man in the room, slowly, deliberately, finally deciding to dare them. He looked back to Glen Torten.

"Perhaps you can direct me," Dylan Price said. "I am looking for a man named Roman Hasford."

Torten's eyebrows lifted, and for the first time since Dylan Price had entered, the pool players moved. Just a shuffle of feet and quick glances between them, and one of the domino players coughed.

"Oh?" said Torten. "Don't many come in my place askin' fer him, huh, boys?"

There was a general murmur from the pool players and maybe a low laugh as well.

"Well now, you just go to the house," Torten said. "He'll likely be there."

"The house?" Price asked.

And there was another shuffling of feet from the pool players, and a low voice that said, "That Gawd damned house."

Glen Torten slowly took a toothpick from some hidden place

beneath the bar, looking at Dylan Price all the while, and began to clean his teeth. Finally, after an inordinate time of scratching at his molars, he spoke.

"Biggest Gawd damned king's mansion in this county," he said. "What's your business thereabouts?"

"It's my business," Dylan Price said, staring into Glen Torten's eyes. His voice was brittle, and Glen Torten abruptly realized that in the interest of peace and dignity, and insurance against having his entire pool hall wrecked in some bout of pool shooters with this new stranger, he should smile. Which he did.

"Why, sure, we can tell you where the house is at," Glen Torten said.

As if on cue, one of the older bearded men, a domino player, rose and came to the bar and stood beside Dylan Price and said, "I can show you where it's at."

"Thank you," said Dylan Price, and looked along the room at all the pool shooters, who were no longer shuffling their feet and no longer saying muted words and no longer laughing softly. And as he walked out, his back to all those still-fox eyes, Dylan Price felt a prickle go up his spine.

On the street, the wind whipping their hat brims, the old domino player said, "I'm John Vain. Used to have a farm out west of town, but it was foreclosed."

"A sad thing," said Dylan Price.

"The house, it's right along this here road." He pointed eastward. "Elkhorn Tavern Road. That's what it is, but nowadays a lot of folks call it the Folly Road."

"A curious name for a road."

"Because that's what a lot of folks call the house. They call it the Folly. The place you're lookin' for. The Folly."

"A curious name for a house."

"Well, it ain't what you'd call a regular house. It ain't like any house around here. It . . . it's got an *inside* privy. Water being pumped up from a well below. One of the best Gawd damned wells in the county. I ain't ever seen that thang, but everybody knows it's there. . . . Anyway, the house . . ." John Vain paused, the dust of the street blowing into his face, making his eyes squint, and Dylan Price was aware, not for the first time, that the squinting eyes were searching him, looking him up and down. "You can't miss it. It's the biggest Gawd damned thing on the road. Couple miles.

Kinda jumps right out like a . . ." He stopped again, uncertain.

"A big house?" Dylan Price asked.

"Yeah, big, like a . . . well, I don't know what it's like. Can't miss it. Not many gets ast to come out there. You been invited to come out there?"

"In a manner of speaking," said Dylan Price, and no more, for he knew that John Vain was acting as agent for all those inside Torten's Billiard Parlor, who would be waiting to ask, "Who the hell was that?" They would be disappointed because Dylan Price had learned in his years of military service when to listen and when to keep his mouth shut. And further, that small communities like this were closed and inbred worlds, resistant to outsiders. After all, he was Welsh, and who better to understand such things?

John Vain started to speak again, but Dylan Price touched a finger to his hat brim and turned, striding quickly away along the street.

He walked east out of the town with his long, steady soldier's stride. And as he walked he thought about the people at Torten's, not so much the instant hostility when a stranger appeared, which was not unusual, but its intensity when he mentioned Roman Hasford.

It was not so obvious, yet stronger on reflection, that not one of them had said Roman Hasford's name. They spoke of "the house" as though it were a symbol for Roman Hasford, as though maybe the house represented something to do with the hostility, as though to these men the house *was* Roman Hasford. And perhaps all of it sewn together with threads of unpleasant memory.

When he came in sight of it, with the lowering sun painting orange along its sides, Dylan Price could see why this place might come to signify a thing either magnificent or obscene. He paused in the wind, staring at it. He remembered John Vain's hesitation in talking about the house, as though trying to explain something he himself could hardly understand. Like trying to explain cholera.

As he stood in the road now, he could feel the force of it, although he knew only a few details of its construction, and nothing yet of how its image intruded on the life of this rural Arkansas hill country. Only sensing that the sight of it was pretension, an abomination to all those who lived in something less than luxury.

Hell, being Welsh, he could understand this kind of monument to wealth for those who had to grub day to day for a mouthful of good food. No, not good food. *Any* food. And not now, but in all the past when such conditions might have existed. As he looked at it, he was himself, being Welsh, repelled. Yet fascinated.

"Ah," said Dylan Price, speaking to the wind in harmony as only the Welsh can do, "it is fit to be a symbol of something or other."

And Dylan Price suspected that the letter inside his jacket would be the means of his discovery about that something-or-other.

And so, the house. Pine shiplap. Once snow white, but now beginning to scale a little, particularly on the north side. And on the upper-floor windows there were the faint signs of brown rust stain below the screens, where the rain had run down.

It had been built on a limestone foundation laid down as perfectly square as measurement could make it and with each quadrant aligned to face exactly one point of the compass.

There were two stories and a multitude of windows, which Dylan Price had already observed were rare, in this northwest Arkansas hill country. The roof was a pyramid, coming to a point at the center. Also something seldom found in this northwest Arkansas hill country. At its apex was a weather vane, black cast iron, with directional spokes permanently fixed, the north one pointing to Missouri just five miles away, the west one pointing to the Indian Territory ten miles away, the east one pointing to the valley of White River some twelve miles away, and the south one pointing to Fort Smith about seventy miles away. Above all this was a moving wind-directional arrow and, mounted on the shaft of the arrow, the silhouette of a running horse.

There was a wide first-floor veranda on all four sides. It was covered by a roof structured out from floor level of the second story, a roof supported with lathe-rounded oak pillars, eight on a side, as in the manner of Greek temples. The corner pillars, of course, counted on two sides, so in all there were twenty-eight pillars.

From any side, the house looked exactly as it did from any other, including seven steps leading up from the yard to the center of each quadrant of the porch. And across the porch from the top of these steps were double doors, the upper half of which had panels of stained-glass windows, in the manner of financially secure Methodist churches, Dylan Price thought.

He would soon learn that there were no such churches in the entire county. There were plenty of Methodist churches and even more Baptist and a few Presbyterian. But none of them boasted stained-glass windows. In fact, the nearest stained-glass window was in the Cassville, Missouri, Catholic church, and it didn't amount to much.

The resemblance to a Japanese pagoda or an Egyptian pyramid or a Greek temple to Apollo or whatever was enhanced because the whole business had been built on a knoll. So no matter from which direction it was approached, one had to look up. The yard sloped gently down in all directions: to the Elkhorn-to-Gourdville road on the south and west, where the gravel trace looped around the property, to the extensive horse barns on the north, and to the line of heavy oak, walnut, and hickory woods to the east.

All about the place, to enclose the road line and the hardwood grove border, were Kentucky-style whitewashed plank fences. There was a great tangle of these, forming corrals and pens and chutes around the horse barns and the hay sheds, the hired hands' bunkhouse and the chicken coop.

At the gate on the Elkhorn Tavern Road was a wooden sign with a burned inscription: CATRINA HILLS FARM.

But Dylan Price had heard the domino player call this place the Folly. Well, he thought, perhaps. And perhaps jealousy. Or something else.

Whatever, after that initial look, standing in the road in the November wind, Dylan Price went on and turned up through the gate and walked through the trees, crabapple and black locust, toward this house, knowing all along that he had been watched for a long time by the man who sat in a rocking chair on the west-side porch, a heavy lap robe covering his legs and feet.

Dylan Price came directly to the porch without any show of hesitation, although he could likely see that in the hard blue eyes of the older man in the rocking chair there was little warmth of welcome. They were hard and bright, even under the shadow of a narrow-brimmed fedora hat. Of course, he had no notion yet that under the shawl the older man held a .45-caliber, single-action pistol, cocked.

Dylan Price stopped directly before the older man's rocking chair and put one foot on the bottom step leading up to the porch.

They took a long look at each other. Not much blinking on either side. The older man saw that the younger one was clean-shaven and that only a sparse growth of sandy hair showed beneath the old campaign hat. The younger man saw that the older one had a heavy mustache, not very well trimmed, gray, and a mop of hair the same color splayed out around his ears beneath the fedora.

Somewhere in the growing gloom of the woodlands to the east, crows apparently had found an owl come out for the night's hunting. They made a dreadful racket. At least it was a dreadful racket where they were making it, but at the Big House where Dylan Price and the older man were taking each other's measure, it was only a distant argument, softened by a west wind blowing in from the Indian Nations.

Part of that measure taken by Dylan Price was that the older man was big, even bigger than he himself, but not nearly so hard-muscled. Although he might have been once, say twenty years ago.

"Seeing no name on your mailbox, and in fact no mailbox at all," Dylan Price said in measured cadence, as though he were reciting lines of poetry, "I can only assume from the kind instructions provided by the natives of your nearby village that you are Roman Hasford."

The older man's head made acknowledgment with only the slightest of nods. Whereupon Dylan Price produced a long, white envelope from some interior pocket and held it up.

"Here I have a letter," he said. "It is a letter of introduction from your nephew."

Roman Hasford bent forward in his rocking chair, frowning.

"My what?" he asked, and his voice was harsh from lack of recent use.

"Your nephew in Fort Smith. Eben Pay."

Roman Hasford sat for a number of heartbeats, still bent forward, without speaking. Then he leaned back in his rocking chair and for the first time looked away from the younger man, off toward the hardwood timber in the east, where the crows were still fussing. This time when he spoke, his voice was softer.

"Why, hell, I haven't heard anything from Eben Pay in years. And I haven't seen him since he was a babe." He looked back at Dylan Price. "Still in Fort Smith, you say?"

"Indeed he is. It was from there I came, riding direct to your local village in a boxcar with two older gentlemen of the road."

"What's your name?"

"Dylan ap Rhys ap Llewellyn. But I have not been known by it for a long time. Dylan Price will do."

"Dylan Price? You a Presbyterian?"

"No."

"Then what religious persuasion?"

"Not much for any. It is my understanding that almost thirty-five years ago, give or take a few, I was baptized in a reform Methodist chapel."

"Well, the last time I went into a church, it was a Methodist one. I can't remember when that was. You vote Democrat or Republican?"

"I have never in my life cast a ballot."

"Have you got a lot of money in your pocket?"

"Only the meager leavings of my mustering-out pay. Barely enough, I would judge, to purchase two or three chickens."

"Well, I don't sell chickens. Horses, I sell those, but not chickens. You like to have some money in your pocket?"

"It is one of my vices to covet the man who has enough coin to feed his belly and keep clothes on his back."

"Well, the clothes you got on your back now ain't gonna do you much good around here in a couple weeks or so because it's gonna get cold as a witch. Where you from?"

They were still staring square into each other's eyes, measuring. Dylan Price still held the white envelope at shoulder level. And the older man still held the pistol out of sight under his shawl.

"From Wales, at the first, but many other places now in between."

"I knew you wasn't from around here anyplace, the way you talk. What's in that letter?"

"It's a personal message."

"Well then, open it and read it. My specs are in the house."

Dylan Price paused a moment and a smile touched the corners of his wide mouth. He dropped the knapsack and ripped open the envelope with long fingers, and the older man could see they were very hard fingers. Dylan Price drew from the envelope a long sheet of white paper and unfolded it.

"Here is the letter," he said.

"Read it."

"Fort Smith, Arkansas, November 17, 1898. Dear Uncle Roman: This is to introduce a Mr. Dylan Price with whom I served during the recent war in Cuba. I believe him to be honest and trustworthy. He is seeking employment and expressed an interest in raising horses. I would appreciate any consideration you might give him.

I am, respectfully, your nephew. Eben Pay. Assistant United States Attorney, Western District of Arkansas."

When he looked up, Dylan Price could see the older man bent forward.

"Is that all?" the older man asked.

"Yes sir, it is."

After a moment, Roman Hasford sighed and sat back in the rocker, looking now again toward the darkening line of hardwood timber to the east, where the crows had finally stopped their chiding. Then he looked back toward the west, where the dying sun was marking a deep red background to the black lace of leafless trees on the lift of ground beyond the road.

"Why, hell," Roman Hasford said, "you'd think a man's nephew might have more to say than that."

Dylan Price could hear the disappointment behind the words, more profound than the words themselves, and he suspected that it was disappointment not only at the brevity of the letter but at other things as well. As though maybe disappointments had accumulated over the years of Roman Hasford and each new one was nothing less or more than an addition to an already crowded ledger.

Dylan Price replaced the letter in the envelope, allowing Roman Hasford to finish his struggle with frustration. It didn't take but a moment, and Dylan Price suspected that Roman Hasford had long practice in struggling with frustrations.

"That's a damned impressive title he's got, wouldn't you say?" asked the older man.

"I would indeed."

"I never knew exactly what it was he did down there in Fort Smith. I haven't seen him in a long time. Well, I haven't seen him since he was a babe. His mother died, you know. In St. Louis. My sister, you see?"

"Yes."

"Well, do you know anything about raising horses?"

"No."

"I figured you might have been in the cavalry. I had a short stretch in the cavalry. Chasing Cheyennes in Kansas or thereabouts. A long time ago."

"No, I have been infantry all my days."

"You on a pension?"

"No."

"You said army all your days."

"I served much of that time in the British army. Wearing the red coat for good Queen Vic."

"Aw. I know about her, of course. You like to read?"

"Only where necessary."

"Lot of books in there." He waved a hand over his back, indicating the house. "Books all over the place. I like to read. Takes up the time. Well, then, my nephew said you're honest and trustworthy. Is that true?"

"Where necessary."

"You drink hard spirits?"

"A dram has passed my lips on occasion." Again the fleeting smile passed across the younger man's mouth.

"Well, then, we'll pass a dram now, if you please." He turned his head back and spoke a name, not very loudly, as though he knew the person he called was standing just inside the door, waiting: "Orvile!"

At once, one of the double doors with the stained-glass panels opened, the screen door as well, and there appeared a large black man, slightly stooped, with hair whiter than Roman Hasford's but with arms inside the sleeves of his cotton shirt that bulged the cloth with muscle. He was a milk-chocolate-colored man, broad-featured and with great white teeth.

"Yeah, Mr. Roman."

"Bring two tin cups from the kitchen," said Roman Hasford, and as the black man disappeared back into the dark house, allowing the screen door to slam shut, the older man looked down at the younger one and smiled for the first time. "When I sit on my porch," he said, "I most generally just drink from the jug. But company deserves cups. Have a seat."

He reached under the shawl where it draped down around his feet on the porch floor and withdrew a half-gallon crock jug and said, "Sour mash. I know the man who makes it. He's got a clean still and a good farm south of here. I hold a mortgage on the place."

The black man reappeared with two tin cups, took the jug from Roman Hasford, poured each cup about half full, all the while glaring with bloodshot eyes at Dylan Price.

"Orvile," Roman Hasford said, "see that there's cover on the bed in the east bedroom upstairs. Mr. Price will be staying in tonight."

"Covers is always on the beds, Mr. Roman."

"And set out another plate for supper."

"Mr. Roman, you tol' me you dint want nothin' to eat tonight, so they ain't no supper except that beef stew we had last night and some cold cornbread and some buttermilk."

"That's ample, ample."

"You want me to dust off the big table in the dining room and lay out the good plate and light candles?" There was the cutting edge of sarcasm in Orvile's voice, but Roman Hasford chose to ignore it.

"No, Orvile, we'll just sup with you in the kitchen."

"Well, I can open a jar of them cucumber pickles I put up last summer," the black man said, contrite now.

"That'll be just fine. And build a fire in the stove in that east bedroom upstairs. It's going to get a little nippy tonight."

"Mr. Roman, we gotta get a couple ricks of wood out here," Orvile said. "I been tellin' you we ain't got enough wood to last November, much less all winter, and I'm too old to go choppin' around in the timber for firewood, and that dumb Colby Hert down at the horse barn, he'd cut off his foot with the ax if he tried to do it, so we gotta buy some wood in town or someplace."

"I'll manage it tomorrow, Orvile, I'll manage it tomorrow."

"Well, I just been tellin' you is all." Again somewhat petulant. Then he was gone back into the house, the screen door slamming again.

By now Dylan Price had seated himself on the top step just beneath the level of the porch floor, where he had deposited his knapsack, and he and Roman Hasford took sips from the tin cups.

"Aw," said Dylan Price. "It does warm the belly indeed."

"The first sip is always the hottest," said Roman Hasford. Then, smacking his lips and looking into his cup, he continued, "I am going to hire you, on the strength of my nephew's recommendation. If you want to know horses, that old colored man can teach you. He knows more about horses than anyone I have ever known. Except for a friend who was murdered some years ago. And maybe he will even teach you how to be a blacksmith, which he was when I found him in Kansas.

"I have a young man working in the horse barns who has trouble learning anything. He is there mostly to shovel out the shit. I have only a few horses left, from better times. But I am going to hire you.

"Now, tonight you are a guest in my house. Starting tomorrow you will be an employee. We will make a place for you in the bunkhouse down by the horse barns, and we will go into town and purchase suitable winter work clothes for you, the cost of which will be deducted from your pay. We'll talk about pay later. But these clothes will be cheap because we will get them from the best mercantile store in town and I own a mortgage on it."

"I am much beholden," Dylan Price said, lifting the tin cup to his lips once more, his eyes steady on the older man's face. "And I assume that by your words you also imply that you no longer have to hold that pistol under your shawl to protect yourself from me."

Roman Hasford's eyes widened and suddenly he laughed. He pulled the pistol from beneath the shawl. "Do you know what it is?"

"It appears to be a Colt single-action, I would say a .45 caliber."

"Correct. One never knows who might come to one's door. The Indian Territory being close by and all."

"That's true. And one other thing, Mr. Hasford. I much appreciate being a guest in your house. And I much appreciate your offering me employment. But let me advise that no man has ever held a mortgage on me. Nor will you."

Each took a sip from his cup. Their eyes locked. Each man had seen a great many things and a great many people, and each seemed satisfied with what he saw now.

"I rather expected that I would not," said Roman Hasford.

Old soldier that he was, Dylan Price appreciated the sudden bonding between men, even in the space of a single breath, because some fire in one struck the metal in the other, inexplicably. So in this moment, sealed perhaps by the signature of the nephew on the letter, sipping sour-mash whiskey on the porch of "the house," Dylan Price felt a camaraderie he had known with other disparate men, and now with this master of Catrina Hills Farm. And was convinced that Roman Hasford felt the same.

The spell was broken by Orvile's shout from inside the house.

"This here stew's ready to eat!"

They rose, Dylan Price with his knapsack and Roman Hasford with the pistol in one hand, the jug in the other.

The meal at the great round oak table in the kitchen, which had a cast-iron cookstove huffing in one corner and cutting tables and a butcher's block and utensils hanging from hooks along two walls, was not a particularly convivial repast. It was mostly a matter of each of the three men around the table spooning the food into their mouths as fast as they could, as though afraid some bugle would blow them to other tasks, although the only one of them who knew about bugles was Dylan Price.

For whatever reason, he ate with studied intensity, soaking up the last of the juice with hunks of cornbread while Roman Hasford ate with a salad fork, taking a sip now and again from the tin cup beside his bowl, which he resupplied as needed from the jug sitting on the table next to the pistol. Which had now been effectively disarmed insofar as any threat was concerned, although of course it was still loaded. All six chambers in the cylinder.

The black man ate with a large wooden spoon, watching the new man throughout, his eyes showing bloodshot in the light from the three lamps hanging in a bracket above the table. Dylan Price knew the feeling of being closely scrutinized. It had happened to him many times before, when he had joined new battalions and all the old, established men searched for any threat to their own standing with the commanding officer.

"I had directions here in an establishment called Torten's," said Dylan Price between sups of stew.

Orvile Tucker grunted. More a growl than a grunt, Dylan Price decided.

"White trash," Orvile said.

"Old Glen's no admirer of ours," said Roman Hasford.

"An old bearded gentleman who was playing a game with dominoes was good enough to walk out into the cold and point me in the proper direction," Dylan Price said. "I can't say that I recognized the game."

"Probably playing Moon. A kind of card game, only with dominoes," Roman Hasford said. "Likely it was old man Vain."

"Yes, that's the man."

"White trash," Orvile muttered.

"Well, the Vains, they don't admire us much, either."

There was no further conversation until Dylan Price, his meal completed, said, "Now I can sleep, with a belly well filled. And good stew."

Roman Hasford was still picking at his food, more interested, it seemed, in the cup of sour mash, his fedora still pulled down over his hair, his eyes directed into the bowl of stew as though trying to determine its contents. "Top of the stairs, first door to the right," he said, without looking up. "Orvile, give him a lamp to carry up to his bedroom."

Dylan Price went up, and found the privy John Vain had told him about. There was an oak-seat pot that had water rushing through it on the pull of a chain, the water coming from a brass tank under the peak of the pyramid roof, the water being pumped up from a well below. Vain's "best Gawd damned well in the county." This house was as well advanced in the science of indoor privies, Dylan Price reflected, as he had seen anywhere, in London or New York or Florida.

As he moved along the hall to the east bedroom, he heard them speak in the kitchen below.

"Who is that man?" Orvile Tucker asked. "He look like he ought to be in jail. You see that dove tattoo on his arm?"

"Orvile," Dylan Price heard Roman Hasford say, "he is a friend of family. Now clean up the kitchen."

Dylan Price lay under his feather tick that first night in the house, listening to the rising November wind under the eaves, hearing the oak beams creak and whisper as they cooled and contracted. He thought of what he had seen and heard, and of what he'd expected to see and hear.

But most of all, he thought of what he'd found in this room. A dressing table with a vanity set of expensive combs and brushes and hand mirrors inlaid with silver. And a porcelain figurine, five inches tall, of a girl in a flowered bonnet, a shepherd's staff held beside her, and a sleeping lamb at her feet.

Dylan Price had taken the figurine in his hand, noting the fine sculpture, the subtle tints of color on the face of the little shepherd girl, the pink cheeks and dark, wide eyes. He thought it strange that such things would be here, objects so feminine he could almost hear a lady's sigh as he held the little figurine in his rough soldier's fingers. Objects so delicate they seemed incongruous in a house so starkly masculine.

After he'd blown out the lamp, he heard Roman Hasford mount

the stairs slowly, then heard a door close. Already he had his mental image of this master of the house. Gruff, cynical, a jug of whiskey close to hand, and holding a pistol under his lap robe even while sitting on his own porch.

Dylan Price wondered why, with such a man and in such a house, there would be a silver-inlaid vanity set and a German figurine that seemed to hold the odor of sweet talcum powder, even though he had the sense that these objects were long unused, unseen, abandoned. Like a flower dropped long ago and forgotten in the passage of other events.

PART ONE

COMING HOME

1

Wolf Cove Mill, on Little Sugar Creek, was pretty much the same as it had been on that terrible day in 1862 when the original proprietor was hanged by partisans. There was the mill and the race and the wheel and the ragged line of rocks across the stream to form a millpond. And the road coming in from the main valley. A road that stopped at the mill and went no farther. Facing the high mill structure across that dusty strip was a matchbox house, and behind that some goat sheds, and behind those, up the slope where sassafras trees grew, the lines of box beehives.

But over the past eight years, this place had become much more efficient than it ever was under the old owner, who was drunk some of the time and off wandering around in the woods at other times. There was whitewash on all the buildings, and the weeds were kept hacked down around the hives, and in summer an old washtub at the door to the matchbox house was filled with moss roses, which, during sunlight hours, provided a splash of brilliant relief—red, orange, yellow, and white—to the green and limestone gray predominant in this small valley.

There were still blue jays and red-headed woodpeckers in the tall sycamores along the small stream, and wrens in the eaves of the mill, and cardinals nesting in the wild cherry trees just beyond where the road stopped, in season, and always crows that flew overhead on their way to do whatever crows do in more densely wooded areas.

There was always the gentle whisper of water in Little Sugar Creek across the rocks of its bed, a whisper made in this valley before there had been any human ear to hear it. Before the Cherokees, before the Osages, before some nameless folk even before that. An eternal sound, beginning before time and going on forever.

In summer, after the corn was ripe and dried, and then the late wheat and barley, there was usually a wagon or two in the widened space of road next to the door of the mill. Two mules, heads down, or maybe only one mule. While inside the grain was being ground on the great wheel, then carried to the wagon in burlap bags by the man, or sometimes the woman. They mounted their wagon seat and wheeled their lazy team about, heading for Wire Road in the main valley.

And usually, in addition to those burlap bags of meal or flour, under the wagon seats there was a small crock jar filled with rich honeycomb. And even, incredibly, a covered can of goat milk. Incredible because goat milk was not the most popular thing to set on the supper table in this northwest Arkansas county.

There was something else, though the residents of the county said, You've got to get there at the right time. If you got there at the right time, in addition to the meal or flour and the honey and the goat's milk, there was the red meat, carried off triumphantly wrapped in cheesecloth or some reasonable facsimile.

The right time was always a couple of days after one of the goats in the herd had become too old to do much of anything, whereupon he or she was killed and cooked. This proprietor of Wolf Cove Mill cooked his goat in great chunks over a bed of hickory coals, then simmered it in large cake pans in the oven of his stove in the matchbox house. He simmered it in a gravy composed of tomatoes, onions, vinegar, brown sugar, salt, red and black pepper, and God only knew what else. After this operation, when a knife finally touched the meat, the blade went through as though slicing warm lard. When a bite of this came to lip, the glands behind the tongue leaped out to embrace it. Sometimes the eyes watered. Sometimes the roof of the mouth had a distinct stinging sensation. But always, always, one bite demanded the next.

Everybody said you could eat it on Tuesday and still taste it the following Sunday.

This proprietor of Wolf Cove Mill had a special talent for certain things, no doubt about that. Maybe there was a pinch of voodoo. Maybe a dash of African recall so old in his blood that he could remember it only with the hands that performed the miracles.

Or maybe it was just something he learned from having had the time to experiment, for three years after the Battle of Pea Ridge, when things along Wire Road came to a standstill, cloistered there at Wolf Cove with nothing better to do than figure out how to make an old goat edible or how to discourage domestic bees from going out to swarm in the woods, keeping them in those box hives where the honey was so easy to harvest.

Whatever the talent was, the Old Settlers knew and accepted it. He had been a part of their lives for a long time, a known quantity and respected for what he could do.

Many of the newcomers after the war did business with him because he ran the best mill in the county, but they didn't accept him. To many of these, he was "that Roman Hasford nigger at the mill." And then just "that Hasford nigger."

A lot of these new folk had come from the north, Missouri and beyond. But there was a legacy among them of distrusting people of color because from the start of the slave question they had been worried about being set upon by a bunch of freed black men who would take their jobs, their farms, their towns. And the few of them who had fought for the Union had fought for exactly that and no more—for restoration of Union, and not for freeing any bunch of wild Africans to come and take the bread right out of their mouths.

And although he could not read or write, although he knew nothing of politics, although he was what many of his day would have regarded as a primitive savage, his mind was capable of putting two and two together, even though he could not write it, and his ears were large and receptive. So he knew many things that the white men of the valley had no idea that he knew.

His name was Lark Crozier. He had taken the last name from the former proprietor of Wolf Cove Mill, the one the partisans had hanged, because the old man had befriended him and because he couldn't think of anything better. He was tall, and bony and ebony black, and in 1870 he was not even vaguely aware of the Thirteenth Amendment to the Constitution, which had freed him, because nobody had ever told him. And besides, he had considered himself free after the battle around Elkhorn Tavern and even more after the tavern was burned, the tavern having been the site of his bondage for as long as he could remember.

So he was Lark of Wolf Cove Mill, and more than that, he was Lark Crozier, citizen and property owner, right after Roman Hasford returned home to the county and made the necessary surveys and claims and dyed-in-the-wool real legal documents with the circuit clerk's office in Gourdville. Of course, Roman Hasford himself didn't make the surveys or any legal claims. His lawyer did, the best lawyer in the county at the time. At first, reluctant to accord property rights to what he called a "field-hand nigger," the lawyer was informed by Roman Hasford that if he didn't do it, not only would an attorney be brought in from St. Louis to handle the paperwork, but also he, the county man, whose name was Hershel Bactrum, might wake up one morning with both his legs broken.

That was the first indication to the Old Settlers, after Roman Hasford came home, that he could be pretty hard in getting what he wanted. They thought it was all right. After all, the things he'd endured with his mother during the war would make any man a little hard. He deserved everything he could get, they said.

But to many of the new people, it left a very sour knot in the stomach, this Hasford making clear and legal a piece of prime property for a black man. So after that, when Lark went into Gourdville, there were always a few who said to him, "Hey, nigger, don't stay here after dark." Or, "Well, lookee here, we got that Hasford nigger lover's boy comin' in to take over the whole town."

Lark knew. Without any details, he knew. Hasfords had been heroes in this county, Martin going off to fight with Lee's army—although Lark didn't really know it was Lee's army, just *an* army—and Ora staying home to hold it all together when the soldiers and then the partisans came. But, hell, this new bunch didn't care about that. This new bunch, Lark knew, reckoned Martin was crazy and were downright hostile to Ora, because if only she'd left the county when danger came, like everybody with any sense would have and did, then that Hasford farm would be lying fallow and unoccupied and ready for anybody to take, like other deserted farms. But no, Ora Hasford had been bullheaded about the whole thing and had stayed through the war and the partisans and everything else, and now her damned son was back with a lot of money and seemed to support on every hand, along with that man of his, Elmer Scaggs, the notion that Ora Hasford was as good as any man—which everybody knew wasn't true, according to Genesis.

Oh yes, Lark knew all this—perhaps in hazy terms, but he knew. And it served only to solidify his loyalty. He made a point of remarking to other customers at the mill that Ora Hasford got the

best cuts of that baked goat and the jars of clearest honey, and
that he ground her grain without taking his usual 10 percent payment of the resulting flour.

Which, of course, the Old Settlers understood, patting Lark and
saying, "It's good." But the new people didn't understand it and
said, "Who the hell them Hasfords think they are?"

They never said any such thing to Ora Hasford or to Roman,
face to face, because of the possible consequences. But they said it
increasingly to one another.

The thing between Lark and the Hasfords went back a long
spell. He'd always been a friend to Roman, when Roman was just
a tad. Ora would come to Elkhorn Tavern to visit Lark's mistress.
They'd sit in the kitchen with dishpans in their laps, breaking beans,
what they called string beans, but a lot of Yankees called green
beans. And they'd gossip, as women breaking beans have always
done.

And outside, sitting back against one of the outbuildings, would
be Lark and Roman. And Lark would tell Roman what the blackbirds said when they flew above the hawk and tried to peck his
head. Or about the tricks a mama cat used to hide her kittens from
the tomcat so he wouldn't find them and kill them. And he'd tell
Roman about how the spirits of the dead buried in the Leetown
graveyard would come up out of their holes on moonless nights and
sit on the limestone outcrops along Pea Ridge and sigh and wail
and moan.

As time passed, Lark kept his senses tuned to the Hasfords:
Martin, head of the family, going off to fight in the war for one
army or the other, Lark wasn't sure which, and didn't care; Ora
holding that farm together through the war until Martin came home;
Calpurnia, the daughter, marrying that Yankee soldier who lost a
hand in the battle around Elkhorn Tavern; then, after Martin came
home, Roman leaving. Gone to make his fortune in Kansas, Lark
would tell his goats. He had no notion where Kansas was or even
what it was, but he knew the word because he'd heard Ora Hasford
say it. Gone to make his fortune in Kansas. The goats probably
understood as much about it as Lark did.

He continued to visit the Hasford place as he had during the
war. Not inside the house, of course, but just out back, he and Ora
Hasford sitting on the edge of the porch, barefooted in summer,
their feet in the dust, black and white.

Martin never came out to join them.

Mr. Martin, he all right, Lark would tell his goats. But since he come back from that war, he got a sundown look in his eye and a padlock on his mouth.

Then Roman came back, just for a short spell, and brought that little black-eyed girl and left her with his mama. That girl, she was no bigger than a chicken mite, Lark told the goats. Pretty as violets. Sweet as sugar syrup. Martin Hasford acted like he did before he went off to the war, Ora sang in her kitchen, and everybody talked about Roman having gotten rich in Kansas and soon coming home for good, to marry that little black-eyed girl.

Happy times, Lark said to the goats.

Then the screech owl he knew, the one that lived in the high beams inside the mill, died. Lark found him one morning when there were thunderheads coming up from the Indian Nations, lying like a little fluff of feathers with two great, bulging eyes, in the meal dust on the mill floor beside the great wheel.

It started turning sour then, after the owl died. Lark didn't mention it to any of the white people because he knew they wouldn't believe the owl had anything to do with what was happening. But he knew.

Martin Hasford took more and more to his Bible and let his fields go to weed. Each time Lark went to the back porch of the Hasford house with a jug of honey, the little black-eyed girl would be there, looking at him, pretty as ever, fresh-clean as ever, with Ora standing before her. But when Lark looked into Ora Hasford's eyes, there was that muddy trouble, and when he went away, thinking about the little girl, a cold chill went up his back. So he'd go back to his goats and his hives in a hurry, and try to forget what he felt now in the Hasford backyard.

Then there was a new screech owl, a young one, to take up the place in the high beams of the mill where the old one had marked out his spot. He didn't sound the same, late at night, as Lark lay in his bunk in the whitewashed shack, listening. He didn't sing with the wind. He didn't sound like he cared if he caught a mouse or not. Leastwise, that's what Lark told the goats. He didn't care a good God damn, that new screech owl.

So Lark knew something was wrong.

Then Roman came home for good, with this man Elmer Scaggs. Roman wasn't a boy now, he was a full-grown man. And everybody in the valley said he was rich as hell. Lark thought this was good, because when he saw Ora Hasford look at her son, there was a great light on her face. But then when she looked at the little black-eyed girl, it was gone. And when she looked at her husband it was gone too, except for those times when this man named Elmer Scaggs was there, talking to Martin and making jokes and being gentle as only a large, ugly, mean man can be gentle.

Sure, Lark told his goats, Roman Hasford made his fortune in Kansas. He'd heard all about it. Made his fortune selling livestock to the army when they were going out to fight the red Indians, starting a big packing house to cure hams and bacon, partners with railroad people, which Lark wasn't sure about because he didn't know what a railroad was, never having seen one. But he understood horse breeding, and Roman Hasford had done that, too, and had brought home a string of horses the like of which nobody in this county had ever seen.

Sure, Lark told the goats, Roman Hasford was back, wearing good clothes, too, and shiny shoes.

Then Roman went into Gourdville and sent off letters, and then all kinds of things started to happen. That was tougher for Lark to figure out. He said to his goats that he'd just as soon Roman Hasford would settle down for a little farming instead of all this other stuff, and the goats apparently agreed, looking at Lark with their great black-agate eyes.

But Roman didn't just settle down. He bought that old limestone building on the north side of the town square, and men went to work there with lumber and brick and mortar and glass to make a bank out of it, some said the second bank in the whole state of Arkansas, the first being down in Fayetteville, established only the year before. And the word went out that a man could borrow money in that new bank in this money-starved county. With appropriate interest.

Then two men came down from St. Louis, wearing good woolen suits and derby hats. They brought their families, and houses were waiting for them, houses that Roman Hasford had bought with cash. The men were there to run the bank and see about all that interest. And mortgages. And all the kinds of things banks do.

Lord God Almighty, Lark said. And the goats looked at him.

But the bank was only half of it. The other half was the horse farm. Roman bought the old McBrighten place just off the western edge of Pea Ridge, and most of the men in the county who weren't working on the bank in town started working there, razing old structures, putting up new ones. Lumber and shingles and glass and screen and nails and paint were coming down Wire Road from Missouri on wagons, turning into the Elkhorn-to-Gourdville road and then onto the McBrighten place. Nobody had seen such a string of wagons on that road since 1863, when the Yankee army was supplying its troops to the south with all the things armies supply their troops with.

By now it wasn't called the McBrighten place anymore. It was called Catrina Hills Farm. Because that was the name of the little black-eyed girl. Catrina. Living in the loft of Ora Hasford's house. Waiting.

Goats, Lark said, bad luck comin' quicker'n Jack Robinson. And not a single goat disagreed.

Elmer Scaggs, the man Roman had brought from Kansas along with the money and the horses, was as big a man as Lark had ever seen. He was a kind of boss over the men working on the Big House at Catrina Hills Farm.

This Elmer Scaggs was a special kind of friend to Roman Hasford because he'd been in Kansas with Roman and helped with that packing house and all the rest. And maybe now, Lark told the goats, this Elmer Scaggs was watching out for all the money they'd brought from Kansas, money surely buried somewhere on the Hasford farm until that bank was ready to put it in a great iron box.

More than that, too. He protected Roman Hasford from hurt, from bullies, as if Roman was a little boy on a school ground by himself, and Elmer Scaggs there to see nobody hit him on the nose. Ora Hasford just laughed and told Lark that Elmer Scaggs was like a big mother hen. "Ready to flog anybody who comes near my boy," she said. Sometimes Elmer Scaggs even carried a sawed-off ten-gauge shotgun.

Mighty big and ugly for a mother hen, Lark said to the goats. He'd heard Elmer Scaggs talk mean to some of the workers at the new horse farm when he thought they weren't doing what Roman Hasford wanted. But it didn't matter, talking mean or being ugly. He came and went at the Hasford farm just like family.

And for good reason.

Elmer Scaggs was the only one who could get Martin Hasford to talk and laugh. Lark had seen them on the front porch, Elmer

telling a story and Martin laughing, then Martin telling a story and
Elmer laughing.

And Ora, hearing the laughter of her husband for the first time
in many months, always smiled, with a special glow on her face
when Elmer Scaggs said, "Yes ma'am, no ma'am, Miz Hasford."
And she'd make him a gooseberry deep-dish pie that Elmer could
carry back to the horse farm and eat at night before he went to
bed.

Often when Roman came to the Hasford farm to have his supper
at his mama's table and then sleep the night, Elmer Scaggs came
too. Sometimes, in good weather, Elmer slept on the back porch.
In bad weather he slept in the barn, where Roman was keeping
his horses until the Catrina Hills Farm stables were finished. That
barn bulged with fine horses.

Roman slept in the parlor. Because the upstairs loft, where he
and his sister, Calpurnia, had had their rooms, was all taken up by
that little black-eyed girl.

Lark told the goats, Miz Ora say that girl come from Kansas.
She say that girl ain't got no mama or papa and Mr. Roman taken
pity on her and brought her home. She say that girl named Catrina
Peel. A poor little orphan with no mama and papa. I wish Mr.
Roman take her back to Kansas and leave her there.

And that horse breeding. Roman even brought a man for that,
named Orvile Tucker. A colored man, who was a blacksmith as well
as a horse breeder and hog raiser and gardener and God only knew
what else. Lark didn't like him, having seen him only from afar.
Maybe part of that was because now Lark could no longer claim
that he was the only colored man in the valley.

One of them Yankee niggers, Lark told the goats. And of course
they agreed, looking at him with those unblinking eyes.

Then came the day that Roman married the little black-eyed girl.
The marriage was performed on the front porch of the Hasford
farmhouse, just as Calpurnia's had been during the war when she
married that Union officer who lost his hand in the Battle of Pea
Ridge.

Almost everybody who counted in the county came. It was
springtime and the black locusts along Wire Road were in bloom.
Everything smelled like honeysuckle, and there were already larks

calling from the fields across the road. The slope before the Hasford house was filled with saddle horses and buggies and wagons.

A Methodist minister came down from Cassville to do the ceremony. Not because there weren't a number of men in the county who claimed to have the call, but Roman wanted a reverend to marry him who had a necktie and a decent suit of clothes.

As soon as the "I now pronounce you man and wife" part was said, Catrina Peel Hasford went into the house and up to her loft room and stayed there the rest of the day. Roman just joined everybody else, eating carrot cake in the yard, or roasted chicken on the back porch, or dancing on the front porch. There were a fiddler and a banjo picker from Gourdville. And sometimes Roman's daddy, Martin, joined in the music-making with a Jew's harp, but with not much vigor or imagination. In fact, Martin spent most of the day sitting at one end of the porch behind the banjo picker, staring out across Wire Road, his lips moving as he spoke silently to himself.

Once Elmer Scaggs came and took Martin's arm and led him off the porch and down through the yard and into the little hollow, and they sat by the spring, Elmer Scaggs telling some of those stories that made Martin laugh. And soon Lark could see that Martin was telling stories too, and Elmer was laughing.

In back of the house that day, Lark and Orvile Tucker, the only two persons of color at this affair, sat with backs against the wall of the chicken coop and drank elderberry wine. A few times Roman came out to sit with them, but he brought his own jug and he was drinking something a hell of a lot stronger than elderberry wine.

It was while they were sitting there, Lark and Orvile Tucker, that Lark made an accommodation to the new black man in the valley. He learned that Orvile Tucker had been a slave in Tennessee, wherever that was, and had run off to Kansas, wherever that was, and there met Roman Hasford.

Some of the citizens of the county, late in the afternoon and drunker than Hooter Tom, came back and insisted that one or the other or both niggers come to the front porch and do a jig for everybody's amusement, but Roman Hasford said they didn't have to, and Ora Hasford, when she heard of it, clouded up like an Indian Nations cyclone and would have run some of the guests off except that her son and Elmer Scaggs talked her out of it.

"Well," Ora Hasford said, "I'm not having those two men make a show on my front porch if they don't want to."

"It's all right, Mama," Roman said. "They won't."

"Well, let's go in the kitchen and let me have a sip of what you and Elmer have got in your jug, because elderberry wine makes me sick to my stomach!"

"Yes, ma'am, Miz Hasford," Elmer Scaggs said.

So, seeing the way things were, even the drunkest of the guests let Lark and Orvile Tucker alone because nobody was willing to risk Roman's rage, Elmer Scagg's fist, or a verbal lashing from Ora, who could grow a tongue like a blacksnake whip when she was in foul disposition.

Toward sundown, with the white dancers still kicking dust off the floor of the front porch and the fiddler fiddling and the banjo picker picking, Lark and Orvile Tucker staggered away. Back through the woods, over the ridge, down into the valley of Little Sugar Creek, to Wolf Cove Mill. And there, in celebration of Roman Hasford's wedding, Lark killed a kid goat and cooked it as he always cooked goat. Late into the night he simmered it in his red gravy in the oven until it was ready to eat. Which was dawn, and he and Orvile Tucker were by then very drunk, smelling the aroma of the meat that filled the valley with a smell that made the juice flow around the teeth and tongue.

They carried the meat over to the mill where they could sit in shade and cool, the new day's sun rising on them, and there they consumed the kid goat. Every bite. And finished the last jar of elderberry wine, to the last swallow, before lying down to sleep on the grain-dusted floor beside the great wheel.

When Lark woke at sunset, he found Orvile Tucker gone. And was glad. Because although he had come to know this other man of color in the valley, he was not ready for any more of this wild drinking and eating. So he rose from the mill floor, his clothes coated with corn dust, went up the hill behind his shack and milked the goats, and then, as darkness fell, went to his little one-hole privy and sat there most of the night, listening to that new screech owl in the high beams of the mill house.

"A fine weddin', a fine weddin'," Lark said aloud, sitting on his toilet hole.

But he could hear that owl. And see in his mind the black-eyed girl. Who, after the vows, had disappeared. Oh yes, Lark had been there in the yard. He'd seen, before the elderberry wine had begun at the chicken coop with Orvile Tucker.

"Like a scared mouse," he said aloud. "Like a scared mouse hiding behind a sack of grain over in my ole mill. Scared because the owl is up there to kill it, to eat it."

2

Gallatin Delmonico was probably the first person in the county to suspect that the marriage of Roman Hasford and the child-woman Catrina Peel had not been consummated during all the time Roman and his bride lived at the Hasford house on Wire Road waiting for the Big House on the old McBrighten place to be finished. Which took about a year.

Gallatin Delmonico was not curious by nature. Nor was he in the confidence of Roman Hasford, except in matters concerning the new bank. So his discovery of this calamity, which is how he characterized it in his mind, came completely by accident and was a thing about which he would have preferred to remain ignorant. But there it was!

Less than a month after the wedding, Gallatin Delmonico was in Ora Hasford's parlor at the big table, Roman across from him, and they were making plans for the bank. There were stacks of ledgers and legal documents before them. It was not the first of such meetings, and it wouldn't be the last.

Gallatin Delmonico, who had never been a party to any violence more severe than mashing his finger with a hammer while installing a kitchen shelf for his wife, gazed from time to time at the bullet hole in the glass front of Ora Hasford's china cabinet. This cabinet stood in one corner of the large room and inside it were the various plates and platters and vases and other things a woman keeps in such places, but none of this held any interest for Gallatin Delmonico. The bullet hole did. A very large bullet hole with spiderweb cracks running out from it in all directions. And as Gallatin Delmonico looked at it, he was constantly reminded that the Civil War

Battle of Pea Ridge, or Elkhorn Tavern as the locals called it, had surged and pulsed just outside the front door.

Gallatin Delmonico had been brought to Gourdville by Roman Hasford, after Roman had made various inquiries among his Kansas railroading friends—those who were not in jail for various kinds of fraud. Railroaders knew good bankers. But that day, as they sat in Ora Hasford's parlor, this Gallatin Delmonico had not seen a single penny of the money Roman Hasford said was there to capitalize the bank. The only money he knew for certain was available was his own nearly five thousand dollars, which he had pledged as investment in the business for consideration of a one-fifth interest.

Still, Roman Hasford had assured him that more than twenty thousand dollars was available for the purpose, and Gallatin Delmonico believed him. Not that he was gullible. Rather, before he seriously considered Roman Hasford's offer, he had made inquiries of his own, among Kansas businessmen, who told him that Roman Hasford's word was his bond. So he had made his decision to come to what he suspected was a savage frontier, and nothing he had seen since had convinced him he was wrong.

But that other money. Gallatin Delmonico thought he knew where it was, even if he hadn't seen any of it. Not exactly where it was, but in general terms. Buried on this Hasford farm. It was the kind of thing these people would do. And who better to guard it until the bank vault was ready than Ora Hasford and Elmer Scaggs?

Ora Hasford was a kind of woman Gallatin Delmonico had never seen. He'd heard the stories, sometimes told with admiration, sometimes with a sneer. About her ability with a muzzle-loading shotgun. About her being able to hit with her fist like any man. And all one had to do was look at Elmer Scaggs to see the potential for unspeakable things. Unspeakable, at least, to Gallatin Delmonico, but apparently acceptable in this crazy hill society.

They were astonishing, Ora Hasford and Elmer Scaggs, and terrifying as well. Not that Elmer Scaggs had ever given any hint of hostile intent, except perhaps in the best interests of Roman Hasford, which Gallatin Delmonico hoped were his own best interests too. But he came from a different world. And maybe the same was true of Ora Hasford, who made no bones about letting Gallatin Delmonico know that he was an outlander and therefore had to earn her respect.

So maybe because Gallatin Delmonico knew that he had not

earned it yet, but was still an outlander, he was terrified of her.

Throughout all their work that day, Gallatin Delmonico could hear low conversation from the kitchen, where Elmer Scaggs was talking with Roman's father, and from time to time there was Ora's voice, and from time to time, too, laughter. But all of it stayed subdued, as though the ones in the kitchen realized that great things were happening in the parlor and they should not disturb it.

This Elmer Scaggs was an enigma. An unschooled, rough man of no credentials that Gallatin Delmonico could discern, yet he was a part of this household. Like an old drunken uncle who had reformed. Or an older brother come home from the penitentiary. And Gallatin Delmonico could not help but observe that there was an intense loyalty, a loyalty beyond his comprehension, between this family and Elmer Scaggs. And the other way round as well.

Yet the older Hasfords had not set eyes on this Elmer Scaggs until Roman brought him home to northwest Arkansas. Gallatin Delmonico could understand the bond between Roman and Elmer Scaggs because from what he had heard, this old roughneck had been instrumental in many of Roman's ventures in Kansas. So it became obvious to Gallatin Delmonico that when Roman Hasford put his stamp on somebody, his mother asked no questions. If it was good enough for Roman, it was good enough for her, without further testing. A rather frightening prospect in itself, he thought.

Anyway, on that day the work extended into what Ora Hasford considered suppertime in her house. So she came out of the kitchen, cleared away the ledgers and documents, set places with bone china and real silver, all of which appeared very new, and laid down boiled pinto beans, fried potatoes, and bacon, with buttermilk, cucumber pickles, hot biscuits, and a large rhubarb cobbler.

"During the war, all we had was goat's milk," Roman said as he tucked a napkin into his collar. "I hated that goat."

"Well, the Yankee army killed the cow," said Ora. "And a lot of other things."

"Now there's another cow," said Roman.

"Not much fat in the milk, though," Ora said. "Takes half the day to churn out a pound of butter."

"We'll get another cow, Mama," Roman said.

Catrina came down from the loft, moving like a small cat, and sat at one corner of the table. She said nothing, just sat silently throughout the meal, eyes downcast. Martin Hasford came and took his place at the head of the table, his due as the man of this house. Once he looked around the room, as if there had been a sudden sound, and twice he asked between bites, "Where's Elmer gone?"

"He had to get back to the horse farm, Papa," said Roman.

Trying desperately to become a part of this, Gallatin Delmonico said, "And a fine horse farm, I might say."

"What horse farm?" Martin asked, but went on eating as though he expected no answer. It was the extent of Martin Hasford's contribution to the dinner conversation. Not that there was much conversation to contribute to, even though Gallatin Delmonico tried.

"It's certainly too bad about that bullet hitting your fine china cabinet," he said.

"Better that than one of the children," Ora said. "Roman, take more potatoes. You're eating like a bird."

Being with this family made Gallatin Delmonico very uncomfortable. And not only because of Ora Hasford's coolness. It was Roman. Delmonico knew this young man as a hard-driving taskmaster in the work of building the bank on the Gourdville square, brooking no nonsense, sure of his own mind, with perhaps a studied hardness. But Delmonico had noticed that the very instant Roman Hasford walked into this house where he had been born, and into the presence of his mother, it was as if he became a child again. As though all the years of maturing were shucked off, placed aside until Roman rode away again and became, with each succeeding step from this place, more independent.

Gallatin Delmonico, with his quick and accurate banker's sense of the reality in such cases, could see that Ora Hasford was disturbed by it. Yet she was unwilling to change it. Maybe she had no notion how.

Gallatin Delmonico could not help but believe that Catrina Peel Hasford—sitting across the dinner table, wrapped in her own silence—was at the root of this, having been brought here like a wet, cold, abandoned puppy dog and left with Ora to be nurtured. Everybody in the county knew that. And so, each time afterward, when Roman came face-to-face with his mother, he was as anxious and apprehensive about her acceptance and approval as is any boy who brings in a stray puppy to mess his mother's clean floors. Each of them knowing, too, that even though the boy would always consider the pup his own, it would be the mother who must clean and feed it.

Added to which, Gallatin Delmonico thought, this particular

puppy dog had a deep, disturbing light in its eyes that defied description or understanding. The kind of light that receded to greater distance the closer one tried to approach it.

It was another of those situations in which Gallatin Delmonico would as soon have been left in ignorance. Because he could taste their agony.

"These are fine beans, Mrs. Hasford," he said that night.

"Just the regular kind," Ora Hasford said, looking at him with her brittle blue eyes.

"Yes," he said, recognizing that everything at Ora Hasford's table was supposed to taste good, so no need to discuss it. And so he gave up all further efforts at small talk.

Uncomfortable, and irritated as well, he thought, Here I am, a vital part of this new venture of the son in this house, but treated like a stranger while Elmer Scaggs enjoys the warmth of friendship, what almost amounts to kinship. Gallatin Delmonico supposed that Elmer Scaggs was like that china cabinet with the bullet hole in the glass, and all the violence it symbolized. Incomprehensible, yet a part of the normal pattern of life to these hill people.

When the meal was finished, Catrina Peel Hasford went back to her loft room. Martin sat staring at the lamp as Ora cleaned the table. Roman poured a glass of elderberry wine for Gallatin Delmonico and Martin and himself, and passed a cigar to each.

"Got to get those posts cut," Martin said.

"That's right, Papa, now why don't you go help Mama in the kitchen?"

"When are the rest of the men coming back from hospital, Doctor?" Martin asked, looking directly at his son.

Ora was there then and led her husband out, without a word, without touching him, like a fly fisherman moving the trout before the lure. Roman wiped his face with the palms of his hands and sighed.

"Papa's got a lot on his mind since the war," he said.

It was another thing to which Gallatin Delmonico would as soon not have been a party. But there it was.

So they went back to their work. But only for a little while. Then Gallatin Delmonico was up and out, into the brisk October night where a dog was barking someplace along Wire Road, a dismal, lonely sound under a moonless sky. He drove away in the buggy that had come with his job. Buggy and horse and the house behind the limestone building on the Gourdville square, all came with his new position in this savage land. He hurried along with the whip because he knew his wife and his three children would be waiting, anxious about him out in the night, even though they already knew that when Roman Hasford wanted to speak business, schedules were thrown into chaos.

He had driven almost a half-mile when he remembered that he'd left an important ledger back there and wheeled the buggy around. When he arrived on the porch and stood at the door, it was impossible not to observe that Roman Hasford was already abed. In the parlor.

Not just a pallet on the floor. A bed. Gallatin Delmonico had seen the bed there beside the bullet-scarred china cabinet, and now Roman Hasford was in it, sleeping.

Ora Hasford, who brought him his book at the door, was obviously not very happy at his seeing the sleeping arrangements in her home. Groom in the downstairs parlor, bride in the upstairs loft, and Gallatin Delmonico sensing that this was no temporary arrangement.

He said nothing to anybody about his discovery. It was not to avoid the wrath of Ora Hasford, although that was frightening enough. It was something deeper, a sense of honor. Honor in that just because he happened to have found his nose in a certain crack, there was no requirement to run around the county talking about what he'd smelled.

Gallatin Delmonico was a rare breed, a man who wanted to lead his own life and allow others to lead theirs. His wife even scolded him about his detachment, saying it would somehow or other end them in the poorhouse. At which times he always smiled gently and said, "Missy, go melt some cheese to put on my toast."

Gallatin Delmonico was a Swiss. A third-generation American, he was perhaps related to those other Italian Swiss who had begun a restaurant trade that would make its mark on the eating habits of the whole country. Like cutting away bone and fat from a slab of beef rib and calling it a rib-eye steak. Or a Delmonico. When Gallatin Delmonico came to northwest Arkansas, those distant cousins, if in fact they were cousins at all, had their cafés at Twenty-five Broadway and at Forty-fourth Street and Fifth Avenue in the city of New York, where Presidents came to eat.

Any possible relationship had to be far removed. Gallatin Delmonico hardly knew a lamb chop from a corn fritter. His was a banking family, come to the United States of America after the war of 1812, and Gallatin himself decades later, named after the Swiss who had been Secretary of the Treasury when Mr. Thomas Jefferson had bought Louisiana from Napoleon, and who, some said, was instrumental in the process.

So one might suppose that Gallatin Delmonico yearned to make his final mark in the world at some spot in the old Purchase. Which gave him a wide range of choices, had it really been the case.

But none of this had anything to do with Gallatin Delmonico coming to Roman Hasford in northwest Arkansas. For this man had never made a decision based on sentiment. Everything he did was according to the credits and debits on the ledger of his mind, including marrying an Irish wife who came with a dowry he felt he deserved, being at that time a chief teller in a Cincinnati bank.

The marriage was as solid as a granite tombstone, for once he had made any contract, only an act of God could amend it, and thus far God had not seen fit to do so. And certainly their three children sealed it, as did their love for each other, which grew with the years.

So there was no sentiment attached to this little Swiss moving to northwest Arkansas. A place where he was as foreign as a snow-capped peak would have been, with his black hat, its brim almost as wide as his narrow shoulders, with his mustache and goatee as black as the hat, and with his delicate fingers that had never shucked an ear of corn or butchered a hog or held the handles of a plow. He came with Roman Hasford because he saw the opportunity to make one hell of a lot of money in a place short on cash and long on agricultural potential.

He said, "Missy, I think we should go to Gourdville."

"Do they have streetcars there?" she asked.

"My dear, I doubt they even know what a streetcar is."

And he brought more than his own experience. He asked, and Roman Hasford said yes, if he might bring this tall, blue-eyed man who he said was the best natural banker he had ever known, a certain Judah Meyer, just married, twenty-five years old, a man who could compute figures in his head faster than most men could use one of the new machines that created such a rattling clatter when the crank was pulled down. And thereby Roman Hasford acquired a bank cashier who was honest, efficient, and only incidentally a Jew.

Gallatin Delmonico was aware that Roman Hasford did not know at first that Judah Meyer was a Jew, didn't think about it, didn't care. But some of the newcomers to the county cared, and said so. Not to Roman Hasford, but sometimes to Gallatin Delmonico, who reacted as calmly as he could.

"It is my understanding that you had a Jewish person in this county once, and he was murdered by partisan bandits at Wolf Cove Mill," he would say.

And the other would answer, "Yeah, and look what he left us. An uppity free nigger!"

There was the day, on one of his frequent visits to the courthouse on bank business, when Gallatin Delmonico overheard Sheriff Yancy Crane say, "Looks to me like the Hasfords are tryin' their level best to repopulate this county with niggers and Jews." Upon which one of the courthouse hangers-on was heard to laugh and say, "Hell, Yancy, whatta you care? You ain't gonna let any of 'em close to a polling place on election days anyway."

Gallatin Delmonico tried to pass such incidents off as minor irritations, even though they were much more than that. But he had other important work to do, other things on his mind. Getting the bank in order, the new safe shipped in from St. Louis, potbellied and with two sets of dials on its round face. Getting the black and white marble mosaic floor tile laid, the iron grillework on the counter before the two teller cages bolted in place. And then the gray stone set into place over the front doors, and cut into that stone, so that anyone could see it from the far corner of the square, the word HASFORD. And on the window facing the street the gold-leaf words placed there by a man brought from St. Joseph, Missouri, just for that purpose: FARMER'S AND MERCHANT'S BANK.

Standing in the little wooded area at the center of the square and looking at it, Roman Hasford said, "Gallatin, don't you think it's showing off a little bit?"

"Absolutely not," said the little Swiss. "You must remember, Mr. Hasford, this is an institution, not a pool hall."

A lot of the Old Settlers who had known the Hasfords since before Roman was born were proud of that gray stone and those gold-leaf letters. Just like one of the big banks up north, they said.

But if the Old Settlers and Gallatin Delmonico didn't think it was ostentatious, a lot of the newcomers did. Just like that house he's buildin', they said. It looks like the kind of place a common man gotta pay money just to walk in the front door.

3

One of the few newcomers who even knew the word *ostentatious* and what it meant and how to spell it was Major Corliss Buckmaten, editor and publisher of the *Democrat Advertiser*. The image of a Northern-style bank diagonally across the square from his newspaper office, which he had to look at each day as he stood in his bay-windowed newspaper shop, was much more than ostentatious. It was evil.

Corliss Buckmaten loved a fight. At least the kind of fight involving antagonists wearing fancy uniforms and responding to drum and bugle call. He had proven that in the recent war. But now that kind of fight was finished. Now there were only political fights. And maybe Corliss Buckmaten loved those more than the ones involving powdersmoke and shot. For one thing, it was the kind of combat when a man could sleep in a comfortable bed each night with nothing more troubling than his thoughts. And his wife's snoring.

Corliss Buckmaten had established himself as what the Old Settlers called a "newcomer" to northwest Arkansas when he arrived after the war was over. There were others in the county who had arrived after the war and were not called newcomers, but Corliss Buckmaten was not one of these for a lot of reasons, the main one being that he was always kicking up dust where the Old Settlers could not remember dust ever having been kicked up before.

Corliss Buckmaten had been one of southern Arkansas's plantation aristocracy before the war but had left his native Garland County because it had become infested with vipers. Things like carpetbaggers and scalawags and Freedman's Bureau people and soldiers wearing the hated blue uniform of Lincoln's armies. He was heard to say that he would rather plant his intellectual seed in contested ground, albeit among ignorant hill folk, than among Republican assholes.

Of course, he did not print these things in those exact terms. Well, in fact he did print them, all except the part about ignorant hill folk, for reasons of survival in a land of sensitive people. Or the asshole part, in the interest of good manners.

He started the first newspaper in the county and called it the *Democrat Advertiser* for obvious reasons. It was the usual kind of weekly newspaper for that period, a tabloid-sized, four-page document in which editorials were hardly distinguishable from what purported to be news. And throughout its pages on succeeding weeks were none-too-subtle hints that the editor and publisher loathed not only Republicans but bankers, big business, big farmers who had never used slave labor, railroads, and everything else that Corliss Buckmaten associated with Yankee money and Yankee ideas, which covered a lot of ground.

There were other things on his list of repugnances: able-bodied men of the South who had not bled for Jeff Davis; anybody who voted for U.S. Grant; and most particularly any man who at the time of trouble or immediately thereafter went north of Mason and Dixon's Line to learn how the Yankees connived to convince God's individuals concerning their obscene ideas about how civilization was supposed to work.

My God, Corliss Buckmaten often thought, we knew how it was supposed to work, and then the Yankee industrial tycoons crushed us.

In northwest Arkansas, all of this produced curious paradoxes, not only for Corliss Buckmaten but for a lot of people. But maybe he, more than most, was aware of them.

Reconstruction in that area was little more than horror stories from farther south. But it was still part of a state run by an invading army and its government. So when the Union occupying forces left, one would have supposed that Corliss Buckmaten would return whence he had come, where old Confederate cronies and Democrats were back in power.

It wasn't that simple. Corliss Buckmaten was a lot of things, but simple was not one of them.

By 1874, when the last of the Federal troops were withdrawn, it was too late for Corliss Buckmaten to go home. How, he might have said to himself, can I find a Republican now in Garland County to rail against? And so he stayed. Despite the paradoxes.

One of which was Yancy Crane, the county sheriff.

Yancy Crane had followed the invading army into Arkansas from Missouri. He became one of their appointed peace officers because he had never worn the uniform of rebellion, he had been a town constable in Sedalia, and, most important, he knew how to ingratiate anyone who might put money in his pocket. A lot of the Old Settlers called him Butt-sucker Crane. A lot of the newcomers thought of him as Good Old Yancy.

Anyway, once the Federal government left the county so the natives could run their own business, Yancy Crane stood for sheriff and was elected mainly because nobody else wanted the job. And Yancy Crane, whom many people may have thought of as an opportunist son of a bitch, was no fool. He figured that northwest Arkansas, like all the rest of the old Confederacy, would turn into a solid Democrat stronghold. So he ran on a Democrat ticket. Not only initially, but thereafter, even though he had first been established as peace officer by the occupying Union army without any election at all.

In that time and place it was not unusual for those with political aspirations to change labels with the ease of a Lark Crozier billy goat jumping a low fence. Nobody was sure what the political labels meant yet, so being a Republican one day and a Democrat the next was common on a stage still confusing and contradictory.

Of course, Corliss Buckmaten supported Yancy Crane during every election because Yancy claimed to be a Democrat, no matter what he might have been in the past. Why, hell, the Old Settlers said, Corliss Buckmaten would have supported a red-assed baboon if the thing had pissed once on a Republican.

But Corliss Buckmaten did not like Yancy Crane or a lot of people who were his close supporters. Even though he was a Democrat, and this was going to be a Democrat county, by God.

Well, Corliss Buckmaten was wrong. Because it became one of the few areas of the old Confederacy that was *not* solidly Democrat.

Initially, just after the war, politics in the county were so fluid that nobody knew what anybody else was, and didn't care, and further, nobody was really sure what a Republican or a Democrat stood for or looked like or which church they went to or how far they could spit.

No matter. Here was the exact kind of fight Corliss Buckmaten loved. Although originally a Catholic he was now seen each Sunday in one of the Baptist churches, and then the following Tuesday in his newspaper he would name certain citizens of the county who had not gone to any worship of the Lord Our God at all. Like Roman Hasford.

Corliss Buckmaten was well aware of the dividing sentiment in the county as a result of new arrivals. The Old Settlers viewed everything in the perspective of how it was before the war. Newcomers didn't give a damn how it had been before the war.

So here was another paradox. Many Old Settlers were Republicans; many newcomers were from Missouri and were Democrats. Corliss Buckmaten found himself associated politically with a lot of people he would have otherwise regarded as damned Yankees.

Perhaps just as distasteful, Corliss Buckmaten could no longer be the champion of plantation aristocracy, because there was no such thing in northwest Arkansas. Hence, the people whose banner he bore were mostly common dirt farmers or small merchants or casual riffraff. The people in the county who owned most of the property, Corliss Buckmaten's natural brothers, were decidedly Republican or moving that way, having gotten off to that start before the war, when they blamed down-South slaveholding cotton power brokers for getting everybody embroiled with war in the first place. These people had never owned slaves or big plantations either, because northwest Arkansas could not sustain that kind of economy.

Some of those people had even fought in Union armies. Others had fought with the South, not for any issue dear to the hearts of slave owners but rather as a protest against what they perceived to be a strong central government trying to tell them how to live their lives. These people were so intensely individualistic they didn't even like *local* government, much less something as far away as Washington.

Mother of God, Corliss Buckmaten often said to himself, what kind of a place is this? Yet maybe that was part of the fun, trying to figure it all out while taking his ink-pot shots at one or another of them.

Like Martin Hasford. Corliss Buckmaten thought about him a great deal. A man who had fought with Lee. The only man in the county who had been in the Army of Northern Virginia. And thus a very large positive symbol in Corliss Buckmaten's mind. Yet, Martin Hasford was certainly no down-South aristocrat. And he'd sired a son who not only failed to answer the colors, even as a drummer boy, but, once the shooting was finished, ran off to Kansas, that festering boil of Free-Soilers, where he learned how Yankee industrialists fleeced Southern agrarian gentlemen, then came home to do it right here in the county, by God!

Some nights Corliss Buckmaten hardly slept at all, thinking about the fact that he was lying abed so close to Mason and Dixon's Line. Geography had a lot to do with the situation, he knew that. The northwest corner of Arkansas was not directed toward the cotton South but toward the Indian Nations and Missouri. It was easier to travel to Muskogee, Indian Territory, or Joplin, Missouri, than to struggle along the bad roads south over the mountains to the state's capital.

So, as a result of understanding more about the county's political and economic status than perhaps anyone else, Corliss Buckmaten never seemed in good temper, which he enjoyed like a man who cannot make conversation without speaking of his upset stomach, as if it was his heritage to be that way.

Some in the county called him Little Corliss because he was small and delicate, like a chicken wing. But somehow tough as a boiled crow. Olive complexion. Eyes burning, like his intent. And although no resident of the county, and certainly not Corliss himself, had ever seen a natural-born journalist, he was that. Always on a mission, seeking out tidbits of information under each fence railing, whether or not he would ever use them in his pages.

The first Buckmaten in his lineage was shown on various shipping ledgers in New Orleans at the time of the Purchase. Only it wasn't Buckmaten then. It was Brieuc. That name, from Brittany, was changed by Corliss Buckmaten's grandfather to ease business transactions when he moved upriver and founded a plantation that straddled the line that would become a state boundary between Louisiana and Arkansas. A large plantation, cotton-growing, slave quarters, a private dock on the Bayou Bodcau to load bales for shipment down to Red River and then on to the Mississippi and New Orleans.

That had been Master Buck, a man not noted for his kindness to field hands in his cotton patches, and little more for his consideration toward what he called his house animals. In 1840, Corliss was born to the eldest son of this man. Which made him the magic age of twenty-one when Sumter was fired upon, and by then Corliss was so viciously bitter about Yankees and the industrial North that his mother became frightened when he spoke of it.

So, when war came, Corliss dashed off to join what was supposed to be an elite Louisiana artillery battery who wore powder-blue pantaloons because he said cannons could kill Yankees faster than rifles.

Corliss had two older brothers. They rushed to the colors, too, and neither came back.

Corliss spent four years under the command of people like Braxton Bragg and Joseph E. Johnson, shooting his cannon at the bluebellies. When it was over and he came home, there were a lot more of the bluebellies occupying the land. And sitting in the Little Rock state house was what was called a provisional governor, meaning he had been placed there and supported by Yankee bayonets. Isaac Murphy was this man's name. And he was not only a Republican and a carpetbagger but a Goddamned Irishman besides, all of which threw Corliss Buckmaten into a blind rage.

Corliss was small, but his rages were monumental. His black French eyes seemed to grow larger than the small face that held them. His tiny pencil mustache seemed to bristle, making quivering shadows of a sword's point across his olive-colored cheeks. He frightened his mother more than ever.

Maybe to avoid such trauma, his mother provided him with a poke of gold money she had from her father-in-law, old Master Buck. Corliss Buckmaten's grandfather had had an unusually strange attachment to his elder son's wife. Corliss asked no questions about reasons for his mother having such a bounty but took it, along with the only horse the Yankees had left in the stable, and rode as far away from cotton country as he could, with the vowed intention of continuing the fight with words instead of artillery.

Having risen to the rank of major in the forces of rebellion, he was required to take a loyalty oath to the newly reconstituted Union. Otherwise, it would be impossible to move about freely in that time immediately after the war.

He took it, grinding his teeth. And afterward told his wife, Melissa, that when he wrote his name on the hated document, he had his fingers crossed.

None of which Melissa understood, being a pale young lady whose only claim to any kind of recognition lay in the auburn curls that danced down along either side of her wide blue eyes. No more sense of politics, Corliss said of her, than a Texas boll weevil.

So Corliss Buckmaten arrived in Gourdville. And, with Melissa, remained childless—due, according to Corliss Buckmaten, to some sort of internal malfunction of Melissa's reproductive parts. Never, even in his late-night introspection, did he consider that maybe the malfunction was in him and not in her.

He was a Democrat because he had always been one. Perhaps not to have been a Democrat would have meant being a Republican. Republican? The party of Lincoln. The party of Reconstruction. The party of the Freedman's Bureau.

And never did it occur to him that the most powerful Republicans of the North were exactly like him. Elitist, committed to power and profits as he had been before the war, they in metal, he in fiber, both exploiting a labor force, they in immigrants at starvation wages, he in slaves. The major difference being that, at least to his thinking, those Yankees had won, he'd lost. And he did not take it with good grace.

And so Corliss Buckmaten came to the day when he stood in his newspaper's bay window and looked out and saw HASFORD graven in stone and knew that he would now share this Gourdville square with a man who represented almost everything that he despised.

Blood of Jesus, Corliss Buckmaten said to himself, he has come back with more than Yankee greenbacks. He has come back and brought foreigners. A freed nigger, a big-city Jew, a Yankee bodyguard, a strange little female, a prissy Shylock with a black hat, and God only knows what else to come.

In the first issue of the *Democrat Advertiser* after the HASFORD stone went up, Corliss Buckmaten used the word "ostentatious." He used other words as well. Like "money-grubbing" and "racial-mixing" and "turncoat."

"Well," said a domino player in Torten's Billiard Parlor who'd read the piece, "I 'spect Roman Hasford ain't gonna take too well to this."

"Nor old Ora," said another.

"Ora? Yeah, I don't wanna think about that."

Corliss Buckmaten had not enjoyed himself so much since the last time he had attacked the Yankee business tycoons who bribed

Congressmen to obtain money for building railroads, becoming obscenely rich in the process. Because now there was a target closer to home. It was so much more convenient to have something ready at hand to hate. And Roman Hasford was it.

The first of these pieces that the Old Settlers came to call the Tirades and the newcomers hailed as Uncle Buck's Gospels was published on the same day that Roman Hasford and his wife, Catrina, moved into their new home.

Ora Hasford watched her son turning down the black locust slope from the house, then off onto Wire Road, driving his shiny new hack with red wheels, drawn by a big sorrel that Elmer Scaggs and Orvile Tucker had decided wasn't good enough to stand stud at Catrina Hills Farm, and so had gelded. Ora knew this because Elmer Scaggs had told her. Elmer kept her advised of just about everything that happened at the new horse farm, probably at Roman's suggestion, because Roman was so preoccupied with getting the bank into form that he had little time to do it himself.

This was supposed to be a happy day, her son taking his bride to his new home. But it didn't feel like a happy day. Only a small part of it was her inability to accept that this son of hers now called home a place where he had not been born and reared. The larger part had to do with Martin's mind slipping away into some shadow land called senility. And more than that, too. All those months after the wedding, Catrina locking herself in the loft room each night when she should have been sharing her husband's bed.

At least the move had been done in a hurry, Roman showing all the enthusiasm of a man who had just said the marriage vows and was now taking his bride to honeymoon even though it had been a year since the event. Loading the luggage, talking a blue streak, then Ora kissing Catrina's cheek and Catrina smiling that small smile that was so sad, then being handed up into the hack, and Roman turning the gelding back toward Wire Road and waving and shouting, "We'll have a housewarming before long, Mama."

"Good," she said. "But don't forget the way back here."

She was sorry she'd said it. As though she might be really afraid that her son could forget such a thing.

She went back into the house and sat in the kitchen, looking at her husband sleeping on the kitchen bed as he did each afternoon. Watching Martin's heavy breathing, Ora Hasford remembered the times they had been in that bed together, before the war, hearing the mockingbirds in the walnut trees across Wire Road, smelling the black locust blossoms in spring, hearing the pop of trees ice-coated in winter. Her children had been conceived in that bed. They had been born in that bed. Yet she knew that these days when her husband woke he would have no notion of where he was or why he was there.

Except once in a while. She always hoped for such moments. Martin's lucid times came unexpectedly, to emphasize how he once had been. As with the mushrooms, only the week before.

It was late April and there had been a hard little rain in the afternoon, then clearing, the clouds running off toward White River in the east and the sun coming through a brilliant blue sky from the Indian Territory. It was that magic time in the Ozarks when everyone leaned forward, expecting the next instant to hear larks or see the north-migrating yellow warblers.

Martin Hasford, in his rocker on the front porch, had called, "Mama, somebody coming."

When Ora came out of her kitchen, wiping flour from her hands on her half-apron, Roman was pulling up at the foot of the steps, and behind him was Elmer Scaggs on a mule.

"Elmer," Ora asked, "won't he let you ride anything but that mule?"

"Miz Hasford," Elmer said, grinning and taking off his hat to show his tangled mop of graying hair, "me and this mule, we know each other."

"Mama," Roman said, "with that rain, I thought there might be mushrooms, so I broke away from the bank early."

"I'll get a bucket," she had said.

They didn't say anything else. They didn't need to. They walked, leaving Elmer Scaggs to sit on the porch and talk with Martin. They went up the familiar slope behind the house, past the barn, to an old apple orchard where there were only a few trees left now, gnarled and untended. As they walked they could hear doves calling from cedar thickets not far away, the low, sighing call that many locals said was made by rain crows. To the east, far off, near White River, they could hear jays.

They found a great many morel mushrooms in the old leaf mold, sprung up with their spongy peaks after the rain. They thought it only ordinary because they had found them all their lives, not realizing that in places such as Gallatin Delmonico's cousins' establishments in New York, such things were more expensive than gold.

With each mushroom he found, Roman laughed, as he had done so many times a long, long time ago. And Ora laughed with him and took each one and put it in her pail.

"You always fried them in butter, Mama," Roman said. "I never tasted anything like it all the time I was in Kansas."

"I'll fix them that way tonight."

"In the butter," Roman said, bending to another. Still laughing.

"Yes, in the butter."

And Ora Hasford could feel the beating of her heart as she had when she'd first come here with her son, when he was only a boy, and with his sister, and she showing them the morels. This orchard was younger and she was younger and they were all younger, those days before the armies came and before Martin walked away down Wire Road and before so many things. And that afternoon a week ago, hearing Roman laugh and feeling the texture of those mushrooms and smelling the rain fresh on the sumac and cedar, it was suddenly the old days once more.

But as Roman bent to pick more mushrooms, Ora knew it was not the old days. Because even as she delighted in Roman's laughter, she could not help but be aware that just back down the slope on the front porch of her home was Martin Hasford and Elmer Scaggs, this man from Kansas whom her son had brought, a man who now seemed to have taken her place and that of her son, her entire family, within that ever-constricting chamber of her husband's mind.

She had cooked the morels in butter and it was a wonderful supper. Elmer Scaggs was laughing and Catrina was smiling and Roman was cramming mushrooms into his mouth with his fingers.

Then suddenly, from his place at the head of the table, Martin had said, "Roman, you remember that time when we came back from White River with a string of blue catfish and your mama and sister had gathered mushrooms, and while we were eating, lightning struck the old sycamore in the spring hollow?"

Startled, Roman gulped down a morel and nodded. "Yes, I remember that, Papa."

"I don't know who squealed loudest," Martin said, laughing, "our new farrow of pigs or your sister."

Just that one quick glimpse into Martin's memory, and then it was gone.

Now Ora Hasford watched her husband sleep and thought of her son and his new wife, that strange little girl who seemed to grow more distant the closer Ora tried to come.

The pride she'd felt for her son, bringing that hapless child home to safe haven, marrying her because he loved her, or at least felt such an obligation to her that it could pass for love until real love came over the years.

But then, about the time Martin's mind had begun to slip, Catrina had begun her withdrawal, creeping into a tiny shell from which only her eyes showed, black and tragic. It broke Ora's heart, but no matter what she did, no matter how gentle she was, nothing changed it, any more than her soothing fingers diverted Martin's errant thinking.

She knew Roman saw it as well. After all, a part of it had been her retreat to the loft each night, hadn't it? So now Ora Hasford thought of her son, going to his new home with his wife. With a troubled child whose wounds Ora had been unable to heal. And now she suspected that neither could Roman.

On that day when he brought his wife home, Roman Hasford had on the face of confidence. Everybody at Catrina Hills helped beyond his fondest hopes. As they pulled up to the west-side porch, Elmer Scaggs ran out of the house, bounded down the steps to hitch the sorrel, assist Catrina from the hack, and get down the luggage. Roman almost choked with astonishment. Elmer was wearing a necktie! It looked as though it had been fastened about his throat with a square knot, but it was a necktie sure as hell.

"You step right down, Miss Catrina," Elmer said. "Step right down and see this pretty house we built for you."

And at the door, a beaming Orvile Tucker, bowing and scraping like a sultan's slave and wearing a new cotton shirt, his great biceps about to split the sleeves, holding the door open.

"Welcome to home, Miz Catrina, welcome to home," he said.

Roman looked at her and saw she was smiling. A real teeth-revealing smile. He could not remember ever having seen such a smile on that small face.

"Orvile," Roman asked, laughing, "have you people gone crazy, all these good clothes and Elmer wearing a tie?"

"Mister Roman, it taken that big dumb Elmer half the mornin' to get that thang 'round his neck."

"Get on in, you field hand," Elmer shouted, laughing as well. "Show this lady the pretty house we built her."

Joy and gladness, Roman thought. Just as he'd willed it, everything falling into place like the figures on one of Gallatin Delmonico's ledgers.

Orvile conducted a tour of the downstairs while Elmer carried luggage to the second floor, then came down the staircase, sounding like a herd of stampeding horses, to join them. He and Roman remained back, allowing Orvile to reveal all the marvels.

Catrina was animated, exclaiming as a child might with a new toy, which was about what it amounted to, and she kept saying, "Oh, look. Oh, look!"

It became difficult for Roman Hasford to swallow the hard knot in his throat as he watched her, thinking of the old mule-shed home in which he'd first seen her.

It's joy, he thought, watching her. It's joy. I knew I could put it there.

Catrina held her hands clasped, looking at each new wonder. The large rooms, the hardwood floors, the Persian rugs, the tables with delicately curved legs, the hanging brass lamps, the kitchen sink with a spigot where water ran with the turn of a knob. Orvile pointing, glaring at Elmer Scaggs as Elmer interrupted. "That came from St. Louis." Or, "That came from Cincinnati." Or, "That one there came all the way from Philadelphia."

When they had gone through all the rooms of the first floor, Orvile Tucker and Elmer Scaggs stood back, grinning, and Roman knew they expected him to extend the tour to the bedroom floor. Which he did, holding her arm as they mounted the wide staircase.

He showed her the indoor water closet, the great four-poster bed in the big room, the chiffoniers, the mirrors, the cedar chests, the polished bedside tables, the globed lamps.

"The mattresses are all cotton batting, not straw or feathers," Roman explained.

But she had become subdued now, away from the others. Roman tried to regain the exuberance, but it flowed away like sour milk through a hole in the bucket.

"I'm tired," she said.

"Well, I know you must be, so just take a nap, just get on the bed and take a nap," he said.

She didn't say anything. She stood before the window that faced north, close by the horse barns and pens, beyond the wooded lift of the west end of Pea Ridge, which was clothed now in the lacy green of April foliage. Then Roman took from his pocket a small porcelain figurine, painted in soft colors, a figurine he had bought in Leavenworth before coming home, only now making his gift of it to her.

"Here's a Little Bo-Peep for you," he said. "A little girl with a lamb. I thought you might enjoy it on your dresser."

Roman placed it on the dressing table beside a set of combs and brushes and a hand mirror he had ordered only two months before out of St. Louis. On the white bone back of each brush and the mirror was a large C inlaid with silver.

Catrina didn't look at them. Her face remained turned to the window.

"Just take a nap," he said, and left her and went down the steps to his people, Elmer Scaggs and Orvile Tucker, who were still grinning expectantly. He looked at them for a long time, trying somehow to think of a way to express his appreciation for their effort, then finally said, "Orvile, get a bottle of that Kentucky bourbon out of the pantry and let's all have a drink. Miss Catrina's taking a nap."

"She tired out, Mr. Roman," Orvile said.

"But she sure likes this house, boss," said Elmer.

"Get the bottle," Roman said.

The joy had evaporated somehow, impossible to hold in his hands.

When he had first discovered Catrina Peel in that old mule barn on the outskirts of Leavenworth, living in filth and squalor with a drunken father, Roman Hasford knew at once that she was being beaten, because the fist marks showed on her face. She had been a child, tiny and delicate, with a heart-shaped face that seemed to emphasize the ugly bruises on her cheeks and the blood-caked, swollen lips. Her dark eyes had shown a depth of misery and resignation such as Roman had never seen.

He had no idea how old she was, but certainly she was a child. Over the next five years he saw her from time to time, often taking fruit or clothing to her, and she seemed to remain a child. She grew, but not much, remaining tiny and delicate. The old bruises and swellings faded and were replaced by new ones. And the terrible eyes remained constant. Roman, remembering some of his reading, imagined they were like the eyes of those condemned souls who passed beneath the archway that proclaimed, "Abandon all hope, ye who enter here."

At first, Roman Hasford did not suspect anything else.

He did learn on inquiry that there was no regular machinery of government to rescue mistreated children if there was a surviving parent who made at least some dismal effort to nurture. Sometimes a group of church ladies would bring a basket of food or a toy at Christmastime, but that was about the extent of it.

Catrina's father was a tanner named Crider Peel. Or that's what he had been before he was murdered by one of his associates with a large clasp knife.

Having long since assessed the character of Crider Peel, it was no surprise to Roman Hasford or to anybody else when it was revealed that Catrina's father had been an accessory before, to, and after the fact of armed robbery, during the course of which two express company employees were bludgeoned to death. It was on account of his possibly having revealed, in a state of opium euphoria or alcohol bravado, certain details of these atrocities committed by border ruffians from the Indian Territory, that Crider Peel met his end.

Good riddance to bad rubbish, most citizens said. And they universally approved of Roman Hasford taking the new orphan off the state's hands, thereby avoiding anyone's bad conscience for having to stuff another urchin into a very ugly and very crowded system of destitute children's asylums. Besides, they said, that girl's likely not even a minor anymore.

Actually, Roman had the girl out of the state before anyone

thought of going to the old mule-barn home of Crider Peel and seeing to her welfare. And that suited everybody, too, because then they could plant Crider Peel in potter's field and forget the whole unsavory business.

The clasp knife never had to be brought before a jury because the man who had used it on Crider Peel didn't come to trial. He was shot dead by railroad and Pinkerton detectives during the course of another express office robbery. It was just an ordinary bone-handled knife with two blades, the kind of knife most men carried for whittling, or sharpening tent pegs, or lancing boils, or cleaning fish and fingernails. But, of course, it was not an ordinary knife. It had been the instrument of last resort for one of Crider Peel's friends, who'd stuck the larger of its two blades into his body a number of times; and when Roman Hasford moved his wife to Catrina Hills Farm, to the Big House, that same knife was upstairs. For Roman, there was a perverse kind of fascination having in his trunk the weapon that had released Catrina so he could carry her away, bring her to Ora's hearth.

But there was more to it than that, and the very thought made Roman uncomfortable. The knife also represented a kind of brutal justice, for, by the time it had been put to its bloody work in Leavenworth, Roman had become convinced that Crider Peel had been doing more to his daughter than hitting her with his fists.

From his Old Testament readings, Roman called it the Sin of Lot. Those were the cleanest words he could put to it. Of course, he knew it wasn't exactly the right connotation, because although Crider Peel often enough had been plied with hard spirits, as had Lot, it wasn't Crider Peel's daughter who had provided the whiskey. It was Crider Peel himself. And it wasn't Catrina who had desired the result, as it was written that Lot's daughters did, but Crider Peel himself.

And so Roman Hasford came to the bedrock foundation of Crider Peel's degeneracy, and there evolved in him a burning passion to make it right, to prove to this small, delicate child that there was a gentle man in the world for her, and a gentleman as well, all wrapped up in one person. Himself. No longer horrifying fury and lust, but normal love and tenderness. Himself. And what better place than in the bosom of his own family?

There had always been something about Catrina's face, her furtive movements, her disturbing eyes, that drove Roman Hasford very nearly mad with pity. He never saw any passion in it, and he wasn't even sure there was love in it. He was only sure that he could take the terror from this child's mind and put gladness in its place. Himself. So he would do it.

The motives for such a task involved things of which Roman Hasford was only vaguely aware, if at all. Maybe he was atoning. For a lot of things. For leaving his mother once Martin had come home, gone from her side in that cruel time when Martin's mind began to slip. When she needed her strong son beside her as surely as she had when the night-riding partisans came through the county.

Or maybe for not having served in the war. He'd seen a lot of veterans who had fought when they were only seventeen. Yet, when asked, he had to admit that he had stayed home, and not gone with his father—no matter that his father had not wanted him to go and that staying at home was sometimes as dangerous as going to war. But whatever the reasons, he had not gone.

Or maybe he was atoning for coming back to the county with a lot of money, in some eyes a sin in itself. He could remember the parable of Jesus which said that for a rich man to get into heaven was akin to passing a camel through the eye of a needle. Roman Hasford was hardly a religious man, and certainly not a church man, but he could recall that statement about the rich man from his father's having read it to him from the great Book.

More than that, too: his coming home rich while his old friends and neighbors could only dream of the things he had learned in Kansas about making money, devil take the hindmost. And once home, not being able to hide it, to allow it to rest, but rather having to make that money work. So, a sin of pride, maybe.

Taken altogether, his old hill-country morality rebelled a little against many of the things he had done and stood for, and maybe, just maybe, he was taking the mission of redeeming Catrina Peel as payment for the liability to his own soul.

It would be no easy task, he knew. The very idea that stood as the basis for the whole business was repugnant. Each time he looked at Catrina, he felt it. And said to himself, It wasn't her fault. It wasn't her fault! She was *not* Lot's daughter!

The sun had gone, and all the shadows around the house on the knoll had disappeared. Now there was nothing but a cool violet haze. From the horse barns came the gentle muttering of horses feeding and making ready for the night's sleep, and beyond that, on the wooded ridge, a whippoorwill was calling. There was a smell of spring, of fresh growing things, and across the yard, beneath the crabapple and black locust trees, there were the yellow blinking tails of lightning bugs, hundreds of them. And above, in the little glow of sun remaining, the barn swallows swept on pointed wings through the evening air and made their little *chee-chee* calls.

By then, Roman Hasford had taken three drinks of the bourbon whiskey, and when he went to the master bedroom to wake her, she was not asleep but lying on her side, face to the wall. Roman sat on the edge of the bed and touched her shoulder. She pulled away, quickly.

"Catrina, it's time for supper. Orvile's made some fried chicken. You always liked fried chicken."

"I'm not hungry. I don't want anything now."

"You need to eat," he said, and reached to touch her again, tentatively. She drew away and faced him, and her eyes in the half-light of the room were luminous, wide, frightened.

"I don't want any now," she said.

"All right, just get some sleep then."

He rose and left the room and went down the stairs, furious with himself that he'd had whiskey before going to her, knowing how the smell of it must bring back the image of her father.

That first night, Orvile set the dining room table for two, and then, as Roman was going up to fetch his wife, went to the horse-barn bunkhouse, still grinning, still thinking of this man and his wife having supper together.

But Roman ate alone.

Orvile Tucker was making breakfast, not because he had been told to, but because he sensed that if he didn't, nobody else would. Working over the great cast-iron cookstove, he heard Roman Hasford's boots along the floor directly above, could trace the path of the footsteps along the hall to the master bedroom, but only to the door, and then down the stairs.

He saw Roman's face, puffy from lack of sleep, and chose to ignore it. "Mister Roman," he said, "you gotta hire somebody to run this kitchen. I'm tryin' to breed horses and run that forge and put out garden and raise up some pigs, an' I ain't got time to be runnin' up here to the Big House all the time, makin' grub fer you and Miz Catrina."

"As soon as I can find somebody," Roman said. "Give me some coffee."

"I am, I am. Mister Roman, I can't teach a man but so much, and them four men you got down there handlin' horses, ain't one of 'em knows how to boil eggs."

"I said I'd find somebody," Roman said testily. "Why, hell, Elmer Scaggs can cook for a while, can't he?"

"Elmer Scaggs? Elmer Scaggs? Mister Roman, holy God, Elmer cook like a Comanche. He think you just throw the meat in the fire, and when it's black, you eat it."

That ended their conversation for the time being, because Catrina came in and sat at the table across from her husband. Orvile noted with a scowl that Roman Hasford reacted like a sleepy dray horse touched with the whip, suddenly coming to life with talk, clattering on, Orvile thought, like old white ladies discussing the weather and the geraniums and the barking dogs that kept them awake at night. Both picking at their eggs, Orvile noted, Miz Catrina nodding and muttering yes and no and nothing more, looking into her plate.

Elmer Scaggs burst into the kitchen like a gusty wind, smelling of alfalfa hay and horse manure, announcing in his loud voice that he was ready to show the new Missy around the horse barns so she could see all those wonderful mares and studs. Then he allowed, in a smaller voice, this time to Orvile, that all they'd had to eat for breakfast at the horse-barn bunkhouse had been corn-meal mush, at which Orvile glared at Roman. And began breaking more eggs into the skillet.

"Just let 'em cook a mite right side up," Elmer said.

"You get 'em how I cook 'em."

"All right, if I ain't got no selection, I'll take 'em shells and all if you say so."

Elmer laughed then, and looked at Roman and his wife at table for some appreciation of his wit, but neither seemed to have heard.

Orvile said, "You gonna get a horse up here so Mister Roman can go to his work in town?"

"Saddled and hitched outside," Elmer said. "Throw some of that sausage on the plate, too, and a dab of that hominy."

All of it just joyful, ain't it? Orvile thought. Kitchen smell good of cooking meat. Cool breeze through the open windows. Man and woman eating together. Then the man going off to his labor, kissing the forehead of his wife. I wonder where at is that big smile we seen yesterday.

Elmer, having bolted the massive meal Orvile laid in front of him at the little side table, escorted Catrina out to show her what she had come upon. But she was back within twenty minutes, before Orvile had finished cleaning the pots and dishes. And went straight up to her bedroom. Already, within twenty-four hours, to Orvile the master bedroom had become Catrina's room. Not Roman's.

Orvile Tucker watched it coming, like a hailstorm on the prairie. Each day, after Roman went into town, Catrina was in the kitchen, touching things: the hanging copper pots, the knob on the sink spigot that made water come and stop, the smooth surface of the chopping block. But she never made any move to help prepare her husband's meals. And before it was time for Roman to come home, she always went back upstairs. And when Roman did come, and it was time for dinner, it was always the same: Orvile serving, Catrina back down from her sanctuary, Roman talking a blue streak.

Talkin' about thangs she don't know about, don't care about, Orvile thought. Usually the bank business, arguing with Gallatin Delmonico about investments, about the slow pace of depositors, about loans to people who want to start a sawmill or a livery stable or get credit for seed. Or talking about the herd, the mares being made ready for standing studs so foals would drop in the spring, already men from Cassville coming to look at the stock, admiring the big red stallion that Roman called Junior, the one they'd brought from Kansas that Elmer Scaggs said was half Morgan, half mountain lion. Or talking about railroads being built into Arkansas from Monet, projected to line out all the way through the mountains to Fort Smith, Arkansas, and Paris, Texas. Or the one being built from Seligman, Missouri, to Eureka Springs. Or the ones being built into the Indian Territory.

All that talk, Orvile thought, just to get this little lady to talk back, strokin' some itch, like with a hound dog, but no itch there.

Once Roman challenged her directly.

"What have you been doing today, Catrina?"

"I didn't bother anything."

"I know that. I just wondered how you spent your day."

"Oh, watching the blackbirds."

"Are you still working on that sampler Mama started for you?"

"Sometimes."

"Do you need any more thread? They've got a lot of pretty new colors down at Caulder's store."

"I don't need any more thread."

Finally, in utter frustration, Roman rose and stamped out into the gathering night, muttering something about seeing to his mares. And Orvile Tucker, who had seen this man's temper flare violently, knew Roman was struggling to hold a close rein.

With Roman just gone, Catrina picked at her cherry cobbler or whatever it was, then rose and went upstairs to the master bedroom.

Orvile Tucker began to clean the kitchen. Talking to the stove, to the pans, to the hot dishwater.

"Bought that little red-wheel cart, and she ain't drove it once. Got her that gentle li'l pony, and she says she don't like to ride horses. She come all the way from Kansas astraddle of a horse, and she ain't rode that pony once. Got her that new sewing-machine contraption, and after one look she put it back in the box it come in and it ain't been out since. Mope around upstairs. Mope around down by the woods, all by her own self, even in the rain. All in her own li'l world and won't let nobody else inside it."

He stopped talking to himself when he heard Roman's heavy footfalls across the porch. Roman went through the kitchen and into the parlor where the bookshelves were, took down a volume, put it back, took down another, put it back.

He ain't gon' read none of them words, Orvile Tucker thought. He ain't read none of them words for a long while.

Every evening, when Roman went upstairs, Orvile took his time cleaning the kitchen, listening. Footfalls to the master bedroom, then out again and down the stairs. Roman then in the parlor, glowering into an open, unread book, a glass in his hand, and beside his chair on the floor a bottle of the Kentucky bourbon he'd told Orvile always to have there, ready.

And so, each evening, seeing this whole thing played out again and again, Orvile would finish his kitchen and stalk out and go to the horse-barn bunkhouse.

Get back to the horses, he thought. Get back to the horses, who got some sense.

Orvile Tucker understood horses. But white people? He knew he would never understand white people.

Throughout that hot summer, Roman Hasford tried. Every night after coming in from the bank, after his conversation at the kitchen table while Orvile Tucker laid down the food, after she went to her room, after he resisted the temptation of whiskey, he went to her. Sitting on the edge of the bed, he reached to touch her, talking gently about anything that came to mind. Dusty roads, cool west winds, calls of quail from across the Elkhorn Tavern Road.

She listened and sometimes responded in a soft voice, but when he actually touched her, she drew away. Not violently or even obviously, but just a sort of pulling into herself, like a terrapin slowly retracting its head into some kind of hard shell. He thought she was like a hunted creature, terrified at his nearness. Terrified as though, even without the whiskey on his breath, he gave off an odor of danger.

So, each night, back downstairs to his books and the bourbon, and saying to himself that tonight it was a little better, tonight was better than last night, but knowing it wasn't. Knowing it was not better but worse.

He knew that Orvile Tucker was watching, and Elmer Scaggs as well, both with some agony showing in their eyes because they realized there was no man and wife here, and both men put great store by such things. Both were solicitous to the point of embarrassment, even when Roman spoke to them rudely and abruptly. And afterward, lying awake in his bed, he was furiously ashamed that he had so abused these two whose loyalty had always tested true.

Roman Hasford's good intentions—and maybe his guilt, because guilt was better than helplessness—restrained his naturally volcanic temper until the first week of September.

The evening the eruption came began like all the others since April: the dinner where he did all the talking, the escape from rage by going to the horse barns, his return to the master bedroom—which, like Orvile, he no longer thought of as the master bedroom but as "her room."

Catrina was at her dresser, combing her hair. Roman entered with considerable thumping of boots, having long since decided never again to come onto her unexpectedly. He moved behind her and placed his hands on her shoulders.

"I've always liked looking at your black hair," he said. And started to say more, before she twisted from beneath his hands, dropped the brush on the floor, and rose to start for the bed. The bed Roman had come to despise because it was not the place of husband and wife as it should have been; it was Catrina's refuge, the cave into which she crawled to look out with those dark, accusing eyes.

In a sudden, blind fury, Roman leaped after her, once more taking her shoulders in both hands, but roughly now, spinning her around to face him.

"Stop it!" he shouted. "Stop it! Don't you know I'm your husband? I'm not going to hurt you, for God's sake. Give me a chance to be near you! To . . . to touch you. As a husband can . . . as a husband should!"

He was shaking her. Her hair fell into her face and her mouth sagged open. Roman stopped himself just short of slapping her. Keeping his hands on her shoulders, he caught his breath, then relaxed his grip.

"God, please," he said. She hung forward under his hands, unresisting, her face showing no expression at all, like a doll's face, everything painted in place. "I wouldn't hurt you. I . . . I . . ." But he couldn't bring himself to say it, didn't know how to say it.

That he was different from her father.

He tried to draw her to him gently, and again felt her body tense, go stiff with resistance. Even though her face remained the same. Blank, like the surface of a porcelain vase.

And then she said one word, softly. "No."

A soft word, but it rang in his ears like a scream, as clear and metallic as a tiny hammer striking a tiny anvil. A word forever.

And again, "No."

Roman dropped his hands. He was trembling. Not with any passion now, just defeat. She didn't turn and run to the bed as he had expected. She still stood, bent a little forward, a little toward him as though he were still holding her. He reached up and touched her cheeks with his fingertips and felt the moisture of tears.

"I'm sorry," he said. "I'm so sorry."

Then turned and walked away and down the stairs, in a rush, grinding his teeth. And would never know for the rest of his life whether in that moment his rage was against himself or Catrina.

Orvile Tucker met Elmer Scaggs in the dark yard, midway between the Big House and the horse-barn bunkhouse.

"What the hell was that?" Elmer Scaggs asked. "Did I hear somebody yell?"

"No. You never." Orvile said. "You stay out of it."

"Now Gawd damnit, what was that? And where are you goin'?"

"I'm sleepin' in the bunkhouse tonight," Orvile said. "And you never heerd nothin'."

"The hell I never. I'm goin' up there if the boss needs me."

"He don't need you. But if you goin', you'll find some of his bourbon whiskey in the pantry behind the bean bin. He'll need that."

Elmer Scaggs found Roman at the kitchen table, his fists knotted before him, his face a mask of anger that Elmer hardly recognized. Elmer got the whiskey from the pantry, a quart bottle of it, brought it out, poured a water glass full, and placed it on the table along with the bottle, beside the salt and pepper shakers. All without a word.

Sitting on a three-legged stool behind the great cookstove, Elmer watched as Roman began to consume the whiskey, glass by glass. Twice during the night, Elmer Scaggs rose and put wood into the stove because it was getting cold in the room. Once he left the kitchen, went down through the north yard to the barn bunkhouse, and found Orvile Tucker in one of the bunks, still awake in the darkness.

"What is it, Orvile?" Elmer Scaggs whispered.

Orvile Tucker rose to one elbow and reached up and took the front of Elmer Scaggs's shirt in his massive blacksmith's fist.

"Don't you ever say. But Elmer, Mister Roman sleepin' ever' night in that west bedroom. He ain't ever had his lady with him in his husband's bed. You hear?"

"Hell, I figured that from what I seen. Only nobody ever said it till right now."

"Don't you ever say nothin' about it to nobody. It's Mister Roman's sadness. No wife."

"It ain't right. I don't know what to do about it, though."

"Hush. You talkin' too loud. It's Mister Roman's sadness, that's what I think."

"Well," Elmer Scaggs whispered, "it ain't right. I'm goin' back up there."

"Don't you ever say nothin'," Orvile said. "To nobody."

When Elmer Scaggs came back into the kitchen, Roman Hasford glared at him. Elmer saw the bottle was half-empty.

"Where the hell you been?" Roman asked.

"Just had to take a little leak is all."

Roman drank from his water glass, made a horrible face, and gasped.

"God!" he said. "Elmer, you remember Kansas?"

"Why sure, boss, I remember all of that."

"Elmer," Roman said, taking another swallow, "you remember that Morgan mare, that big, beautiful Morgan mare?"

"Hell, yes, I remember her."

"Elmer?"

"Yes, boss?"

"I wish we were still in Kansas."

5

It should have been a good time. The bank was functioning under the steady hand of Gallatin Delmonico. Roman had hired a new man at the horse-barn cookshack, so Orvile Tucker became a permanent fixture in the Big House, even sleeping on a bunk in the pantry behind the kitchen. Often, Roman could hear Orvile and Elmer Scaggs talking in that little room, planning the day-to-day business of breeding good horses.

As he had promised his mother, Roman held a housewarming. In addition to family, Roman invited Gallatin and Missy Delmonico and Judah and Rebecca Meyer, and they ate in the dining room, using bone china and sterling flatware and linen napkins. Catrina answered the compliments to her house with "Thank you" and a small smile. She seemed to attend much of the conversation, though she added nothing to it. The men spoke of coming prosperity, and Martin Hasford grasped a few moments of reality and said the crops would be good this year. The Northerners complained of chiggers and ticks, and Ora Hasford said the best remedy for such tiny varmints was to rub the legs with coal oil before going into infested places. The bankers' women spent most of the evening casting furtive glances at Roman Hasford, at the head of the table, trying to measure at close range this strange man about whom they knew so little but who controlled the destiny of their husbands.

As for Roman himself, it was two hours of apprehension, waiting for his father to wander off into some Virginia battlefield or for Catrina to pull back into her protective shell.

But Martin Hasford did well, even commenting on the tenderness of Orvile Tucker's pork cutlets and the sweetness of this year's watermelons. And though she said little, Catrina's eyes were not hooded, nor was there the usual dark depth of preoccupation there.

But the next morning, as on so many other mornings of late, when Roman Hasford arrived at the bank in Gourdville, he needed a shave and smelled like a bin of soured apples. Gallatin Delmonico was much relieved when the president of the Farmer's and Merchant's Bank marched directly to his office, went inside, and slammed the door. And stayed there all day, finally emerging looking even harder than he had when he went in. Without a word he marched back across the lobby and out to the red stud Junior, who had been tied all day to the hitch rail in the street, mounted, and turned for home.

By then, clouds had come in from the Indian Nations, low and black, and it had begun to rain. One of those drizzling, cold September rains that would continue all night and into the next day.

Gallatin Delmonico moved to the plate-glass window with the gold-leaf lettering and watched Roman Hasford ride around the corner of the square and out of sight along the Elkhorn Tavern Road, slouched in the saddle, the rain gray around him. And Gallatin Delmonico could not help but think that it was appropriate. He had an idea what was happening. Had had it for some time, ever since that night at Ora Hasford's house when he'd had to return for his ledger.

Judah Meyer joined Gallatin at the window, both of them standing in their fine suits, hands in pockets, watching the people rush about in the rain across the street at the courthouse.

"The Old Man was as dismal as the weather today, wasn't he?" said Judah Meyer.

Gallatin Delmonico almost laughed. The "Old Man" was only three years older than Judah Meyer. But Gallatin Delmonico didn't laugh. And in later years he suspected that as he and Judah Meyer stood looking at the rain through that gold-leaf window, Judah Meyer's comment was perhaps the first time anyone in the county had referred to Roman Hasford as the "Old Man."

Instead of laughing, Gallatin Delmonico said, "Judah, when you are as rich as he is, you may smell and act as you please, too."

"Of course," said Judah Meyer. Laughing.

* * *

It was during that same September that Elmer Scaggs got drunker than he knew he should have. So drunk, in fact, that afterward he could not remember precisely some of the things he might have said as a result of his long anguish over the situation of his boss at Catrina Hills Farm.

When he had first arrived in the county, Elmer Scaggs had made discreet inquiries in the pool hall and around the courthouse and at Brown's Tavern concerning the availability of what he termed a professional lady. For although many people might have thought Elmer Scaggs was well past the age of carnal urges, on something like a monthly schedule the juices rose in him as though he were a twenty-five-year-old man.

There was indeed a woman to satisfy such urges, for a price. Gourdville was not unlike any other town of that size on the edge of what was still a frontier. Her name was Matie Luten and she had a house north of town on the Baxter Springs Road, a house on which Gallatin Delmonico had written a mortgage—one of his first official acts in the Farmer's and Merchant's Bank—after Matie Luten expressed a desire to improve her home. Gallatin Delmonico knew a good risk when he saw one.

The citizens of Gourdville and the county at large, being of similar mind to citizens of other such places, tolerated a whore. In fact, many were secretly glad she was there. Even though she was condemned in public discourse and from various pulpits, in private the decent ladies of the community, realizing the animal nature of all men, saw her as a safety valve for the violent lusts of the male population, lusts that might have been released on them if Matie hadn't been there.

As for the male population in question, they were most generally glad to have her for obvious reasons. Besides, she always paid her bills and never paraded brazenly on the streets of Gourdville or tried to show off better clothes than local wives and widows could afford.

Elmer Scaggs began a regular routine with Matie Luten to relieve his periodic calls of the flesh. Often he would ride into town with Roman Hasford in the mornings to visit, as he put it, then hang about and talk with various citizens at the bank or at Torten's Billiard Parlor—although he knew he was not particularly popular there—or at the courthouse, or with travelers from the Indian Nations in the lobby of the hotel. And on those days when Elmer

Scaggs was feeling the need of warm companionship beyond conversation, he would give a nickel to Bobby Joe Felcher, the lad who came to the square each day to deliver milk and butter to the hotel from his father's dairy on the Baxter Springs Road. At the same time, Elmer would instruct Bobby Joe to call on Miss Matie Luten on his way back to the dairy and inform her that payment was due on her note at the bank.

Of course, this message had nothing to do with Matie Luten's payment on the note. She knew it and so did Bobby Joe. What it meant was that Matie should turn aside other customers for that evening, if there were any, because Elmer Scaggs would be coming with a bottle of fine whiskey, some candy, and a lot of money. Matie Luten always complied because of the money, but also because she liked Elmer and his bumbling, gentle, bearlike lovemaking, and maybe even more than that, she liked the stories he told about Kansas and other whores he had known.

Elmer Scaggs had taken great pains to keep his boss from knowing about these little bouts with passion, but Roman Hasford knew, as did almost everyone else in the county. In fact, because of his rough appearance, Elmer Scaggs was pointed out in private conversation among respectable ladies as the perfect example of the public service Matie Luten performed by keeping this great, hairy, ugly roustabout from having lewd designs on the county's virginal or not-so-virginal women.

So it was on a September evening that Elmer Scaggs arrived at Matie Luten's door in a state of drunken despondency, having already gone the rounds of every saloon in Gourdville, even to Brown's Tavern on the Indian Nations Road, where he was no more welcome than at Torten's Billiard Parlor, in both places being considered the bodyguard lackey of a rich man.

The next morning, as he rode his mule around the edge of Gourdville and on toward the Big House, his head was pounding and his mouth felt as though it were lined with cotton seeds. But the worst part was that Elmer Scaggs could remember little of what had transpired the night before. He had no recall of the usual sweaty contacts or of funny stories exchanged.

Worse still, he did vaguely remember talking at some tearful length about the trials and tribulations of his boss since the little wife had arrived. He had the terrifying feeling that he had said his boss really didn't have a wife at all.

Since the beginnings of his elephantine trysts with a not-too-petite whore, Elmer Scaggs had felt twitches of guilt because he was doing such things and then going about his usual business with all the Hasfords, whom he mistakenly assumed would condemn his occasional base pleasures as a Sodom-and-Gomorrah depravity. But such minor concerns paled in comparison to the possibility that he had told a prostitute what he knew was a Hasford family secret, and maybe even a family shame, that Roman had never bedded his wife. Elmer Scaggs saw such a thing as disaster. A violation of the greatest trust he had ever been asked to bear.

So he was more miserable than he had ever been, in body and mind. For he knew that the hint of such a thing in this hill-country community would be seen as a measure of Roman Hasford's inadequate manhood.

A bad winter followed. There was more ice and snow than usual. And hard winds blowing in from the Nations, bringing evil-looking gray clouds and low temperatures.

Elmer Scaggs stayed in a constant state of anxiety, thinking about his last visit to Matie Luten. Orvile Tucker, now established in what he was calling his own kitchen in the Big House, tried during the blistering cold weeks to develop sympathy and affection for Catrina, but the harder he tried, the more he saw her as the cause of Mister Roman's discontent.

Everything was in retreat, inside and out. The country looked dead, the great hardwoods with their skeletal branches bare, their nakedness only emphasized by the scattered clumps of green cedar. In the fields, July's cornstalks were dry and brown, rattling in the wind like the last breaths in an old man's throat.

Many horses came down with distemper. None at Catrina Hills Farm, but Elmer Scaggs went to three neighbors' farms to help force the horses to inhale the vapor of smoldering crushed cedar leaves under a hood of burlap or canvas.

In Gourdville, the rooms at the hotel were empty. Missouri drummers and salesmen would avoid the ride south until spring, after the cold had gone. Business at the bank was almost at a standstill, and payments on loans were always late.

Gallatin Delmonico foreclosed a mortgage on a small farm on the west side of the county, near the Nations, and Corliss Buckmaten's newspaper spent the major portion of three issues railing against Yankee systems of squeezing out honest farmers. Sheriff Yancy Crane refused to serve an eviction notice, but it didn't matter. The farmer and his wife who had defaulted on their loan loaded everything into a wagon and, with one bony mule pulling it, lit out for Texas. Or someplace south. So, after a month of frustration with the machinery of county government, Gallatin Delmonico got the property on the tax rolls as a holding of the Farmer's and Merchant's Bank. All of which was coldly distasteful to a lot of people.

Each Sunday morning, Roman Hasford and Catrina drove in the hack to the old Hasford farm for dinner, even in severe weather, bundled in heavy lap robes and overcoats with fur collars. It was always a large meal, in the manner of well-to-do hill families on Sunday, but subdued. The conversation was carried by Roman and his mother, who talked mostly about the winters they had spent alone together on this farm during the war. Martin Hasford seldom came up from his netherworld. Catrina showed more interest in what Roman and his mother were saying than in the food, which Roman took as a good sign, but of course Ora complained that her daughter-in-law was eating like a bird.

Then, in midafternoon, Roman and Catrina would drive back to their home, wordlessly, and into the routine that had become established since that evening when Roman had almost struck her, had fallen into the very violation he'd so despised in her father.

Roman never went to the master bedroom now. And Catrina never appeared in the parlor where Roman sat with his books and bourbon. They ate breakfast together, and sometimes supper, in the kitchen. It was their only real contact. But since it had become clear that certain areas of the Big House had been marked out silently for each of them, Catrina began to talk a little. Not much, just a little. She liked to watch the birds that came to the west porch where Orvile Tucker put out bread crumbs for them, and she would talk about them sometimes, asking Orvile what kinds of birds they were, and he would tell her.

Once, during January, Elmer Scaggs said he saw the pug marks of two wolves in the snow behind the horse barns, on the slopes of Pea Ridge, and Catrina was obviously frightened and became actually animated in asking about what wolves did and where they lived and what they killed. And Roman found some satisfaction in reassuring her that she had nothing to fear from wolves even if she wanted to walk in the yard, which he knew she often did during the day when he was at the bank.

It had all become very civil, Roman thought. Never joyful, but civil. At least, he thought, she is warm and well fed. He had done that for her. And for now, he decided, that was all he could do for her.

That winter Roman read through Mr. Gibbon's book on the Romans once more, already knowing it well, but at least Mr. Gibbon took up a lot of time. And he needed something to take up a lot of time. Desperately. Often he took a small-bore shotgun and went hunting for squirrel along Pea Ridge. Orvile Tucker fried squirrel and then made a brown gravy, and Catrina seemed to eat that better than most things.

Roman hired some men to dig another well on the property, this one just behind the horse barns. They had to use black powder to break through the strata of limestone rock, which scared hell out of the horses, so it was abandoned before water was struck.

He thought about building a new house for Lark Crozier at Wolf Cove Mill, but winter wasn't the time for such things, any more than it was the time for building a new stone spring house in the wooded draw just south of his mother's house.

But something. Anything. To consume time. The bank didn't do it. Delmonico and Meyer had that so well in hand that Roman felt like a bridle without a bit when he was there. He set the policy, but the other two did the work. And the horse farm didn't do it. There was only so much time a man could spend exercising mares and rubbing them down when there were people like Elmer Scaggs and Orvile Tucker seeing to feed and procreation and stall cleaning.

Finally he made a decision. With spring coming and time to get out and make another mark someplace, like a dog putting its scent on the boundaries of his territory, he decided to get involved with politics. Which he should have known that a man in his position would have to do eventually anyway. But being Roman Hasford, son of Ora Hasford, whole-hog-or-die, he would not go about it in some minor way. He would jump in thrashing and kicking from the start, just as a baby, never having seen the water, might be thrown in to sink or swim.

And just maybe, in his innermost mind, Roman Hasford had had all the sinking he intended to take after his failure with Catrina. From now on, he was going to swim.

Two of the people closest to Roman Hasford took the same view, but in different ways.

Elmer Scaggs said to Orvile Tucker, "Listen, if you know anything about how thangs really work, like me and the boss did in Kansas, you got to be close to the catbird's seat."

Gallatin Delmonico said directly to Roman himself, "Mister Hasford, it's best not to *own* those in public office. Bad things can accrue. But it doesn't hurt to hold a mortgage on their tenure."

6

Politics was a volatile vocation in northwest Arkansas in the decade after the war. There were still old Civil War wounds. And a lot of people enjoyed picking at them to keep them bleeding. No matter which side of a public or even a private decision a man came down on, there were plenty of citizens ready to brand him with a red-hot iron. Too Yankee or too Rebel. Too Reconstruction. Too fence-straddler. Too Democrat. Too Republican. And combinations of all these. It was not difficult to work certain segments of the community into righteous wrath over anything seen as contrary to their best interests, collectively or individually. And usually it wasn't too clear what their best interests were. But feelings could run deep, even if it was nothing more than a stubborn resistance to any idea held by any man perceived to be a dyed-in-the-wool son of a bitch.

Alcohol didn't help. A few citizens would imbibe too much peach brandy or sour-mash whiskey from one or another of the three distilleries in the county, or maybe sip too often from a jug of corn moonshine cooked in any of numerous wooded hollows, and suddenly remember past prejudices that seemed appropriate to resurrect. Heated arguments ensued on the public square, with many parties coming close to resorting to knives or firearms.

There was a jail in the basement of the courthouse, with two cells, where those disposed to public drinking could be placed until rambunctious spirits dried out. And once more the courthouse had become the center of county business, as it had been before the war and the Yankee occupation. Because it was clear now that the Yankee government, as everyone considered that Washington city apparatus to be, was getting tired of fiddling around with the South. So now everybody could regain control of their own destiny.

Nobody in the county knew how this was working in the rest of the old Confederacy. Nor did they really give a damn, just so long as bushwhackers and freebooters and carpetbaggers and scalawags and Northern do-gooders stayed clear of them and let them tend to their own business.

Court was in session across the street from the bank about four months out of the year. On the bench was a Republican named Jacob Rich. He was not one of those crazy Reconstruction Republicans, so he was well entrenched with the electorate. A circuit judge who sat in three counties and a resident of Fayetteville, he was also the first man on record in that area who wore a toupee. It was supposed to be a black toupee, but somehow it bleached out now and again, so His Honor had to touch it up with lampblack to keep it in proper color, and then when he perspired there were lovely charcoal etchings down his cheeks and into his beard. Because of this, people called him the Zebra. But they voted for him nonetheless.

Each county had its own prosecuting attorney and sheriff, and the Gourdville pair were not firmly entrenched at all. Both were Democrats having some rumored connections with downstate scalawags.

The prosecutor was Timothy Burton, who had served in the first Reconstruction legislature, which was mostly a Republican forum. It made his tenure a little shaky.

And there was Yancy Crane, the outlander sheriff from Illinois who lived occasionally with his wife, Claudine, a mule of a woman in both temperament and size, in contrast to Yancy, who reminded some of an overweight rat.

For some time, Yancy Crane seemed to have spent most of his waking hours, and some of his sleeping ones, too, at Courtland Brown's tavern, a mile west of town on the Indian Nations Road.

Brown's Tavern wasn't anything like the old Elkhorn Tavern. It was owned and run by old Courtland and his wife, Sarah, and their three sons, Drake, Essex, and Becket. Although old Courtland made no pretense of a knowledge of history, Sarah did, being inordinately proud of her English ancestry as evidenced by the names she gave her sons. She was quick to tell anyone who cared to listen that her husband had nothing to do with the naming, that she herself had done it. Like her last-born being such a beautiful, blue-eyed child, she had felt compelled to give him a handle once used by an Archbishop of Canterbury. Had old Henry II of England been able to see Becket Brown, he would have had a great laugh. Because that old archbishop of Henry's had been rather intelligent, according to all reports, while Becket Brown was so dumb that sometimes he had to be told which direction was east, so the folk of the county said.

Which was an injustice, because Becket Brown knew which direction was east. It was where the sun came from each day. It was only north and south that gave him trouble.

Anyway, citizens of the county said that if you had trouble at night, when most trouble came, there was no use sending for Sheriff Yancy Crane, because he'd be out there at Brown's Tavern and wouldn't budge from his five-card stud game with Drake and Essex and Becket, the four of them drunker by sundown than boiled cats, and violently resistant to all interruptions.

So Roman Hasford, who had tasted a little of the political stew in Leavenworth, Kansas, decided that prosecuting attorney and sheriff provided a good place to start.

Instead of going at it one barrel at a time, Roman determined to make a run at both offices at once. So he had a party at Catrina Hills Farm. He invited a group of people who were either Republicans or, whatever their party, were disenchanted with the incumbents. A lot of people in the county said later that this gathering was the very moment when Roman Hasford started taking control of their lives.

He didn't intend it that way. Why, hell, he said to himself, I'm not even a Republican. I don't know what I am.

But the two incumbents were Democrats, and to challenge them meant branding himself, to many, with the mark of Reconstruction and the Freedman's Bureau. Well, Roman reckoned, neither of those things are so all-fired important in northwest Arkansas anyway.

Which, he was to learn, was a miscalculation of the strength of hidden hatreds. But no matter. Republican brand it was, and devil take the hindmost.

It was a male gathering, women having no vote. Some of the men claimed later that they saw the face of Catrina in an upstairs window as they came up to the Big House, where one of Roman Hasford's horse-barn employees took the reins of their horses. They reported it as a small, valentine face, large-eyed, pale, tentative, behind the white lace curtain.

The gathering took up two quadrants of the porch, in the shade. There were barrels of ice and two long tables with cole slaw and fried fish set alongside a few modest pitchers of lemonade, just for appearances, before a forest of bourbon and sour-mash bottles. Orvile Tucker was there, in a starched white shirt and black vest, not much warm welcome in his bloodshot gaze for the various guests.

Among those were Harley Stone, who owned the Stone Hotel on the same side of the square as Roman's bank, and who was establishing a reputation for fine food in his hostelry, Sunday dinner for only two bits, all you could eat. The ice in the barrels along the porch came from his ice house, which was as heavily mortgaged to the Farmer's and Merchant's as was the hotel itself.

Then there was Anson Greedy, the barber, an old resident of the county who had sat around a ridge fire many a night before the war and listened to the fox dogs running while talking about God with Roman's father, Martin. And Isaac Maddox, a Scots-Irish tobacco farmer, also an Old Settler, and mortgaged to the hilt with Roman's bank. And Doctor Hazlet Cronin, a young Missouri medico who had come down from Jefferson City five years after the war and who everyone said looked like Abe Lincoln, God forbid, with his black chin whiskers and moles all over his face. And Jefferson Caulder, who owned the best mercantile store in the county and had five daughters and a wife who together, many said, could start their own female legislature if so inclined, and run the state better than it was being run now.

Courtland Brown and his sons were not invited. For obvious reasons. Nor was Major Corliss Buckmaten.

It was summertime, but the heat was bearable on the wide porches, what with the barrels of ice. There were meadowlarks doing a great song from the fields across the Elkhorn Tavern Road, and jays made their presence known in the hardwood timber east of the house. Now and then one of Roman's stallions gave a small whistle from its pen, as though not wanting to be completely ignored, and from that same direction there came on a soft wind the scent of horse droppings, sweet and musty. A smell all these men understood and appreciated.

Guests of honor, although not identified as such, were Terrance Shadbolt, a young lawyer from Fort Scott, Kansas, in the county less than a year, and Hamlin Bidd, a threadbare farmer who'd lived in the county all his life except for a short stint in the Cherokee Nation as a deputy United States marshal out of the Federal court in Van Buren, before the court was moved across the river to Fort Smith.

Shadbolt was a small, intense man, dark of features and hair, who had some trouble keeping food on the table for his wife and two children. He tried to sustain them with fees from writing wills and doing probate, and bringing a suit now and then against somebody whose pigs had rooted through a fence and into a fresh turnip patch.

Bidd was a big, lanky man, straw-haired and pale-eyed, with a large jaw, a bachelor trying to gain headway on an apple orchard north of Gourdville and just barely making ends meet by doing odd-job cabinetwork and gunsmithing. It was said that he was the best shot in the county with the possible exception of Roman Hasford.

Roman didn't make a big ceremony of it. After all his guests were in mellow disposition with the icy drinks, he invited Shadbolt and Bidd into his parlor, where all the books were, and they had a few sips alone together, the two men obviously very nervous and wondering what the hell was going on. Roman remarked on the dry weather and then about the railroad coming soon, and the other two nodded, holding their drinks in front of them like some kind of protective shield. So at last he told them.

"Some of the citizens of this county have decided that you two gentlemen are going to be our next prosecuting attorney and sheriff."

It was as though someone told them gold had been discovered on their property. Or else that someone had hit them between the eyes with a ten-pound sledgehammer.

Roman escorted them out onto the porch and made a little talk. His guests enthusiastically welcomed the announcement, and there was much back-slapping and many vows of support and parades back to the tables where the bottles stood. At one point Terrance Shadbolt said, "Why should I do this thing?"

And Isaac Maddox replied, "To keep from starving, man."

Everyone on the porch that day understood what Roman had learned in Kansas. Political power was not necessarily held by those in office, but by the ones who put them there.

And so Roman Hasford stayed in the background. Or at least he tried to. Making no speeches. Beating no drums. His contribution was his pocketbook. Which meant that throughout the campaign, he called the turns.

Out front of it all was the County Committee Against Courthouse Corruption. That was the name of it; a campaign committee composed of two men: Harley Stone, of the Stone Hotel, and Isaac Maddox, the farmer. One from town, one from the land, as Roman pointed out, so a citizen could feel his interests were being protected no matter where he lived.

The last part of that name, the Courthouse Corruption part, was the inspiration of Jefferson Caulder of the mercantile. He knew from conversations he'd heard over the bean bin and the thread box in his store that people suspected many things of Sheriff Yancy Crane, true or not. Maybe there was some money collected for taxes that never got to the county treasurer. Maybe there were a lot of fines that went into a Crane pocket.

"By God, you listen," Caulder shouted in his great, booming voice. "You arrest a drunk man on Saturday night. You lay him in the jail until next morning, when you turn him out before breakfast. Then you bill the county for two days of grub for this drunk, and you haven't fed him a single corn dodger! It's easy."

"You mean Crane's been doing that?" Dr. Cronin asked.

"Who gives a good God damn whether he's been doing it or not? It's got the appearance of it, hasn't it?

"And tar the prosecuting attorney with the same brush. You don't have to accuse anybody. Just a hint here and there. The people in this county will put it together in their heads. Just explain the system. A sheriff can get rich. Just explain it and the people will make the accusations at the polls!"

Harley Stone said, "Now, gentlemen, there are a lot of good people in this county who are Democrats."

"Name me one," said Isaac Maddox, to everybody's laughter.

"No, truly, Isaac, there are. You know that."

"Yes," said Isaac Maddox. "I know that. And I also know, Harley, that since the war those good people haven't had much chance to vote for anybody worth a damn, have they? So we put up a good slate, we'll get most of those Democrats you think are good."

It was going to be one hell of a campaign, Roman reckoned. First, some decent clothes for the candidates, both of whom were pretty threadbare. You couldn't have a man asking for the votes, it was said, if his ass was showing through a ragged hole in his britches! Nothing at all ostentatious, of course, nothing expensive. Just clean, honest clothes, no patches on the elbows. Hard-working clothes. Deduct the cost of them from the loan outstanding to Caulder's mercantile, the loan outstanding at the Farmer's and Merchant's Bank.

"By God," shouted Jefferson Caulder when presented with the idea, "I can put a good suit on those two men for seven dollars apiece!"

"Too uppity," Isaac Maddox said. "Give 'em the four-dollar ones."

"Well, the shoes are gonna cost two dollars. And that's my price!"

Grooming. Each candidate was sent to Anson Greedy's barbershop once a week to get trimmed and powdered. But none of that expensive-smelling bay rum. "So all right," Anson Greedy said, "Who pays? I ain't cuttin' hair for the absolute fun of it."

"Roman Hasford pays. He comes in about once a month, he pays for all those trims and shaves and talcum powder. But no paper on it and no receipts. Just do them as contributions to the candidates, and then when Roman comes, a little cash in the hand."

"That's fine," said Anson Greedy. Although his barbershop was one of the few places in Gourdville not mortgaged to Roman Hasford, Greedy remembered Roman's daddy before Martin had gone senile. "That's fine."

"We need to get that alto band down here from Cassville," Isaac Maddox said. "I hear they're real good and play loud."

"They ain't comin' for nothin'," said Anson, and everybody looked at Roman.

"We'll get 'em down here. Feed some good pork to those boys and whatever else they want. We'll get 'em down here."

"I just thought of something else. Watermelons," said Jefferson Caulder. "Isaac, you know folks out in the county got good watermelons?"

"Why, hell, yes."

"Ought to have a big watermelon supper. Right on the God-damned square. Right in the middle of town."

Everybody looked at Roman.

"We'll pay top price for the watermelons," he said. "Penny a pound? Whatever it is. Big watermelon supper. Right in front of the bank. Gallatin Delmonico can cut the first one."

Everyone laughed.

So the fight was joined. At first it seemed the Democrats had a great advantage. The only newspaper in Gourdville was the *Advertiser*, and Major Corliss Buckmaten wasted no time firing off weekly blasts at what he called the Scalawag Social Club, with Roman Hasford's name always prominently displayed.

But Corliss Buckmaten had a real problem of conscience about the campaign itself. It put him in the position of having to fight for Yancy Crane, whom he despised. Always before it had only been a matter of endorsing the Democratic slate, not actually *fighting* for it. Because there was no real opposition. Now there was opposition. So it was fight for Yancy, which, to Corliss Buckmaten, was much like fighting for smallpox, or else give the ticket to the Republicans. Like hell he would!

And there was something worse, if that was possible. Roman Hasford's campaign had forced Corliss Buckmaten to sit himself on the same bench with the Browns of Brown's Tavern. And if Yancy Crane was smallpox, the Browns were the black plague.

But by God, the fiery little editor thought, any kind of Democrat is better than a Republican!

Corliss Buckmaten hadn't counted on what amounted to an *organized* political campaign. He was aghast to learn that Terrance Shadbolt and Hamlin Bidd went about the county talking to people. Dressed in their honest suits and riding mules, not horses, because mules (bought from Catrina Hills Farm on credit) had the proper humility.

Even Corliss Buckmaten didn't realize the depth of this thing. As with Isaac Maddox drawing up a list of voters according to religion and then instructing the candidates . . .

"Don't ever talk about dancin' with Baptists. Don't ever refuse a little sip of grape juice from a Methodist. And if a Presbyterian gives you a cup of elderberry wine, don't gulp it, and put in a good word for John Calvin. And for God's sake, don't talk about Revelations with any of 'em!"

And then the *Committee Correspondent* began to appear in Gourdville. Each Saturday, when a lot of farmers were in town. Distributed by freckle-faced urchins, free of charge. A single sheet of paper printed on both sides, it gave some of those hints Jefferson Caulder had spoken of, extolling the virtues of Shadbolt and Bidd. And at the bottom of each sheet was a coupon that any kid could take to Caulder's mercantile store to be redeemed for a licorice whip. Those licorice whips? Once more, without anyone but Jefferson Caulder and Roman Hasford knowing it, their cost was deducted from that loan, a penny at a time.

The paper was printed in Joplin, Missouri. Each Monday morning, Elmer Scaggs rode away from Catrina Hills Farm with the next issue's copy and the cash to pay for the words to be set in type. The next day he'd be back, with a small bale of the broadsides.

The copy was written each Sunday in the parlor of the Big House, Roman and Harley Stone and the two candidates putting the words together. Most of the phrases were Roman's, borrowed liberally from the books on his shelves. But nothing fancy, nothing too high-toned.

It was more fun than Roman had had since the time he'd won a turkey in a pistol shoot at Fort Leavenworth. And there were many hours when he completely forgot that Catrina was upstairs in her room, the door closed.

The printer in Joplin provided other things, too. Like samples of the ballot that citizens would see in November, with great red checks in the right places. These were scattered all over the county and produced screams from Major Corliss Buckmaten in the columns of the *Advertiser* that the scalawags were sowing the seeds of Satan.

Or people would rise to a new morning and find large placards nailed to trees or to barns or to chicken coops, lettered large: "Vote for Shadbolt." "Elect Bidd." "Terrance and Hamlin, Your Honest Men!"

After it was all over, Isaac Maddox said, "Hell, that damned Brown's Tavern bunch didn't have a chance!"

And he was right.

The fall smelled good that year. There had been a lot of slow, gentle rain on the earth, and then a quick little frost that turned the persimmons golden brown and sweet. The trees along the ridge behind old Elkhorn Tavern and Catrina Hills Farm were ablaze with color as the leaves turned pink and red and yellow and orange.

Often Roman Hasford went onto his south-side porch, a heavy shawl over his legs, a bottle of Kentucky bourbon beside his rocking chair on the floor, and watched the sun leave, the trees turn more and more each day from the great, blooming green mushrooms of foliage to skeletons of bare limbs. He would smile then and sip the bourbon and think how wonderful it was to buy a whole county.

Why, hell, it's easy when you've got a bank.

PART TWO

THE TROUBLE

7

The great national panic and depression that came in those early years of the Hasford Farmer's and Merchant's Bank slowed business to a crawl. When the Jay Cooke banking empire in the East went bust, along with a lot of other outfits that had been operating the way Cooke had been, the shock waves spread like an Indian Nations cyclone. But Gallatin Delmonico had reason to smile a little.

There were going to be a few tobacco farmers and lumber people who had overreached, and it would mean foreclosures as the markets shrank. And Gallatin Delmonico knew that once the country's financial crisis was past, the property thus obtained would be worth a lot more than it had been when mortgaged for Hasford cash.

And, second, the Farmer's and Merchant's capital was invested in the county, a thing for which Gallatin Delmonico could take full credit and pride, having dissuaded Roman Hasford in his desire to sink a lot of that money in railroads. Because when the crash came, a full 25 percent of the country's railroads went bankrupt. And once the panic was past, and a little money started moving again in places like St. Louis and Cincinnati, the railroads would begin building once more, because the country wanted and needed railroads. After the scare of the crash, boards of directors would be very cautious and conservative, and would establish a solid base of business in which Roman could put some of his money if he continued to have this sentimental attachment to coalsmoke and crossties.

Besides which, a couple of the county sawmills that Gallatin Delmonico knew would go broke and be foreclosed would make large profits for the bank in operating those mills to provide white oak crossties for the St. Louis–San Francisco Railroad, which was building south from Monet all the way to Texas and on to the Pacific Ocean. The line surveys had already been planned right in the county.

More than that, some of the real estate the bank was about to acquire, owing to mischance of fate and finance, was smack in the middle of the railroad right-of-way. And Gallatin Delmonico was well aware that such land sold at premium.

"Missy," he said to his wife, "it seems Mr. Hasford is most assuredly unlucky in affairs of the heart, but when it comes to making money, he is the most unconsciously blessed son of a bitch I have ever known."

"Mr. Delmonico," she replied, "watch your language in front of the children."

But the crash brought something else with which Gallatin Delmonico was not so ready to deal: a wave of unemployed and desperate men, come to the end of rail lines in Missouri, riding the rods or empty boxcars, and then filtering south. Looking for food. Looking for anything better than what they had, which was nothing.

Never having lived alongside a railroad line, the people in the county were not accustomed to hobo traffic. But there was considerable sympathy for these vagrants who had been working men before the panic, particularly among hard-shell Democrats like Corliss Buckmaten.

Generally, these wanderers were considered a nuisance but not much more. Until two things happened. First, people got the intelligence from a Joplin newspaper that groups of such men had banded together in various places, and one such outfit had virtually taken over a southern Illinois town, running off the people and sleeping in their beds and eating from their larders and vandalizing the town's businesses. A lot of the county's citizens said this was going a piece farther than nuisance.

Then the second thing. One of the migrants in northwest Arkansas had a horse. The two people who had seen it said it didn't amount to much—just a little gray gelding on its last legs and with ribs showing through its hide like a Monday washboard—but a horse was a horse, and a horse conjured up images of the past for the Old Settlers. Images of riders who claimed to be partisans for one side or the other during the war but who were actually nothing better than bands of savage outlaws.

"He likely ain't one of the honest working men," said Isaac Maddox. "Just like in the war, he's likely some peckerwood taking advantage of the circumstance."

"No matter how it's reckoned, people don't like it," Sheriff Hamlin Bidd said. "A lot of them are hearing a horse at night and next day a pig or a mess of chickens are gone. We can't track the son of a bitch because he uses roads and hard-packed trails. And if you can't track him, you can't find him. Why, there's enough timber in this county to hide fifty men until who-shot-John!"

That realization sent a shiver up the backs of old residents. It wasn't a pleasant thought, a lot of horseback vagrants coming into the countryside and laying out in the timber all day, maybe as far away as the Nations or White River, then slipping in to take a man's livestock at night.

"These newcomers don't know what it was like during the war," Harley Stone would say to anybody who paused in his hotel lobby for a little visiting. "But some of us know what it was like. I don't feel too comfortable about that horse out there. I thought we'd come to the time when we knew every horse in the county and who rode it. No sir! I don't feel solaced about that horse."

Still, the new people who hadn't lived there in the years immediately after the Battle of Pea Ridge had no sense of dread. Major Corliss Buckmaten wrote in an *Advertiser* editorial: "These poor men, victims of Yankee viciousness and Republican greed, must be welcomed and given succor. They should be taken to our hearts. Remember the Good Samaritan."

"Bullshit," said Isaac Maddox. "I'm out there on a limb, just me and the old lady and all my young'uns growed and gone off and three hired hands who'd run like scalded dogs if a wolf howled clear over in the Nations. And I seen in 1862 what these roving outfits can do if they're mounted. You have too, Roman."

"If any of them come mounted, we'll handle it," Roman said.

"Hell, boy, they already *have* come mounted!"

Roman remembered. How the partisans had ravaged everyone. How livestock had had to be hid in the woods or else it would fall to bushwhackers' cleavers. How one band had held the bare feet of a farmer in the coals of his fireplace until he told them where he'd hid the money, the only problem for the farmer being that he didn't have any money, hidden or otherwise. How another band had hanged old Tulip Crozier at Wolf Cove Mill, hanged him with baling wire right there beside his big wheel inside the mill, because he had had the guts to tell them to get the hell off his property.

Roman remembered.

The vagrants kept coming. In twos and threes, sleeping in the woods, asking for handouts at back doors—anything, a chunk of cold salt pork used to cook last night's beans, a crust of corn bread, and always a drink of cool water from the well.

"We'll draw it up, ma'am," they always said. "But we don't want to drink out of your bucket, so have you got a dipper?"

More and more were seen on the county roads, usually late in the day. Furtive as pregnant foxes, most people thought. Slipping off into the woods when anyone approached.

More and more citizens thought they heard a horse at night, too late for anyone who was an honest man to be out riding. And soon there were rumors going around that there was more than one horseman. People started going armed, even in the middle of the day. Caulder's mercantile store started selling a lot of bolts for doors. And a lot of ammunition.

It was springtime, and the smell of the hills was as it always was, like fresh lettuce, and the trees budding out even looked like lettuce, fresh green, fluffy, exploding into what would soon become hardwood jungles. First there was redbud, lilac-colored and delicate, then wild plum, pink and radiant, and finally dogwood, cotton puffs of pure white scattered along the hillsides among the oak and walnut and hickory.

The black-eyed Susans growing wild along the Elkhorn Tavern Road did not have Roman's attention on the afternoon he rode to his mother's house. Although he was usually alert to the new juice of spring, there were other things on his mind that day. And certainly, riding behind him on the mule, Elmer Scaggs was unaware of the exploding splendor around him.

Roman had a gift for his mother. He gave it to her on her front porch, Martin sitting there in his rocking chair, calling him "Doctor" and complaining of back pains. Elmer Scaggs was still on his mule about halfway down the slope before the house, Wire Road behind him.

"What's the matter with Elmer?" Ora Hasford asked. "Does he think we're gonna bite him?"

"I guess he's mad at me," Roman said. "I told him he had to stay here with you and Papa for a while, until all this business of outlanders wandering through slacks off."

"Roman, you're takin' him away from those mares just when they're about to foal. I don't blame him for bein' mad. Tell him to come on up here, and I don't need anybody to look out for me. Now or never."

Roman started to argue, then remembered that this was not some hired hand or horse buyer but his mother, who brooked no arguments, especially from him.

"All right," he said. "But anyway, I brought you something. It's time for you to get shed of that old muzzle-loading blunderbuss you keep in the kitchen."

"Blunderbuss? It stood us in good stead a lot of times."

"Times have changed, Mama."

"More's the pity."

"Well, here it is."

It was a new double-barreled Remington shotgun, twelve-gauge, full choke, exposed hammers. With two boxes of ammunition, one of number-eight shot, the other of double-ought buck.

Ora accepted it as most women would accept a hand-painted teapot.

"Well," she said, opening the breech and looking down the barrels.

"Now, Mama, if you want to shoot some doves or maybe a squirrel, use the eights. But at night, keep it loaded with the buckshot."

Ora laughed and placed a hand on her son's shoulder.

"I'm sure glad you told me that," she said. "I never would have known what to do if you hadn't told me."

"All right, Mama, all right."

"Now get Elmer on up here to the house," Ora said. "Your papa wants to talk to him, and besides, I've got some oatmeal cookies just out of the stove and we can have a few. And thank you for the nice shotgun."

It was a short visit, Ora telling them that her garden was planted, with lettuce and radishes and Irish potatoes and cabbage.

"I sure hope you put in a lot of cabbage, Miz Hasford," Elmer said. "So you can make about a ton of that kraut again."

"Well, maybe not a ton, Elmer, but enough."

Nobody mentioned Catrina. Nobody ever mentioned Catrina

now. But watching her son and Elmer Scaggs ride away, Ora Hasford thought about Catrina, and her thoughts were not nice. The pretense of a happy marriage was gone now. Ora Hasford didn't know all the details, and maybe she didn't want to know, but it was obvious to anybody close to Roman and life on that horse farm that there wasn't much marriage.

It infuriated her, because here was her opportunity for grandchildren. She doted on any child, and the only grandchild she had was Calpurnia's, in St. Louis, a little boy named Eben whom she had never seen and now never expected to see, this woman who would have welcomed a dozen grandchildren. To love and cuddle them, to feed them and sew for them and tell them the stories she had heard Martin tell but was no longer capable of telling, or even of remembering. To show them the wood violets sprung up, to help her churn the creamy white milk until, magically, there was butter. To tuck them into one of her own beds under one of the comforters she had quilted with her own fingers. To listen with them as the little frog-songs announced the coming of spring. To make them gingerbread men for Christmas.

Maybe what was worst of all was that Roman's compassion for a mistreated child, which she recognized came largely from herself, had turned to bite them both. So, in place of grandchildren, she had a new breech-loading shotgun.

Roman had rearmed himself, too. He and Elmer Scaggs and Orvile Tucker had come from Kansas with a couple of large-bore repeating rifles, Elmer's scattergun, and an old Navy Colt that Roman had had for years. Now he had a rifle rack in the hall of the Big House, well equipped, and two Colt single-action pistols, both .45 caliber, one with a four-and-three-quarter-inch barrel, good for hiding under a coat, and another with a seven-and-a-half-inch barrel, complete with heavy belt and holster. When he bought that last one from Jefferson Caulder, he had remarked that it was primarily for bear-hunting, and laughed.

"So," said Jefferson Caulder, "if you miss the son of a bitch, you can always beat him to death with this massive thing."

"I don't miss," Roman snapped, no longer laughing.

It infuriated him. Not what Jefferson Caulder had said, but his own reaction to it. More and more, Roman was allowing his irritability to surface, to structure his words. And he wasn't proud of it.

Why, hell, he thought, Jeff Caulder was only joshing me, and I acted like a cranky old man.

A large part of his bad disposition he laid at the door of Corliss Buckmaten and that newspaper, in the columns of which Roman Hasford had been called a great many unflattering things. Surprisingly enough, perhaps the epithet Roman most resented was "Republican." Not because he supposed there was anything inherently bad about Republicans, but because he didn't consider himself a Republican or a Democrat or anything else, any more than he considered himself a Methodist or a Baptist.

As Roman saw it, he was just a citizen who wanted to put in public office men he perceived to be good and honest.

Getting a haircut in Anson Greedy's barbershop, he asked the question of Isaac Maddox, who was waiting his turn.

"Isaac, what is a Republican, anyway?"

"Me," said Isaac. "I'm a Republican. I'm for Union and free enterprise."

"Why, hell, the war's over. Everybody's for those things."

"They ain't either."

"What about before the war?" asked Anson Greedy, snipping with his scissors.

"Well, what about it?"

"Your daddy before the war, he was a Democrat," Anson said. "I don't know what he is now."

"Martin Hasford's always been my friend," said Isaac. "But before the war I was a Whig."

"They wasn't no Republicans before the war," said Anson.

"They was Whigs, though," Isaac said. "Now we're Republicans."

"But what the hell *is* a Republican?"

"He's a man who never votes for a Democrat," Isaac said, and he and Anson laughed.

"You're not doing a damned thing to clear my mind, are you?" Roman said with considerable heat, enough to cloud Isaac Maddox's face with anger and send him stomping out of the shop without waiting for his haircut.

Roman's evil temper fed on itself, too, because each time he was abrupt to someone, he spent the rest of the day in silent self-reproach and irritation. It seemed so much harder than it once had to lift himself out of such moods.

Well, sometimes there were good things that did it.

As happened on the day he bought the big pistol from Jefferson Caulder and went home to find that Orvile Tucker had baked a pigeon pie. Pigeon pie was Roman's absolute favorite meal.

For some time, two Cherokee boys had been coming into the county selling pigeons. Over in the Nations, these boys caught the pigeons in their night roosts with a fishnet. They brought them to Gourdville in burlap bags, alive, and sold them for two pennies each to Harley Stone at the hotel and to Orvile Tucker at Catrina Hills. Sometimes when the boys came, their burlap bags bulged with two hundred pigeons.

"I make a good pigeon pie with six pigeons," said Orvile Tucker. "But it's better if I use twelve, and a lot of butter. Mr. Roman can eat one of those pies all by his ownself."

The boys were Poco Jimmy and Kingsnake. At least, that's what the white people called them. After a day of enterprise in the county, they usually went to Raymond Ort's bakery, just off the square at Gourdville, and bought a loaf of bread. With that, and a couple of pigeons they'd held out, they'd go into the woods and build a fire and roast the birds over it and eat. And the next morning they'd walk back to the Indian Nations.

From time to time, Roman had left a few little gifts with Orvile Tucker for the boys—pocket knives, a large bag of marbles, metal whistles. Sometimes he saw them and talked to them, usually about a man named Spavinaw Tom, a Cherokee whom Roman had known a long time ago, during the war. The man, in fact, who had given Roman that old Navy Colt revolver. Spavinaw Tom was in Going Snake, Indian Nations, trying to grow a little corn and sorghum. Twice, Roman had given the boys a ham, hickory-cured by Elmer Scaggs, to take back to the Nations for Spavinaw Tom. Roman didn't know if those hams ever got there or not.

Even if not, Roman Hasford thought of the two boys as good friends because they never sold all their birds in town but saved a few and walked the extra distance to Catrina Hills Farm, so that Roman could have his pigeon pie.

Two days after Roman had brought the shotgun to his mother, he found Orvile Tucker waiting for him on the west porch of the Big House when Roman rode home from town, and standing behind Orvile Tucker were Poco Jimmy and Kingsnake, looking big-eyed as only Indian children can look.

"Boys got a story to tell," Orvile Tucker said.

"All right," said Roman. "Tell it."

The boys glanced at each other, then Poco Jimmy, whom Roman judged to be about ten years old, told it.

"We sleep on the big hill last night."

"Pea Ridge?"

"Yes. We seen this fire."

"Where?"

"On the road. Close to the road. The road that goes by your mama's house."

"Wire Road?"

"Yes."

"What kind of fire?"

"Campfire. Lot of men. We sleep in the woods. Then, next day, we see 'em."

"What did you see?"

"Lot of men. White men."

"How many?"

Poco Jimmy and Kingsnake conferred, whispering, heads close together, eyes darting back and forth from Roman's face to Orvile Tucker to Elmer Scaggs, who had just come up onto the porch.

"Maybe forty."

"Fox hunters?"

"I don't think so."

"Did they have guns?"

The boys conferred again, black eyes darting.

"Maybe."

"Long guns? Handguns?"

"We didn't see that."

"Were there any horses?"

Poco Jimmy's face split into a great, toothy smile because he knew the answer to this one quick.

"Yes. One. A very bad horse."

"What color horse?"

"A gray. An old gray gelding. A very bad horse."

Roman turned to Elmer Scaggs. "Get back to town and tell the sheriff I want him out here with half a dozen men, well mounted, well armed. Quick."

"Quick it is, boss," Elmer Scaggs said, and turned and bounded down the steps to his mule. Roman turned back to the boys.

"What happened then?"

"We just watch awhile. Some of them white men wander off. Some just lay around. They had a pig."

"A pig?"

"Yeah, a pig. They was roasting this pig on the fire. It wasn't a very big pig."

"What then?"

"We come over here." Poco Jimmy waved to the hillside to the north, behind the Catrina Hills Farm horse barns. "We lay down in them woods and watched your horses. Good horses."

"All day, you watched the horses?"

"Sure."

Roman stood there, looking at the boys. They looked back, unblinking, unafraid. Somewhere to the east, close to Wire Road, a chuck-will's-widow was calling.

"Orvile," Roman said finally, "give these boys a dollar and something to eat. They can sleep in the horse barns, they like those horses so much."

"I ain't got a dollar," Orvile said.

"All right," Roman said, taking out his pocketbook. "Have you got something to eat for them?"

"I always got that."

"We'll just go on home now," Poco Jimmy said. "We'll take the dollar, but then we'll just go on home."

"Suit yourself. You're welcome to stay."

"No," said Poco Jimmy. "We'll just go on home. It looks like some white-man trouble around here. We'll just go on home."

"Suit yourself."

By the time Sheriff Hamlin Bidd arrived with his little cavalcade, it was fully dark and Roman Hasford was waiting, Orvile Tucker with him. Fresh horses were saddled and hitched at the west porch quadrant of the Big House. Orvile Tucker was holding one of the large-bore repeating rifles they had brought from Kansas. Under Roman's jacket was the obvious bulge of a pistol.

Roman was not personally acquainted with any of the men Sheriff Bidd had brought, but he noted with satisfaction that they were all riding what appeared to be decent horses, and they were all carrying rifles. None of them dismounted. Hamlin Bidd and his men sat in their saddles, looking at Roman Hasford, who stood on the porch before them. The orange glow of lamplight from the windows of the Big House lit all their faces like October pumpkins. The chuck-will's-widow somewhere to the east was making his mournful call. As the horses settled down and stopped snorting and the bit chains stopped clinking, the men could all hear the Methodist Episcopal church bell in Gourdville, a distant peal, marking the end of the Wednesday-night prayer meeting. Closer, probably at Ephraim Tage's hardscrabble farm on the Gourdville Road, a dog was barking.

"Sheriff, we're going to scald some people out of the county," Roman said.

"Elmer told me," the sheriff said. Just behind him, grinning a little, was Elmer Scaggs. Roman noted that his shotgun was in the boot under the saddle fender, and that Elmer now held what appeared to be a Marlin lever-action rifle.

"Elmer, where'd you get that rifle?" Roman asked.

"Sheriff loaned it."

"We've got rifles here."

"This one was kinda new," Elmer said, still grinning. "And it's county ammunition in there."

Roman snorted.

"Sheriff, can we count on these people you've got here?"

"We sure can, Mr. Hasford."

"All right. We'll ride over to my mother's place and stay the night." Roman looked at the sky. It was shining black with stars. "Good night to sleep on the ground. Then in the morning, just at dawn."

"I understand, Mr. Hasford."

"No fires tonight. We want this to be a surprise party."

"I understand, Mr. Hasford."

"Your people eat yet?"

"Yes sir, they did."

"Well, Orvile's got a sack of oatmeal bread and some cold bacon we can munch on. But no fires. And, Sheriff Bidd, no whiskey."

"I understand, Mr. Hasford."

As they rode off, Orvile Tucker carried two lumpy burlap bags tied to his saddle horn. Riding down the slope to the Elkhorn Tavern Road, he looked back and saw the lighted window upstairs and the silhouette of a small head and a hand holding the lace curtain aside.

They found Ora Hasford on the slope in front of her house, standing in the black locust grove with her new shotgun cradled in one arm, completely unperturbed.

"I knew you'd come," she said to Roman as he rode up and dismounted.

"Why, Mama, we've got a nose for this kind of thing, haven't we?"

"We ought to. We had enough of it when your papa was gone during the war. Anyway, I seen the fire last night. You can see it now. There's not supposed to be a fire there."

To the north, along Wire Road, past the old, blackened foundations of Elkhorn Tavern, hidden now in the night, they could see a tiny wink of firelight. They looked at it a long time, that little orange eye in the night. And to Roman and Sheriff Bidd, it created sensations long forgotten. A fire, around which were gathered strange men.

"Sheriff."

"Yes sir."

"I want some men awake all night here. I don't want that bunch knowing we're going to visit them at first light."

"I understand, Mr. Hasford."

"And, Hamlin, make it clear. Any of those people come onto this farm to steal something tonight, kill them."

"I understand, Mr. Hasford."

And Ora Hasford, listening, shotgun in her hand notwithstanding, could not help but think, This is my baby boy.

It was just short of dawn when they rode out of Ora Hasford's yard. She stood on her porch to see them away. "I'll be back soon, Mama," Roman said.

"I hope so," she said.

On the high ground behind the Hasford barn they could hear the first chirping sparrows and, farther east, toward White River, an early jay fussing. Nobody talked. As they rode north along Wire

Road, there was only the creaking of leather and the clinking of bit chains and the occasional snorting of horses.

They found the camp just off Wire Road, about a mile north of old Elkhorn Tavern. There were cocoon blankets where men were sleeping, ashes of a fire, pork bones scattered about, and a single horse, head down and observing them with detached interest, and on his back an old McClellan saddle. He was gray and a gelding. His ribs showed and he was ground-hitched, reins from his head drooping to the weedy sod. There were saddle sores on his back.

Jesus, Roman thought, anybody who'd treat a horse like that!

It was gray dawn, just enough light to see by, and they arranged themselves around the sleeping men in a crescent. They waited a moment, everyone looking at Roman. Finally he turned to the sheriff.

"Fire a shot," he said.

Sheriff Hamlin Bidd produced a large-caliber pistol from beneath his yellow duster and discharged a round toward the treetops. A rookery of crows just to the side of the clearing fluttered up, cawing angrily, and flapped away. The horses snorted and jerked against the bits.

Men began to unroll from blankets and sleep, coming to their feet with faces puffy and eyes bleary. They were a miserable-looking bunch, and Roman could not help feeling sorry for them. Unshaven, with tattered coats, sweat-stained hats, broken shoes, dirty fingernails.

Except the one near the gray gelding. He didn't look like the others. He had a salt-and-pepper beard, well trimmed, and as he rose from his bedroll he brought out a beaver hat and screwed it on his head, his eyes coming awake, fierce, glaring above the beard as he looked along the crescent line of horsemen with rifles in their hands. He seemed to know what was happening to them, while the others were stunned, confused.

When Roman figured they were all upright and awake, he spoke: "We give you this chance to turn around and go back north where you came from." He turned in the saddle toward Orvile Tucker. "Give these men those bags of grub." And then, to the openmouthed men: "This here is some corn bread and cold bacon and other things. You can eat this on your way back to Missouri. You." He pointed to one of the nearest men. The man stepped forward and Orvile

Tucker tossed him the sacks. The man caught them and held them close to his chest, as though he were cradling a baby, then quickly stumbled back among the others.

Roman looked at the man in the beaver hat. He looked at him a long time, and the man looked back.

"It seems to me I saw a small pistol in your pocket before you pulled on that duster."

"I ain't armed," the man said.

"If you're not, that's fine. But as soon as these others are walking out of here, we'll undress you. And if we find a pistol, like I think you've got under there, we'll hang you!"

The man's eyes fixed on Roman's for a moment, then shifted along the line of men. Along the line of rifles. He reached under his duster and pulled out a small pistol with white bone grips, and dropped it at his feet.

"You're a smart man," Roman said. "Elmer."

"Yeah, boss?"

"The horse."

There was no hesitation. Elmer lifted his rifle, and hardly had the butt touched his shoulder than he fired. The little gray gave a quick, convulsive jerk and collapsed into an unimaginable heap, quivering for a second only. The man in the beaver hat stared down at the horse, and he was panting. Elmer worked the lever, chambering another round.

"And now," Roman said, "all of you turn around and start back up this road to Missouri. Don't come back. Pass the word to others. If they come, we'll be here waiting for them. And while you're walking, we'll be just behind. Anyone tries to go off into the woods, he'll get the same thing as the horse."

And they did, those forty men, escorted by less than a dozen citizens of the county. And leading them was the man in the beaver hat.

Of all those men in the posse, if that's what it was, probably only Hamlin Bidd understood that this whole business was a bit of repayment by Roman Hasford. Repayment for those four years he and his mother had stood in this valley against the transgressions of mindless marauders and never with any chance of help, never with any hope of assistance in protecting themselves and what they'd worked for all their lives. Just waiting to see it sucked away by outlanders for as long as the outlanders could suck it. But now, by God, Sheriff Bidd thought, a different day. Now no more that fear in the night. Now the gun was in another hand. And in this whole business, nobody questioned that Roman Hasford called the tune, least of all the recently elected Sheriff Hamlin Bidd.

When it was over, a lot of people slept more soundly. And a lot of people said things.

Orvile Tucker said to Elmer Scaggs, "I never seen Mr. Roman's face that hard before. I never knew it could get that hard, like a rock cast in the sea."

"Rock cast in the sea?" Elmer said, cleaning the rifle he'd used to kill the horse. "What the hell's that supposed to mean?"

"Mr. Roman never done like that before," Orvile said. "You remember in Leavenworth, when that Morgan mare come down with Junior, and Mr. Roman cried. Me and him got drunk that night, he was so happy. And now and again, I'd be laughin' and Mr. Roman would be cryin'. You remember that."

"Well, no. I wasn't there, but what the hell's that got to do with chuckin' rocks into the sea?"

"Elmer, you are a real ignorant white man."

Elmer laughed. "Yeah, that's what the boss told me."

And when she heard about all the details, Ora Hasford thought, I'm sorry about the horse.

So was Gallatin Delmonico. In fact he was physically sick, throwing up in the alley behind the bank. And when Judah Meyer came to help him, bringing a small towel that had been wetted from the drinking barrel always kept in one corner of the Farmer's and Merchant's lobby for customers with a thirst, Gallatin Delmonico said, "My dear Lord, Judah. I'm glad I wasn't there. It makes me sick to think about it."

"Yes," said Judah Meyer, "it obviously does. Take the towel. And remember, never buy a small gray gelding." And laughed just as Gallatin Delmonico threw up again.

Major Corliss Buckmaten wrote in the *Advertiser:* "Now the citizens of this county have seen the monster. A party of poor, destitute, downtrodden travelers on the rocky road laid down by Republican vultures and big bankers find not the love and comfort they deserve in our fair county but only threats and gunshots and must flee for their lives before the Tartar hordes of the man who holds this place in bondage. The Thirteenth Amendment does not apply here, dear friends. You are not niggers, who are freed. You are slaves to the King of Catrina Hills and to his elected vassals."

Roman Hasford ignored the major's diatribe. In fact, it rather amused him to think of Corliss Buckmaten caught in this trap of politics, forced to defend people he traditionally would have termed Yankee white trash, and all just for the sake of attacking Roman Hasford and Sheriff Hamlin Bidd.

At least, Roman thought, he didn't call me a Republican Reconstructionist for a change.

But Elmer Scaggs did not ignore it. Three days after the scathing editorial, Elmer left his mule behind the bank and walked across the Gourdville square to the office of the *Democrat Advertiser*. He accosted Major Corliss Buckmaten, explaining in extremely obscene and profane language what a dyed-in-the-wool son of a bitch the major was. And to emphasize his point, he lifted the squealing little ex-Confederate and threw him into a tray of type.

All of which infuriated Roman because it only exacerbated an already bad situation. For almost a week he refused to let Elmer Scaggs ride behind him on the mule.

Major Corliss Buckmaten sought legal action for assault and battery. The prosecuting attorney, Terrance Shadbolt, refused to bring charges owing to lack of eyewitnesses to the alleged offense. Well, there had been two employees of the *Advertiser* in the shop when Buckmaten collided with his type tray, but each had a sudden loss of memory when they thought about Elmer Scaggs and the man he represented.

Once Roman's rage had subsided somewhat, he asked for an audience with Elmer Scaggs. In his own living room, sitting with a book open on his lap and a glass in his hand, already emptied a number of times and refilled, he glared at Elmer and finally said, "Elmer, you are a dumb son of a bitch!"

"Hell, boss, I know that."

Roman looked at him. This man, he thought, looks like one of those pictures I've seen of apes. Long arms, hairy, eyes close together, no neck. And is the most loyal person I have ever had in my association.

"Don't ever go near Buckmaten again."

"Well, all right, boss, but the little bastard didn't have no call writin' them bad things about you. What the hell's a Tartar, anyway?"

"Oh, Elmer. Why hell, you keep on, you'll have people out here trying to lynch me."

"They'll pay hell."

"Oh, for God's sake." Roman slammed his book shut. "I'm going to bed."

"Well, good night, boss."

Roman was at the foot of the stairs and realized the book was still in his hand. He dropped it on the bottom step and spoke without turning his head.

"Elmer."

"Yeah, boss."

"Have a drink from my bottle."

"Well, I was just thinkin' about how nice that'd be."

God save me, Roman thought, and went up to his room.

In the next edition of the *Advertiser*, Elmer Scaggs was named as the Prince of Tartars, knee-bending to King Roman. Elmer was so taken with the idea of seeing his name in print, which had never happened before, that he had no trouble resisting the urge to pay a second visit to Corliss Buckmaten.

"You can read, can't you?" Elmer asked Orvile Tucker.

"Enough to know what you're about to tell me."

"Tell you? Hell, man, there I am. Right in the newspaper. I bought seven copies."

"Good Lord God Almighty!"

"Yeah. That's about what I said."

The Old Settlers understood killing the horse. Put a marauder on foot, they said, and you ain't got a marauder no more. You got a bum.

But not everybody shared such a view. Them men hadn't done nothin', they said, just begged a meal here and there.

Of course, the ones who disparaged the threat most loudly were those who had little to steal. Or those who hadn't been in the county during partisan raids. Or who simply saw the whole situation as an opportunity to scald Roman Hasford. Chief among these was Yancy Crane, who blamed Roman Hasford for his exit from the county's political scene.

"A real brave man, ain't he?" Yancy Crane was heard to say at Brown's Tavern. "Goin' around killin' honest people's horses, when he's got all them armed elected officials sittin' beside of him."

"Yeah," said Becket Brown. "Elected officials."

Of course, only one horse had been killed, but it sounded better when Yancy and others who took up the story made it plural. Made it sound as though Roman Hasford spent his idle hours riding around the countryside with an armed guard, looking for horses to shoot. That is, they said, when he wasn't fleecing honest people out of their money.

"Yeah," said Becket Brown.

Like any such story, it got better as it went along. At Brown's Tavern and Torten's Billiard Parlor and even in the livery stable and across a few backyard fences. That's right, certain people said, this Hasford Reconstruction Yankee's brave enough with armed men behind him, but then why ain't he man enough to get in bed with his own wife?

Nobody admitted knowing where that part of it had started.

Matie Luten knew. And one night in her little house on the Baxter Springs Road with a regular visitor, she brought it up.

"Yancy," she said. "I told you not to say nothin' about that, what I told you."

"Yeah, well," said Yancy Crane, "then you shouldn't have told me, should you?"

8

Nobody in the county had the nerve to say anything directly to Roman Hasford about the Catrina Hills story. His volcanic temper, once thought by Old Settlers to have been a function of adolescent survival in a rather violent Gourdville schoolyard, had not mellowed much with aging and had, in fact, taken on various tones much more serious than a bloody nose administered by a young boy behind the school outhouse.

And they knew pretty well what his reaction would be when he did hear it, because they could imagine hearing such a thing about themselves.

So everybody acted as though it didn't exist when Roman was within hearing. But still circulated it just the same, neighbors and pool shooters and drinking companions and even Roman's friends in the hotel or the courthouse or Anson Greedy's barbershop. After all, it was too good a story to keep quiet about, maybe especially for some of Roman's friends, who saw it as a chance to bite into that inordinate pride that Roman—and Ora as well—was famous for. Besides which, manhood was involved, a very large thing in the thinking of most citizens of the county, old and new, man and woman alike.

There was, too, the fact that it had a certain biblical resonance about it, because a lot of people in the county, men and women alike, while they might consider marital mattress-pounding a sin, being perhaps unknowing students of old Saint Augustine's teachings, nevertheless thought it a requirement of true matrimony. In their view, the man did it to the woman whether she wanted it or not—one of those punishments, along with the pain of childbirth, handed down to all women as a direct result of the first woman's disobedience to God in that Genesis Garden. A punishment like having to work, maybe—thus responding to God's command to go forth and multiply.

None of these folk, of course, were willing to argue about, much less admit, the contradictions involved. That was how it was, so that was how it was.

Elmer Scaggs was in agony as the story proliferated. And he was unable to avoid his agony, because every time he appeared on the town square in Gourdville, one or the other of Roman Hasford's friends took him aside and whispered, "Is it true?" Elmer, knowing it was true and that he had initiated it on the night of his crying drunkenness in the company of Matie Luten, pleaded ignorance.

"It ain't none of my business," he'd say.

Well, Roman's friends said, that's a strange little creature, from what I seen at the wedding. Like a scared mouse. You ever see her come to town to buy dress material or a broom for her kitchen?

Well, some of Roman's enemies said, she must be glassy-eyed crazy. That's why he keeps her cooped up all the time.

If she's so crazy, they said, why'd Roman Hasford marry with her? It ain't done him no good.

Who knows what happens to a man, they said, when he goes to places like Kansas?

Elmer Scaggs heard all this but struggled to go his normal way, which was to serve his boss. He even went his normal way in the business of going to Matie Luten's from time to time. Of course, he never mentioned the story to her and she didn't to him, both mortified by their parts in it, both acting as though it might evaporate like spring mist in the pastures if they could just ignore it. For a lot a reasons, chief among them being that the ramifications of the story scared hell out of them both.

Never once did Elmer Scaggs think of reproaching Matie Luten. He had known a lot of whores in his day and understood that sometimes they didn't behave like everybody else. He reproached himself, however, and was grateful to Matie Luten for never bringing the subject to hand during, before, or after their sweaty couplings. Thus the silence between them was a kind of mutual accommodation, which, to Elmer Scaggs, was the only good thing about the whole sordid business.

But once the story became broadcast, Elmer found it harder and harder to go about his life normally, because he couldn't avoid torturing himself with the thought that he himself had opened a Hasford closet door that should have been left closed. So he found help where he could, which was mostly from Roman Hasford's liquor cabinet. But the pilfered bourbon helped not at all, and in fact seemed to make it worse. He became more frantic with the burden of it, maybe even beginning to believe that, without confession, hell's fire was opening up before him.

And so, one evening as Elmer leaned against one of the lathed pillars of the Big House porch, and Roman came from town and found him there and asked what kind of stomach cramps were putting such a frown on Elmer's face, Elmer told him. Maybe as a kind of bungling way to clear his soul's debit ledger. Yet not really going so far as to admit his own part in it.

"Boss, some of the people in town and around this damned county are sayin' things about you and the little Missy."

"There are some people who are always saying things about me," Roman said, but already his voice had taken on the sharp edge of a crosscut saw. "What are they saying about Catrina?"

"They're sayin' that you and the little Missy ain't never been man and wife."

Roman made a low, guttural sound, spun toward the door, and smashed his fist through the stained-glass window. Elmer Scaggs leaped off the porch and backed away and stood in the yard, hearing Roman, now inside the house, bellowing wordlessly, then saw him reappear with one of his new magazine rifles, shoving ammunition into a jacket pocket and scattering some across the porch floor, where the cartridges rolled about like brass cigars.

"Get a fresh horse saddled!" Roman screamed. "Get a fresh horse saddled!"

Elmer Scaggs was immobile, staring, as Roman ran toward the horse barns. Orvile Tucker and the hired hands had heard him from there. They ran out, saw him, then ran back inside and brought out a young stud sired by Junior, throwing saddle gear onto him, with Junior himself at the porch hitch rail where Roman had left him, prancing and snorting, and Elmer still standing without moving, watching, his mouth hanging open.

Roman mounted and began to whip the horse, past Elmer Scaggs, down the yard, onto the Elkhorn Tavern Road and toward Gourdville, whipping with the ends of the reins, still bellowing,

Junior at the hitch rail at the porch, trying to pull free and run after them, and Orvile Tucker shouting.

"Get Junior, Elmer, get Junior, don't let him hurt hisself!"

"Gawd Almighty," Elmer said aloud, "the boss gonna set the town on fire!"

Halfway into Gourdville, Roman Hasford pulled in the stud with a hard yank on the reins. The horse threw a lot of gravel with his hooves and snorted and grunted, maybe in protest at the whipping, maybe in disappointment that the driving run had stopped just as it was getting started. They were directly in front of the dilapidated farmhouse of Ephraim Tage, and Tage's dog ran out into the road and barked at them. Roman sat in the saddle, panting, feeling the froth of the horse's mouth on his face from the hard run to this point. And felt a complete fool.

Hell, he thought, I don't even know who it is I'm supposed to shoot!

So he reined the stallion around, thinking he should at least shoot Tage's dog, still barking at the horse's hocks. But he didn't, feeling the hard metal of the rifle in his hand and ashamed he'd whipped his horse as he had.

When he rode into the low slope of the horse barns at Catrina Hills, there were all his people. Orvile Tucker and Elmer Scaggs and the hired hands were throwing saddles onto horses so they could follow and help in whatever it was Roman was doing. And because this seemed to emphasize his foolishness, he lost his temper again. They all stood wide-eyed, like children caught in some naughty act in the woodshed, while Roman screamed at them.

"What the hell is this, anyway! Get the saddles off those horses. Get those horses back in the stables where they belong."

Then he swung down from the saddle and stalked up the slope to the Big House, stiff-backed and suddenly glad that it had gotten too dark for them to see his face.

In the parlor, Roman didn't light a lamp. He didn't take off his hat. He still held the big rifle in his hand as he threw himself into the easy chair where he usually read, and reached in the growing darkness for the bottle.

If it was only a lie, maybe a man could abide that. But it's not a lie. And the next thought came overwhelmingly, the absolute mortification of having people talk about this private, personal, family secret. As though perfect strangers had crept into his home and lifted the bedcovers to have a peek underneath.

A man can be a drunkard or ugly or ragged or outright hateful, he thought, but there is a pride of family.

Not just for him, either. For all the men he knew in this hill country, humiliation before a man's neighbors was almost unbearable.

Why, hell, he thought, any man I know would rather be hit in the mouth with a shovel than be embarrassed.

But the next leap of mind, after the second quick glass of bourbon in the dark parlor, was this: How the hell did people know?

You couldn't hide such a thing for long among family, Roman thought. So there was his mother and Orvile and Elmer. They all certainly knew or suspected. But the idea that anyone had said anything was so distasteful he wouldn't even consider it.

There were the hired hands, who may have heard something, or seen lights in the upstairs of the Big House, lights in two different bedrooms. Anybody passing along the road could see that, so maybe somebody just guessed. And guessed right.

That had to be it, he thought. Just a random guess, and with a lot of telling becoming truth, which it was anyway.

He wouldn't consider any other possibility. It was the only way he could come to terms with it. But he knew, also, that a man, a Hasford man, faced up to anything. That family pride. Level gaze, firm mouth. All a man can do is just go on, devil take the hindmost.

But he knew, too, as he went up to bed that night, he would never again be able to look at anybody in this county again, friend or foe, without suspecting that they had been one of those gauging the extent of his impotence. He understood that he had the same surging desires that most men did, and he could recall how from the time of his adolescence he had often been as randy as one of Lark Crozier's billy goats, with the rising flesh to emphasize it. But who knew or understood that?

Hell, he thought that night, a man can't go around Gourdville proving such a thing.

And maybe that night, and certainly a lot of nights thereafter, the humor of it helped, along with the bourbon. Roman Hasford lying in his bed, sometimes fully clothed, fantasized about opening his fly on the Gourdville square and showing all passersby how rigid he could be, shocking the ladies, astonishing the children, amusing the men, and evoking envy among various preachers.

"There, you see that?" he'd say. "Take a look at that!"

With such thoughts, and maybe a little laughter, though bitter laughter, he'd fall asleep.

Ora Hasford came at the story a little more obliquely than Elmer had. It happened on the day Roman was at the old Hasford farm, telling his plan for Lark Crozier at Wolf Cove Mill. They were on the Hasford front porch, Ora and Martin in rockers, as they had sat so often when Roman was a boy, and Roman sitting on the top step as he had done so often in those old times.

Roman had a handful of pebbles and was tossing them at the guinea hens scratching about in the yard, looking for bugs and spiders and worms. The late-afternoon sun glinted on their feathers, as though they were sprinkled with gold dust.

"Not too much more porch-settin' this year," Ora said. She was putting cross-stitches of red thread in a white muslin pillow slip. "Chill in the air already."

"Get down to Brandy Station before the Yankees," Martin said. "Old Hood's back in Richmond now, you know."

"Yes, Martin, we know," Ora said, without looking up. Her heavy fingers worked quickly, efficiently. She sighed.

"Well, what do you think, Mama?"

"It's a fool thing to do," she said. "But you've always been so bullheaded, once you set your mind to something there's no sense arguing with you about it. But it's a fool thing to do."

"It may be," Roman said. "But Lark Crozier was one of the best friends we had during the war. And now he's over there at Wolf Cove all alone. He deserves a wife."

"Let him get one, then."

"Where's a colored man going to find a wife around here?"

"Well, it seems strange that you've taken on yourself so much of what's really somebody else's business."

"He ought to have a chance to have a wife."

"So when you take this coach all the way down to Fort Smith, what will you do then? Just up and buy yourself a colored woman? I didn't think you could do that anymore."

"I won't buy anybody." Roman's voice was a little testy. "It'll just be like offering her a job."

"And what if this woman don't want Lark Crozier, once you've got her up here?"

"She can go back to where she came from."

Ora Hasford lay the pillow slip across her knees and sighed again and looked out at the fields across Wire Road. The sumac along the fence lines was blood red, and already the black locusts on the slope down to the road were dropping their little spearpoint leaves, making a carpet of yellow on the ground.

"There's something in your own business you need to think about," she said. "You need to think about Catrina."

It was the first time in more than two years that Roman had heard that name pass his mother's lips. It affected him as though a hot poker had been laid along his spine.

"Oh?"

"I know the stories. Mother Caulder has told me. It's been eatin' me up, vicious things like that being said. They may be true, but it's nobody's business."

"All right," Roman said, his back stiff, his tone bellicose. "You want me to take her off down in the woods and shoot her?"

Ora laughed abruptly, but it was a hard laugh. "You've been good. You've been good, bringing her away from all she had to face up there in Kansas or wherever it was. That wasn't any mistake. That was good. But marrying her, that was a mistake. I don't hold any with divorce, but a lot of people nowadays do. All those friends you've got over in the courthouse, a divorce wouldn't be hard."

"A divorce would just make it worse," Roman said, some of the belligerence gone from his voice now.

"Well, I don't know. But something. You've got to do something. You've to get her out of that house. For your sake. For her sake. For all of us."

Roman stood up and showered all the pebbles in his hand out into the yard. The guinea hens scrambled around with their frantic pot-rack calls, then quickly settled back into the serious business of looking for bugs and spiders and worms.

"Well, I'll think about it. But I still can't help feeling sorry for her."

"So do I. But you can't build anything on sorrow alone. And these stories going around the county have to stop."

"I know where they start," Roman said bitterly. "But I can't prove anything. I better get on."

Quickly, embarrassed with his feelings, Roman stepped across the porch and bent to kiss his mother's forehead. Then he moved to Martin and kissed him too.

"Be careful, son," Martin Hasford said.

It had been a long time since Martin had recognized his son. Ora turned her face away so that Roman couldn't see her eyes, but when he mounted Junior and looked back, he could see her lower lip trembling.

"I'll bring you a pretty little parasol from Fort Smith, Mama."

"I don't want a parasol. I just want you back safe. I don't like them big cities."

Roman reined Junior around and rode down the slope to Wire Road.

"God love him," she murmured.

"Little Powell Hill's coming up on the right," Martin said.

So Ora knew that after that one brief moment of reality, Martin had slipped away again. She wiped her eyes with the backs of her hands and picked up the pillow slip and the needle.

Damned red thread is off-color, she thought.

So Roman Hasford went to Fort Smith on the coach that was running its last gasp generally along the old Butterfield route before the St. Louis–San Francisco railroad got its tracks laid down through the mountains.

Fort Smith was pretty much like Leavenworth had been. There was no big military installation there, but the Federal court for the Western District of Arkansas had moved into town from Van Buren, and that had created a lot of action, what with Judge Isaac Parker hanging people frequently. It would be another fifteen years before Roman's nephew, Calpurnia's son, Eben, arrived here to make his mark. But what he would see when he got there was about what Roman saw when he went for Lark Crozier's wife.

From his Kansas experience, Roman knew where to spread a little money around—chief of local police and a few of the better saloon keepers and a couple of the best madams along the bordello strip by the river—and was thus put on the track of a small black woman who was about twenty-five years old, give or take five years, whom he hired on what might be considered a consignment basis with the understanding that if she didn't take well to Wolf Cove Mill, Roman would pay her passage back to Fort Smith or anywhere else she wanted to go.

Her name was Renée and she spoke with a decided French accent, having come upriver all the way from New Orleans less than a year before. She'd kept body and soul together over that year by doing housemaid work, first for the brothels along the river bottom, and then, when Roman found her, for the German Jewish families who were establishing some of the finest businesses in the city, mostly cafés and jewelry stores. Roman's negotiations were not at all hindered by the fact that he had a strong German heritage himself, which he played to the hilt with the Fort Smith Jews, and it resulted in a few pleasant evenings in their homes, where he was treated to some of the best food he had ever eaten, especially the rye bread and the chocolate layer cake.

Yes, Renée was ready for migration beyond the valleys of big rivers and the humidity and mosquitoes, so long as she could take her half-dozen voodoo dolls, and her eagerness to quit Fort Smith and go with Roman was enhanced considerably when he displayed a fat roll of greenbacks and fistfuls of gold and silver coin. She was a talker, as Roman found on the coach ride north, and a lot of it he couldn't understand, but she was a nice-looking woman, he thought, with a complexion like weak-brewed coffee, close-cropped hair, and eyes as shining as good bone china, with irises as brown as the frosting on some of those Jewish cakes.

Back in northwest Arkansas, it was all a little disappointing and anticlimactic. Lark Crozier took the whole business in stride, and the woman began at once ordering him around and started cleaning up his little house.

Roman got the Gourdville Methodist preacher to Wolf Cove Mill to say the wedding ceremony, so that all of this wouldn't be conducted in sin, although that was three days after Roman had taken Renée to the mill, and he suspected that the sin had already taken place. Anyway, Ora Hasford came, and Elmer Scaggs and Orvile Tucker, whose bloodshot eyes gave no hint of either approval or disapproval, and Sheriff Hamlin Bidd, at Roman's specific invitation, which was no invitation at all but an order.

Immediately after the ceremony, wagons began arriving with lumber and shingles and glass windows so that Lark could start building a place for his bride, because that little matchbox house he'd been living in wasn't big enough to scald a cat in, as Ora said. Of course, there was no new house. Lark just attached a room here and there to the matchbox house, so that the whole thing eventually defied description and looked more like a casual scatter of children's wooden blocks than anything else.

Nobody really knew if Renée thought this was all a good idea, but at least she didn't bolt. As for Lark, despite his apparent lack of interest at first, he soon began to act twenty years younger than everybody knew he was. As he told Roman, "Mr. Roman, ain't a single bee stung that woman. It's lak she was born to be right here at Wolf Cove."

And later, Roman said to his mother, "You see?"

"All right," Ora Hasford said. "Sometimes that bull head of yours works."

But it didn't work everywhere. There were a lot of people in the county, and now not just the newcomers, who said, "For God's sweet sake, what's he tryin' to do? Start a colony of niggers? A couple of colored men might be all right, but now we got a breeder. Next thing, we'll be just like one of them south Arkansas cotton patches, little pickaninnies runnin' all over the place. Who the hell's he think he is, anyway?"

So Lark Crozier and Mrs. Crozier became fixtures in the county, suddenly and amazingly a family, like it or not.

"Mistake, mistake, mistake," Gallatin Delmonico said to his wife. "Why can't he just sit calm, without doing all this foolishness?"

"I think it's rather touchingly sweet," said Missy.

"Sweet Savior! How can you be so Goddamned naïve?"

"Little ears, Mr. Delmonico, little ears. Remember the children."

"Oh, for Christ's sake!"

In only a few weeks Lark came to Ora Hasford's back porch with a crock of honey, his face beaming, and announced that his wife was with child.

9

In April of the bad year, with foals ready to drop, Roman Hasford rode Junior to Cassville, Missouri, for talks with certain gentlemen interested in breeding some good horses seeded out of the Catrina Hills herd. He took Orvile Tucker with him, claiming, as he always had, that Orvile Tucker was the best horse man he'd ever known.

Whether or not Roman's absence had anything to do with what happened was a matter of speculation in the county for years to come. Maybe it was just spring juices rising in certain loins, or maybe it was because word had gone around the county that in about September there would be a child at Wolf Cove Mill, a new little black face in the mostly white world of northwest Arkansas.

For those who cared to reconstruct it, and a great many did, the whole business started in the hotel dining room with Glamorgan Caulder, old Jefferson's third-eldest daughter, who was trying to make a little money waiting tables for Harley Stone, saving most of her pennies so that by next year she could pay her tuition and board at a young women's seminary and teachers' college in Carthage, Missouri.

"Daft ye be, daughter," said old Jefferson, who often fell into his own parents' Welsh constructions when addressing one of his children. "Tuition and board, is it? Does not your old Da have the money to pay your way?"

But being a Caulder, and hence as independent as an Ozark wood tick, Glamorgan, though only fifteen, said she could handle her affairs. "But thank you, Da, and maybe from time to time you can pick up the slack."

"Slack, is it? Slack? How can a man know what the young are speaking of these days?"

Anyway, on the Saturday night in question, Glamorgan Caulder was serving Cato Fulton, a tobacco warehouse man, and John Vain, a farmer whose property lay west of Gourdville, close to the Indian Nations. In the process of handing down platters of fried Irish potatoes and pork chops smothered in white cream gravy, it was impossible for her not to hear some of their conversation.

And having heard it, Glamorgan Caulder went directly back through the hotel kitchen, out into the alley, and around the building to the lobby entrance, running most of the way, to find Harley Stone leaning across his guest register, discussing the next presidential elections with a hemp-rope-and-baling-wire drummer from Decatur, Illinois. Glamorgan began a series of frantic signals designed to attract Harley Stone's attention, which they did, and knowing that Caulders did not act this way without good cause, he broke off his talking and came to her where she stood beside the potted palm Harley had just imported from Memphis, and which was now the showpiece of his lobby.

Having heard her tale, he went quickly through the glow of spring sunset across the square and directly into the office of Sheriff Hamlin Bidd, on the first floor of the courthouse. Hamlin Bidd was there, as were his two deputies, Nathan Bridger and Colin Hamp, both twenty-some-odd years old and at present addicted to the dime novels of Ned Buntline and Prentiss Ingraham, which dealt with the exploits of Indian frontier heroes like Kit Carson and Buffalo Bill Cody and others of that sort. Both young men were from old, established families, families who had been in the county since before the war.

When Harley Stone finished his recitation of what Glamorgan Caulder had heard, Sheriff Bidd instructed Deputy Bridger to run over to the Lugi livery stable and saddle three horses. And he told Deputy Hamp to unlock the gun rack and get down three ten-gauge shotguns and to fill all available pockets with shells, buckshot, and number-four.

What Harley Stone reported was that Cato Fulton and John Vain had been having a few sips around town and had come into his place for an early supper. And they were careless with their talk, what with the sour mash clouding their judgment. None of this was a surprise to the sheriff, knowing that both men tried to break clear of Puritan-directed wives at least once a month to drink some whiskey. And the careless talk was to be expected, too. Less than a month before, Sheriff Bidd had found it necessary to place Cato Fulton in the jail for being rowdy and loudmouthed in Glen Torten's Billiard Parlor, just off the east side of the Gourdville square. Most of that conversation had dealt with Cato's opinion of Roman Hasford and his imperial ways and money-grubbing—which was to be expected, too, because Cato's tobacco warehouse was mortgaged heavily at the Farmer's and Merchant's Bank. A transaction designed by Gallatin Delmonico, of course, but one in which Roman Hasford was certainly a co-conspirator, so Cato yelled. And hence into jail to sober up.

Sheriff Hamlin Bidd had always reckoned Harley Stone to be an old gossip, worse than any woman in town. And so, this night, when the hotelkeeper rushed in red-faced and panting and smelling of sweat-activated bay rum, the sheriff paid scant attention to the words that poured from Harley's mouth. Until the word *Klan* came out.

That's when Sheriff Bidd's boots left the top of his desk and hit the floor with such emphasis that both his deputies dropped their dime novels (which described in gory detail the manner in which Wild Bill Hickok had dispatched a great number of people named McCanless with weapons ranging from pistols to butcher knives).

"The Klan? What the hell do you mean, the Klan?"

"The Klan, for God's sake," Harley shouted. "They said it was about time we had a chapter of the Klan, maybe should have had it a long time ago."

"Listen, Mr. Stone, this ain't the cotton South," Hamlin Bidd said.

"I know that, Hamlin. I'm just telling you what they said. And according to them, we've got a Klan now. They even laughed about the pillowcases and sheets Jeff Caulder has been selling so many of at his mercantile. And they said tonight's little visit would be a good place for the Klan to get started in this county."

"Little visit? Where, a little visit?"

"Where else? Wolf Cove Mill."

"Shit," Hamlin snorted. And that's when he instructed his deputies about the horses and shotguns.

"How many?" the sheriff asked.

"I don't know."

"Does this girl know what she's talking about?"

"Glamorgan Caulder? Did you ever know one of those Caulders who didn't know every minute what they're talking about?"

When Hamlin Bidd had been a United States deputy marshal in the Territory, everything had been pretty straightforward. Somebody committed murder or rape and they had to be brought in and hanged. This Klan business was a different load of manure. He wasn't sure he knew how to fork it.

But one thing Hamlin Bidd did know. Roman Hasford himself had invited him to be present at that wedding there on Little Sugar Creek. Over and above his oath to keep the peace, Hamlin Bidd knew to whom he owed his increased social and financial status. And if something unpleasant happened to old Lark Crozier and his little wife, there would be seven kinds of hell to pay.

I hope there ain't forty or fifty of these Klan bastards, Sheriff Bidd kept thinking as he and his deputies rode to Catrina Hills Farm.

Elmer Scaggs was still sulking because the boss had gone off to Missouri and left him behind. There was salt in that wound, too. The salt was Orvile Tucker, who got to go. But when Sheriff Bidd and his two men arrived at the horse-barn bunkhouse and asked for whatever assistance Elmer could give, Elmer sprang into action.

Elmer Scaggs hadn't been drinking very much—it was only a little past sunset—but enough to frighten the four hired hands, who knew how Elmer could get when he'd had a few sips. He started ordering them around like a mule-train wagonmaster, at the top of his lungs. Get horses saddled, Elmer shouted, and he'd go to the Big House for weapons. Watching the whole performance, Sheriff Bidd and his deputies, still sitting there motionless in their saddles, wondered if maybe once Elmer Scaggs and his four hired hands got armed and mounted, they might be more dangerous to public safety than the Klan was.

They rode along the Elkhorn Tavern Road to Wire Road and turned south along that to the valley of Little Sugar Creek, then east along the narrow trace through the timber that led to the mill. Just short of the mill, Sheriff Bidd stopped them and disposed his men under the sycamores beside the road that followed the line of the creek.

"If there's trouble," he said softly, "For God's sake try not to shoot each other."

Sheriff Bidd thanked God for the full moon that night. It helped to be able to see something, anyway. The bright light filtered down through the leaves and patterned the roadway like the hide of a dapple gray horse. The new frogs were croaking their amazement at still being alive, what with all the copperhead and rattler-type snakes around, and there were various crickets and cicadas and other bugs adding their tune. Over this whole scene was the flood of moonlight and, from the shadows under the trees, the sound of water running smooth over round pebbles, a whisper beneath a veil of silver.

Knowing it was always better to shoot from a solid platform instead of a horse's back, Sheriff Bidd ordered his men to dismount. If there's a whole peck of these people, he thought, we'll need all the advantage we can get.

So they stood, listening to the night. Smelling gun oil. Itching. It wasn't tick or chigger time yet, but just standing there listening to all the bugs, they itched.

Then they heard it. From Wire Road, horses coming toward Wolf Cove Mill. The surface of the trace was deep with loam and new grass, so the steel-shod hooves made only the kind of faint sound that stocking feet make, going across a smooth pine floor. There was the soft rattle of bit chains and a horse snorted, but that was all.

Then they saw them in the speckled moonlight beneath the trees. They wore white pillowcases over their heads, with eye slits cut. They looked ghostlike, ephemeral, like wisping smoke.

Sheriff Bidd waited until they were very close, and then he stepped out before them, his shotgun up, drawing back the hammers as he spoke.

"Well, howdy, boys."

The horsemen drew in on the reins, a sudden movement that made the horses blow air through flared nostrils. There was a muffled oath. Along the treelines on either side of the road there was the metallic click of hammers being drawn back, and these riders heard it. Sheriff Bidd had not been able to tally them yet, but neither did the riders know how many men were in the dappled shadows with cocked weapons.

"Where you goin', boys?" Bidd asked. "Little moonlight ride?"

"We got bidness up ahead," somebody said from under a pillow slip. "You best stand aside."

"Not hardly, boys," said Bidd. "You turn around now and go back home and we won't ask you to take them pillercases off your faces."

"Let me kill one of 'em, Sheriff," somebody said from the shadows of the sycamores.

"Not yet. Maybe in a minute," Bidd said. "Well, boys, best turn around and go back home."

"Aw hell, Sheriff, we're just gonna have a little fun," one of the riders said. "We ain't aimin' to harm nobody."

By now, Sheriff Hamlin Bidd could see that there were no more than a dozen of these masked riders, and it made him breathe easier.

"Boys, we don't want no bunch of grown men ridin' around the county at night dressed silly and scarin' people," he said. "Now, I've got men here in the trees with ten-gauge guns, so we ain't gonna have no serious argument, I hope."

There was another voice then, muffled by the pillow slip, yet clearly heard.

"Are we payin' you good tax money now to stand up for the Hasford niggers?"

Hamlin Bidd saw what happened, but it was too fast for him to stop. Elmer Scaggs sprang from the darkness, holding his heavy rifle by the small of the stock, and swung it at the nearest horseman. There was a soft, moist *chunk*.

The struck man, more surprised than hurt, fell out of the saddle and his pillow slip came off. It was Essex Brown. He thrashed about on the ground, and his horse was pawing and snorting and kicking.

"You son of a bitch," Elmer Scaggs said, and he lifted the rifle again, like a club.

"Get back in your place," Sheriff Bidd yelled, and it had enough force in it to make Elmer Scaggs pause, then slowly back off into the trees, shifting the rifle into a firing position once more.

"That crazy bastard hit me with his gun," Essex Brown shrieked, clawing his way upright, holding on to a stirrup. His horse was shying away from him.

"Hold his horse for him, Courtland," Bidd shouted. It was just a guess, of course, but immediately after Bidd said it, one of the other riders reached over and took the bridle on Essex Brown's horse and held him until Essex could get back into the saddle.

"Crazy bastard," Essex bellowed. "He hit me."

"You brought it on yourself, Essex," the sheriff said. "Now, the whole bunch of you, get the hell out of here and back home and sober up. You must be drunker than a fried owl, out here in the night tryin' to scare folks. Get now, I mean it, get."

It was like a school of fish, all moving at the same instant, flowing around silently, horses turned back toward Wire Road and then going off into the speckled darkness.

"We'll have your ass, Scaggs," somebody shouted back through the moon-patched darkness.

"Elmer, stay put," the sheriff said.

Then, in five heartbeats that seemed like as many minutes, the sounds of the night riders were swallowed in the night and gone.

"Dear Jesus," Sheriff Bidd said, but not loud enough for the others to hear. He eased down the two hammers on his shotgun.

"Elmer."

"Yeah, Sheriff?"

"Take your men back over to the hill. I'm beholden for your help. But Roman Hasford ain't gonna be too overjoyed with you hittin' Essex Brown."

"I wisht I'd hit him again."

"Elmer."

"I'm goin', Sheriff."

After Elmer and his Catrina Hills hired hands had gone the way of the pillowcase riders along the trace to Wire Road, Sheriff Bidd said to his deputies, "Stay here the night. If you gotta sleep, do it in the middle of the road so nobody gets by. I'm goin' back to Roman Hasford's place to be sure none of them peckerwoods decide they wanta burn somethin'."

But as he found his horse among the sycamores and rode out, he thought, And mostly to keep that damned crazy Elmer Scaggs from traipsin' around the county tonight, lookin' for somebody to kill.

Alone with the frogs and cicadas and the moonlight, Deputy Colin Hamp said, "Who you reckon all them others was?"

"I'll bet you a big wet bug you'd find 'em all real shortly out there at Brown's Tavern on the Nations Road, havin' some more of that popskull they were drinkin'," said Nathan Bridger. "You wanta sleep first, or me?"

* * *

East of them, less than half a mile away, in the house across the road from the mill—the house that was beginning to look like a heap of unpainted kindling wood, thanks to Lark Crozier's ideas about enlarged living space—it was dark. There was the occasional soft bleating of a goat from the hillside behind the hives. There was the sound of water over the pond dam, and the screech owl making his quavering complaint from above the mill wheel.

It was a good and peaceful night at Wolf Cove. And with the sun, the two rose and had some goat cheese, then went up to the hives with the pans of sugar water that would feed the bees for another few weeks until the blossoming of spring flowers that would provide the natural foundation for summer's honey.

And there, Renée kissed her husband and smiled at him and said in words he only partially understood that this was her special place. But whether or not he could understand the words, Lark Crozier knew what she meant, and they stood by the hives in early morning sunshine and looked down across the little valley, and then, after a while, decided this was a good place, right here on this slope, in broad daylight, to join together again.

April mornings in the Ozarks were a blaze of light and new color. There were more shades of green in the new-leafed trees than could be counted. Shadows cast by the cedars along the spur of Pea Ridge were blue-gray in the clear morning air. Everything the sun touched grew a halo of brilliant orange light.

Elmer Scaggs's eyes were clear enough to see all this, but he took little note because he was still fuming about the previous evening.

Dirty scum white trash, he thought. I don't know why I ever went out to that Brown's Tavern for a drink of whiskey anyway.

Of course, before Roman Hasford had found him in a Leavenworth livery stable and brought him to his full potential, Elmer Scaggs himself would have been counted dirty scum white trash by the decent folk in any community. Throughout most of his life, he had had more in common with people like the Browns and Yancy Crane than with respected citizens like the Hasfords. And as with many reformed rowdies, he now had only contempt for men who were what he once had been.

Elmer stayed away from the Big House that morning. If Orvile or Roman wasn't there, he was uncomfortable in the place. Because of Catrina. He'd liked her at first because she was the wife of his boss. But now she was the cause of all his sleepless nights.

With Orvile up there gallivanting around in Missouri, Elmer thought, maybe she'll have to come down and fix her own breakfast for a change. Probably up there now, peeking from behind her curtains, tryin' to spy on me, tryin' to see if I go inside and have a sip of the boss's whiskey. Sneaky little bitch. Shoulda left her in Kansas.

Because if they'd left her in Kansas, there wouldn't be that story going the rounds, the one he had turned loose. So Elmer had begun to degrade her in his mind, to make her responsible for his guilt. It didn't help much.

This place gives me the creeps, he thought, with Orvile and the boss not here.

There was always the bank. He could go there, tie his mule at the back door as he sometimes did, and go inside and sit by the boss's door. But, hell, the boss wasn't in there. And he'd have to put up with that little pussyfoot Gallatin Delmonico and that young, high-toned son of a bitch Judah Meyer.

He tried to busy himself with the horses. He even fed Orvile's hogs and weeded Orvile's garden, hoping each moment that he'd see Roman and Orvile riding along the Elkhorn Tavern Road from town. But even though the sheriff had told him he should stay around Catrina Hills Farm until Roman returned, two days after the Little Sugar Creek episode Elmer saddled his mule and rode into town and stopped at the first place that served beer. Glen Torten's Billiard Parlor. And as he walked in, Elmer came face to face with Drake Brown, who was buying gumdrops at the front counter.

Major Corliss Buckmaten recorded his version of what happened in the columns of the *Democrat Advertiser*.

On Monday last, the local ruffian E. Scaggs assailed Mr. Drake Brown in the recreational emporium of Mr. Glen Torten, inflicting grievous harm about Mr. Brown's head with a pool cue.

The vicious attack was completely unprovoked, and Dr. H. Cronin was called into attendance. E. Scaggs, the well-known bully of Catrina Hills Farm, was taken into custody by Sheriff Bidd and presently is safely incarcerated in the county jail. Prosecuting attorney Terrance Shadbolt has filed a charge of assault and battery.

Mr. Brown is a member of a well-known and respected family in the county. At last report, he was still confined to bed at his home, where he lives with his parents, west of this town on the Indian Nations Road.

Decent and law-abiding citizens in this county will not be safe so long as brutes such as E. Scaggs are allowed to roam at liberty, preying on the innocent.

When Roman Hasford came home from Missouri, the first place he went was the Gourdville courthouse, to lay down bail for Elmer Scaggs. Sheriff Bidd gave a detailed account of the Klan business in the valley of Little Sugar Creek, and as much as he knew about the pool-cue business in Torten's recreation hall.

"He wouldn't say nothin', Mr. Hasford. He like to have gone crazy, I guess. We had to arrest him and charge him."

"All right," said Roman, his face bleak. "Let's get up to the clerk and pay him out of here."

Roman didn't speak a word to Elmer Scaggs, not coming out of the cell, not going across the sunlit square to Ennis Lugi's livery, where the county had boarded Elmer's mule, not on the Elkhorn Tavern Road, riding home. And all the way, Elmer dragged behind, like a contrite six-year-old who'd been caught tasting somebody's stale beer.

But when they were at Catrina Hills Farm and Roman was crossing the porch to the door, Elmer spoke.

"Dammit, boss, I just told that man to keep his filthy mouth off my family."

Roman Hasford stopped, one hand on the doorknob, and stopped for a long moment before turning. He looked at Elmer Scaggs.

"What family?" Roman said, his eyes temper-fired. "You haven't got any family."

Elmer Scaggs leaned forward, mouth open, but he didn't speak, seemed incapable of speech. His eyes were wide and bewildered as he returned Roman's gaze for only a second, then turned his head one way, then the other, as though searching for something lost.

"I thought I did," he said at last.

Roman shuddered, shaking himself like a dog shedding water.

"God, Elmer, you bring discredit to us all. You can't keep your hands off people."

"I know it, boss."

"Well, tell me what happened."

"Them boys who come to Little Sugar Creek. They said 'Hasford nigger.' "

"They said that?"

"Yeah, and I busted one of 'em. It was Essex Brown."

"Hamlin Bidd told me all that," Roman said, his voice harsh with impatience. "What about at the pool hall?"

"That was Drake Brown."

"I know that," Roman shouted, and Elmer jumped.

"They yelled they'd get me, when they come to Little Sugar Creek. So when I seen Drake Brown, I just went up to him and said here was a fine time for him to try it, and he said I wasn't worth the trouble, bein' as I was just a butt wart on a man who didn't have no gonads."

"Gonads? Drake Brown said that?"

"Yeah, and that's when I waded into him with a pool cue."

Elmer Scaggs felt scalded by Roman Hasford's gaze, but he looked directly back into Roman's eyes now and was astounded to see that Roman was about to laugh.

"Gonads?"

"That's right, boss. The son of a bitch!"

Roman looked away quickly, staring down across Elkhorn Tavern Road and into the trees beyond. Somewhere there, among the low sumac and cedars, a cock cardinal was trilling, staking out nesting territory. Roman's face had gone soft. It wasn't exactly what Elmer Scaggs would recall as a smile, but the mouth was soft now.

"Elmer?"

"Yeah, boss?"

"Remember the day we left Kansas, and the cardinals were raising such a fuss?"

"Yeah, I remember all about when we left Kansas."

"Me, too," Roman said. Then he wasn't listening to the cardinals anymore. "Elmer."

"Yeah, boss?"

"I want you to stay here on the farm until after the trial. You understand?"

"Yeah, boss."

"And Elmer—"

"Yeah, boss?"

"You've got a family."

Then, as though embarrassed at what he'd said, Roman quickly went inside, leaving Elmer Scaggs with his mouth open once more, speechless, yet thinking, By Gawd, I wisht I'd hit ole Drake a few more licks with that pool stick.

On the west side of town, Courtland and Sarah Brown watched their eldest son with dismay and despair and rising fury. Drake Brown was up and about now, but the left side of his head would never look the same again. Appearance wasn't the bad part. The bad part was that he had serious trouble trying to do sums and subtractions, this son who had been the one to keep his father's business ledgers since he was ten years old. And he had trouble holding a pencil in his right hand, and he often dropped his cup or his knife at table and had to use his left hand to turn a doorknob.

The increasingly hot Brown rage wasn't cooled by the results of Elmer Scaggs trial in late summer, when Judge Jacob Rich was sitting on circuit at the Gourdville courthouse.

Prosecutor Terrance Shadbolt suggested to Roman that Elmer Scaggs enter a plea of guilty.

"Mr. Hasford," he said, "I'm not confident we could empanel a jury in this county without having about six or eight men in the box who wish you ill will. So have him throw himself on the mercy of the court."

Exhibiting extreme humility, dressed in a new suit of clothes Roman Hasford had bought him at Caulder's Mercantile, and not even offending the court by bringing in some high-priced attorney from Fayetteville or some such place, Elmer entered his guilty plea. Thus no jury needed seating.

Throughout this short procedure, Roman Hasford sat just behind the prosecuting attorney with an expression that could only be described as cloudy and with his eyes, as hard and blue as his mother's, fixed on Judge Rich's face.

His Honor, Judge Jacob Rich, sentenced Elmer Scaggs to three years at hard labor.

Suspended.

"Well sir," it was said in Anson Greedy's barbershop, "it sure shows you who's astraddle of the wheelhorse in this county, don't it?"

Roman Hasford displayed no elation over Elmer's good fortune, still punishing the big man with cold stares and only minimum conversation. But Elmer knew his boss well enough to understand that this couldn't last. He began measuring the moments until he found one with the right dimensions for getting away, satisfying that always rising urge to visit awhile with Matie Luten.

By George, Elmer thought, Ole Matie'll believe I fell in a hole somewheres. Gotta get out there, see that lady. Send that kid to tell her the payment's due. Let her know when to splash a lot of that rose water on the soft parts. Pretty soon now. Boss said I was family, so he ain't really mad.

He had almost forgotten the story, in the rush of other events. Besides, like most such stories, it had run its normal course and was dying out. Elmer Scaggs could never understand that such a story would never really die out completely, because it left a scar on family honor. Now he was not concerned with family honor. He was concerned with that urge of his, and throughout the summer he and Orvile worked on the new foals, worked on the mares, showed horses to buyers from Missouri, stayed busy enough to make the weeks slide past into fall, but knowing that soon now there would be time for the rose water.

10

It was one of those cold, drizzling October days, gray as death. In the kitchen at Catrina Hills Farm, Roman Hasford and his wife sat at the kitchen table having their breakfast, Orvile Tucker laying down eggs and pork tenderloin and hominy and coffee. As had become the norm, there was little or no talking, just the sounds of fork and knife against bone china plate and the huffing of the huge cooking range, the damper wide open so that the hickory wood inside blazed hot to send warmth to the far corners of the room as well as to sizzle the meat in the cast-iron skillet. At the center of the table was an open mason jar, deep red with the wild plum jelly Ora Hasford had sent over from her larder a few days before, as she always did at this time of year. Along with her homemade sauerkraut and cucumber pickles and string beans. All this came in mason jars Roman bought at Caulder's Mercantile, except for the sauerkraut. It came in a gallon crock covered with cheesecloth, and this crock, sitting now in one corner of the kitchen, sent a pungent, gland-tightening aroma through all the house. And reminded Roman of his boyhood along Wire Road before the war.

"Somebody comin'," Orvile Tucker said.

It was Deputy Sheriff Colin Hamp, riding slouched in the rain, hat pulled over his ears, wearing a split-tailed yellow slicker that came down all the way to his ankles. As he pulled up at the west quadrant of the porch, Roman was there to meet him, wiping his mouth with a white linen napkin.

"Colin," he said.

"Mornin', Mr. Hasford," Colin said. His face was as dreary as the weather, and Roman Hasford already knew something terrible had happened. "Sheriff says you ought to come along with me so he can show you something."

"Show me what, Colin?"

"Well, I'm afraid it's Elmer Scaggs."

Roman didn't ask any more, and as he turned back into the house he could hear Orvile Tucker yelling down to the barn, instructing somebody to get Junior saddled.

"What's the matter?" Catrina asked.

"I don't know," he said, throwing his napkin on the table as he passed through to the stairs. "Finish your breakfast."

They rode toward Gourdville, Roman beside Colin Hamp. Neither of them spoke another word. They crossed the town square and saw no one, this being very early on a Sunday morning. Out into the road north toward Baxter Springs. There was little timber here, alongside the road, all of it having been cleared to make plow ground and to grow corn. A little less than a mile from town, Roman could look ahead through the gray mist and see a group of horses in the road, near the edge of a field where the summer cornstalks still stood, brittle and brown and waving little pennants in the northeast wind. As they came closer, Sheriff Hamlin Bidd moved out from the group of men in the field and came onto the road to meet them.

"Mornin', Mr. Hasford," he said.

Roman didn't say anything. He looked at the men standing off the road, all wearing slickers and staring back at him. Deputy Bridger was there, and Dr. Cronin and Criten Lapp, the county coroner, and some others, including Tilman Lapp, the coroner's brother and Gourdville's only undertaker. Roman dismounted. He already knew what he was about to see.

"I left everything just like it was," the sheriff said. "I wanted you to see."

"Then let's see," Roman said.

Sheriff Bidd led him over to the group of men, and into the edge of the old cornfield. Roman was very close before he saw it. The man was lying facedown, but his clothes and bulk left no doubt that it was Elmer Scaggs, and Roman could see some jagged tears in the back of Elmer's coat.

"Kid comin' into town this mornin' before daylight with a can of milk from Felcher's dairy found him," Sheriff Bidd said. "Somebody shot him all to pieces, Mr. Hasford."

Roman looked north along the road and could see the dim outlines of a small house, with a lot of fences in back. Matie Luten's.

"We talked to her," Sheriff Bidd said, seeing the direction of Roman's eyes. "She didn't see him all night."

"She hear the shooting?"

"She said no. But it was done right here. Ground's been wet since yesterday afternoon, and there ain't no sign of his being shot somewheres else and drug here."

For the first time, Roman saw Elmer's mule, standing with the other horses in the road. Once more, Sheriff Bidd saw where Roman was looking.

"Mule was right there, in the road, when we got here."

"In the road?"

"Yeah, I think they shot him off the mule and he got over this far into the field and they shot him some more. That's about how I got it figured."

"Shotguns?"

"Yeah, but there's some bigger wounds in him, probably from heavy-bore rifles."

Roman looked at Dr. Cronin.

"How long dead?"

"Hard to say, Mr. Hasford. Stiffened up. I'd guess sometime before midnight last night."

Roman looked at Criten Lapp, the coroner.

"Homicide by parties unknown, Mr. Hasford."

"Unknown, hell!" He turned to Tilman Lapp. "Get him a new suit of clothes at Caulder's and have him out to my place as soon as you can today. We'll bury him there."

"Mr. Hasford," said the undertaker. "I can't do much about his face. It's shot up pretty bad. If you like, I'll show you."

"No, don't show me. Just get him cleaned up and in the box and seal the box. Make it a good box, you hear?"

"I will, Mr. Hasford."

"Hamlin," Roman said to the sheriff, "get one of the preachers. I don't care which one. He wouldn't care either. Have him out to my place, too, and you come along, because I want to talk."

"I was plannin' on that, Mr. Hasford."

Roman went back to Junior in the road, and all the others watched him, graven images, solid in the drizzle that had turned to cold rain, silently watching as Roman mounted the big red stud and turned back toward home.

Catrina was waiting for him downstairs, which was a shock, or would have been if there was anything else this day that could shock him. She stared at him with her great, luminous black eyes.

"Is something bad?"

"Yes. Very bad. Somebody shot Elmer Scaggs."

"Is he hurt?"

"He's dead."

Roman was facing away from her and did not see her short movement toward him, did not see her ready to speak. But she stopped without touching him, without a word, then turned and went upstairs. Roman went to the parlor and took down a bottle of his best whiskey and cried before he took the first drink.

It was late afternoon before the funeral procession came along Elkhorn Tavern Road to Catrina Hills Farm. It didn't amount to much. Leading was Tilman Lapp's glass-cased hearse pulled by two black mules with black plumes set above their heads in the black harness. Following were Sheriff Bidd and his deputies and Tilman Lapp's brother, the coroner, and old Jefferson Caulder and Mother Caulder and two of their daughters had come, all the women riding sidesaddle. Terrance Shadbolt, the prosecuting attorney, was bringing up the rear with the barber, Anson Greedy.

The hole had been dug long since, on the rise of ground behind the last of the horse barns, just short of the line of white oak timber that clothed the top of the ridge. The four hired men of Catrina Hills, who had dug the hole, stood well back, wet with rain and sweat, their trousers spattered with red mud.

As the procession came onto the yard, Roman and his wife and his mother and father and Orvile Tucker came from the house and walked up to the grave and met the oncoming black wagon. On the seat of the wagon was this Methodist preacher from town, whose name Roman didn't even know; the man preached on Sunday and taught school the rest of the week with one of old Jefferson Caulder's daughters in the local school.

They all arranged themselves around the grave, as people always do, and the four Catrina Hills hands hoisted the polished oak box out of the windowed hearse and lowered it into the ground by ropes. Ora Hasford was standing next to her son, holding above her head the dainty parasol he had brought her from Fort Smith.

"I never knew this man . . ." the preacher started, and with that Roman turned and walked away, slapping his hat onto his head, and went on back down the slope, past the horse barns and up to the Big House and inside. Everybody else stayed.

When the others came from the grave, Ora Hasford had a moment with her son in the kitchen. She touched his arm, and in her eyes he could see not sorrow but the hard glint of anger, and knew his mother well enough to understand that, like so many hill women, she defeated grief with rage.

"He was a rough-cut man," she said. "But he was our friend and he was so good with your papa."

"Yes, I know," Roman said. "He was good with Papa."

"Whoever did this needs to hang," she said, softly but fiercely, and Roman could not help recalling all those times during the war when this woman, by her will alone, had held the Hasford farm together.

"I promise you, Mama, somebody's going to pay for Elmer."

"An eye for an eye, a tooth for a tooth."

"I know the Book, Mama."

"Good."

Then, in his parlor, with his books behind him and a glass in his hand, Roman sat, morose, dark, his mother and father and wife and the sheriff in the room, and Orvile Tucker standing back by the door. There was a tray of buckwheat cookies on the table, which nobody touched, and Sheriff Bidd stood in the presence of all this Hasford clan with his hat held before him in his hands.

"Tell me what you know," Roman said. He waved his hand to encompass the room. "These are all people you can talk in front of, so tell me what you know."

"Not much, Mr. Hasford."

"Did you ask anybody today?"

"I know who you mean, Mr. Hasford. Courtland Brown said Essex and Becket went to the Indian Nations three days ago, with Yancy."

"With Yancy Crane? That old sheriff? Why did they go there?"

"Courtland Brown said they wanted to talk to some Cherokees

about raising cattle to sell to that railroad line building down through the Nations."

"Hamlin," Roman said, looking into his glass of whiskey, swirling it around, "Elmer told me somebody threatened him that night on Little Sugar Creek."

"That's right."

"And you know the Browns were there."

"I know Essex was, we seen his face. I suspect Courtland was, but I couldn't prove it in a court of law."

Roman swirled his whiskey more violently, almost spilling it. He rose and began to pace the floor, one end of the room to the other.

"Time to get posts cut," Martin Hasford said.

Ora, sitting beside her husband, reached out and placed her hand on his arm. "Not now, Martin."

"You can't arrest Courtland Brown on suspicion?" Roman asked.

"Couldn't hold him. He's already said all he'll say to me. I asked Terrance Shadbolt about it. There must have been a dozen people seen Courtland at the tavern last night, all through the evening. Drake, too, and besides, Drake wouldn't be able to do it, I don't think, condition he's in."

"And I guess you haven't seen anybody who's willing to say they saw the other two boys or Yancy Crane the last two, three days?"

"I've tried that too. Not a soul's seen any of the three of 'em. Of course, they could have been upstairs out there at the tavern and nobody would have known it."

"Yes," said Roman. "If they were planning this, there wouldn't be much problem staying out of sight until it was done."

"That's right, but it's something else Terrance said he couldn't use in court, just suspicions. Only thing would be if one of those three admitted doing it. And if it was Becket, any decent lawyer could show a jury right off how crazy he is. So even if I could get my hands on 'em, I doubt much would come of it."

"Do you think they did it?" Roman asked, standing still in the center of the room.

"Yes," said Hamlin Bidd. "But even if I got my hands on 'em, they wouldn't confess anything, you know that."

"So what you're telling me is that you haven't got much chance of arresting anybody on this."

"That's right, and even less chance of convicting them, the way things stand now. I've already sent a letter to the Federal authorities in Fort Smith, telling them these men are in the Nations illegally and if they catch 'em I want to talk to 'em, but I doubt anything'll come of that. Those deputy marshals over in the Territory got more serious things to do than roust out illegals."

"But Courtland says his two boys went over there three days ago? With Yancy Crane?"

"That's what he said. Just him and Sarah and Drake out there at the tavern now."

"They played hell going to the Nations three days ago," Roman said. He lifted his glass and drank all that was in it, then looked at Sheriff Bidd and said, "Thank you."

"Yes sir. Good afternoon, Mrs. Hasford," bowing to Ora. "Good afternoon, Mr. Hasford," bowing to Martin, who sat with glazed eyes and an expression of complete detachment. "Good afternoon, Mrs. Hasford," bowing to Catrina. And turning toward the door, "Good afternoon, Mr. Hasford." Roman lifted his hand and nodded, then poured himself another drink from the crystal decanter on the library table.

After the sheriff was safely away, Ora Hasford rose, shaking her ruined parasol.

"Little old thing wasn't any good for real rain," she said. "We'll go now, Roman."

And after kissing Catrina on the cheek, she took Martin's arm and went out to the buggy provided by her son, and drove back to Wire Road. Catrina quickly and silently went to the stairwell, but paused there and waited.

Orvile Tucker took up his cookies and started to carry them out, but then turned at the door. "I'm sorry, Mr. Roman."

"Hell, Orvile, he was always asking for somebody to do it."

"Yes sir," Orvile said.

After he was gone, Roman said to himself, But I'll scorch whoever did it, because if it wasn't for things I've done, Elmer would still be here now, to talk with Papa and eat Mama's gooseberry pie and josh Orvile and follow me around like a good dog, ready to do anything I asked. I'll scorch whoever did it!

He went to the steps, and Catrina was still there. She looked at him, big-eyed.

"Mr. Hasford?" she asked.

"Yes."

"Send me somewhere they can teach me to read and write."

Roman looked at her, remembering the first time he had seen her, in that mule-barn house in Leavenworth, her face blue with bruises.

"Of course. We'll see," he said. He bent and kissed her cheek, and Catrina smiled, fleetingly, and turned and ran up the steps.

"Oh God," Roman breathed, holding to the banister unsteadily. He could hear the rain outside now, coming harder, and he knew his mother and father were caught in it somewhere toward Wire Road, but he knew as well that rain was nothing to match his mother's iron will, and suddenly he laughed bitterly.

In his upstairs room he lit a lamp against the gloom of approaching evening and sat at his desk, listening to the rain. Trying to make his mind work.

So, he thought, Matie Luten didn't hear anything. Why, hell, her house isn't more than two hundred yards from where they got him, and it must have sounded like a war starting from the way Elmer was shot all to pieces.

Well, he thought, if Matie Luten won't talk to anybody around here, I know somebody she'll talk to. I'll bet it was her place Elmer was goin' to when they caught him on the road. All heated up like a stallion. Not looking for anything bad to happen, not suspecting anything bad to happen.

So finally he took paper and pen, and wrote a letter.

To Mr. Jared Dane, in care of the Kansas Pacific Railroad, Topeka, Kansas.
Sir:
I would appreciate an audience with you soon in someplace away from my home where we might discuss the fact that I need you.

And on it went from there.

The next morning, Roman Hasford placed the letter in Orvile Tucker's hand for him to mail personally. And riding into Gourdville, Orvile Tucker saw the addressee.

"Oh Lord," Orvile said to the horse, "he sendin' to Kansas for that one-arm man. Somebody gonna be in a peck of trouble. Real trouble."

*   *   *

On the Tuesday following the dispatch of Roman's letter, Renée Crozier at Wolf Cove Mill on Little Sugar Creek delivered herself of a seven-pound baby boy while Lark stood outside in a driving rain, waiting for it to be over. And after it was, and he had gone in, dripping, to see the new face and to stroke his wife's head, Lark was back in the rain again before his house, dancing a wild dance in the mud.

11

When he'd first brought Catrina Peel to his mother's house, Roman Hasford had assumed, without even thinking much about it, that she would be taught to read by his father, as Roman and his sister, Calpurnia, had been before they ever attended school. It hadn't worked out that way. Catrina was not Cal, and Roman's father was not the same father he had been before the war, his two children at his feet each evening when he took down the Bible or Mr. Gibbon's *Rise and Fall* or one of the books borrowed from Tulip Crozier at Wolf Cove Mill.

It was obvious that Catrina would have been eager for such tutoring. And maybe, Roman thought, had it gone as he expected the girl might have become a real woman instead of the frightened animal that she remained.

But it was too late, and Roman thought that since he'd come home, everything seemed to become clear only after it was too late. Too late to undo a wedding. Too late to distance Elmer Scaggs from a loyalty that became deadly. Too late to change a lot of his own actions that had created irritation and anger and even hatred among some of his neighbors. Always too late, Roman thought.

So because of all this, when Catrina actually crawled out of her shell long enough to make her wishes known, Roman Hasford thought of little else, seeing it as an opportunity to correct a lot of mistakes, taking it as a chance to heal his own wounds.

But how the hell does a man do this? he thought. During the week after they buried Elmer Scaggs, he lay awake each night, struggling with it, sober and resisting any temptation toward the bourbon, knowing he needed help. And finally he decided that there was only one person who could give it. Gallatin Delmonico.

"Of course, Mr. Hasford," Gallatin Delmonico said. His dark little face was working with either compassion or reluctance to be brought into this thing. Roman couldn't decide which it was, but no matter, the little banker plunged into it. "There are many places where a young lady can be schooled."

"I don't want one of the local ones, like in Fayetteville or even Fort Smith."

"Of course, I understand," Delmonico said. "There's a fine school of which I am personally aware in Jefferson City. It's called St. Scholastica Seminary."

"Catholic?"

"Of course."

"But she's not a Catholic."

"It doesn't matter."

"Is it a convent kind of thing?"

"There is a convent associated with it," Gallatin Delmonico said. "The nuns do most of the teaching. It is administered by the Society of Jesus. Great teachers, those Jesuits. Young women go there for retreat but also to learn. Not only the forms you would expect in a regular school, such as grammar and syntax and Latin and figures and geography, but also the tilling of flower gardens and needlework of all kinds."

"What's this 'retreat'?"

"It means getting away from the world. The young women there are cloistered, their whole universe enclosed within the school, its books, and its teachers. There are no outside influences."

"Well, I like that idea. Are they well fed?"

"Nothing extravagant, of course. Good, solid diet, I am told."

"And they might take a married woman?"

"Of course. Their doors are open to all. Their purpose is not to make nuns of all the pupils."

"How much does it cost?"

"I have no idea."

"Find out, would you, Gallatin? And if I could enroll my wife there. Soon."

"I understand. I will initiate correspondence with them this afternoon, as soon as I have completed an appointment on a loan."

"A loan to who?"

"James Chesney."

"The man who's got that tannery out there on Oak Creek, along the south property line of my place? Pretty hardscrabble, isn't it?"

"He wants a loan to start a small slaughterhouse and a sawmill."

"Well, all right. But don't forget the letter to this St. Scholastica."

"Of course not, Mr. Hasford."

Roman would never know what Gallatin Delmonico wrote in his letter to the Missouri seminary. He assumed there was a great deal made of the fact that Roman could afford to pay considerable amounts of money to the Society of Jesus, because the reply came immediately. At least as immediately as the postal service allowed.

It was only after Catrina's acceptance to the seminary was concluded that Roman told his mother. He didn't expect any opposition from her, and he didn't get any.

"I'll need to take her to Caulder's for some clothes. Everything she'll need," he said.

"I'll do it," Ora said. "This needs a woman."

Roman hesitated, but he saw in his mother's pale eyes that gritty determination he had seen all his life when her mind was made up and she would brook no argument.

"Mama, I don't like you going in there with her."

"Listen, none of that rowdy, loudmouthed scum in town will say anything to *me*. Nor to her, when I'm with her!"

When Ora Hasford took Catrina into Gourdville, they drove along Elkhorn Street, passing Glen Torten's Billiard Parlor, Ora holding the reins of a bay mare that drew a new buggy with a black leather top and yellow-spoked wheels. On the sidewalk in front of Torten's stood a group of men, overcoat collars turned up against the cold, chewing tobacco and talking about the things men standing in front of billiard parlors always talk about. As the buggy came near, they stopped their spitting and talking, and a few of them, as the buggy passed, tipped their hats and said, "Good morning, Mrs. Hasford."

In response to which Ora Hasford made no sign that she had heard, and as the rig passed on toward the Gourdville square, everyone looked after it, still chewing, and now beginning to spit once more, registering on their minds the image of these two Hasford women in fur-collared coats, so that later they could tell their wives, or anybody else who cared to listen.

"By Gawd," said John Vain, "I never seen that little chippy before. Right smart little piece there."

Everybody laughed and spit.

"Yes sirree," said Ephraim Tage, who owned the subsistence farm just west of Catrina Hills on the Elkhorn Tavern Road, where he tried to grow enough corn and melons to sustain himself and his grown son, Ausbin. And, some said, he helped it all along by slipping over into the Indian Nations each winter to steal a cow or two. "Sittin' up there with the old lady like a little lamb beside of the sheepdog."

"Ora Hasford's got a lot of stout juice in her," John Vain said, spitting. "She's mighty uppity, 'specially now her own boy's got that bank and all, but that's the kinda old sheepdog you get bit by if you tie into it."

"Well," said another spitter, "there's one tough old sheepdog amongst them Hasfords we don't hafta worry 'bout no more."

"Yeah. Elmer Scaggs," said Ephraim Tage. "Good riddance, too."

Everybody nodded, chewing thoughtfully, spitting.

Glen Torten, just a mite of a man, came to the door of his pool hall then, and he was disturbed.

"Gawd dammit!" he yelled. "You people get your spit out in the street. I'm tired of tryin' to mop it all up offen my new cement sidewalk ever' day."

"Aw hell, Glen," John Vain snickered. "We ain't hurtin' nothin'."

"The hell you ain't. You're specklin' up my new sidewalk with all that juice. What's a lady gonna think, she wants to come in here?"

They all laughed.

"A lady? In here?"

It was a terrible experience for Roman, that trip to Jefferson City. They went by coach to Cassville, and Roman insisted that Gallatin Delmonico accompany them. It was cold, a late-November wind whipping bits of wastepaper along the street in front of the Stone Hotel, which was also the coach station.

Ora Hasford was there, and she'd brought Martin, although he had no idea what was happening. Before Roman and Catrina and Delmonico mounted the coach, Ora kissed Catrina on the cheek, and then Roman in the same way, a short, undemonstrative peck.

The ride was bumpy, and even though they had heavy lap robes, their feet were chilled before they got out of Arkansas. Catrina talked a little, looking from the windows of the coach, seeming to enjoy it all. Roman recalled her this way when he'd first brought her down from Kansas, and it made a hard lump in his throat. She had been so small then.

Why, hell, he thought, she's so small *now*.

That had been spring, when they'd come down from Kansas. Now it was winter coming on, the landscape pretty dismal and gray. They saw a lot of blackbird flocks and a lot of hunting hawks. And a lot of corn stubble in the fields and a few lonely cows, watching them pass.

They spent the night in a Cassville inn, Roman and Gallatin Delmonico in one room, Catrina in another. The whole arrangement obviously was a great embarrassment to the dark-faced little banker. The next morning they boarded the railroad cars for Jefferson City, and Catrina was even more animated, watching the southern Missouri landscape slide by, and it made Roman a little sick that perhaps the farther away she got from his own ground in northwest Arkansas, the happier she was.

The seminary made Roman's skin crawl. It was so austere, so barren. The old nun who received them reminded Roman of a railroad conductor. He was glad when finally Gallatin Delmonico could complete all the forms and hand over an envelope bulging with money and they could leave.

"I'll write you a letter," Roman said to Catrina. "The nuns can read it to you."

"Soon I can read it myself," she said, and she was smiling.

Roman bent and kissed her on the forehead, and as he turned quickly to leave, she said. "Thank you, Mr. Hasford."

God, he felt like hell.

Outside, he pulled the fur collar of his overcoat up around his ears and stood a moment, smelling the night, feeling the icy wind that seemed to be coming all the way from the western high plains.

"Gallatin," Roman said, "I want some very strong whiskey."

"I know just the place, Mr. Hasford. And they also have fine beefsteak," Gallatin Delmonico said, and for the first time since this whole thing started he appeared vastly relieved to the extent that he showed his Swiss cheese-colored teeth in a smile surrounded by the black beard.

The next morning, with Roman feeling the effects of too much of the strong whiskey and too little of the fine beefsteak, they stood together in the Jefferson City railroad depot and Roman said here was a parting of the ways. Gallatin Delmonico would return to Arkansas, but Roman would take a later train to Topeka and there meet with an old acquaintance.

Even with his minimal capacity to perceive what was about him on that morning, Roman realized at once that he had thrown the Gourdville Farmer's and Merchant's Bank vice president into a complete panic. Roman laughed and took the little man's shoulders in his hands, as he might have a child's, and tried to explain.

"Gallatin, it doesn't have anything to do with business. It doesn't have anything to do with the bank. I'm going to see an old friend whose profession has nothing to do with anything you'd understand."

It seemed not to reassure Gallatin Delmonico at all.

"For God's sweet sake, Mr. Hasford, don't do anything precipitous. Remember, advice from those who trust and honor you is the foundation of intelligent decision."

"Why, hell," Roman said, jerking his hands away from Gallatin Delmonico's shoulders, "can't I do anything without you thinking you can stick your finger in?"

He half turned away but turned back and bent quickly so that his face was close enough to that of Gallatin Delmonico's for the little banker to smell the sour, morning-after odor of too much whiskey.

"I'm sorry I said that. I shouldn't have said that. But just get on your Goddamned train, and I'll be home in about a week or so."

Then Roman walked away, furious with himself, furious with his apology, furious that he had said anything in the first place that required an apology.

He'd as much as accused Delmonico of meddling yet knew the

little man wanted nothing so much as to stay clear of his personal life.

It was me got him into this thing about Catrina, Roman thought. He didn't ask for it, and I could tell it made him uncomfortable as hell. Why can't I say things right? Here I am past thirty, and I haven't learned yet how to keep my boot out of my mouth! Roman fumed. I'm getting another man involved in our personal life, just like with Elmer. I've got to stop that. I've got to distance Gallatin from all that now, after Elmer.

Then he had to laugh, thinking of Elmer Scaggs and Gallatin Delmonico together in the same crib, like identical ears of corn.

I doubt if Gallatin is going to start going around bashing people on the head with pool cues, he thought.

And felt a little proud of himself that now, even after so short a time, he could think about what happened to Elmer and still find something to laugh about.

A man needs to laugh more, he thought.

He walked back to the place of strong whiskey and tender beefsteak, and when the bartender saw him and remembered all the money passed across his board the night before, he smiled, nodded, and brought forth his best brand of Kentucky bourbon whiskey.

"Never hurts to soothe a day like this with hair of the old dog," he said.

"Well, maybe just a tad," Roman said.

Later, his stomach soothed but more likely anesthetized, he rode the railroad cars west to Topeka and could not shake the vision of St. Scholastica from his mind. The seminary, cold and gray, the cell-like windows as narrow as railroad ties, the pitiful little smile on Catrina's face. That small face with the terrible eyes.

Even so, he knew it was better now. She would be cared for and possibly moved to interest in the things those black-robed sisters tried to teach her. Maybe better, after all, to be nurtured by strangers than by family, maybe strangers she could accept simply because of their distance from her.

God Almighty! With Jefferson City's morning whiskey wearing off, he felt miserable.

Gallatin Delmonico, riding south, allowed his mind to race from one awful possibility to another. What is Roman Hasford doing with our bank? Going to a big railroad town, with that crazy thing he's got about railroads. Going to invest Farmer's and Merchant's money in a damned railroad, maybe two, maybe three. My God! Mortgages are so good when one is on the right side of them, but so bad when one is on the other.

All the way to Cassville, on the railroad train, Gallatin Delmonico chewed his fingernails. God, how he hated railroad trains! From Cassville into Arkansas, on the coach, he did not bite his fingernails because the ride was so bumpy over the rough roads that he had to cling to the seat with both hands to stay in place.

Gallatin Delmonico leaped from the coach in front of the Stone Hotel on the Gourdville square, bursting from the door and running, not walking, across the square to the bank. There was a fine mist of swirling snow, but Gallatin Delmonico was not aware of it. He was aware only that behind the gold-leafed window of the bank, Judah Meyer was waiting, and it terrified him.

Something was wrong. Something terrible had happened in Kansas. It didn't occur to him that he himself had arrived back in this town quicker than any bad news from Topeka might have.

He slammed into the bank, and Judah Meyer had him by the lapels. Oh sweet Jesus, something is wrong, Gallatin Delmonico thought.

"Where's the Old Man?" Judah said.

"What?"

"Mr. Hasford, Mr. Hasford, for God's sake. Where is he?"

"What?" Gallatin Delmonico could not perceive what was happening. Perhaps even where he was.

"For God's sake, Mr. Delmonico, Mr. Hasford's mother has diphtheria. Dr. Cronin has quarantined that Hasford farm!"

"What?"

"God damnit, Mr. Delmonico, Mr. Hasford's mother is dying. Where the hell is *he*?"

"Aw," Gallatin Delmonico gasped, dropping his black valise onto the floor and shaking himself free of Judah Meyer's grasp, feeling a great, lovely relief that it was only Ora Hasford sick, and then immediately ashamed of himself and shouting, "I'll go out there, I'll go."

"You can't do that," Judah Meyers said. "It's quarantined."

"What?"

"Mr. Delmonico, we need to get Mr. Hasford here."

"He's in Kansas. I don't know how to get in contact with him."
The tellers in their cages were staring at them, wide-eyed.

"But I'll go, I'll stay in the barn, I'll go," Gallatin Delmonico
shouted, and, leaving the valise, in which there was still a great
deal of money, he ran back through the bank, out the back door
and into his own house, kissed Missy, then ran to Ennis Lugi's
livery, where his buggy and horse were kept, and after a few
moments of Ennis getting the horse into the stays, Delmonico
mounted the buggy and whipped the startled horse across the
square and out along the Elkhorn Tavern Road.

"My God," said Judah Meyer, watching all of it from behind the
gilt window of the bank. "What have I got myself into?"

Ora Hasford died exactly three weeks to the day before Christmas.
Her son came home a week later. But he knew. In Cassville, where
there were those certain gentlemen interested in his horses, they
had heard, and told him, as gently as possible. He handled himself
well, riding into Gourdville on the regular coach, without hurry,
because he knew that his mother had already been buried, five days
before. He sat in the coach for that ride with two other men and
a woman, none of whom he knew or cared to know, and he had two
quart bottles from which he drank from time to time. It seemed to
have little or no effect on him.

When the coach drew up before the Stone Hotel in Gourdville,
he stepped down and saw the lines of people waiting to see him,
standing far back, their collars up, mufflers across their faces, some
of them enemies, some of them friends. The wind blew little flurries
of ground snow across the sidewalks. Only one person came up to
him. Orvile Tucker.

"I got Junior at Ennis Lugi's stable," Orvile Tucker said. "I'll
bring him over. You goin' to the bank?"

"No. We'll walk together."

Harley Stone was standing in the doorway of his hotel, and
Roman looked at him, but Harley said nothing. So Roman said it:
"It's the passing of something, isn't it, Harley?"

Harley nodded. But did not speak.

Orvile Tucker talked all the way to the stable. Yes, Miz Ora
was laid down where Roman had said her own folks was laid down,
right there on the oak ridge behind the farmhouse. Yes, she went

peaceful. Yes, Orvile had been waiting every day since for each coach from the north, not knowing when Mr. Roman would be there, but waiting for each one. By the time they had the horses, Junior for Roman and one of Junior's colts for Orvile, he was quiet, and they rode out into the blowing snow and across the square. And there were still all those people, enemies and friends, standing at the Stone Hotel, watching silently.

They rode out the Elkhorn Tavern Road, side by side. Neither of them said anything until they were abreast of Ephraim Tage's house set back off the road behind its ragtag snake-rail fence.

"Ever'body come to the funeral," Orvile Tucker said. "We laid her down where you tole me your other folks was laid."

"That's good, Orvile."

"Ever'body there to pay respects to Miz Ora. Lark and Renée brang that new chile and he cry all the time. Reverend Kirkendall, he says a good funeral."

"That's good, Orvile."

"Ever'body there."

"Not a few, I'd guess," said Roman, holding a wing of his coat collar across his face against the wind. "Not the Browns."

"None of them scum, Mr. Roman," Orvile said. He sounded offended.

"Where's Papa?"

"I brang him to the Big House."

"That's good."

"He's all right. We get to talkin' sometimes, me and him. He eat pretty good."

They were at Catrina Hills Farm by then, and before he turned Junior in at the gate, Roman stopped and sat and looked in the bleak afternoon toward Wire Road in the east, toward his mother's house and toward his memories.

"I'm going over there now," Roman said.

"I'm goin' with you," said Orvile.

"I figured you might."

On the way, Orvile said only one thing:

"They quartered her."

"Quarantined her," Roman said. "I understand that."

When they came along Wire Road to the old Hasford place, Roman reined in and looked at it as the day faded away into December coldness. There was the gentle slope up from the road to the house, the black locust trees there stark and lifeless now, their fallen leaves having long since been swept away by wind, and at the base of their trunks a crescent of white snow.

Beyond the locusts was the house, the house Roman knew so well, every log and beam and rock and pane of glass. But knew more than that, too. Knew its sounds and smells and colors and soul. It was strange now, because it was dark, no light shining in the windows. He could not remember when, even during the war, there had been no light in this house.

"Where's the livestock?" Roman asked.

"We brang it to your place, Mr. Roman. Them guinea hens is hard to catch."

"Yes. I remember that."

He nudged Junior up the slope and into the yard, but didn't stop here, didn't even pause. He rode on around the house and past the barn and across his mother's old garden and into the edge of white oak timber that stood on the rise of ground where, in the last light, he could see the new soil on a fresh grave close beside those sunken ones where he knew his grandparents lay.

Roman Hasford dismounted and walked to stand beside this new grave and look at it, trying to imagine what lay there. Somewhere to the east, near White River, there was the harsh cawing of a crow. And no other sound except the whisper of wind as it touched a small stand of cedars along the fringes of the real timber.

Roman Hasford took off his hat, and the wind whipped his hair about like unbaled hay. He went to his knees and bent down and placed a hand on the grave. His breathing and the breathing of Orvile Tucker and of the two horses made little clouds of vapor that were quickly eaten by the wind.

With his hand still there on the ground, growing cold, Roman Hasford looked down the slope to Wire Road. Where he and his mother had seen the old Butterfield stagecoach line operating, and where the men put up the telegraph poles for a line that gave Wire Road its name, though it was doomed never to operate because of the war. The two of them had watched armies go back and forth, and the two of them had seen the first partisans come into this valley. They had also watched Calpurnia ride out with her husband, and never come back.

It was the final, devastating culmination of the most tormented moments of his life. In doing what his mother had said he should, get Catrina out of the county, he had taken himself away at the exact time when his mother needed him most. When he should have been sitting in that room, that warm kitchen, beside that great bed, with her hand in his. Instead he had been in Kansas, drinking whiskey with old railroad cronies, trying to forget St. Scholastica in Jefferson City. When he should have been here, where he could hear the owl call from the spring hollow.

"Orvile," he said softly.

"Mr. Roman?"

"Who was with her at the last?"

"Doctor, he was here. Miz Caulder. Miz Caulder says she don't give a damn about that yellow flag nailed to the door. She gon' be here. So she was."

"Good. Anybody else?"

"Mr. Delmonico, for one day. He stayed in the barn. Like to froze. So doctor tole him to go on home. And he done it."

Roman dug his fingers into the loose dirt of his mother's grave, as though trying to hold it for a moment in his hand.

"Goodbye, Mama," he said.

He rose and replaced his hat on his head. Orvile Tucker was watching him closely, and he saw no tears. But he thought: Tears inside too big to find a hole to get out of.

Roman mounted Junior, and when he and Orvile Tucker turned their horses about toward the house they saw a quick, furtive movement on the porch. Roman's hand went under his coat to the pistol there, and he was aware for the first time that Orvile Tucker was armed, because now a cocked pistol appeared in Orvile's hand.

"Who's that?" Roman called.

"It's me, Mr. Roman."

Roman kicked Junior up to the house. Lark Crozier came out to meet him, and even in the pale dullness of the December evening, Roman could see the shine on his black cheeks. Lark Crozier came off the porch, and as Roman drew rein, Lark put a hand on Junior's neck. Behind him, Roman knew that Orvile Tucker's pistol had disappeared as quickly as it came to hand a moment earlier.

"Mr. Roman," Lark said. "I been watchin' out for Miz Ora's stuff."

"That's good."

"Mr. Roman, no tellin' who come by, all this riffraff in the county, like buzzards, steal thangs, chuck rocks through the winders. I got Miz Ora's shotgun in there."

"Thank you," Roman said. "But you go on back to Wolf Cove Mill. And tomorrow, come back and take anything you want here. Except the china cabinet. I want that and everything in it."

"Awright, Mr. Roman. Awright. I'll brang that china closet over to your place."

Then Lark was silent, his hand still on Junior's neck. After a while he looked up at Roman, and his eyes were shining.

"You mama gone now, Mr. Roman."

Roman took Lark's hand, and their fingers gripped hard for a moment.

"You go back to your wife now, and that new child," Roman said.

"Awright, Mr. Roman."

Roman pulled Junior away and started around the house, then stopped and looked back. There was Lark, even in the December darkness a shining blackness, and Roman said. "Lark, what did you name that new baby?"

"Why, we name him Hasford Crozier, Mr. Roman. Hasford Crozier!"

Roman violently pulled Junior about and rode away around the house and down the slope to Wire Road. That was when the tears came.

12

The new year began with a gray, cold January. The wind seemed always to blow from the northeast, pushing dark clouds before it, and the Old Settlers said that usually meant snow. It did. Not that it stayed on the ground very long. The sun returned on alternate days, but it brought little warmth and only emphasized the lack of red in the glass column of the big thermometer on the front of the Stone Hotel.

There were many migrations of blackbirds, working the brown stubble cornfields as they passed, making a sharp, friendless chorus of chirping and scolding, and there were cardinals in the patches of cedar along the edges of the leafless hardwood timber, male and female feeding together now in flocks, with no concern for territory until April. And hawks grew fat because field mice coming aboveground in the barren furrows found no green growth to hide them as they foraged for summer's overlooked grains of wheat and barley.

Squirrels were out at dawn, looking for sunlight so they could lie spread-eagled on some large branch and soak up heat. They went to den early, last year's young still curled and entwined with the mother sow in old leaf nests or hollow hickory tree trunks, another two months before she would drive them out to find their own place.

Foxes in the backwoods searched for overlooked persimmons and wild grapes, and raccoons came boldly into the backyards to run their delicate little hands through human trash to find a bite of bread or potato peel. And some of the Old Settlers said they had heard wolves in the night, over toward White River, lamenting the lack of cottontail rabbits.

It was a cruel time.

Yet a good one for the people of the county. A lot of things had changed since the past summer. A lot of tension had gone, if only for a little while. Elmer Scaggs dead. Two of the Browns over in the Nations somewhere, who knew for how long. Catrina Peel Hasford off someplace in Missouri to go to school, as if she needed school. Old Ora Hasford in her grave. Her husband suffering from advanced senility, which most of them charged to some kind of mental weakness, proof of which, some even said, was evident in Martin's having gone off to fight with Lee in Virginia during the war. And Roman not seen so much in town, spending a lot of time at the Folly with that colored man, Orvile Tucker.

Whether they counted any or all of this as good or bad, at least everyone had to admit it was nice about that tension fading. It was nice to think the whole top wasn't about to blow off the thing between the Brown people and the Hasford people.

Yet it was difficult not to take sides in that mutual hostility; most people couldn't help doing so. And that made them uneasy, apprehensive about maybe being accosted on the street by one of the Brown faction for favoring the Hasfords, or else the other way around. Even though most of that threat had disappeared, what with the most volatile men either down to the Nations or murdered.

Of course, there was still old Courtland Brown and Roman Hasford himself, both of whom could be pretty mean-spirited. And with good reason, old Courtland having a son disfigured and crippled, and Roman having a close family friend slaughtered on the Baxter Springs Road. Everybody knew who had assaulted Drake Brown, and everybody supposed that Elmer Scaggs had not been casually killed by some passing stranger. Neither of those wounds would ever disappear. But at least they had begun to scar over a bit, people hoped.

For the present, everybody had plenty of good hardwood for fireplaces and stoves, and the newest *Farmer's Almanac* out of Chicago indicated that next growing season would produce bumper crops.

And before long, they all said, the railroad would come and a lot of money would be moving throughout the county. So even though the weather was what the Old Settlers called a bull bitch, it wasn't a bad winter for most folk. There were, of course, a few exceptions.

Each morning, like everyone else, Matie Luten put on her heaviest coat and her boots, put a shawl over her head, and went out back to kick the ice off the surface of pails and troughs where her livestock was supposed to water—her chickens and pigs and two goats and her shaggy little saddle horse and her milk cow. It was a good time for Matie Luten, because in this kind of weather not many men were willing to freeze their noses just to come warm up other parts of their anatomies. She had a snug little house and plenty to eat, what with the milk and eggs. So it was a good, lazy time for Matie Luten.

It was therefore somewhat of a surprise that on one of the worst days in a bad month there was a midafternoon knock. And more than a surprise. An irritation.

But Matie Luten opened her door to him and allowed him to come inside because it was in the nature of her business to open her door to men and allow them to come inside. Otherwise, she would have had a meager income indeed.

He was a strange man. And a stranger besides, a man she had never seen before. His clothes were expensive. They were not what Matie Luten would describe as city clothes. They were trail clothes, or camp clothes, made for long and rough wear. But very expensive. Corduroy pants and a heavy, long coat with a split tail for riding and a fur collar. Made of some sort of duck material Matie Luten had never seen before. Low-heeled boots, very expensive boots. A hat almost like a planter's hat, with a wide, flat brim and a low crown, but of heavy gray felt. And beneath it all, a white linen shirt, buttoned tight at the neck.

This man had only one arm. His left sleeves were empty. A veteran from the war, Matie Luten thought. He wore a gray suede glove on his right hand, and once inside he pulled it off with his teeth. His hand was white but strong-looking, with long fingers as supple as the tentacles of an octopus, Matie Luten thought, although she had never seen an octopus. As he shed his hat and long coat on a chair, she saw the butts of two pistols at his waist. Ivory, she suspected. One butt forward, the other back, so that he could reach either of them with his one hand.

A little chill went up Matie Luten's back, but then she had been in this business a long time, and the sight of two pistols was certainly not going to disturb her too much.

"Would you like a little drink first?" she asked.

"Yes," he said, with a flat, hard little voice. "Tea."

"Tea?"

"Then coffee."

He had a very pale complexion, the kind that is violently burned by slightest exposure to sun. His hair was short, rust-colored, and he had no eyebrows. He had a wide, thin-lipped mouth. And blue, metallic eyes that seemed never to be quite in focus.

Sleet rattled against the glass panes of Matie Luten's windows. In back, the milk cow bawled, a protest against the cold.

"You can put your horse in my shed," she said, having seen this man's absolutely magnificent black tied at her gate when she opened the door to him.

"It's no matter," he said. "He's a winter horse."

She thought it was a funny thing to say. But the man's hard, flat voice and his hard, flat eyes made it very difficult to laugh about anything.

"I'll get some coffee for you," Matie Luten said.

"For yourself as well," he said. It was a command, not a suggestion.

Matie Luten went to her cookstove and brought down cups and saucers and poured from the pot that was always on the back of the cast-iron kitchen range. And she began to tremble. Behind her, she was aware that the man was going from window to window of her house, peering out, then looking around the small room. It was the only room in the place, with a small alcove behind the stove where Matie Luten had her stock-in-trade. A large bed.

"Well, there we are, sir," Matie Luten said, placing both saucers and cups on her oak-topped table.

"Sit down," he said. She did.

He went to her utility table, opened the drawer, fingered about until he found a butcher knife. He laid it aside, found the stove-lid handle, took off a stove lid, and thrust the point of the knife into the coals of the fire.

"Now," he said. He came to the table and sat down, stretching his legs and sighing. He lifted the cup Matie Luten had brought for him and sipped the coffee. He held his little finger out away from the cup as he drank. He sighed again, replaced the cup in its saucer. "Good coffee."

His hand slid under his coat and then out again, with a roll of bills. He flipped it open and began to peel off greenbacks, one after another. Fifty-dollar greenbacks. Matie Luten counted as he peeled them off until he had a ragged stack.

Sweet Jesus, Matie Luten thought, there's a thousand dollars there.

It was more money than she'd see in a year. Maybe two years.

"Mister," Matie Luten said, "I don't know what you want me to do for that kind of money, but I'll be willing to discuss it."

"Good, good."

He rose and went to the stove and lifted the butcher knife. The tip of the blade had turned glowing red.

"Aw," he said. He turned to look at her with those eyes that did not focus. "Matie, have you ever felt hot metal on your lovely flesh?"

"Dear God, I don't want to do nothin' like that."

"No, we're not talking about gratifying my appetites. We're talking about something entirely different."

"Listen, I'll do anything you want, mister, but don't touch me with that hot knife."

"Aw," he said, and thrust the knife again into the red coals, came back to the table, sat down, and took another sip of coffee, the cold, hard eyes fixed on Matie Luten's face. "It is not pleasant for me, either, Matie."

"How'd you know my name? I ain't ever seen you before."

He said, "You'd best pray God you never see me again, Matie."

She was panting now, finally realizing the kind of peril in her house, and tears began to run down her cheeks. She was not crying, exactly, she just understood that within a short time she might be horribly dead, and the tears came of their own accord.

"Would you be willing to talk truthfully to me, Matie?" he asked.

"Yes." She looked at the bills on the table. Even now, terrified, she had to look at those bills. The corners of his lipless mouth turned up slightly.

"Oh, Matie, those are all yours. Or the knife."

He suddenly leaped up and in two steps was at the stove and yanked back the knife. Its wooden handle was flaming and the blade was white-hot. He dropped it on the stove top, and Matie Luten sat there, mesmerized, looking at the glowing blade. He came back and sat down, taking another sip of coffee.

"Matie," he said. Then, with one finger of that long, white hand, he flipped the stack of greenbacks so that they made a leafy pattern across the top of Matie Luten's table. No matter her jeopardy, no matter the glowing blade of that knife, she could not help but think: A thousand dollars!

"Talk to me, Matie," he said.

"All right. But don't hurt me."

"Of course not, Matie. Listen." He bent toward her, and his eyes were as metallic as the blade of that knife. But not hot as the blade had been, still was. They were cold. "Listen. Elmer Scaggs."

"Oh my God." Matie Luten threw her head back and felt the shock of fear turn from unknown to something as real as this room, as real as that knife on the top of the stove with the handle burned off. "Who are you? Who are you?"

"Matie!" And he may as well have said, "Red-hot knife."

He reached across the table and took one of her hands and placed it on the scatter of bills. She was panting harder, tears running, her nose running. He gave her a white cotton handkerchief. She wiped her face with the handkerchief, using the hand that was not on the money. It was hard to take her hand off the money.

"He come now and again, Elmer did." She looked at one of her windows, where the sleet was beating, making a hissing sound. She could smell the burned wooden handle of the butcher knife. She had one hand on the table, the greenbacks beneath it. And he held his own hand on hers. Patting it gently.

"Yes, Matie, this is all better than the hot knife."

"I never knowed they was gonna kill him," she said. She kept looking at the window. She could feel his hand, patting hers. "He come now and again is all. He'd send this kid up here from town, some kinda message about a bill I owed at the bank. It was a message. You see? Just a message. It meant he'd be here that night."

"Of course, Matie."

"Elmer wasn't bad. He was just a big dumb man. Like a little child, that's what he was. He'd come here. He always had lots of money. I didn't care. He was just like a little child."

Matie Luten wiped at her nose again with the handkerchief, and sniffed and still looked at the window as though expecting some kind of rescue.

"Then he got in that trouble in town and they had him in jail and in court." She wiped at her nose again. She'd lost the handkerchief and used her hand now, but she didn't seem to know the difference. And his hand had left hers on the table, but hers was still lying on the money, beginning to clutch it.

"They come then and said they'd just give him a little calf-rope. Just rough him a little. Just fun him some. I never knowed they'd kill him."

She broke a little then, covered her face with both hands and shook and wiped at her mouth and nose and changed her gaze to another window. She didn't look at him, across the table.

"So they said they wanted to know when Elmer'd get here. Just to play a little calf-rope with him. One of 'em rode over here ever' day from Brown's Tavern, to see if it was time."

"Who rode over?" the man said.

"Yancy Crane. Or Essex."

"Essex?"

"Essex Brown. Hell, Becket Brown never come, that dumb bastard. But he was with them others when we talked about playin' a little calf-rope with Elmer. They was all three here then. But he never come back after, that dumb Becket. Just the other two. Ever' day. Until the kid come from town, and I told Essex that day when he come that Elmer'd be here. Then, Jesus Christ, I heard all them shots down the road and I knew then it was somethin' besides calf-rope."

The man was up now, seeming to straighten all his clothes, his face calm, no more expression than had been there when he first came into Matie Luten's house.

"What did they pay you for telling them this, Matie?"

"Seven dollars."

He was looking down at her then. And she finally looked back into those hard, metallic eyes, and she was shaking and her hand had forgotten to clutch the bills on the table.

"Please, mister, just shoot me, but don't put no hot knife on me."

She covered her face with both hands and began to sob, her shoulders shaking.

Had it not been for the cold blast of air that came in when the door opened, Matie Luten would not have believed she was suddenly, abruptly alone. When she moved her hands away from her face, he was gone. The shock set in and she shook so badly she thought her heart would pound its way right out through her chest. In her profession, she had known many men, some close to madness perhaps, many dangerous and unpredictable. But she had never seen a man like this one. And the thought of his coming back terrified her.

She lay her head on the table and wailed, thinking, Dear Jesus, only you can protect a woman like me. But after a moment she was up, running to the front window, looking out. The fence lines along the fields across the road were dim in the sleet that slanted before the northeast wind. But the man and his horse were gone. She tried to see as far down the road as she could, eyes squinted, trying to penetrate the icy curtain. But as far as she could see in any direction, there was nothing but the windswept land. He was truly gone. But the money was still on the table.

"Dear Jesus," Matie Luten said aloud. "Don't let him come back for a little while."

She ran to her small wardrobe and pulled out a wicker suitcase, a sidesaddle, bundles of clothes, hangers of clothes.

"Don't let him come back, don't let him come back."

Her means for escaping this whole mess was lying there on that table in the scatter of green. But quick, quick. Even in this weather. Even in any weather. The sleet and wind were terrible, but not so terrible as a white-hot knife blade.

Courtland and Sarah Brown served their customers in a large room with a short oak bar across one end. All along the place were wooden tables, many with initials cut into their surfaces, and straight-backed chairs. Opposite the bar was a fireplace that didn't draw too well, and as a result the place was always clouded with smoke.

On that icy winter day, in midafternoon, Courtland and Sarah were behind their tavern bar, she wiping glasses with a towel, he bent over the bar trying to read the latest edition of the *Democrat Advertiser*, but with little success, not only because the light was bad but because Courtland Brown had only a rudimentary knowledge of the English language, and a lot of Corliss Buckmaten's fancy prose escaped him completely.

There were three men at a table near the fireplace, playing cards. One of Sarah's cats, of which there were five, was on the bar and from time to time approached Courtland Brown with the apparent intention of sharing the newspaper. Courtland Brown would swipe the cat aside with a halfhearted oath.

When the strange man came through the front door, everyone already in the room suspended whatever they were doing and stared with the same intense interest they would show any unknown person in this place. They watched as the man took a chair at a table near the door, his back to the wall, and pulled a gray suede glove from his right hand with his teeth. He did not remove his overcoat or his hat, and there was no outward indication that he was armed.

The man was well dressed and apparently a gentleman and a veteran of the war, being of the right age and also having only one arm. They watched as the man glanced quickly about the room, his eyes pausing for only an instant on the cardplayers, the ice-glazed windows, the double door at the rear of the room that led to living quarters and to a stairwell up to the attic, where two rooms were kept for passing travelers desiring to spend the night. And finally, his eyes paused for a longer moment, before he looked down at the table before him, on Courtland and Sarah Brown.

"Who's that peckerwood?" Courtland asked his wife.

"I'll see."

"No, I'll do it."

Courtland Brown was a handsome man, in a horsy sort of way, his features exposed without any beard to hide the massive, coarse terrain of his face. He was of average height and weight, although now he had begun to develop a pot belly that was emphasized by the fact that he wore his trousers draped below it.

"Howdy," he said to the stranger, stopping before the table with his hands on his hips. "You want something?"

"As a matter of fact, I was looking for a Mr. Courtland Brown."

Courtland's heavy eyebrows lifted for a moment.

"Well, you've found him."

There followed a conversation that nobody else in the room could hear, even though Sarah Brown tried very hard. During the course of that conversation, the one-armed man dropped a roll of greenbacks on the table, at which point Courtland Brown sat down at the table and, in time, called for Sarah to bring a bottle of good sour-mash whiskey, as opposed to a pitcher of the usual less-than-a-month-old popskull aged in woodchips that most customers were served.

Later, there were bowls of beef stew and baking-powder biscuits. Courtland Brown was fascinated with the efficiency of this pale man's single hand in the performance of duties normally requiring two. The conversation continued with increasing intensity as they supped together, and Sarah Brown, behind the bar, was beside herself, wondering what it was about. And wondering why her husband had become so obviously enthralled with this odd-looking stranger.

Outside, the wind was whipping under the long eaves, making a mournful wail in the growing darkness. The three cardplayers finished their game and left, still staring at the stranger as they passed him. No one else came in. Sarah Brown polished glasses furiously, glaring at her husband. Drake Brown, with his strangely disfigured face, came in from the back and found himself a stool behind the bar and sat there near his mother, but they had no conversation.

After a while, Drake went across the room to throw more logs on the fire, using his left hand. He looked like a stamped-out metal copy of his father, or at least that's what he must have looked like before the disfigurement. The room filled with new smoke, its aroma blending harshly with that of sawdust, raw whiskey, and old grease.

Courtland Brown would remember that conversation for the rest of his life, playing it over and over again in his mind until he reckoned he wore it out, but then it would pop up unexpectedly.

It started with the man introducing himself as John Smith, from Cairo, Illinois. Courtland Brown did not believe the name, but he could understand how a man sometimes needed to use various handles. This was followed by Mr. Smith explaining that he was interested in joining men familiar with the Indian Territory for the purpose of establishing a cattle trade with the railroad construction companies that were starting to move through there. Railroad construction people ate a lot of beef, Mr. Smith explained, and if a man was careful in obtaining his cattle so they didn't cost too much—implying all kinds of things to Courtland Brown—then there were large profits to be made.

Further, he understood that Courtland Brown was acquainted with men of the same purpose, and that he might be helpful in directing Mr. Smith to them. It was at this point that Mr. Smith accidentally dropped a large roll of bills from a coat pocket, and quickly picked it up again, embarrassed at his clumsiness.

It was also then, seeing the greenbacks, that Courtland Brown took a seat opposite Mr. Smith. He began to pose questions, not too subtly. And he was delighted that Mr. Smith gave all the right answers. Mr. Smith gave all the right answers because he had received the necessary information in Topeka from Roman Hasford, but, of course, Courtland Brown did not know this.

Yes, said Mr. Smith, the arm had been lost at the Battle of Shiloh, while he was serving in the forces of Albert Sidney Johnston, who happened to have been one of Courtland Brown's great heroes for various vague reasons.

Actually, Mr. Smith had never been on a battlefield in his entire life. He had lost his arm as the result of his participation in a gunfight in a railyard in Kansas, where his two assailants lost not limbs but their lives.

Yes, Mr. Smith said, he was a devout Church of England man, but unfortunately, true Episcopal churches in which he could worship were hard to find. This, of course, was a very large item to Courtland Brown, not only for him but for his wife, who placed such store in an English heritage, whether real or imagined.

In fact, Mr. Smith could not remember the last time he had been inside a church, Anglican or otherwise.

Yes, said Mr. Smith, he was a businessman, a former banker in Illinois who wished to capitalize on the possibilities of large money in the project of railroads building through the Indian Nations. The profits from which, Mr. Smith said, he hoped to use in opening a bank right here in northwest Arkansas to compete with the bloodsucker who was already in that enterprise here, and of whom he had heard as far away as Illinois.

Courtland Brown marked this as an item of even greater interest than the Anglican church, and it was at this point that he called for Sarah to bring the bottle of good whiskey.

Actually Mr. Smith had never been a businessman. He had, from his earliest memory, been a troubleshooter and enforcer for a very wealthy railroad tycoon with interests from Baltimore to Denver.

Yes, Mr. Smith said, he was a Democrat.

Another splendid item.

In fact, Mr. Smith was without politics of any kind and had never voted in his life, and the railroad tycoon he'd been with all these many years was one of the biggest anti-labor, tight-money Republicans in the country.

Yes, said Mr. Smith, he had become aware of Major Corliss Buckmaten's wonderful newspaper and looked forward to meeting him someday. But of course, for the present, Mr. Smith explained, he needed to stay in the background—unknown, as it were—until he could come back with all that money he'd make in the Nations.

In fact, Mr. Smith had never read a word written by Corliss Buckmaten and had no interest in doing so.

Yes, Mr. Smith said, the hill country should be kept lily white, with niggers being sent back to where they came from, even if force was required.

Actually, Mr. Smith's close friend and confidant was a very black man named Fletcher who had been the cook for the railroad tycoon for almost as long as Mr. Smith himself had been the railroad tycoon's bodyguard.

Yes, said Mr. Smith, the story of this Arkansas county's czar of finance was well known in southern Illinois, so notorious had he become with charging usurious interest, buying political officials at the polls, and keeping ruffians about him to terrorize decent citizens.

Courtland Brown was so delighted with this entire recitation that the thought of deceit never entered his mind, this rather small man before him was so sincere, so knowledgeable, so in step with what *he*, Courtland Brown, thought.

So even in Illinois they know about Roman Hasford, thought Courtland Brown.

In fact, Mr. Smith had not been in Illinois since 1866, having had at that time to leave in some haste because local authorities were interested in placing him on a scaffold with a rope around his neck, inasmuch as he'd found it necessary to shoot and mortally wound a man disenchanted with the wages and company store prices of the railroad. This action took place in a roundhouse in Cairo.

Sitting in that smoky tavern with Courtland Brown, Mr. Smith was rather proud of having come up on the spur of the moment with a name for Roman Hasford. Ivan the Terrible.

"That's what he's called in southern Illinois," said Mr. Smith.

"Ivan the Terrible? In Illinois?"

"That's correct."

"By Gawd, I like that. Who the hell was Ivan the Terrible?"

"A vicious, spiteful man who wore good suits."

"By Gawd, I really *like* that."

And so, after all this cornucopia of wonderful items, Courtland Brown was willing to admit that he did indeed know three men in the Indian Nations, there with the same purpose in mind that motivated Mr. Smith's mission. Of course, Courtland Brown was incapable of phrasing it like that, but what he said meant the same thing.

Yancy Crane, Essex Brown, and Becket Brown. Operating out of a place called Hawk's Hole, a crossroads near the proposed right-of-way for the Missouri, Kansas, and Texas railroad, and regularly receiving from him, Courtland Brown, little messages delivered to a place much like the tavern in which they were now sitting, a tavern called Hawk's Hole Recreation Hall.

"It's not far from Tahlequah," said Courtland Brown.

"Good," said Mr. Smith. "Might I have from you a letter of introduction to these gentlemen?"

Courtland Brown withdrew somewhat, not because he had changed his mind or had any suspicions, but because when it came to writing anything he was on foreign ground.

"I'll be glad to write it," said Mr. Smith. "Just a letter to let them know where my sympathies lie, and that I do have funds to finance any venture we might desire."

"Hell, I'll sign it," Courtland Brown said. "I like that part about bringin' the money back here. We need some money on our side, Mr. Smith, so maybe we won't be affeared to brang our boys back home."

For a moment Courtland Brown thought he had said too much, but Mr. Smith's expression did not change. His face was calm, as though he had missed any implication that it might be of interest to local law-enforcement officials if the Brown boys and Yancy Crane reappeared in the county.

"Yes, I'll sign a letter," Courtland Brown said, thinking of that roll of greenbacks inadvertently exposed, and how it would help in the enterprise of railroads in the Indian Territory to produce more money, and how it all might end with Courtland Brown and his friends and sons having a friendly bank around. Thus putting the boot in the county on the other foot, as it were.

So it was all done, and later, in their bedroom, Courtland Brown said to Sarah, "It's like a gift. Jesus God, love, we got this dumb son of a bitch ready to help the boys and Yancy. He'll go off over there to the Nations tomorrow and the whole thang is gonna start for us, right there, with the boys and Yancy. Next time Poco Jimmy comes, we'll send a little note to the boys so they can be on the lookout for this one-armed man, and we'll make a real mark before it's through. I'll tell you what to write to the boys."

"You always do," Sarah said testily, still smarting from all that time in the tavern barroom, wondering what the hell was happening. "But I don't trust that Poco Jimmy. I don't trust any of them Indians."

"He's all right, that Cherokee, since he's got too big to be foolin' around with catchin' birds. Now he's carryin' better thangs back and forth."

"That's another thing," Sarah said. "Usin' that Indian to carry whiskey over there. Them Federal marshals in Fort Smith don't take much to people runnin' whiskey into the Territory."

"Hell, love, the kid's takin' all the risks. And we make most of the money. Poco Jimmy, he's all right. He likes money, too. Better'n sellin' pigeons."

"I don't like it," Sarah said.

"It'll be fine, love, and by Gawd, I gotta go in town tomorrow and tell Major Buckmaten about this fine gentleman who knows all about him and his newspaper. All the way up in Illinois."

"I don't like Corliss Buckmaten, either, and you know he don't like us."

"It'll be fine, love," Courtland Brown said.

In one of the attic rooms of Brown's Tavern, the stranger sat on the edge of his bed, laughing silently at how he'd savaged his friend Roman Hasford. And made Courtland Brown believe every word.

Nor was he concerned that Matie Luten would be rushing about telling everyone about their little meeting. In fact, he was convinced that even now Matie Luten was likely far gone from the county. He knew whores and he knew his own business.

And thinking of his business, he looked at the two pistols now lying on the night table under the coal-oil lamp. They were not the pistols he would have preferred. He liked Colt pistols. But a man with only one hand had to make concessions. These were custom-designed Smith & Wessons, paid for by that railroad tycoon and manufactured in Hartford, Connecticut.

They were breakdown pistols, with a special latch that he could operate with a single hand. As the pistols broke open, they ejected the spent cases, and then could be thrust into his waistband, where he could reload them. He had practiced this many times and could do it with his eyes closed. Of course, with two revolvers loaded, a total of twelve rounds, reloading wasn't much of a problem. He had never known a situation in which he needed as many as twelve rounds.

But anyway, there they lay, under the yellow glow of the lamp. Vicious weapons, double-action, .44 caliber, the lamplight shining on them, ivory butts gleaming creamy white, stubby barrels gleaming blue-black, gold-inlaid cylinders gleaming yellow. This last item was a concession to his vanity, perhaps, somewhat like his mania for having the part in his rust-colored hair exactly straight and exactly centered down the middle of his head.

Well, he thought, he had never shot anybody with these very expensive pistols. All that shooting of people had been before he'd lost the arm. During the Colt pistol days. Which he had assumed were past.

But sitting there in Courtland Brown's cold attic on this January night, he thought maybe such times were not past at all, and before blowing out the lamp he looked at those pistols, feeling renewed, feeling as though he had a place once more. A chance to bring back more exciting times, and do a service for an old friend, thought Jared Dane.

PART THREE

PROGRESS

13

Even in the raw frontier period, a post office was often the single most important place in a town. And as growth and civilization set in, it became more so. Not only because it was a link with the outside world, but because it was a daily visible symbol of the Federal Union, the only symbol that citizens of hill country like northwest Arkansas could accept, hill-country people having by nature such a fierce streak of individuality as to mistrust most any form or appendage of government.

But a post office, that was different.

When a post office was first established in a community, the name of that place went right into a big book they had in Washington, District of Columbia. A book with the names of all post offices, no matter if they were in Florida or Delaware or California or Vermont or other such unlikely place. After a time, the community's first postmaster received a copy of this book and people could come into the post office and look at it in its light gray cover, could marvel at its thickness and even thumb through the pages and find the name of their own town right there, listed in alphabetical order by state or territory.

To most of them, the fact that their own town was there among all the others became proof of their affiliation with the rest of the nation, more solid proof than the flag or statute law or the Constitution or George Washington cutting down a cherry tree.

The post office lost no portion of its exalted position when and if a railroad was built, because much of what came in and went out on the cars did so through the post office. And the railroads, not usually willing to share anything with anybody, admitted this marriage of progress, this partnership of value. A contract to carry mail by the trains came as a matter of course, much to the chagrin of stagecoach lines, and once trains began to run regularly, each one had a mail car. It was really just a baggage car with a small section devoted to the mail, but the railroads called it a mail car.

Even in these little burgs, people said, where the train didn't stop unless a red flag was up to signal a waiting passenger or freight, a man could send a letter or a bill of sale or a form to one of those new mail-order houses in Chicago or Kansas City—asking for a plow, say—and the stationmaster would just put it in a heavy canvas bag, the bag was hung on a pole beside the tracks, and when the train came through, this man in the mail car raised a hook that was built right on the side of the car and that hook snatched the bag off the pole and into the mail car to be put in one of those little pigeonholes. Then away it went, they said, to Chicago or Kansas City or wherever.

If that ain't progress, they said, I'll buy your blind cow.

If our town's gonna amount to a hill of beans, they said, we gotta have a post office and a railroad.

The post office in Gourdville was a raw oak lumber building, sided with limestone rock to add some stability and dignity. It was on First Street, directly across from the Sample Cider and Vinegar Works, which was owned by Omar Sample, who, not coincidentally, also owned the biggest apple orchard in the county.

Postmasters were appointed by a rather convoluted system that went all the way to the White House. Sometimes a President actually appointed a few in places where the position was considered a plum. More commonly, even though the warrant might have the President's name on it, the position of postmaster was a reward held out to locals who had done something good for politicians who ended up in the Congress.

So, right after the war, this meant Gourdville's postmaster would likely be a Reconstruction Republican. Which was indeed the case. But once Reconstruction was at an end, the next steward of the gray book with all the post office names was likely to be a Democrat. Which indeed he was.

Walter Matt was appointed postmaster during the first six months of the administration of Rutherford B. Hayes. He was a young man, too young to have been involved in the war and hence without a store of partisan bitterness. He was a political innocent, and maybe that's why he got the appointment. A man who wouldn't kick up rage and roaring from either side. But he was a Democrat, a Missouri Democrat who had come into the county with his wife, Stella, and infant son, Adam, ten years after the war was over.

Walter Matt became a close friend of Corliss Buckmaten, even though their backgrounds were dissimilar. The Matts were often the Sunday dinner guests of the Buckmatens after they had attended services together at the biggest Baptist church in Gourdville. Walter went because he and Stella were Baptists, and Corliss because, though he had once been a lukewarm Catholic, since there was no Catholic church in the county at the time, he felt he was now required to find something else.

Not that Corliss Buckmaten had in his soul some burning desire to find God through an organized church. It was, in fact, a cynical and secular requirement. How could he constantly publish cutting remarks about Roman Hasford not bending his knee to the Almighty if he himself did not? And certainly, from that first election in the county, when Roman Hasford had financed that slate of officials who won and had been winning ever since, Corliss Buckmaten had been banging away at Roman Hasford's godlessness.

"In a God-fearing community," he often wrote, "when was the last time any pious citizen here has seen this man, one of our supposed community leaders, in a church pew?"

Comments such as that had become so much a matter of course that a lot of people had come to expect them every week. As sure as fleas on a yard dog, they said.

The friendship between Walter Matt and Corliss Buckmaten provided the editor and publisher an insider's sure knowledge of who was writing to whom. The sharing of such information became a part of their casual conversations, as usual as gossip between housewives in backyards on washday. It was a function of Walter Matt's innocence and Corliss Buckmaten's journalistic curiosity.

Corliss Buckmaten originally may not have had ulterior motives in cultivating the postmaster, but there were obvious advantages to such an arrangement, which Corliss couldn't help but appreciate. Even though, as he was to find, his knowledge of traffic in the postal system could set him off in directions that were disturbing and maybe even dangerous.

*   *   *

When Courtland Brown appeared at the *Democrat Advertiser*, Corliss Buckmaten was not overjoyed. Corliss had frequently quoted to his wife that old bromide, "Politics makes strange bedfellows." But bedfellows or not, Corliss avoided courting the company of any of the Brown's Tavern bunch, whom he considered to be white-trash riffraff.

He listened, however, and, having listened, dismissed the whole thing as the result of one of Courtland Brown's great bouts with demon rum. There were, of course, interesting journalistic possibilities. That someone as far away as Cairo, Illinois, was saying wicked things about Roman Hasford. That his own words had been read and admired there. But, being an intelligent man, the more he thought about it, the more skeptical he was.

"Someone is blowing smoke up Courtland Brown's rear end," he said to Melissa in their bed. "Blowing smoke for some purpose as yet unknown."

After all, Corliss Buckmaten reasoned, why would anybody in Cairo, Illinois, give a good God damn about Roman Hasford, and why would anyone there read a little newspaper like the *Advertiser*, even if a copy of it should somehow happen to drift that far north?

Yet he couldn't shake it from his mind. There were such intriguing ramifications. Perhaps Roman Hasford had strong Yankee connections in Illinois or Missouri or one of those other strongholds of Lincoln Republicanism. Corliss Buckmaten lay awake at night, beside the snoring Melissa, wondering about it. Listening to the cold winter wind outside and wondering.

There had been that Hasford trip some time ago, with the purpose, as everyone soon knew, of placing Roman Hasford's wife in a school of some sort. Roman Hasford, his wife, and Gallatin Delmonico departing by coach for the north and Delmonico returning soon after. And Roman Hasford not coming home until much later. What the hell was he doing up there? Corliss Buckmaten wondered.

That period was well set in Corliss Buckmaten's mind because while Roman Hasford was gone, his mother had died. He'd published an obituary, of course.

Mrs. M. Hasford, of the county, died last week and was placed to rest on the property of her husband, who is an honored veteran of the war of Yankee aggression but is now himself suffering from the abuse of time and other things. The service was said by the Rev. Kirkendall.

Nobody who read that had any doubts about the phrase "and other things." The reference was clearly to Martin's son, Roman Hasford, as implied in so many column inches of the past.

So perhaps because his curiosity was driving him mad, as the curiosity of good journalists is supposed to do, Corliss Buckmaten began steering his conversations with his friend Walter Matt in the direction of that strange trip. And had little trouble discovering that Catrina Peel Hasford had departed the county after correspondence between Gallatin Delmonico and a Catholic school in Jefferson City, Missouri.

A Catholic school. That was some small triumph in itself. A school of his own old faith. So perhaps he took it as a sign, a sign of revelation. Or maybe his inquisitiveness simply overwhelmed him.

"Melissa, we're going to take a vacation," he said.

"Now? It's still dead of winter in this horrid place."

"Now is the best time," he said. "Pack some clothes, warm clothes. We're going north."

"To Yankee country? Corliss, are you out of your mind?"

"Pack some warm clothes."

So off to Missouri, a state he would not have ventured near ten years before, because Missouri had not seceded from the Federal Union when the opportunity presented itself. But now to Missouri, and to Jefferson City.

They toured the capitol building and rode past the governor's mansion in a coach and four. They dined on rack of lamb with mint jelly in their hotel, a repast unheard of in northwest Arkansas. Corliss got a little drunk and Melissa giggled.

They went to St. Scholastica but could not gain entrance, having no proof of relatives therein, and in fact they were refused their request to know if one Catrina Hasford was cloistered inside. No matter, Corliss thought. She's there. It gave him some satisfaction to look at the buildings and to remark to Melissa that it looked somewhat like a penitentiary.

"It does not," she said. "The trees are lovely."

"The trees are as bare as last year's bones," he said.

"They'll be green soon," she said.

In Jefferson City, Melissa shopped for a spring hat. While she was thus engaged, Corliss displayed his considerable charm when so required, his inconsiderable credentials as a journalist, and his roll of money that was somewhere in between. Speaking with other members of the Jefferson City newspaper fraternity, he soon became aware that the czar of Catrina Hills Farm may have been infamous in Cairo, Illinois, as Mr. Courtland Brown's one-armed stranger said, but nobody in Jefferson City had ever heard of him or of the *Democrat Advertiser*.

Still, the assistant ticket agent at the Missouri Pacific passenger depot was most informative, particularly after the encouragement of greenback bribes, and he said that he did indeed recall a certain tall gentleman, distinguished and a little drunk, who had arrived from the south in company of a man with a black beard and a very small woman. This ticket agent recalled it so vividly because of the striking appearance of the small lady, with whom the tall gentleman had arrived but without whom he had departed. And without the man with the black beard, instead purchasing a round-trip ticket to Topeka, Kansas.

When the ticket agent mentioned Topeka, Kansas, all kinds of sparks were set off in Corliss Buckmaten's mind. On that instant he forgot Illinois or Missouri or any other of those places now called the Land of Lincoln, and forgot as well whether or not anyone in such places was familiar with his newspaper.

"Why in hell was he going back to Kansas?" Corliss asked Melissa.

"I'm sure I don't know. Go to sleep."

"There may be a lot of reasons. But I don't know any of them. So we're going to Topeka."

"Topeka!" Melissa shouted, rising up from her bed. "These people up here don't have any hats we'd put on scarecrows in Benton County!"

"In Topeka they'll have hats," he said.

It was a long ride. All the way Melissa complained about the quality of Yankee headgear, all the way Corliss Buckmaten silently came to doubt more and more the "Mr. Smith" of Courtland Brown.

In Topeka they toured the capitol, rode past the governor's mansion in a coach and four, and dined on Rocky Mountain oysters in their hotel, although Corliss Buckmaten did not explain to Melissa what Rocky Mountain oysters really were. The next day, as she searched for a hat that would be acceptable in Benton County, Arkansas, Corliss Buckmaten visited the two newspaper offices. And discovered very quickly that if Roman Hasford was not known in Jefferson City, Missouri, or Cairo, Illinois, he sure as hell was known in Topeka, Kansas.

"Why, yes," one editor said. "That's the young man the Kansas Pacific was about to sponsor for the state legislature some years ago. And you're a friend of his?"

"Oh yes," said Corliss Buckmaten. "We know each other well."

Corliss Buckmaten learned a great deal about Roman Hasford, who had grown to wealth in this state and was a hero of Beecher's Island. And he learned, too, that Roman Hasford had become a close associate of the man who was bodyguard and hired killer to one of the state's great railroad men.

The hired killer was named Jared Dane, and he had one arm, after a small shooting in the Topeka railyard. And had departed Topeka shortly after the last visit of Roman Hasford. For parts unknown, they said, which was not unusual for Jared Dane.

Corliss Buckmaten tried not to choke, because he remembered suddenly what Courtland Brown had said about this Mr. Smith. A one-armed man.

"Why are you pushing me, why are you pushing me?" Melissa said.

But it was back in a hurry. Back to Jefferson City and then to Cassville and then the coach to home, with Corliss Buckmaten on the edge of his seat all the way.

"What's the matter with you?" Melissa asked.

"Look at your new hat."

"It's a terrible hat," she said.

Once home, with Melissa and her new hat established in their small house behind the newspaper office, Corliss Buckmaten hired a hack from Ennis Lugi's stable and, for the first and only time, rode to Brown's Tavern on the Indian Nations Road.

Courtland Brown didn't believe him at first. But as Corliss Buckmaten laid it all together, like a professional cabinetmaker gluing

and doweling and screwing together the bits and pieces of walnut
wood, he was convinced.

"So warn them what they're facing," Corliss Buckmaten said.

"I will," Courtland Brown said. "My God. That son of a bitch.
I will. We got a way to do it."

"I'm not interested in any way you do these things."

On the way back to town, Corliss Buckmaten had second
thoughts. In fact, as this thing was shaping up, it occurred to him
that he had become involved in what could be a very serious game
indeed. Corliss Buckmaten was certainly no coward, as he had
proved during the recent war, but fighting with a military unit—
clanging a sword about and waving a battle flag and wearing
powder-blue pantaloons—was entirely different from the prospect
of some savage from Kansas appearing unexpectedly to inquire
about Corliss Buckmaten's curiosity.

He wheeled the hack about, drove back to Brown's Tavern, and,
finding Courtland and Sarah Brown in agitated conference together,
explained that his part in this must be kept from public knowledge,
or dire consequences would result. Courtland and Sarah Brown
agreed, and Courtland added that he wasn't too anxious for anybody
to understand his own involvement.

And so they made a pledge of silence, like schoolchildren who
had just invented a secret handshake for their tree-house club.

Then back to town went Corliss Buckmaten in the hack, feeling
in no wise reassured. Because he didn't trust Courtland Brown any
more than he trusted Roman Hasford.

"Why do you dislike Mr. Brown and Mr. Hasford so much,
honey?" Melissa asked.

"I have tried explaining it to you until I'm tongue-tied with it.
Just remember one thing. Courtland Brown is a scoundrel and
Roman Hasford is a Republican, which is the same thing. But Courtland Brown is stupid and Roman Hasford is very smart. Which
makes him the more dangerous of the two."

"I don't understand."

"Go to sleep, for Christ's sake."

Corliss Buckmaten was torn between pride at having done such
brilliant detective work—better, he suspected, than a Pinkerton
could have done—and the utterly frustrating certainty that he
couldn't print anything about it because if he did, it would reveal
him as a man who might now be, or in the future could become,

accessory to some very distasteful violence. Maybe even to the extent of murder.

And just as surely, he thought, I cannot go to the law with what I know, with the knowledge that at this moment there is likely a very bad man in the Indian Territory looking for the Brown boys and Yancy. Because then the prosecuting attorney will ask some very embarrassing questions, with a view, perhaps, toward charging me with obstruction of justice, believing, as they surely will, that I know more than I do.

Besides, Corliss thought, if I went to the law or printed any of this, that Jared Dane person would surely hear of it. And would not take kindly to it.

So Corliss Buckmaten could only lie awake at night, beside the snoring Melissa, hoping and praying that the Brown boys and Yancy would simply depart the Nations for Colorado—or, even better, California. Hoping and praying as well that Courtland and Sarah Brown would keep their mouths shut about all that brilliant Buckmaten detective work.

14

Nothing could exceed the excitement of a railroad's first scheduled train into an area that had been thinking about it for twenty years. Gourdville had been thinking about it for that long at least, having subscribed five hundred dollars to promote such an enterprise before the Civil War. But then the project was set aside to accommodate invading armies instead of locomotives, and by the time things struggled back to normal, the emphasis on tracklaying was directed toward east-west lines instead of north-south ones; and all those, like the Union Pacific and the Northern Pacific and the Southern Pacific, were either too far north or too far south to touch the Ozark hills, which weren't designed for easy railroad construction anyway. And then, just when it appeared to the big railroad companies that there might be profit in running a few north-south roads, the money crisis of the 1870s put all of it on the shelf for another ten years or so.

All of which made it that much sweeter when it did happen.

None of the preliminaries took the edge off anticipation. In fact, each step heightened it, and there were a lot of preparatory steps in railroading itself before that first engine came down the tracks belching black smoke, making metallic noises never before heard across a virgin countryside, scattering cinders and setting woods on fire, and scaring hell out of the livestock.

First was land acquisition. In northwest Arkansas, it wasn't exactly like building a line across Nebraska in 1869, when most of the terrain there was public domain. All the acreage in the county was owned by somebody, recorded in the office of the circuit clerk, and anybody who wanted to traverse it had to buy it or make some sort of easement proposition.

After the land was in hand came the survey teams. This didn't kick up a lot of dust, because it usually amounted to a couple of wagons and some mules and a few men with transits and stakes and engineering tape. But even though it was a quiet operation, everyone knew about it. And what it meant. It meant bigger things to come.

The grading crews. Now the dust was kicked up. Now there were more mules than anyone had ever seen. Plows and scrapers and shovels. And men. A lot of men, most of whom spoke English in a strange sort of way, if at all. Men with picks and shovels and more transits and stakes and engineering tape. Of course, there was a requirement to feed this invading army that was falling on the local population to their great delight. Hay and grain for the mules, and potatoes and beefsteak for the men.

More than that. Whiskey and beer for the men's leisure time.

More than that, too. Because these were men alone, without their women, if indeed they had any in the first place, and so it was like any other invading army. And anybody who knew about invading armies realized that one of the most important aspects of leisure time was women. Women who were as professional as the men they entertained.

So even though Gourdville lost Matie Luten to Baxter Springs or someplace—nobody ever knew why—she was now replaced by half a dozen others. Maybe more, nobody was ever sure. They didn't cause any trouble. They didn't mingle with the townsfolk, God forbid. And when the railroad work crews left, so did they, because the local population could never support that much licentious recreation. Although some of the male citizens of the county would have been willing to try, had they been financially capable of it.

It was toward the tag end of the roadway work that something else started to happen. The telegraph crews arrived and began to set in poles, screwing green glass insulators like doorknobs onto crossmembers and stringing wire, because a railroad had to have telegraph lines all along its course, no matter whether the railroad did the job itself or left it to Western Union. Western Union did it mostly, because they knew how better than anyone else, and besides, they had a monopoly on such things.

The telegraph line that paralleled the tracks was much more than a communication link between trains. It was a system citizens could use, for a price, which meant that once it began its click-click operation, a whole new world was no farther away than the railroad depot where there was a window with a Western Union sign above it, and inside, a man wearing a green eyeshade, with his hand on the key.

The depot. That was the next step, and it meant a lot of work for local stonemasons and carpenters and common laboring people. And big orders for bricks from the local kiln. Rust-red bricks, as in the manner of all railroad depots.

Then the arrival of important railroad men, pointing, waving their arms, to be sure there was a spacious baggage room, a waiting area for passengers, with benches like church pews, good privies not too far removed from the depot, a ticket window with a cast-iron grille in front, freight-loading docks, and two small houses, one for the stationmaster, the other for the section foreman who would see to the maintenance of the line.

A lot of money coming in and a lot of excitement building. A lot of beans and overalls and water buckets and horses and paint and screwdrivers being sold.

And finally, the real railroad builders. The men who laid down the crossties and spiked the steel rails to them. Huge, mule-drawn wagons to bear the ties, eight feet long, square-cut, and each one bought from locals, hacking down the oaks as fast as they could, then off to the sawmills. A land-rush business.

The rails. Stacked on flatcars that were pushed ahead of a little locomotive, extending out mile by mile. The gandy dancers driving in the spikes for one section of steel, and just behind them the flatcar with more, carried up, laid down, spiked in, the little locomotive running on the new-laid steel before the last spike had cooled from being driven into the hardwood crossties.

Every kid in the county came to watch. Every family in the county came to watch.

It was amazing, these ribbons of shining metal, so neatly defined by the crossties under them, and the telegraph poles alongside, set at precise sixty-foot intervals, the new wire from one crossmember and one green-glass insulator to the next, like the web of some great metal spider.

God, it was exciting!

Of course, there was some bitching and carping about the placement of things. The track passed through the edge of town on the east, only a short distance from Glen Torten's Billiard Parlor, and Glen was already building a second floor onto his establishment where he would have four rooms to let for travelers or for railroad people coming into town to inspect sections of the track.

James Chesney, who had the new slaughterhouse on Oak Creek, had bought some land just outside the city limits and alongside the right-of-way and was clearing ground for a tie yard, because a railroad always needed ties. In fact, the St. Louis–San Francisco, which happened to be this particular railroad, was putting in a siding track there so that boxcars could be dropped off and left to sit until loaded with oak ties.

A lot of people were furious with James Chesney because they hadn't thought of a tie yard first.

Finally, all of this activity passed on to the south, and Gourdville had to content itself with the running back and forth of work locomotives carrying rails and other things to the head of construction, the engine's whistle shrilling constantly as it ran along First Street. Dogs and children would get out of the way, though sometimes it seemed just to frighten the teams of horses and mules always standing at the rear of Newton Black's feed store.

It was a time of impatience, for everybody understood that the rails would have to reach Fayetteville before the Frisco sent a real train with passenger coaches down the line. As that day approached, the railroad posted colorful placards on the sides of buildings announcing various things, like the fact that freight would be accepted at the depot once passenger service began. Accepted at the new warehouse, actually, a building that stood just north of the passenger terminal, where a loading dock and another siding were being built, in a somewhat more leisurely fashion than the main line had been.

Local farmers were already rubbing their hands together and heading for the bank for more loans so they could expand, whether in pigs or peaches, cotton or cucumbers, beans or bulls, because they could see new markets opening to them in Missouri, all the way to St. Louis.

Thus was the romance of steam-and-steel railroads based on solid economics.

The banner day arrived, announced in red, white, and blue

broadsides nailed to every barn. The first passenger train would arrive from Monet en route to Fayetteville on Independence Day, July Fourth, a Sunday that year, with the arrival of the train in Gourdville timed just at noon, after services in all the various churches. Everything would be draped in red, white, and blue crêpe-paper bunting, even the locomotive. Which in the event had been known occasionally to catch fire from hot cinders, the fire then having to be slapped out by train crewmen using wet burlap bags carried in water barrels on the tender.

Speeches already prepared for Independence Day were enlarged to get the railroad into the patriotic phrases. One would be given by the mayor, who at that time happened to be Harley Stone of Stone's Hotel, and another by Circuit Judge Jacob Rich, everyone expecting His Honor's face to be streaked with black sweat from the excess coloring of his toupee for the event. The additional references were to Progress, which was expected to be tangible, what with the locomotive and its two passenger cars appearing from the north and grinding to a halt at the depot platform, sparks flying, bell clanging, whistle blowing, release valves spurting steam into the crowds of squealing kids.

From the volume of his trade in firecrackers, Jefferson Caulder predicted the place would sound like the second Battle of Pea Ridge. And, of course, added to this childish bedlam would be the firing of pistols by young men too frequent at the bottle when they should have been in church, disregarding the safety of livestock. And Ennis Lugi, at the livery stable, firing his anvil in the smithy behind the stalls with black powder at least half a dozen times during the day.

So, at a little past noon—late, because the train had had to pause for a flock of sheep on the track near Seligman, the fireman having to dismount from the locomotive cab to shoo them away with his hat and very obscene language—the funnel-stacked locomotive appeared, exploding black clouds of smoke toward a cloudless blue sky. The people alongside the tracks cheered. Mules brayed. All the churchbells in the town were ringing. The kids were almost hysterical with delight, throwing firecrackers beneath the train as it screeched to a halt at the depot platform.

Then from the coaches descended the two Distinguished Citizens of Gourdville whom the railroad had brought to Cassville to board the train there and ride into Gourdville on this first run.

Two more disparate Distinguished Citizens could hardly be

imagined. But the railroad knew what it was doing, buttering its bread on both sides, as it were. For one of the honored gentlemen was Corliss Buckmaten, publisher of the *Democrat Advertiser*, and the other was Roman Hasford of the Farmer's and Merchant's Bank and Catrina Hills Farm.

If there were two men in this county who loathed each other more than these two did, nobody was able to name them.

The Frisco officials had had sense enough to place their guests in separate coaches on the ride from Cassville, and the additional foresight to avoid mentioning to either one that the other would be there. So each discovered the fact only as he mounted the train in Cassville, too late to back out, to refuse the free ride in honor of northwest Arkansas Progress.

The Frisco officials had counted on these circumstances to stay their two honored citizens' hands from pulling revolvers, which everyone suspected each would be carrying, and dispatching each other on the spot. Progress! Even the most bitter of enemies would be reluctant to open fire in the presence of Progress, particularly when it was all in public view amid red, white, and blue bunting. And with a band playing, besides. A band stationed on a flatcar coupled between the two passenger coaches and honking out martial airs from the moment the train departed Cassville until it came to a steamy halt at the Gourdville depot. And every mile in between, startling pasturing cattle and horses alongside the right-of-way.

The speeches were made from the rear platform of the last coach, and, as was the custom with Fourth-of-July oratory, they were too long, and hardly half of what was said registered even faintly on the minds of those who were supposed to be listening.

Then the dignitaries from Fayetteville, who had arrived the night before and spent a pleasant evening in the mayor's hotel, guests of the owner, boarded the train so that they might alight in their own city, where a crowd was also waiting. The whistle blew, the bell clanged, the steam shot from piston and valve in a great cloud, the drive wheels spun, and the little train was off to the south, followed by further barrages of firecrackers thrown by Gourdville kids as long as they could keep up with the thing, running down the tracks and screaming like Comanches. Only then did people begin to disperse, going their own ways, to tables soon to be set with fried chicken or pork, fresh tomatoes, and mashed potatoes, each and every one feeling a part of history.

There were amazingly few ugly incidents connected with this event, most certainly the largest Fourth of July Gourdville had ever experienced or probably ever would. Only one team of horses bolted amid all the explosions of firecrackers, running wildly across the square, dragging behind them a careening cart wagon, on its side the words FELCHER'S DAIRY in black letters. The eight-year-old son of Brian Felcher was thrown out of this vehicle and suffered a broken arm, which Doc Cronin set free of charge in honor of the day and of Progress.

The volunteer firemen had to put out only one fire, started in the shed beside Ennis Lugi's blacksmith shop when he spilled a bit of black powder while preparing to shoot his anvil; the powder was set blazing when Ausbin Tage, a little unsteady from too much beer in Glen Torten's Billiard Parlor, flicked a hot ash from his cigar. It was a disgrace, the ladies of the Presbyterian church said, their reference being to the son of a member of their own congregation, Mr. Ephraim Tage. For although they found little about the elder Tage to brag about, at least he was a devout predestinationist, a man whose shortcomings through the week could be overlooked so long as he appeared in church every Sunday.

The younger Tage appeared in church, too, except for that Sunday of the train's coming.

And besides, the ladies said, Ephraim Tage had some license to be a crabby old son of a bitch, what with having lost his wife, a fine, upstanding Calvinist, the poor woman dying right in the midst of trying to raise a son. Ausbin had no such excuse.

But if the ladies of the Presbyterian church were embarrassed, it was nothing compared to what happened to the Methodist Ladies' Aid Society. The ladies were selling lemon pie and layer cake on the sidewalk of the Stone Hotel that day, trying to raise enough money to build a belfry on their church, when directly before them in the street two local dogs began to engage in sexual congress.

The disgraceful spectacle was brought to a damp conclusion when Tilman Lapp, the undertaker, ran all the way across the square from his funeral parlor with a bucket of water and doused the miscreants.

As Tilman Lapp returned to his emporium of death, red-faced and carrying an empty bucket in his hand, a group of young men standing on the corner near the newspaper office made hissing sounds, and one even shouted to ask if the bucket had been filled with formaldehyde, these young men having lost all sense of decency, it was said, due to imbibing large quantities of peach brandy distilled right here in the county by Benjamin Tark, who everybody knew represented Satan in his worst possible guise, being not only purveyor of intoxicating spirits but a godless man and living in sin with a Cherokee Nations woman not his wife and having a large dose of Indian blood in his own veins besides. In fact, some said, Ben Tark was the biggest atheist anyone had ever known. Except, of course, for Roman Hasford.

Corliss Buckmaten knew Roman Hasford was not an atheist. Having the big ears of a born journalist, Corliss had heard it said that Roman Hasford, when invited to services in various of the local churches early after his return from Kansas, had declined with the explanation that his was the religion of Thomas Jefferson.

Most people didn't know what this meant—the issue being further confused by Roman's annual contribution to the Methodists, which some said was because his papa had been a Methodist before the war and others said it was just a case of Hasford showing off his money, but Corliss Buckmaten knew exactly to what Roman was referring when he mentioned Jefferson. He knew that Roman believed the universe had been set on its course by some great, majestic, unknown power and then allowed to go its own way according to rational but yet undiscovered natural laws. Not predestination in any sense, either, because within these natural laws where things happened logically, like water boiling if enough heat was applied, individual human beings had free will, control of their own fate.

Corliss Buckmaten knew that Roman Hasford was a Deist.

Yet it was never even hinted that such was the case in the columns of the *Democrat Advertiser*. Corliss simply wrote that the czar of Catrina Hills Farm was not to be found in holy places of worship on Sunday mornings. Which was true. And Corliss often called Roman Hasford a godless man, which, under the definition of the word according to most hill folk, was also true. But Corliss never wrote anything about Deism. Because although Deism was not a widely accepted or even a known philosophy in the county, it couldn't have been as terrible to the locals as atheism. And in this instance, Corliss Buckmaten was certainly not going to cloud his readers' thinking with facts.

After the Fourth of July celebration of the coming of the railroad, there was another thing Corliss Buckmaten knew as fact but never wrote about either. It had to do with political party loyalty, an issue over which Corliss Buckmaten could become so infuriated that he frightened his wife when he spoke of it, just as he had frightened his mother years before when he discussed Yankees.

When that train came into Gourdville, shrouded in red, white, and blue bunting, Corliss Buckmaten had noted a curious phenomenon. Everybody had lined up on one side of the track or the other, naturally, but unnaturally, all the Democrats were on the west side, all the Republicans on the east.

Into the Republican group went Roman Hasford, taking his station as soon as he alighted from the train (although Roman was never sure exactly what he was, and Corliss Buckmaten likely knew that, too). With Roman stood the Caulders and Isaac Maddox, Anson Greedy, Terrance Shadbolt, Sheriff Bidd, and all the bank people and their families; and behind everybody else, just in front of the section foreman's house, was a buggy, and in the buggy were Orvile Tucker and the Croziers with their baby.

"It's a calamity, ain't it?" some men said. "That little tick gonna grow up to be a nigger."

But a lot of the women said, "I tell you, they ain't nothin' in the world cute as a little colored child."

On the west side, the Democrat side, stood Corliss Buckmaten, the Browns (not counting their two sons off somewhere in the Indian Territory), John Vain, and Ennis Lugi, lawyers Bactrum and Burton, Ephraim Tage and his son, Ausbin, Cato Fulton, Raymond Ort, and a lot more.

Corliss Buckmaten looked at the distribution and thought of the last election. All the candidates put up by what the *Democrat Advertiser* called the Scalawag Society had won, even though Roman Hasford had been taking less and less of an active part since that very first election when Yancy Crane got thrown out. Then Corliss, counting up the two groups, reckoned that a lot of people had been lying when they said they had voted as Democrats. The truth of the matter seemed to be that whatever the labels, people in the county were voting for whomever they considered the best man, and not for the ticket. Which was a disaster, as far as Corliss Buckmaten was concerned, a disaster he laid directly at Roman Hasford's door.

PART FOUR

DANE

15

Nason Grube wasn't supposed to be in the Indian Nations, and he knew it. It made him very nervous because if one of those United States deputy marshals found out about it, they'd put iron on his wrists and legs and haul him up before Judge Isaac Parker in the Federal Court at Fort Smith. Nason Grube would then be spending a lot of time in a penitentiary at Detroit or some such place.

The thought of Judge Parker and a white man's penitentiary did more than make Nason Grube nervous. It scared hell out of him!

Under the law, there were only four kinds of people who could be in the Indian Nations. And although Nason Grube was not an educated man, and in fact couldn't even read and write, he knew each of the categories. And that scared hell out of him, too, because he didn't fit into any of them.

A member of the Five Civilized Tribes whose ancestors had come there during the Jackson administration under various removal policies, or an Osage or a Ponca or any one of a number of other Indian people who had been dumped into the area since the Civil War, they could be there.

A man or woman, black or white, who married into one of the resident tribes, they could be there. Nason Grube had never married anybody because the thought of having a wife frightened him even more than Judge Parker and the penitentiary did.

Any former black slave in one of the Five Civilized Tribes could be there. With ratification of the Thirteenth Amendment, and under various associated Federal statutes, a person who had been chattel to a Cherokee or a Creek or a Seminole or a Choctaw or a Chickasaw became a free member of that tribe. Even though he or she was not an Indian, but was, in fact, an African. Well, Nason Grube was an African, all right. But his bondage had been in Tennessee.

Finally, anyone with a work permit issued by a Federal court could be in the Territory. As in the case of railroad builders.

When the steel began to inch south out of Kansas into the Indian Territory, a lot of work permits were issued. But there were some common laborers, pick-and-shovel people, who had none. A jobber for one of the lines would hire crews of unskilled men. The railroad paid him; he paid his crew. Sometimes the jobber would forget to file requests for work permits. Then the jobber would pocket large chunks of his crewmen's pay, and if they complained the jobber would threaten to expose them as being in the Nations without legal sanction.

Like Nason Grube, who was one of these unfortunates, the men so exploited needed work. And knowing nothing of law, they had no notion that if this whole thing came to law, the jobber would be at the head of the line in front of Judge Parker. And so they worked. For pennies, with back-breaking labor and fear and bad food.

But after a while, Nason Grube stopped.

He didn't leave the Indian Territory, mostly because the Cherokees treated him just like any other man, red, white, or black. And even more because he didn't have anywhere else to go.

Nason Grube found a deserted shack south of Hawk's Hole on Mud Creek, a small stream that emptied into the Verdigris River, about a mile away. He kept body and soul together in summer by growing a vegetable garden and eating everything that came from it, including the roots of onions and the stalks of corn. In winter it was more difficult. He managed by carving little dolls from walnut wood and selling them to the Cherokees. And he milked their cows, too, taking in payment a small part of the milk, and each day stealing a pocketful of bran or oats from the Cherokee barns to take home and make mush.

His shack had only a single room, furnished from whatever Nason Grube could find discarded from some of the more prosperous Cherokee families in the area. An old settee covered with straw-stuffed burlap bags. A stained mattress. A heating stove that Nason Grube also used as a cookstove, an old cast-iron Dutch oven on top.

He lived from hand to mouth, and likely would have starved if it hadn't been for the kindness of some of the Indians around Hawk's Hole. Each night he lay on his stained mattress, hungry, wishing he had a drink of whiskey, and wondering if maybe before he woke Judge Parker's deputies would be there to arrest him.

Of course, Judge Parker's deputies had more serious things to do than to roust peaceful illegals out of the Territory. The illegals they dealt with were anything but peaceful. Over a period of time, about fifty of them would be killed in the line of duty. So somebody as timid and law-abiding as Nason Grube actually had little to fear from Judge Parker's law. Only Nason Grube didn't know that.

Things got better for Nason Grube his second winter at Hawk's Hole. But at the same time they got worse.

They got better because three white men came and said they'd pay him a little money and bring him a little meat and whiskey if they could sleep in his shack. They said they were cattlemen and would be traveling around a lot, but they needed someplace to call headquarters, and the tavern at Hawk's Hole was always full when a man needed to lie down and rest his bones.

It sounded like a fine idea to Nason Grube, especially that meat-and-whiskey part. Besides, these men brought in some blankets and bedrolls and said he could go right on sleeping on his own mattress just like always. They also brought two coal-oil lanterns, so now the light in the shack could be something better than candle shine, and they had some skillets and tin plates and forks so nobody had to eat with his fingers. They even threw together a little lean-to on the back of the shack to shelter their horses.

The bad part was that these looked like very dangerous men. They began to look that way to Nason Grube after the initial euphoria of the meat and whiskey wore off and he took more time to inspect their good horses and the many firearms they always had handy. And listened to their talk. They started telling Nason Grube that if he ever breathed a word to anybody about what he heard them saying, they would skin him alive and hang him to a tree with his own hide. They said if he did something they didn't like, they'd heat a poker in his stove and push it up his black ass.

After a few things like that, Nason Grube began to wonder if these men were really his friends. But at least the beefsteak and whiskey kept coming.

The leader among them was the smallest. The other two called him Yancy. With his long nose and little eyes that were as bright as chips of glass, he reminded Nason Grube of a weasel. He told Nason Grube he was a sheriff, but Nason knew a real sheriff wouldn't be going around the Indian Nations stealing cows, and he knew from their talk that that was exactly what they were doing.

The other two were brothers, men who looked like bulldogs. One was named Essex and the other Becket, and Becket was a little touched, Nason Grube figured. Always giggling and sitting around with his mouth open and slobbering. About all that Essex ever said to his brother was "Shut up, dumb ox!"

Nason Grube was afraid of Becket because he figured Becket was so addled he didn't know how mean he really was, and doing something bad to another human being wouldn't mean any more to him than stepping on a cockroach and giggling when it popped.

These three were in and out of Nason Grube's shack all the time. He never knew when they'd leave or when they'd get back. From their talk, he knew they went all over the Territory north of the Canadian River. Over into Creek Nation, to Blue Bird and Nayaka and Muskogee. Into Cherokee Nation, too, to Sallisaw or Fort Gibson. Stealing cattle to sell to the railroad construction crews at Big Cabin or Vinita.

Then the one-armed man came. It scared hell out of Nason Grube because at first he thought the one-armed man was a Federal marshal. Then it scared hell out of him that he wasn't. Yancy and Nason's two other friends were somewhere around Okmulgee then, stealing cows. But Nason Grube knew from the times he went into Hawk's Hole to spend some of the money his friends had left him that the one-armed man was staying at the Hawk's Hole Recreation Hall and Hotel, and that he had a letter he was telling everybody about, a letter to these two brothers, whose name turned out to be Brown, and that he had a business proposition that would make everybody rich.

The whole thing scared hell out of Nason Grube.

When Yancy and the Browns came back from Okmulgee, bursting into the shack before dawn, and Nason Grube told them about the one-armed man, they started acting like pregnant cats, nervous and suspicious.

"You tell him we come here?" Yancy yelled.

"Naw, naw sir, I ain't ever tole nobody nuthin'."

"You better not, you nigger son of a bitch," Essex Brown said.

"How'd he know we was around here, then?" Yancy said.

Becket Brown was giggling, waving a big knife around.

"You tole, you tole," he slobbered.

"Shut up, you dumb ox," Essex said.

"I ain't tole nuthin'. He says he got this letter from you boys' daddy."

That cooled everybody down somewhat, and Nason Grube's three friends sat on the floor and whispered together. Nason Grube couldn't hear what they said.

They left again before noon, Yancy telling Nason to stay out of Hawk's Hole, and that he and Nason's other friends were just going to wait and see about this one-armed man and let him stew awhile in his own juice.

It seemed to drag on a long time—the one-armed man staying in Hawk's Hole, the three friends of Nason Grube coming in for maybe a single night of sleep and then off again, still acting like pregnant cats, skittish and shifty-eyed, their hands always close to guns.

Yancy and the Browns were gone when Poco Jimmy came. Nason Grube knew him. He was a Cherokee boy, about seventeen or so. He'd been there before, and Nason Grube had seen Yancy give him money and one time a Marlin lever-action rifle, .32 caliber, and a box of shells.

Poco Jimmy had a piece of paper that he said was a letter to Essex Brown from his daddy over in Arkansas. Nason Grube asked what it said, not being able to read it himself, and Poco Jimmy said just give it to Essex when he gets back, and then Poco Jimmy left.

It was almost a week before Nason Grube's friends came back again. He gave the piece of paper to Essex Brown, and when he and Yancy read it they went crazy. Essex started beating Nason Grube over the head with a cast-iron skillet lid.

"I don't know what it's about," Nason Grube said, the blood running down into his eyes.

"Get over there on your Gawd damned bed," Yancy said.

Nason Grube squatted on his old stained mattress and his three friends whispered together. But the longer they whispered, the louder it got, and soon Nason Grube could hear what they were saying.

"He's here for us," said Yancy.

"Yeah, and we know who sent him," Essex said.

"Yeah, yeah," Becket giggled.

"For Christ's sake, shut up," Essex said.

"We'll have to kill him," Yancy said.

In the corner, hunkered on his mattress, Nason Grube felt all his insides squirming into a hard knot.

"That's why we're over here livin' like rats with no cheese, because we killed somebody."

"You wanta go over there to Hawk's Hole and try to talk this man out of it?" Yancy asked.

"Hell, Daddy says this is a bad man."

"Yeah, yeah."

"Dammit, Becket, shut up, you big dumb ox."

"Lemme think a minute," Yancy said. The light from the two coal-oil lanterns glinted in his little eyes. Nason Grube felt all his skin tightening on him. He smelled the congealed beef grease in the skillet on the back of the stove and thought it might make him puke.

Yancy took a handful of black cigars from his pocket and passed one to each of the Browns. When they struck the sulfur matches to light the cigars, it made a small cloud of bluish smoke that evaporated as it rose to the naked rafters of the shack but left its odor behind.

"Listen," Yancy finally said, his eyes shining. "This man says he wants to see us. So why don't we just send word to Hawk's Hole that we'll see him?"

"For God's sake, Yancy," Essex said.

"Listen, listen, listen," Yancy said urgently. "We know why he's here now. He doesn't know we know."

Nason Grube moaned, and Yancy turned and stabbed a finger like a pointed gun.

"Nigger, hush your mouth or I'll take a pair of wire pliers to your tongue."

"Yeah," said Becket.

"Shut up."

"Listen, listen. We'll let this big stud from Kansas know we'll talk about his proposition. Hell, he ain't made no secret about that. And we'll talk to him right here. Dead of night."

"You're crazy," Essex Brown said. "He walks in here, he ain't gonna start talkin' no proposition. He comes in here smokin'."

"Listen, listen, listen," Yancy said. Nason Grube thought Yancy's long nose was quivering. Like a ferret near the chicken coop. "We ain't gonna be here. We're gonna be outside, with shotguns. You and me."

"Outside?"

"Listen, listen. Outside. We get him here. He don't know we know, see?"

"All right, then how the hell we get him here?"

Yancy grinned, his glassy little eyes squinting, and he looked at Becket.

"Oh, for God's sake," Essex said, "we can't send this dumb ox over there to Hawk's Hole and tell this man we want to see him."

"Listen. Who better? Best thing in the world. We send good ole Becket and he just goes into Hawk's Hole and tells this jake leg we're ready."

"Send this dumb ox?"

"Listen. He's so plain and simple. You or me go, or this nigger, the man might see right through it. But good ole Becket? Hell, Essex, never nothin' shows on that sweet face."

Essex looked at his brother's face. Becket was grinning, nodding. A dribble of saliva ran from one corner of his mouth.

"Oh God," Essex said.

"Yeah," said Becket.

"Listen, listen, it'll work good."

"Yeah," said Becket. "I'll get that peckerwood."

It occurred to Nason Grube that maybe Yancy was not only sending Becket Brown to reel in the fish, but also as a bait in other ways. If that one-armed man flashed in a hurry, it was better to offer dumb-ox Becket as a sacrifice than get all three of them killed. Nason Grube's insides contracted into an even tighter knot as he finally, fully began to comprehend the kind of friends he'd collected here.

During the next hour, Nason Grube sat on his mattress in the corner of his shack and prayed to all the gods he'd ever heard of to send seventeen deputy United States marshals from Judge Parker's court. Because what was happening scared him worse than anything else he'd ever known or imagined.

Becket Brown went off into the night, grinning. The other two began loading shotguns and told Nason Grube that if he moved from his corner or so much as made a quiver, he would be castrated, impaled, and what was left of him rendered down into soap in his own Dutch oven. And then, each carrying two shotguns, Yancy and Essex went out into the night beyond the light of the open door.

Nason Grube sat, wondering what *impaled* meant, and heard a collecting thunderstorm developing from the west. They'd left the door open, both coal-oil lamps lit inside, and within a few moments there were all kinds of flying varmints attracted to the light, fluttering and buzzing about the shack. He began to hear thunder, far off at first, then stepping closer. He could smell rain, that clear, clean odor. The door after a while was outlined more and more frequently with blue-white lightning. He sat transfixed on his stained mattress, looking at the door, because he knew that just outside were two of his friends with shotguns.

Becket Brown had gone to Hawk's Hole on foot. But when he returned, he was driving a small wagon, a single horse in the stays, and he was yelling and screaming and laughing.

"I done it," Becket Brown shouted. "I done it my ownself."

"Oh my God," Essex said.

Nason Grube was terrified. Becket had pulled the wagon to a halt just in front of the open door, and now, out of the lightning-illuminated night, Yancy and Essex appeared, holding their shotguns.

"Hey, nigger, bring a light."

Becket was holding the reins, jumping up and down on the wagon seat, and in the bed of the wagon was a small, bloody form.

"I just done it my ownself," Becket was shouting. "He rented this here wagon and horse and he never knowed what was happening."

"Shut up, Becket," Essex bellowed.

Nason Grube was holding the lantern above the wagon bed.

"Look at them pistols," Essex said.

"No, no, no," Yancy said. "You want somebody to know we done this because we got them pistols? Leave 'em, leave 'em."

His hands were going through the one-armed man's clothes, hands soon bloody.

"God, look," Yancy said, holding up a roll of greenbacks.

"I just done it my ownself," Becket was shouting. "He was drivin' this rig down here and I just done it."

"I want them pistols," Essex said.

"You leave the Goddamned pistols be," Yancy said. "You, Becket, off your ass and get the horses ready to travel."

"I done it," Becket yelled, leaping down from the wagon seat. He ran around the shack to the lean-to. They could hear him shouting there, and the thunder and lightening growing. It began to rain.

"We'll dump him in the river," Yancy said. "Run this rig and horse off down the way and leave it. Light out of here for a while."

Becket was back, leading the horses, saddled, ready.

"Yeah, yeah," he shouted, laughing.

"You big dumb ox," Essex yelled. "You wasn't supposed to do that."

"It's all right," Yancy said, climbing down out of the wagon bed. "Hell, it's good. It's good."

Yancy grabbed Essex by the coat lapel.

"Listen, listen, this is good. By tomorrow morning he won't even remember that he done it. Now come on."

Nason Grube, holding the lantern in one hand, stood for a moment after they'd disappeared into the flashing night, toward the Verdigris. The rain was beginning to come hard, slanting down across the light of the lantern. The water ran into his eyes. He felt it stinging the cuts on his head where the iron skillet cover had opened his scalp.

Nason Grube had never been a very smart man, could not read and write and figure out why everybody he knew exploited him. But the one thing he could do was run. And that night, he ran.

He dropped the lantern and started after his three friends, not even knowing why—Yancy driving that wagon with the little bleeding corpse, and Essex and Becket on horses beside and leading another horse, going toward the Verdigris. Nason Grube was silently close behind them when they pulled the little wagon along the river's muddy banks. Yancy moved back into the bed and pulled the limp form out and dumped it into the shallows, and then he got back into the seat and whipped the horse away, Becket Brown shouting, "I done it, I done it my ownself!"

Nason Grube splashed into the water, the lightning coming so fast by now that it was almost like day. He felt the wet form, so slight, and pulled it up onto the muddy bank. His hands could not help but feel for the wound, and even Nason Grube, who was no expert on gunshot wounds, knew the heavy slug fired by Becket Brown had cut through the edge of the rib cage of this one-armed man and passed on.

Yet even as Nason Grube felt the wound, in the flashes of white fire from the skies, he could see the glassy eyes of this frail man, eyes open, eyes of a dead man, and thought he had indeed pulled a corpse from the water. But as he bent down, there was a harsh sound, like brass cartridge cases rattling together.

"Thank you," the one-armed man said.

16

When Roman Hasford first saw Diana Chesney, he was stunned by her beauty. Not only by the flowing golden hair and the gray eyes framed in coal-black lashes, but by her very presence, her dignity, her quiet confidence. He had no way of knowing then that Diana Chesney came by such things through generations of hardship and ambition beginning when old James I of England had begun to encourage establishment of a Protestant enclave in Catholic Ireland.

They became known as Scots-Irish, these people who settled Ulster, but they were not Irish, and the new home was no better than the old, and in some ways worse, so a lot of these people began to ship out to the New World. People named Reed and Maddox and Fulton and Lockhart and Buchanan. And Chesney. Most of them were hard and tough and perfectly suited to provide the cutting edge for an expanding frontier.

The Chesney clan had arrived in mid-continent of the Americas well before the Civil War. They saw one of their number, a certain Campbell Chesney, go off to Texas with another Ulster Scot, the former congressman Davy Crockett. This was in 1836. A year later, another Chesney, Hiram by name, was arrested somewhere along the Ohio River and tried for river piracy and hanged.

Yet another, cousin to these two, was James, who had begun his own journey toward Texas when the coming Civil War made such travel uncertain, and then was further thwarted in his design by the call of profiteering in leather tanning. Which was followed by his obtaining a wife, at considerable expense, through one of the many love merchants operating along the big Northern rivers.

This particular wife was Molina Vasilakis, a Greek, who had the most beautiful eyes James Chesney had ever seen and who made him forget, at least occasionally, his bitterness over a clubfoot that kept him out of the fighting.

James could not speak the language of his wife, nor could she speak his, but apparently nothing was required of language for their productivity. By the time James had come into Missouri, toward the end of the war, there was a daughter, whom they named Diana, and sometime later came two sons, Campbell and Hiram, named in honor of the family heroes who had died, respectively, at San Antonio de Bexar, in the Alamo, and on a Louisville gallows.

So James and his brood arrived in Gourdville to homestead a rocky cluster of acres on Oak Creek, just south of the Hasford property at Catrina Hills Farm, having run out their welcome in Missouri insofar as James could see it. Besides, the clubfoot had developed an irresistible itch for moving on, which was typical of Chesney feet, clubbed or otherwise.

James Chesney was as dour and taciturn as any Ulster Scot could be, and he made few friends. He attended the local Presbyterian church but had no truck with the social life of the congregation. His wife, everyone assumed, practiced her own religion with veils and icons and candles, and perhaps she wondered how many trackless miles it might be to the nearest Greek Orthodox priest. Although by this time she and her husband had learned to converse with each other, at least in a rudimentary way, religion and its requirements were never a subject between them.

People in the county knew none of this family well, and some of them not at all.

But in any case, Diana was as beautiful as her mother. She had begun to take on the storied attributes of that stunning woman in the epic poem who made the Greeks go a little crazy and sail over to Turkey and kill all the Trojans they could find. At least that's what Homer said.

From the fair-haired Chesney line, and maybe from some hidden Vasilakis gene that went back to Greek nobility when a lot of them were blonds, the young Diana developed a long, flowing mane of golden hair that was more like that of a Teutonic princess than a Greek. But that illusion vanished once a person saw her thick, coal-black brows and long lashes and gray eyes, just like her mother's.

There was something mysteriously Mediterranean about her.

Some depth nobody could plumb. As though she could see, with those startling eyes, places the county folk couldn't even imagine. As though she could conjure up white marble statues on rocky hills, or smell the olives being crushed to make oil, or hear the emerald waters of the Aegean kissing the island of Skyros or some such place. All these things. And the child had never been east of the Mississippi River.

Hell, the people in the county said, she's downright spooky, that Chesney kid.

When Roman Hasford saw her, he did not think she was spooky at all. He thought maybe she was heaven-sent, just to brighten his day. Most of what had happened to him that year and the year before was certainly not heaven-sent.

It hadn't been a good time for James Chesney either. The club-foot hurt all the time. And when he'd gone into the Farmer's and Merchant's Bank for a loan, he'd had to put up with a lot of fool questions from that prissy little Gallatin Delmonico. But James got the loan, primarily on the strength of the tie yard he was planning alongside the Frisco right-of-way.

That was the day Roman had seen her for the first time. What he saw was no child, but a young woman ready to burst into full bloom. She'd been sitting in her father's wagon in front of the bank, holding the reins, although the old horse in the traces didn't act as if he would go anyplace without violent urging.

Behind her in the wagon bed were her two younger brothers, Hiram and Campbell, as different as two brothers could be. Hiram was tall and fair, like his daddy; Campbell was short and dark, like his mother. But they both had those startling gray eyes, just like their sister.

Roman had been struck by the long, flowing hair as he walked along the sidewalk in front of his bank. And then she was looking straight at him, bold and unafraid, and without a second thought Roman tipped his hat to her, even though it was not his custom to tip his hat to girls who were sixteen years old.

It was over a year before he saw her again. But he did not lose the vision of her, sitting in that old wagon, her eyes seeming to measure him as he strode past. The afternoon sun had woven astonishing lights into her golden hair. He always remembered it as one of those pleasant little moments, somehow surprising. Like finding a lovely purple jack-in-the-pulpit blooming early in late-winter snow. The circumstances leading up to his seeing her again were not so lovely.

It was late summer. Roman had stayed at the bank until midafternoon, arguing with Gallatin Delmonico about investments. When he arrived at Catrina Hills Farm, Orville Tucker met him on the porch, his bloodshot eyes rolling, making gestures toward the living room, and there was a saddle horse tied to one of the hitch rails, from all of which Roman deduced that he had a visitor.

It was a Pinkerton detective, just passing through, he said, on his way to Fort Smith, but doing a personal favor for a friend in Kansas. Then, having convinced himself that this man was indeed Roman Hasford, the detective handed Roman an envelope and departed.

Inside was a strange letter. But Roman understood it. There was no salutation or signature, in fact no proper name written anywhere on the single sheet of high-quality bond paper. There was a letterhead at the top: Kansas Pacific Railroad. And Roman understood why it had been hand-carried and not consigned to the mail, where many eyes would note it in its passage.

Roman Hasford had never seen anything written by Jared Dane, and the sweeping, flowing strokes of the pen amused and surprised him.

They knew. Somebody told them. There are various possibilities. Discreet inquiries will be made. As soon as most recent wound heals. Not serious but painful. If they knew about me, they likely are aware of your part in all this. Be watchful. Go armed at all times.

They believe my body has long since rotted in a muddy river. Efforts have been made not to disabuse them of this. Benefactor and I came here, by night always. A long and painful trip. It was necessary to steal two horses. Once recompensed, benefactor disappeared. A frightened man with little intelligence, but we can be thankful for his compassion.

They will be very hard to find now, at least for a while. They were extremely cautious and will be more so, knowing there is an interest in bringing them to justice. But before putting me in that muddy river, they did not finish their work. It was a mistake. Someday they will make another.

A little chill passed up Roman Hasford's spine. A few things leaped out at him as he reread the words. The justice Jared Dane mentioned had nothing to do with bringing anybody into a court of law. And Roman thought also of how tenuous life would be for a man whose next mistake might produce a visit by Jared Dane.

Maybe I ought to call this thing off, Roman Hasford thought that night, as he lay in bed. But, hell, Jared Dane's got a personal interest now, beyond doing anything for me. Those ignorant bastards gave him that. Jared Dane is not the kind of man who takes injury from somebody and then forgets it.

And in that moment, perhaps without even being aware of it, Roman Hasford shifted responsibility for anything else that might happen away from himself and onto Jared Dane.

I'd sure like to talk to somebody about this, he thought. Maybe I ought to tell Sheriff Bidd.

Then quickly dismissed such an idea. Clearly, somebody already knew Roman's connection with this business. No need, he reckoned, to spread it around any more.

But it was satisfying to find that he'd been right about the Browns and Yancy Crane killing Elmer Scaggs. He knew that Jared Dane had convinced himself of it, else he would never have gone into the Nations looking for them. And of course Courtland Brown and probably Sarah as well were involved, if only through their knowledge of the killing. He wondered if Corliss Buckmaten was involved as well, then decided that although he despised Buckmaten, he didn't figure the little ex-Confederate officer would ever stoop to such violence, however he might encourage it by his fiery words in the *Advertiser*.

Another thing, he thought. I know why Matie Luten left this county. Sure as hell, Jared Dane paid her that visit I suggested when I went to Topeka.

From his years in Kansas, Roman Hasford had come to know how Jared Dane operated. And one way or another, Roman was sure that Dane had squeezed more information out of the woman than Hamlin Bidd could have, because Hamlin Bidd was just a good, solid peace officer, where Jared Dane was a wolf who could scare the hell out of anybody.

And I'm the one who let the wolf loose, Roman thought. It made him uncomfortable. He wrote no more letters in care of the Kansas

Pacific Railroad in Topeka, and he tried to believe that those three men in the Territory would now be frightened enough to move off someplace far away, and that everybody would then be done with the whole thing, because without those three, Courtland Brown wasn't capable of kicking up much fuss.

And Corliss Buckmaten?

Why, hell, Roman thought, the little bastard will just keep right on being a nuisance.

Then he tried to sleep, but it didn't come easily.

After carrying the Jared Dane letter around for three days, re-reading it a number of times, Roman Hasford burned it in his parlor fireplace. Watching it burn, Roman asked the same question he'd asked from the first reading of that letter: How did they know Jared Dane was coming? Who had known? Who had warned them?

The last light was going out of the west-facing windows when Martin Hasford came in, wandering aimlessly, his great farmer's fingers touching all the furniture.

"Sit down, Papa," Roman said. "I'll pour us some brandy."

Martin sat in his favorite chair, the one at the east window. Roman watched his father staring out into the gathering darkness, toward the woodline, toward Wire Road, and he wondered if Martin in his strange mind could visualize the old Hasford farm that lay in that direction, the house on the rise of ground covered with black locust trees, trees growing old now, with rough bark that flaked off when high winds caused the trunks to bend.

"It's good whiskey, Doctor," Martin said.

The next morning, Roman rode into town early and went directly to Caulder's Mercantile Store and bought a shoulder holster for the short-barreled Colt. And three boxes of .45-caliber ammunition. He planned to do a little target shooting, he told Jefferson Caulder.

"At anybody I know?"

"Bottles and cans," said Roman. "It's been a long time since I've done any pistol shooting. Don't want to lose my eye. I won a turkey once, shooting a pistol."

"I know the story," old Jeff said. "I've heard you tell it a dozen times."

Roman adjusted the shoulder holster under his left arm and,

once satisfied, took the pistol from his hip pocket and positioned it.

"If you wax that leather, the pistol will come more readily to hand," Jefferson Caulder said.

"I know."

"In case you run across a bottle or can that tries to get away."

"Yes."

They walked to the front of the store together and paused there. Jefferson Caulder offered a cigar, and they smoked for a short while, silently.

"Is this a great secret?" Jefferson finally asked. "Should I have a bout of forgetfulness on selling you that thing?"

"No," said Roman. "The more people who know about it, the better."

"All right. But you should tell the sheriff, just as a matter of form, if you're going to make a habit of carrying a cannon around. This isn't Deadwood, Dakota Territory, you know."

"I'm going to the courthouse now," said Roman, moving his shoulders, trying to become accustomed to the deadly weight under his left arm. "I expect to have a long conversation with Sheriff Bidd."

"Well, if it's going to be a long conversation with Bidd, I expect that you'll be doing most of the talking."

"Yes."

Roman found a nice little bend in Oak Creek where the bank was thick with sycamores and willows and where he could set up a few cans and bottles against a clay bank cut by the stream during spring high-water time. Each afternoon, Orvile Tucker handed him a burlap bag filled with cans and bottles, and Roman walked to Oak Creek, it being less than a quarter mile from the Big House.

He was happy to see that his eye was still intact. But having established that, he continued to go to Oak Creek almost every afternoon to shoot, because there was some kind of release in this, some kind of satisfaction. Maybe it was just being alone, there beside this free-flowing little stream of clear water. A reassurance of more than his shooting eye. Maybe a resurrection of his boyhood. There alone, among the trees, remembering when he had been in this same country before the war, his mother alive, his father normal and teaching him woodland lore. Before he had ever heard of

Catrina Peel, before he had ever gone to Kansas. Alone, without even a horse standing by. Alone with the trees and the water and the land and the silence emphasized by the whisper of water moving and the call of jays and the rustle of wind in the great flat leaves of the sycamores.

But the day came when he was no longer alone on Oak Creek.

It was April. He had come to Oak Creek right through the winter months, bundled up and blowing clouds of vapor. But now it was mild and smelling of spring, and there were green buds popping along the branches of all the trees.

Roman had just fired six shots and was hulling out the empty cartridge cases from the Colt when she called to him, startling him, making him jump.

She was on the far side of the stream, on the Chesney side, looking at him as boldly as she had that day in front of the bank. Even in his memory, her hair had not been this long and golden.

"It sure makes a lot of racket," she said, and she was smiling. "I wondered who was making all that racket down here."

"I was just practicing," Roman said, almost stammering, feeling as though he had been caught naked or some such thing. The pistol in his hand was still smoking, and it suddenly became very embarrassing to have it there, so he thrust it into the shoulder holster, smoke and all.

"You must do it a lot," she said. "I hear it all the time. I come down in the morning to see the fish."

"The fish?" Roman's boots seemed rooted. Only his body had twisted at her first call. Now, awkwardly, he turned to face her squarely. She was still smiling, as though she understood his embarrassment.

"Yes, the little fish."

"They're just minnows," he said.

"I like them," she said, slipping out of her moccasin-type shoes. "I wade in the water and they swim right around my feet and tickle me."

She laughed then and held up her gingham dress and walked down into the stream. Roman Hasford was terrified.

"That water's still pretty cold," he said.

"I like it. I wade all the time."

Her feet aren't near big enough to hold anybody up, Roman Hasford thought.

She was across Oak Creek quickly, coming directly to him, stepping surely on the rounded gravel of the streambed. Then she was before him, close enough for him to smell her. She looked up at him and smiled again, and in her eyes were lights Roman thought he had never seen before. The top of her golden head came only to Roman's chest.

"You're Mr. Hasford, aren't you?"

"Yes."

"I'm Diana Chesney. My daddy's building a slaughterhouse. And he's got the tie yard. You gave him the money to do it, didn't you?"

"Well, loaned it anyway."

"The boys are helping, and when they hit their fingers with a hammer there's an awful fuss." She laughed, and Roman could see her pink tongue. It was devastating.

Afterward, he wasn't sure he could reconstruct anything that had been said. But it all seemed so damned important, to have some deep significance. When she waded back across Oak Creek and up the timber-covered slope of the Chesney side, Roman breathed a sigh of relief, yet one of disappointment as well. Then he walked back to Catrina Hills Farm, his boots seeming to bounce along the ground.

Why, hell, he thought. And could think no other thing beyond that. Why, hell!

"You want any supper?" Orvile Tucker asked.

"Yes. A big one. I'm starving."

"Well, they's some mail."

One of the horse-tending hired hands always went in and brought the mail out, then left it on the small table beside Roman's chair, in front of his bookshelves. It was the usual thing, feelers from Missouri horse buyers about the breeding season, and notes from other bankers. But on this day came another letter, a letter from St. Scholastica in Jefferson City. From the Mother Superior, or whoever she was, saying that Catrina Peel Hasford was becoming one of the best young lady students in needlepoint and had taken particularly well to the forms of both Latin and English and would soon be writing her own account of things.

The last paragraph reminded Roman that it was time to pay the next season's tuition, and that any additional contribution would be appreciated. And below the sister's signature, in a cramped, tiny scrawl, barely legible, were these words:

"It is good here. Thank you. Your wife, Catrina Peel Hasford."

It was almost full dark when Orvile Tucker came into the large room where Roman Hasford sat before his books.

"Supper ready, Mr. Roman."

"I don't want anything."

"You told me you wanted a big supper. I got it."

"I don't want anything."

"Mr. Roman, you need somethin' in you belly beside that tiger sweat you drinkin'."

"No."

"Well, lemme light a lamp in here. You can't read none in the dark like this."

"No."

Orvile Tucker started to say something else, then turned and went out to the brightly lighted kitchen, muttering. Then talking aloud, "I'm goin' outta here."

Martin Hasford was sitting at the kitchen table, when Orvile entered. His hands lay on the oak surface, fingers working like grub worms, a faded glaze in his eyes.

"I tell you, Mr. Martin, I gonna go outta here. Over to Wolf Cove, live with old Lark and Renée and that little boy. I ain't no cook anyway, an' I ain't gonna put up with all this white man shit misery."

Orvile put a plate of beefsteak smothered in onions on the table before Martin Hasford. Also boiled potatoes and a heap of scalded sauerkraut, the last of what Ora Hasford had sent before she died.

"Thank you, Mr. Tug," Martin Hasford said.

"Mr. Martin, I ain't nobody named Tug," Orvile said. "I ain't ever been that, and you always callin' me Tug. I ain't that."

Martin Hasford looked at him then, his eyes clear, and he nodded.

"Yes. I'm sorry," he said. "Tug was a colored man, like you."

"Well, all right, Mr. Martin. Eat your grub."

"He was killed at Gettysburg," Martin Hasford said.

Then Martin Hasford bent to his plate and began to eat, and Orvile Tucker watched him for a moment, then filled his own plate and slammed it on the table and sat down and took a great mouthful of sauerkraut and talked around it.

"You an' me, eaten' by ourself. He sittin' in there soakin' up that whiskey. But it's all right. You eat up all that grub, Mr. Martin, you ain't been eatin' too good last few days. You eat up. You like that kraut. But I tell you, Mr. Martin, I gonna go live with somebody else."

Martin Hasford paused, looking up at Orvile for a long time before he spoke softly.

"You can't leave my boy here alone."

Orvile stuffed more kraut into his mouth.

"I know it," he said. "Eat your grub."

17

The afternoons on Oak Creek during the summer when Diana Chesney came to him were, to Roman Hasford, chapters in a book he had never read. He had supposed himself in love on at least two previous occasions, both of which in the event were near disasters, and in neither one had he seen anything like Diana's innocent aggressiveness for his favor. Well past thirty now, he had considered himself beyond lightheadedness and giddy dreams, but he realized that he'd been seriously mistaken, perhaps coming to understand that the onset of romantic attachments became more fierce and unrelenting with the passage of years.

He began rising early, having a hearty breakfast, saddling Junior himself, and riding into town for some banking business. But by noon he was back at Catrina Hills Farm, and ate what Orvile Tucker called dinner with a ravenous appetite. Then, with the bag of cans and bottles, he set off for the bend in the creekbed where he expected her to be. And she was always there.

Once, on his return, Orvile Tucker said, "Mr. Roman, I dint hear no shootin' down on the creek today. Is your gun broke?"

"No," said Roman, in good humor. "I was just looking at the fish today."

"Fish? They ain't no fish in that creek," Orvile Tucker said.

"There are fish there as big as Jonah's fish," said Roman, laughing, and Orvile Tucker laughed too, because although he had no idea what Roman meant, he knew at least that Roman was not drunk, and in fact in recent weeks had consumed very little of his bourbon specially ordered from Frankfort, Kentucky. Wherever that was.

There was never any shooting now on Oak Creek. Roman and Orvile maintained the pretense with the burlap bags of cans and bottles every day, but there was no shooting. Orvile Tucker asked no questions, and Roman volunteered no answers.

In place of the target practice, he sat under the willows with her, being drawn out by her straightforward and honest acceptance of him. He talked more than he had in years, telling about times he had never mentioned to anyone, about this valley before the war, about the partisans who had come after the Battle of Pea Ridge, about the things he had seen in Kansas. Diana was especially fascinated with his descriptions of the buffalo.

There was such dramatic change in him that Orvile Tucker began to worry more about him than he had when Roman sat in the dark in his living room, drinking whiskey. Now the master of Catrina Hills Farm seemed to find joy in things never before thought of, like the time he called Orvile to come watch with him as a pair of house wrens built a nest in the eaves of the west porch. Now, each night, Roman was at the big table in the kitchen with Martin to eat his supper, making conversation, sitting afterward as Orvile cleaned the stove, he and his father smoking cigars and sipping brandy.

On days when it rained, Roman was impatient with the weather, but he made light of it. On weekends he was content to sit and read, or to go down to the stables and help groom the year's new crop of horses. Once he even suggested to his father that they go into Gourdville to church, but when Martin showed little interest, that project was forgotten, though cheerfully.

Cheerful was not the word to describe the days when a letter came from Jefferson City. Most especially when one came addressed in that tight little penmanship that Orvile Tucker had come to recognize as Catrina's hand.

My Dear Husband:

We are planting apple trees now. I have learned to read from the Big Bible and Sister Marie helps me. She helps me write this letter. It is very happy here. We can look out our windows and see the river.

Your wife, Catrina Peel Hasford

On those days, and perhaps for a day afterward, Roman would stay upstairs in his room, where Orvile Tucker could hear him pacing back and forth. He didn't come down to eat. And on one of those nights, at the kitchen table, Martin asked, "Where's the Doctor?" And another time asked, "Where's my son?"

Then, after the kitchen was cleared away and Martin was in his own room, on those days after a letter had come, Roman would come down in the dark and sit in the living room before his silent books and drink directly from one of the bottles that came from Frankfort, Kentucky. And Orvile Tucker, behind the kitchen, lay in the dark and said aloud, "Damn letters and writin', like the white man always doin'!"

But it was soon over, each time, and then Roman would be off again to Oak Creek. It was the happiest time of Roman Hasford's life. The letters from Jefferson City always threw him into a deep depression, but they arrived infrequently. Roman would almost have his mind made up to see Judge Jacob Rich about a divorce or an annulment, and then one of those single pages of carefully, almost painfully formed words would arrive, and any thought of breaking the contract would vanish in a bitter haze of Kentucky bourbon whiskey.

It was simply a reluctant concession to old, never-clearly articulated values buried in his soul. Man and woman married, man and woman stayed that way through fire and famine, love and hate, the covenant never broken to the bitter end, to the grave. His mother, once suggesting divorce, had thereby showed that, although coming from an even older school, she had progressed into modern times more than he.

There was no question but that he could support Catrina in anything she wanted, whether he was married to her or not. But once married, it was done. Vow taken, vow kept.

God, he hated it. Yet there remained something in him that prevented him from changing it. Nor was he alone with such thinking in that time and place. Other citizens of the county who were in other ways not willing to concede him anything developed a reluctant admiration for Roman Hasford's willingness to remain husband from afar to "the crazy little woman of Catrina Hills."

Roman seldom thought of Jared Dane that summer. Hearing nothing from the one-armed man—not that he expected to—Roman had no idea where Dane might be, or whether his wound was healed as yet, or if he might be back in the Nations, hunting.

Those three men in the Nations, or wherever they might be, didn't worry him much. Indeed, he had begun to convince himself they were no longer close by but had gone off to Texas as so many people did. So life could go on, with Corliss Buckmaten's vitriolic words in the *Democrat Advertiser* only an irritation like the bite of a horsefly before rain, and the remaining Browns staying close to their tavern where they belonged.

He still carried the revolver, sometimes even in the house, because he knew that whoever had betrayed Jared Dane might still be close, and he remembered Dane's letter warning him to protect himself. But that didn't worry him much, either. Too many good things were happening.

It was one of those warm days of Indian summer. The foliage was still green except for the red gum, its leaves already dark crimson like Comanche spear points colored with the blood of buffalo. There was a constant gentle breeze from the west that brought faint odors of approaching autumn, a kind of sharp, pungent smell of persimmons ripening and fox grapes going black on the vine.

Isaac Maddox drew up his wagon before the Big House about sunset, when Roman and his father and Orvile Tucker were just finishing their supper.

"Hello the house," Isaac called.

Roman came onto the porch, wiping crumbs of Orvile Tucker's first cinnamon apple cobbler of the fall from his lips with a white napkin. Below, in the road at his gate, was not only Isaac Maddox but also beside him on the wagon seat Dr. Hazlet Cronin, and beside the wagon Anson Greedy, the barber, on a saddle horse. In the bed of the wagon was a brown, red, cream, and black mangle of hounds, tails up like buggy whips and all eyes turned toward Roman standing on his porch.

"Howdy, Roman," Isaac called. "Goin' over behind your old farm, let the dogs loose. Ought to be some frisky grays along White River now. Come along?"

"Why, hell, I haven't heard a good fox race for years."

"Doc's brought some cheese. I got a jug of lightnin'. Good night for it."

Just behind Roman, standing in the door, Orvile Tucker said, "I'll get some horses saddled."

"Bring your papa along," Isaac yelled. "He might like to hear the music again."

That was the beginning of the Northwest Arkansas Fox Racing Association.

During its early weeks, Roman paused often on his way to what they called the Deep Woods, east of the old Hasford place, and stood beside his mother's grave. And spoke aloud and unashamed, even though Orvile Tucker was right behind him and could hear.

"Mama, there's light in his eyes again."

The light of which he spoke was that in Martin Hasford's eyes. It astonished Roman and delighted Orvile Tucker, who attended every fox hunt that Roman did, from the very first.

The Association, with Isaac Maddox at its center, grew with each outing until by late November a dozen men would attend each race, sometimes more. Even Lark Crozier, who always brought little Hasford, carrying the child on his hip and grinning as the night went down and the boy's great black eyes stayed wide open, alert to the last moment.

"He don't take to no sleep till the big folks do," Lark said proudly.

About once each week they would go to some high-ridge abandoned field where only scrub sassafras grew, build a fire, and sit and talk until the hounds off in the timber raised a fox and started the run. Then they'd argue about which dog was leading the pack. Warming their butts at the fire, chewing on the rubbery yellow cheese, sipping from the fruit jars of white whiskey. And listening to the sound of the dogs, far off sometimes and faint, close by sometimes and roaring thunder, a music they all understood but could never explain—a chilling, primeval sound that, of all the things they knew, described the beauty of hunter and hunted, these men who knew both sides of that, and about the struggle for survival. And often, though they were reluctant to admit it, they admired the fox even more than they admired the most loved foxhound.

Martin Hasford came alive around those fires. He ate the yellow cheese, he sipped the white whiskey, and he talked. Not about vague battlefields and distant comradeship, but about the dogs, and about which ridge they were coming over in the night, and about the next stream they would be leaping through, and about the pattern of the run the fox was making. Say, a great oval-shaped race from Brewster's old, burned-out farm down Iddy Creek and up across McLain Ridge and the oak flats where Jim Sharnson lived before the war, and into the hollow of Pecan Branch and back across the cedar-covered hogback above Pendleton's deserted mill, and thence right back to Brewster's burned-out farm.

"By God, Roman," Isaac Maddox said one night, "your papa's the best fox-racing man I ever knowed."

Roman knew the dogs were saying a lot more to his father than they were to him. Even so, on those nights around the fire, listening, he felt more chills up his back than Gallatin Delmonico had mortgages in the bank safe.

Once they were back in the Big House, Martin reverted to monosyllables and glassy-eyed stares and vacant comments about John Bell Hood. And always called his son Doctor, which he never did when they were in the woods.

Sometimes, after they came in from listening to the dogs, three o'clock in the morning and Martin safely in his bed upstairs, Roman could hardly contain his excitement. At those times he would call Orvile Tucker into the living room and they would stand before his books and together have a sip of brandy from stemmed glasses, Roman not knowing whether to laugh or cry and perhaps doing a little of both, because he had done both with this powerful black man down through the years and felt no shame about it.

Orvile Tucker would chuckle in his deep chest and his bloodshot eyes would roll, his teeth would gleam, whether Roman laughed or cried or both, and he would say, "It's good. That Mr. Martin, he like to listen to them dogs."

Others did, too. Omer Sample of the vinegar works started coming. He had two dogs of his own. And Criten Lapp, the coroner, who had three hounds. And finally, James Chesney, he being a member of Isaac Maddox's Presbyterian church. Maybe it was because he could hold his head up now that he was making a little money from his slaughterhouse and even more from the tie yard. So he and his boys came, Hiram and Campbell, named for those heroes, nice boys in their early teens and well behaved and never taking a drink of the white lightning. At least not when their father was looking.

It was a strange relationship that developed between Roman

Hasford and James Chesney around these fox-hunting fires. Roman was very tentative, what with seeing this man's young daughter almost every day at Oak Creek, and the crippled James Chesney was tentative as well, though of course he didn't know about Oak Creek at all.

Maybe Martin Hasford brought it all about; he and Chesney hit it off famously from the first. James Chesney, coming from the hills of eastern Tennessee, knew a great deal about fox dogs, and he and Roman's father would put themselves aside, standing just barely in the glow of the fire, and talk about wonderful dogs they had known. And wonderful foxes.

Once, as a hunt was breaking up and Isaac Maddox had blown his cow-horn bugle to call in his dogs, which they would of course ignore, James Chesney said to Roman, "Your papa and me, we think the same in many ways." And Roman knew they had talked of things other than hounds, though he had no notion what.

And so around those fires—Martin Hasford in this way between them—Roman and James Chesney came together, not as banker and mortgagee, but as men who shared the sounds of a fox race.

And it always gave Roman particular satisfaction when, after James Chesney mounted his old wagon and called for his boys, both of them, Hiram and Campbell, before they went to their father, would turn to Roman Hasford and say, "Good night, Mr. Hasford. It's been a good race."

As if, Roman thought, I had anything to do with it. Why, hell, they're not even my dogs.

One time, Roman made the comment to Isaac Maddox, "Papa hasn't talked like that to anybody since Elmer Scaggs died."

"Well now," Isaac said, "ole James, he ain't a rounder like Elmer was, but he hits it off with some folk. Strange man. He got so he's close friends with Ephraim Tage, of all people. Always talkin' to Tage after church, and to Tage's boy, Ausbin. Strange man, ole James Chesney."

"I suppose so," Roman said, thinking of Diana.

Criten Lapp brought a new member for one of those fox races in early December. It was Owen Caulder. Roman had known Owen almost from the time of his issue. Roman's mother had been in attendance at that birthing, about twelve years previously, and Owen's mother had been the one holding Ora Hasford's hand when

Ora died. And old Jeff Caulder, the boy's father, had once said to Roman, "A Sunday-school teacher he will never be, but that Elmer Scaggs is the most faithful friend you'll ever have, Roman. Except me, of course."

So Roman Hasford had watched this boy grow. And soon he would become the nearest thing to a son Roman Hasford would ever have.

18

The genuine, old-line county folk, the ones who had been there before the Civil War, considered the Caulders newcomers. They hadn't arrived until 1869, led into the streets of Gourdville by the patriarch of the clan, old Jefferson Caulder, sixty years old and riding a young bay mule fifteen hands high and weighing more than half a ton.

That's the biggest Gawd damned mule I ever seen, everybody said.

Behind him came a Conestoga wagon pulled by six brindled oxen and driven by Jefferson Caulder's eldest child, Gwendolyn, who walked beside the wagon trailing the hem of a long calico dress in the dust and carrying a twenty-foot bullwhip in one hand and a three-foot willow switch in the other.

The wagon appeared to be bulging with kids, which was an illusion, because there were only five of them, all female, ranging in age from fifteen down to six. Plus, of course, Mother Caulder, as she came to be known, whose real name was Lizbeth, and who, as everyone soon discovered, was as tough as the bullwhip her daughter Gwen carried on that day. She had to be, if she expected to maintain any sort of Christian decorum among so many headstrong offspring.

It appeared to everyone that old Jeff and his wife had a patent on the formula for making daughters. But within a year of their coming they surprised everyone, maybe most of all themselves, by using different ingredients to bring forth a son, whom they named Owen.

These were mercantile people. And most of that stuff in the

wagon, except the girls and Mother Caulder, was buckets, bolts of cloth, ax heads, dye, lantern globes, and everything else old Jeff would need to stock his first store in Arkansas.

He already had the building. It was an empty frame structure just off the town square that had housed a brewery, and it had a second floor with plenty of room for living quarters. And there was a patch of ground in back where Mother Caulder and the girls could grow a garden every summer. Which they did, cultivating, among other things, great, shining leeks, a vegetable almost nobody in Gourdville had ever known.

Damndest big green onion you ever seen, they said.

The transaction for that building took place when the man who owned it ended up in western Pennsylvania in 1868, having wandered there after his Union Army volunteer cavalry regiment was mustered out of service in Louisville, Kentucky. Being a bachelor and still having wanderlust, but getting to the rock bottom of his money belt, he offered the old brewery to Jefferson Caulder for three hundred fifty dollars. And Jefferson Caulder bought it because the requirement to move on had been as strong in his genes as the instinct in mallard ducks to fly south before winter.

The Caulders had always seemed unable to take root for longer than a generation or two. It went all the way back to Wales, before the Hanovers were brought over from Germany to sit on the throne of England, thus avoiding another Catholic Stuart. Maybe that was what started the urge for moving on. Heaven knows, Jefferson Caulder's ancestors were anxious enough to find any excuse to leave their homeland once it had become a part of the Goddamned English-dominated Great Britain.

In that early time, they were not Caulders. They were Cadwalladers. And like the Cadwalladers of Philadelphia, they were merchants, although they were no direct kin. What with signing of bills of lading and deeds and mortgages and other instruments of property and commerce in America, it seemed sensible to have a name more comprehensible to people like wholesalers and circuit clerks. Hence, Caulder.

For whatever reason, the unrelated Philadelphia Cadwalladers never found such a change necessary.

The first real Caulder store in the New World was at Cambria County, Pennsylvania. They went there because it was obviously a Welsh community. Witness the name. They settled in a small town called Ebensburg. And there Jefferson had been born and named for the President of the United States just finishing his second term in 1809, in celebration of the fact that President Jefferson himself had a very large dose of Welsh blood in his veins.

The Caulders were very proficient storekeepers. And throughout the time from their arrival in America until their appearance in northwest Arkansas, the menfolk had managed to stay out of various wars and Indian uprisings, having the better adventure of standing behind their counters and making money.

These Caulders were hard workers, everybody in Gourdville agreed. Not just old Jeff but Mother Caulder and the girls and the growing boy Owen too. They were smart in book ways. They established a small lending library in the back of their mercantile, where a citizen could take a book home for a week if he was willing to pay a few pennies for the privilege. The library ran heavy on things like Sir Walter Scott and Shakespeare, and it was said that each member of the family had read every book on the shelves.

As they grew, usually there were at least two of the girls off in Missouri or in Fort Smith or Fayetteville attending seminaries in order to become schoolteachers. Before one of them attained the status of old maid, say at about twenty-one, she was usually off in one place or another, trying to pound a little education into resistant hill-country kids.

One stayed right in Gourdville and became the mainstay of the town's learning process, far outshining the only other member of the school's faculty, a certain Claudis Kirkendall, who wore a cork leg as badge of his service with Grant at Fort Donelson, and who was also ordained—by whom, nobody knew—to preach in the Methodist church.

The Reverend Kirkendall actually became a part of the Caulder family, in legal terms at least, by marrying old Jeff's daughter Glamorgan, the very same who was teacher in the school day-to-day beside the Reverend.

Old Jeff considered himself to be a Methodist, in a chapel sort of way. But the sight of Reverend Kirkendall's pinched face and beady little eyes upset his stomach, and often at the Sunday dinner table, when the Reverend found it appropriate to quote a line or two from Luke or James, old Jeff always cut him off with the comment that he knew the Book and needed no instruction in it, so just pass the damned sweet potatoes!

Glamorgan was the only Caulder daughter who ever married. All the others became old maids indeed. Citizens around the county said they were all so tough and headstrong that no man wanted to put up with them. Besides, to most of the county's eligible bachelors, many only marginally literate, what could be worse than committing themselves to a life of corrections of their grammar at their own damned supper table? It took a man blind with love or lust or both to take on somebody who expected a Noah Webster *Compendious Dictionary* to be a part of the household furnishings.

Jefferson Caulder died two years after Ora Hasford did, of old age, everybody said. And going as he'd lived, with his daughters all around him.

It left Owen head of the family. Only a boy, but, like all the Caulders, smart beyond his years. And besides, he had the advice and counsel and an occasional backhanded slap from a mother and so many tough sisters he didn't even like to count them.

Jefferson died that early winter when Owen started going to the fox races. When Jeff lay down his load, the old mule died too. There was no real significance in this, because certainly there had been no love between Jefferson Caulder and his mule. In fact, young Owen had learned most of the cusswords he would need for the rest of his life listening to his father addressing the mule.

But in the manner of myths being born, the people of the county told it differently. This mule, in the horse shed behind the Caulder Mercantile, had sensed what was happening in the bedroom on the second floor of the old brewery where Jefferson Caulder lay abed, surrounded by his daughters. And on the very instant that old Jeff gave up the ghost, so the story went, the big bay mule lay down in the straw of his stall and did likewise.

Jefferson Caulder had been mortgaged to the Farmer's and Merchant's Bank, since the bank was established. Not because his business was in trouble, but because he was always expanding. The very month that he died, the mortgage was paid off and Mother Caulder and Owen came in to talk money again. Gallatin Delmonico was waiting and smiling.

But he was not smiling much when Roman Hasford came to Gallatin Delmonico's desk and said, "Same loan. No interest."

There were those who said that Gallatin Delmonico appeared to be having a heart attack. Or at least a massive stroke. There was a confrontation between the desk of Gallatin Delmonico and the office of Roman Hasford.

"Mr. Hasford," Delmonico said, Judah Meyer standing behind him, nodding vigorously, "you cannot operate a bank by loaning money without interest."

"Mr. Delmonico," said Roman Hasford, "I will operate this bank any Goddamned way I please. Give Mrs. Caulder the money, whatever she wants, without interest. But with a mortgage, of course."

"Well, I should hope so!"

It was more than Roman's friendship with old Jeff. It was more than his mother's friendship with Lizbeth Caulder and the fact that Lizbeth Caulder had been at the bedside when Ora Hasford had died. Roman had come to know young Owen and admire him.

That had started some months before, in fact two years before, when Owen had come to Roman Hasford one day as Roman was rushing to the privy behind the bank.

"Mr. Hasford," Owen had said, "could I maybe come and see your library at Catrina Hills?"

"Of course, any time. But now I'm in a hurry, so excuse me."

It was the start of something. Each weekend after that hurried meeting before the bank privy, citizens of the county could observe Owen Caulder walking out the Elkhorn Tavern Road to Catrina Hills Farm and back again, carrying a double armful of books. Eventually, Owen began to take a burlap bag for carrying these books, and everybody in the county said the lad was going to put his eyes out reading all that stuff.

Winter, spring, summer, and fall, Owen Caulder left the mercantile in the efficient hands of his mother and a sister or two, plus sometimes the Reverend Kirkendall, and trekked to Roman Hasford's house. Old Jeff, still alive when this first began, said nothing. But there seemed a satisfied light in his eyes each time his only son came in with a stack of Hasford books.

The day after old Jeff's funeral, at which the Reverend Kirkendall presided in the Methodist church, and which Roman Hasford himself attended, the only time county citizens had ever seen him in a pew, Lizbeth Caulder said to her son, "It's Saturday. Go for your books."

Owen Caulder had free run of the Big House. The only restriction laid down by Orvile Tucker was that he couldn't take any books lying on one of the living room tables, because these were things Mr. Roman was reading. Otherwise, he browsed and took what he wanted, returning them the following Saturday.

Even when Roman was in the house, there wasn't much conversation between them. More and more, as he grew older, Roman was becoming taciturn. But there was a feeling between him and the boy, without words.

Sometimes Orvile Tucker took Owen down to the stables to see a new foal. But he didn't seem too interested in horses. Books were the biggest thing in his life.

Until one day Roman came in and Owen was leafing through a copy of Gibbon's *Decline and Fall.*

"I don't think I could do this one in a week, Mr. Hasford," said Owen.

"Take it for as long as you want," Roman said. "We're going out tomorrow night and let the dogs loose. Would you like to come?"

Owen Caulder at first didn't show much interest, as though he wanted to get started on Mr. Gibbon. But he came with Criten Lapp. And as soon as he heard the first voice of hounds from the Deep Woods, books were no longer first in his heart. Foxhounds were.

It stayed so all his life.

In the dead of winter, just after his father had been buried, Owen appeared one Saturday morning at Catrina Hills Farm with his bag of books. He was bundled and muffled against the cold, his nose cherry red, but nothing to hide the sparkling, blue-eyed joy in his face. Trailing behind him was a hound with splashes of black and tan and red on a coat of white. She looked to weigh about twenty-five pounds and she had a dry black nose, big brown eyes, and a pink tongue that had no end.

Roman went out on the porch to meet them, and Owen stopped, grinning. The hound stood at his heel, grinning as well, looking up at Roman Hasford, her tail whipping.

"Who's your friend?" Roman asked.

"That's Trixie," Owen said.

"Why, hell, boy, looks to me like she might know how to run a fox, you give her half a chance."

"I aim to."

"Where'd you get her?"

"Bought her. Paid two dollars for her."

"Sounds like a good buy. I can't say I recognize her. She from around here?" Roman asked.

"No sir. Cherokee Nation. I bought her from an Indian. Poco Jimmy."

Their breathing was making great clouds of vapor, and Roman shivered.

"Well, come on inside. It's cold out here."

They went into the house, and Owen Caulder began peeling off coats and scarves and gloves, still grinning. Roman stayed at the door, looking through the stained-glass window there, watching the dog inspect his yard and his crabapple trees.

"Poco Jimmy?" he said.

"Yes sir."

"Haven't seen him in a long time. He used to come out here and sell us pigeons."

"He's a good-sized Indian now," said Owen. "I guess the pigeons are mostly gone."

"I guess so."

"Poco Jimmy comes over all the time. I see him on the square. They say he's always coming over to see Courtland and Sarah Brown."

Roman's back stiffened.

"Can I look for some books now, Mr. Hasford?"

"Help yourself."

Roman's nose was almost against the window. He could feel the cold from it. The dog was still running around the yard, sniffing.

Why, hell, he thought, Poco Jimmy was my friend, I always reckoned. What's he doing, going to see the Browns all the time?

A little ripple went up his back, but he shrugged it off as winter chill and went to the kitchen for a cup of coffee.

19

It was a typical Ozark winter. There were the same kinds of storms that had glazed the landscape with ice on the opening day of the Battle of Pea Ridge, back in '62, which some of the Old Settlers recalled. As then, the ice didn't last long, but winds continued harsh, and much of January was marked by at least a little snow on north slopes in the timber.

But it wasn't a bad winter.

Orvile Tucker put out ground suet for the birds, scattering it along the west quadrant of the porch so he could watch the blue jays and red-bellied woodpeckers come to eat as he worked in the kitchen, pausing often to look through the two windows.

"Mr. Roman," Orvile said, "them woodpeckers is brave. They go right at them big jaybirds when it comes to grub."

Birds had become a fascination for Orvile Tucker. There was such a wild profusion of them here on this old northwest Arkansas plateau, even many that had not yet been classified by ornithologists. Locals gave them names anyway, mostly from appearance alone. They called the little migrating goldfinches canaries, which they definitely were not, but Orvile didn't care what they were called. He liked to watch them.

"I been puttin' out oatmeal, too," Orvile Tucker said.

"Put out whatever you want," said the master of Catrina Hills Farm. "Except my beefsteak."

It was said at the supper table, and Orvile and Roman laughed and Martin smiled as he sat chewing on his mouthful of chicken leg.

"I'd like to have some fried squirrel," Roman said. "It's been a long time since we've had that."

"Mr. Roman, I ain't got time to go out and shoot no wildlife," Orvile said.

"Well, I'll take a shotgun out here before long and get a mess of squirrel. Fried, with white gravy."

"I know how to cook 'em, Mr. Roman," Orvile said, and they both laughed again.

The meetings with Diana Chesney along Oak Creek were suspended for the duration of the frigid weather. But Roman was not impatient. It was like having to wait for one of his mother's chocolate cakes when he was a boy. Almost intolerable, but worth the agony in anticipation of the coming taste.

Well, he was impatient, to the point of riding over to the Chesney farm on three occasions during January, but each time, at the last minute he decided against it and stopped short.

Roman forced himself to avoid thinking of Catrina. His mind went only to the next meeting with Diana, and not a single moment further.

Oak Creek and other streams had borders of ice each morning, a milky film along the banks. Sometimes there was a thin layer all the way across, though never enough for kids to skate on. There were a few ponds that grew ice thick enough to hold a little weight, and there was skating there.

Of course, skates were the soles of shoes because this was not skate country. Even children of affluent citizens, like Denny Felcher from the dairy and Alvis Lapp, whose daddy was the undertaker, didn't have real skates. Or real sleds, either. Not the store-bought kind. When there was enough snow for sledding, they improvised. Plow handles for runners, and two-foot oak boards nailed across the plow-handle stems.

Sometimes during that winter there was enough snow to make snowmen in the yards of houses that were scattered now in all directions from the town square. Some of them stood in sight of Brown's Tavern in the west, others north of town in what had been cornfields a few years before. Some with picket fences. Some built with brick.

"Why, this here is gettin' to be one helluva big city," said Anson Greedy, who, like all barbers, recognized his position as town philosopher.

That winter was a terrible time for peace officers. Someone was always trying to get them out into the cold, away from their hot stoves. Not only Sheriff Hamlin Bidd but also Criten Lapp, the coroner, who in the last election had been chosen justice of the peace. It was an office that carried some connotation of policeman, even though Criten Lapp certainly never thought of carrying a gun or pinning a badge to his vest.

Citizens that winter were always harassing these two public servants with complaints about antisocial activity. It seemed to have reached epidemic proportions, especially when snow was on the ground.

Like the day Raymond Ort, who had the bakery on the square and a house on Second Street, north of the post office, came into the courthouse to interrupt Sheriff Bidd's afternoon nap, and Deputy Hamp and Deputy Bridger's reading of the latest Colonel Ingraham dime novel.

Raymond Ort claimed that on three successive days he had been ambushed on his way home at the end of the day by a group of vicious snowballers.

"Ray," said the sheriff, his feet still on his desk, "you gotta stop wearin' that old beaver high hat. First, it's out of style, and second, it makes a target no decent kid can ignore."

"I don't mind the snowballs so much," said Raymond Ort. "But the little bastards use mostly ice balls. Now, Sheriff, that can raise a welt."

"Ray," said Hamlin Bidd, "you gotta go over to Caulder's and buy one of them Russian fur hats and carry a handful of iceballs yourself so you can throw back. What's in that brown poke you got there?"

"Doughnuts."

Hamlin Bidd's boots came off the desk.

"Hell, I think Deputy Hamp's still got a pot on the stove. Why don't you just grab yourself a chair and we'll have a few of them doughnuts and some coffee while we discuss all the nine-year-old criminals we got runnin' around this town."

Or like the day Judah Meyer thought Gallatin Delmonico had gone crazy. Finally, after an hour of incoherent jabbering, Gallatin rushed from the bank and ran across the square, throwing up a plume of snow behind his churning feet. Straight to the undertaking parlor and upstairs to the offices of Coroner and Justice of the Peace Criten Lapp.

Bursting into Criten's small office, Gallatin Delmonico screamed that Cato Fulton's son Noah had to be arrested at once.

"On what charge, Gallatin?" asked Criten Lapp.

"Last night he had my daughter Lucerne skating on John Vain's pond and she fell through the ice and the little bastard ran off and left her."

"Fell through the ice? My goodness, Gallatin, your daughter's more than half growed and that pond ain't over two foot deep."

"She got out by herself. But that's beside the point! She was at the Baptist church quilting party and Cato Fulton's son took her out of there and over to John Vain's pond, and she wasn't supposed to be with him and she fell through the ice."

"I didn't know you was a Baptist, Gallatin."

"I'm not a Baptist, damnit," Gallatin screeched, by now frothing at the mouth.

"Well, did Cato's boy take her out of there at gunpoint or something like that?"

"I don't know, she won't tell me or her mother anything, she just came in at ten o'clock. *Ten o'clock!* Wet as a drowned cat, soaking wet."

"They ain't nothin' I can do, Gallatin. It's out of my jurisdiction. John Vain's pond's outside the city limits. Go see Sheriff Bidd."

"Sheriff Bidd? Sheriff Bidd?" Gallatin Delmonico shouted. "I don't like that son of a bitch and he doesn't like me. You're a peace officer. What are you going to do about this?"

Criten Lapp took off his spectacles and scratched his chin whiskers.

"Well," he said. "I guess somebody ought to go out there to John Vain's pond and post a sign that the ice is too thin for skatin'."

Roman Hasford was well tuned to these things, as he was to all that happened in the county, whether he wanted to be or not. Somebody who owed him money was always volunteering information, as though it might reduce the interest rates. Usually it irritated him. But this winter he didn't mind. For the first time he felt a kind of community spirit. On two successive Sundays he almost went to the Methodist church to hear Glamorgan Caulder's husband, the Reverend Kirkendall, preach, but changed his mind after contemplating sitting for almost two hours on a hard pew, listening to the cork-leg minister. Even though it was likely Roman's money that had bought the pew.

But he did walk one day to Glen Torten's Billiard Parlor and shot a game of Rotation with lawyer Hershel Bactrum. Roman was the only one in the place who seemed to enjoy it. Everybody else stood back against the walls, giving him the fish eye, with Hershel clearly none too happy to have been corralled into the game.

They knew this was not Roman Hasford's territory. No matter that he had come in obvious friendship, no matter that he was holding out some sort of olive branch. It was hard to forget that this place, this recreation hall, was the very spot where Roman Hasford's man Elmer Scaggs had savaged one of the Brown boys, setting off a lot of things that scared hell out of folks.

But that January, waiting for good weather and more walks to Oak Creek, Roman was full of vibrant expectations. It seemed only right to smile at people whom he knew might wish him dead. To speak on the street to Timothy Burton, the long-since-deposed prosecuting attorney. To tip his hat to Stella Matt, wife of the postmaster and close friend of Corliss Buckmaten.

Vibrant expectations or not, there were no visits to the *Democrat Advertiser*. That was one concession to civility Roman Hasford was not prepared to make. As far as Corliss Buckmaten was concerned, it was still war to the death. In each issue of his newspaper he found ways to pillory the czar of Catrina Hills Farm, concentrating on the properties the Farmer's and Merchant's Bank was acquiring.

One such property was a half-interest in the Chesney tie yard and meat-packing company, and the *Advertiser's* comments on that were galling to Roman because he wasn't too comfortable with it himself.

It came about on a terrible day. There was a wind from the north, the kind that bit right through the heaviest coat. As Roman rode Junior into town, Ephraim Tage's yard dog ran out into the road and made a lunge at the horse's hocks. Roman was ready to draw out his .45 pistol when Tage came onto the porch of his shack and called the dog back.

"Mr. Tage," Roman said, trying to hold Junior in, "if that dog ever bites one of my horses, I'll shoot him."

"You kill my dog, you'll deal with me, Hasford," Ephraim Tage yelled.

"That suits me fine," Roman said. "But you best keep the son of a bitch off the public roads."

So he arrived at the bank in a foul mood, his worst temper of the winter, to find Gallatin Delmonico waiting to say that James Chesney was there and would speak with no one but Roman.

"I put him in your office," said Gallatin.

And there was James Chesney, sitting on the edge of his chair, hat held in both hands between his knees. Roman looked at him, thinking only that this was Diana's father.

"Mr. Hasford," James Chesney said, "I can't make the payment on that tie yard mortgage. Railroad's moved off down into the mountains around Weedy Rough, and them folks down there are sellin' 'em crossties and it may be summer or later when we get back into it. Right now, I'm on hind tit."

"You won't lose it. We'll work out something," Roman said, and called in Gallatin Delmonico.

It was embarrassing as hell, listening to Delmonico work. The upshot was that the loan on the tie yard was written off as paid in full. In return, the Farmer's and Merchant's Bank would own a half-interest in the tie yard, plus a half-interest in the slaughterhouse, although there was no lien on that. James Chesney ended up delighted that he was still in business. And a partner with the most powerful man in the county.

Even worse for Roman than the transaction was what James Chesney said to him on his way out, hat still in hand.

"It's a fine thing you're doin'," he said. "Sendin' your wife off to school so she can get educated by the time she's grown enough to start havin' your children. Now, my wife, she's educated. She can talk that foreign tongue as good as you and me talk English. But it's all Greek to me, as they say."

James Chesney laughed at his little joke, or maybe he was laughing because this was perhaps the longest speech he'd ever made, or maybe he was just trying to cover his embarrassment at putting his nose into somebody else's business.

The laugh didn't concern Roman. The speech did. How could he possibly reveal himself now to this man, reveal what had been happening all summer on Oak Creek, with Chesney holding so many of those old values that Roman himself held? Like considering Roman a solidly married man.

Why, hell, Roman thought, if he knew the truth about it, he'd likely shoot me. And I wouldn't blame him!

He remembered times, when he had been a boy, that married

men had tried to take advantage of young girls, how he'd heard his mother mention their names to Martin when she thought the children were not listening. Randy old billy goats! Candidates for the tar and feathers! Or the rope!

He arrived that evening at Catrina Hills in what Orvile Tucker had begun to think of as the sour-water mood. Orvile could spot it as soon as Roman rode into sight.

"We eatin' by ourselves tonight, Mr. Martin," Orvile said.

While Orvile Tucker and Roman's father sat at the big table in the kitchen, Roman stayed in the dark parlor before his silent books, drinking the bourbon whiskey until very late, after his father had gone up to bed, after Orvile had cleaned the kitchen.

At last Orvile went into the parlor, the only light there coming from the kitchen, and touched Roman on the shoulder.

"Mr. Roman, time for bed."

"All right." But he didn't move.

"Mr. Roman, time for bed."

"All right. Help me."

Orvile Tucker lifted him with a powerful hand under one arm, then across the room and up the stairs, slowly. Halfway along, Roman stopped and asked, "Where's Papa?"

"In bed, Mr. Roman. He sleepin'."

"Sleeping?"

"That's right. Come on."

"Yes."

Orvile didn't make a light in Roman's room. He put Roman on the bed, pulled off his boots, and covered him with a heavy comforter. And started to leave.

"Orvile."

"Yes."

"Thank you, my friend," Roman said from the darkness.

"Go to sleep, Roman. Be a good breakfast in the mornin'."

Orvile left the stairwell lamp burning, as he always did, and went into the kitchen to sit for a while at the table, his great hands clasping and unclasping before him. It had begun to sleet, and he could hear the rattling sounds of it blown before the wind, slanting under the porch roof and striking the windowpanes like a flock of blackbirds pecking to get inside where it was warm.

Some kinda thing happen about that little cat-face woman, Orvile thought. Shoulda put poison in her jelly.

He rose slowly, lowered the lamps above the table, blew each of them out, and found his way in the darkness to his pantry bed. The sleet was making a lot of noise now against the sides of the house. And he thought, Good night for sleepin'. Cold out there, warm in here. Good night to jus' forget. First time I ever call him Roman. Not *Mister* Roman, jus' Roman. He won't remember. But I will. Now, though, good night for sleepin'. Warm in here, cold out there.

By morning the storm had blown its way into Missouri and there was a cloudless sky. The limbs and low bushes were sheathed in ice and so dazzlingly bright in the sun that they hurt Orvile's eyes when he looked out. To Orvile's great surprise, Roman was in the kitchen only slightly later than usual. Orvile fried eggs for him, with bacon, and the smell of the meat cooking seemed to revive Roman completely.

"Where's Papa?" he asked.

"He all right," Orvile said. "Sometimes he like to sit in his window up there and watch the sun in the mornin'. He be all right."

Roman ran a finger over his puffy face.

"I think I'll grow a mustache," he said.

Orvile Tucker had a signal he made to the horse-barn hired hands on mornings when Roman was going into town. He hung a dishpan on a nail in the north wall of the house, beside the kitchen door. When they saw that, one of the hired men saddled Junior and had him waiting by the time Roman had finished his breakfast. So it was this morning.

As Roman rode away, Orvile Tucker sighed and grinned and shook his head. That man change quicker than weather, he thought, low feelin' gone in a hurry. But later he remembered an old saying that came out of the slave quarters in Tennessee. Feelin' low, like big, blue grapes. They come off the vine in bunches.

Orvile Tucker knew that this day it was true.

About noon, a new bank of menacing clouds blew in from the Indian Territory. Within an hour, the ice still on the trees from the last storm, it began to sleet, and the big quicksilver thermometer on one of the lathed oak pillars of the north porch fell below freezing.

Before that happened, before there was any warning that it would, Lark Crozier arrived in his spring wagon, with Renée and little Hasford Crozier. Orvile gave them all cold biscuits and crab-apple jelly in the kitchen, everyone sitting at the big table and laughing as the baby licked his fingers, all ten of which dripped with butter. Martin Hasford was there, and he laughed, too.

By now Renée was coming one day each week to clean the Big House. She always left her son with Lark at Wolf Cove, but from time to time, when she came with her husband on business, she brought little Hasford with her, and each time Martin Hasford conducted his tour as though it had never been done before. Or maybe he hadn't forgotten. Maybe he did it because seeing this place with all its shining things, no matter how often, so delighted the child that it delighted Martin.

On that day when the storm blew in, Orvile and Lark hurried back to the Big House, interrupting Martin's grand parade, and Lark drove away toward Little Sugar Creek with his family, little Hasford looking over his mother's shoulder and waving a tiny chocolate hand in farewell, Martin Hasford standing on the porch and waving too.

Finally, Orvile Tucker said, "Come in, Mr. Martin," knowing from experience that Roman's father would stand there on the porch waving, long after the wagon had disappeared into the eastern woods. "It's gettin' cold out here."

It was shortly after that when Orvile saw Roman, riding Junior hard along the road from town, the horse already well lathered. Roman rode past the front gate and on toward the old battlefield and Wire Road, and Orvile knew he was going to the Hasford homestead. He also knew something bad had happened.

Orvile Tucker began to pace, looking out the east-facing windows each time he passed them, then back into the kitchen to pour Martin another cup of hot coffee. Once he sat down at the table with Martin and played a game of checkers, a game that seemed to draw out Martin's interest and lucid memory. Then more pacing, watching the storm grow vicious with sleet.

Two hours after he'd ridden past, Roman reappeared. His hat and coat were crusted with ice. Junior was bathed in soapy lather and blowing hard, his nostrils extended, frost around them and around his eyes.

"Get outta them clothes right now," Orvile said, going out on the porch. "I'll take care of the horse."

Roman said nothing but stomped across the living room and up the stairs, that furious, raging expression on his face.

Orvile got Junior to the barn and rubbed him down with straw, then covered his back with a blanket.

"You let this horse blow down," Orvile said to one of the wide-eyed hired hands, who knew something was wrong from Orvile's glaring, bloodshot eyes. "Then you give him another good rubdown and keep a blanket on him all night. You hear me, white boy?"

"I hear you."

Going back to the Big House through the driving sleet, Orvile muttered to himself, "He's gonna kill that horse. That horse gettin' mighty old, an' him running that horse like he was a three-year-old. Gone crazy, runnin' ole Junior thata way."

Orvile Tucker didn't know what it was and realized tha the probably never would know. But whatever it was, it was bad.

Junior didn't die. But he was never the same horse again, after that wild ride from the Gourdville square to the old Hasford homestead, and then only a short breather while Roman stood or rather stomped around his mother's grave, and then the dash back to Catrina Hills into the face of the wind.

And Orvile Tucker was right. He never did know the details, although he made a lot of wild guesses.

It had been the day for Roman's monthly haircut. At about the time the clear sky began to darken with those scudding Indian Territory clouds, Roman had been in Anson Greedy's chair, and the barber was down to the last few snips with the scissors around Roman's ears. Sitting in the wooden armchairs along the far wall were Coroner and Justice of the Peace Criten Lapp and Newton Black, the feed-store man, waiting their turns.

Conversation on politics and Gourdville's new baseball team, planned for summer, had about run its course and Criten Lapp mentioned that on this day, first crack out of the box, he'd done a marriage ceremony that surprised him a little.

"Criten, all them weddings you're doin'," said Newton Black, "the preachers in this town gonna tar and feather you one day."

"If they do, it won't be because of the money," Criten said. "I only charge fifty cents."

"Who tied the infernal knot this time?" Anson Greedy asked, his scissors snicking around Roman's left ear.

"Ausbin Tage," Criten said. "Your neighbor, Roman."

Roman grunted and everybody laughed because it was an open secret in this county that Roman Hasford didn't hold much truck with old Ephraim Tage, who lived just down the road from Catrina Hills Farm.

"Yes sir, Ausbin married that little blond-headed girl of James Chesney's," said Criten Lapp.

"Was Ausbin sober?" Newton Black asked.

"Couldn't tell," Criten Lapp said. "Everybody was a little shocked, it seemed like. 'Cept for James Chesney. He paid me the four bits. For the ceremony."

"Well, hell," Anson Greedy said. "Ole Eph wouldn't have that much money. Since his woman died, he can't keep a penny to his name."

"Mainly on account of Ausbin drinks it all up," Newton Black said.

"Surprised me a little," Criten Lapp said. "That's a fine-lookin' woman, that Chesney girl."

"Well, James Chesney's struck up a real close acquaintance with ole Eph Tage," Newton Black said. "Sittin' in church together ever' Sunday and talkin' after. With Ausbin, too, I reckon."

"Yeah," said Anson Greedy. "But what I hear, James and his two boys is all goes to that church. I wouldn't know, me and my woman bein' Baptists."

"That's right," said Newton Black. "James Chesney's old lady and that girl never come with James and the boys."

"They tell me that woman of James Chesney's is a Greek," said Anson Greedy. "I ain't ever seen her but twice, come in town with James right after they got here."

"I never seen that girl but about twice, either," said Newton Black. "Stay close at home, them Chesney women, I reckon."

"Well, I'll tell you the truth," said Criten Lapp. "That's a fine-lookin' girl."

"I guess Ausbin can lay out drunk at his daddy-in-law's tie yard now, instead of always gettin' in Ennis Lugi's way over at the blacksmith shop," Anson Greedy said.

Roman Hasford sat deathly silent as Anson Greedy whisked cut hair from his neck and collar and then, using a dry shaving brush, applied talcum powder in a great, snowstorm cloud. Then, abruptly, Roman was out of the chair, throwing aside the catch-cloth, putting a coin in Anson Greedy's hand and going headlong out the door, grabbing his hat and overcoat from the clothes tree on the way.

"Well, Roman looked like he's comin' down with something," Newton Black said.

"Can't ever tell about that man," said the barber, and he opened his hand for the others to see. Roman had left a silver dollar, and everybody knew a haircut was only fifteen cents.

"All right," Anson Greedy said. "Who's next?"

20

Lorton Quint arrived in Gourdville in the spring of 1880 without the usual disadvantage of "newcomer" attached to his name, simply by virtue of the fact that the Frisco railroad had hired him to be the Gourdville stationmaster.

His wife, Sally Agnes, put her own mark on the town by becoming a mainstay in the Baptist church, where she was soon directing the choir, singing all the soprano solos, of which there was one every Sunday after she got there, and forcefully instructing the preacher, the Reverend Zechariah Smith, on points to be made in his sermons, some of which were ill-concealed barbs about the Methodists.

Lorton Quint moved into the house built for him by the railroad, a one-story frame structure distinguished only by a huge black oak tree in the front yard, and located at the intersection of Main and First streets, on the east side of the tracks, within a short spit of the passenger depot, as Anson Greedy put it.

At about the same time, Ansel Kimes, the Frisco section foreman, moved into an identical house next door, except it didn't have a black oak tree in the front yard. He was not so well received as Lorton Quint, because section foremen, it was said, were vile and unwashed men, besides which Ansel's wife, Matilda, attended no church, swore like an army muleskinner, and weighed three hundred pounds. And had a black mustache. And had three daughters, each of whom cussed with as much imagination as their mother and each of whom outweighed the elder Kimes by at least forty pounds.

The horrors to be encountered in such a household were apparently overcome by passion and lust. At least they were in one case. Glen Torten, who was feisty and tough, everybody said, but who weighed only one hundred thirty pounds, married the oldest of Ansel Kimes's daughters within three weeks after the section foreman moved into town. Her name was Thelma, and she was the largest of the Kimes girls, and already a legend of sorts. On the day of their arrival in town, when Matilda and her brood were standing on the station platform waiting for their baggage to be taken off the train, some drunken and very stupid young man from a farm in the western part of the county, in Gourdville celebrating something or other, made an untoward remark to Thelma, whereupon she struck him with a hard left hook that broke his jaw.

Mother Matilda insisted that her new son-in-law live right there in the section house with the rest of the Kimes family, although it was already bulging with amazons. During the tag end of that first summer after they arrived, and after Glen Torten lost his reason and married Thelma, the very best entertainment each evening came when people were standing on the Frisco depot platform waiting for the northbound passenger train and listening to the colorful verbal battles taking place in the section house, Glen Torten on one side and opposed to him his wife, Thelma, and her mother and sisters, with Ansel himself sitting on the porch smoking a pipe. These encounters usually terminated just before the train arrived, when Glen burst from the front door of the section house, sometimes tearing off the screen as he came, and marched across the tracks and on to his domino and billiard parlor.

But those who observed such things said that by midnight little ole Glen would creep back into the section house for whatever wild and sweaty pleasure awaited him in the arms of the great and profane Thelma.

With winter, this public entertainment was of course suspended because nobody came to see the train in, for fear of frostbite. But they all looked forward to spring, when it would all begin again. And most citizens, whatever their attitude to Glen Torten's situation, felt sorry for Ansel Kimes in that cold time of year, because he was either cooped up in the house with all those monsters or else out on the line somewhere with a bunch of his section workmen, freezing his tail off.

As for Lorton Quint, nobody felt sorry for him. They felt respect for his enterprise. And respect for his cap, with the brass plate on the front that proclaimed him STATIONMASTER. It was just a regular billed cap, but nobody else in Gourdville had one. And even if they had, they would not have known the things that Lorton Quint knew.

He knew what all those signals meant on the railroad poles, the lights and the things that looked like canoe paddles and moved up and down. He could tell when the next train was coming, late or not, because he had the best pocket watch in town, a huge thing made in Waltham, Massachusetts. He sold the tickets. He was the telegrapher (for which Western Union paid him a little each month). And being an old railroad man and an old telegrapher, he knew the requirements of newspapers. So he sent little items to them and to the new press associations on the company wire, for his personal pocketbook. He was called, in this capacity, a stringer, and was, in effect, a window on the local scene for the big Yankee newspapers in St. Louis and Chicago and even New York.

Of course, not much that happened in Gourdville was of any interest to St. Louis or Chicago or New York. Except now and then a particularly vicious hailstorm, or maybe a bank robbery, or the birth of a two-headed calf. Some of which was reported whether it happened or not. Lorton Quint reasoned correctly that no one was going to come down to Arkansas from St. Louis or Chicago or New York to check the authenticity of a story about a baby born with the signs of the zodiac tattooed on its ass.

Nobody in Gourdville knew Lorton Quint's politics. They knew that he most certainly was a Baptist, but to courthouse watchers that didn't count as politics. Yet if they knew little about him, he soon learned a great deal about them, because he watched and listened. And almost immediately he knew where the power centers in the community lay.

So on that day in early February the year that Ausbin Tage married Diana Chesney, when Roman Hasford came into the depot, Lorton Quint knew who Roman was, even though he'd seen the president of the Farmer's and Merchant's Bank only from a distance.

What Lorton Quint saw that day was not reassuring. The Hasford mouth was set in a hard line, there were dark, brittle shadows under the eyes, and the eyes themselves were as icy cold as the weather outside. There was a small, bristling mustache, dark brown even though the ample hair that protruded below Roman Hasford's hat was hay-colored going to gray. It was the kind of fine, never-stay-put hair that stood out around the ears like horns when the slightest breeze disturbed it.

The voice, when Roman spoke, was no more tender than the face.

"Round-trip ticket to Jefferson City."

"Jefferson City, Missouri," said Lorton Quint, not as a question but as an affirmation.

"Do you know of any other Jefferson City?" Roman Hasford asked in a voice as frigid as any Lorton Quint had ever heard.

"No sir," Lorton Quint said, and began rolling off the ticket stubs, Cassville to Monet to Springfield, change there, on to Lebanon, then into Jeff City. A string of tickets fully eighteen inches long. And just as many for the return trip.

"That'll be three dollars and eighty cents, Mr. Hasford."

Lorton Quint was paid in silver coin.

Roman Hasford didn't wait in the room where all the benches were, where there was a large stove glowing cherry red from the hickory wood burning inside. He went out to the platform, where the wind was fierce, pulling his fur overcoat collar up around his neck. Orvile Tucker was there, and their two saddle horses at the hitch rail near the track.

"Get on back home, Orvile," Roman said. "No need freezing yourself out here."

"I'll leave Bucky at Ennis Lugi's stable so when you get home, you have a horse straight off."

Bucky was a two-year-old stallion that Junior had sired. And he was even bigger than his daddy. Looking at him, Roman couldn't help but think that Elmer Scaggs would have said he was part Morgan and part wildcat.

"Three, four days. That's all, then I'll be back. Take care of Papa."

"You know I do that, Mr. Roman."

Roman watched the big black man walk off the platform toward the horses, and he noticed for the first time that Orvile Tucker was walking a little slower, with a little more labor in each step. It didn't improve his disposition.

Riding north into Missouri that night, Roman wasn't sure why he had decided to visit Catrina. It certainly wasn't for any anticipated pleasure, nor was he willing to admit that he was reaching out for something, no matter how tenuous, that represented better days. Catrina didn't represent very many of those. Maybe it was sentimentality. But he wasn't going to admit that, even to himself. Most especially to himself.

There was a two-hour layover in Springfield at three o'clock in the morning, and he walked the streets near the station. Everything was dark. The wind howled along between the buildings, and there was snow here, whipped into his face as he walked. It fit his mood. Back in the depot waiting room, he opened a small valise he'd brought, took out the bottle of bourbon, and sipped it. There was one other person in the room. A matronly lady, a bonnet tied to her throat with a garish purple scarf. She glared at Roman.

"Good morning, ma'am," he said, lifting the bottle in her direction. She looked away, her nostrils flaring.

It was just after noon when he arrived by cab at St. Scholastica. He waited in the vestibule, hearing young voices singing somewhere. In Latin, he assumed, not knowing any of that language, despite his name, except what he read on the coins of the United States. There was a haunting quality to the sound, and he thought it was a lot like listening to fox dogs far away. That these voices seemed far away made a chill go up his back. Coming from a great distance and down through the corridors of time, just like the sounds of fox dogs running.

Maybe that's it, he thought. Maybe that's why it's so foreign, listening to the dogs. As though they're sounding in Latin. I'll have to mention that to Anson Greedy the next time we're listening to a race. Then he thought, No, I won't mention Latin to Anson Greedy.

The black-robed nuns were polite, but they made him extremely uncomfortable. After a long wait, explained by the headmistress or Mother Superior or whatever she was by the fact that Roman's telegraph message announcing his visit had only preceded his visit by a few hours, he was put in a room with two small windows through which shafts of sunlight illuminated bare walls and a bare oak table and two bare oak straight-backed chairs.

After a few moments, Catrina came.

Roman rose and met her and kissed her forehead. It was the only thing she presented him to kiss. She looked much as he remembered her when he'd brought her here, except that now there was some distance in her black eyes, as though he were a stranger. Which was how he felt.

Roman gave her his gift, a wrapped box with a fine fur muff inside, the kind that ladies put their hands in on cold days, and she smiled and placed it on the table, unopened.

"Thank you," she said. "I brought some of my things to show you."

"That's good," he said, and the nun who had accompanied Catrina into the room and still stood at the door smiling, hands folded in front of her, nodded in approval.

"This is Sister Marie," Catrina said. Roman recognized the name, recalling it from Catrina's letters as the person who was apparently Catrina's special mentor.

"How do you do."

Catrina had a large bag made of woven rattan, and she began to take things out of it and lay them on the table.

"We thought you might want to see what Catrina has been doing with us," Sister Marie said.

"Yes, of course."

Then they sat across from each other at the bare oak table, Sister Marie at the door, smiling, hands folded. Catrina, once everything had been emptied from the bag, sat staring at him. Waiting for approval, he assumed, and it was unbearable.

But he lifted each object and nodded and said what he thought was expected of him by the nun.

"Yes, very beautiful, very well done."

There were a number of small needlepoint canvases, the colors rather dull, Roman thought. There were two ceramic pots about the size of his doubled fist, a woven straw placemat, a number of sheets of foolscap with conjugations of Latin verbs, all written in the tiny, cramped penmanship Roman had come to recognize from the letters he had received.

"She is excellent in Latin," said Sister Marie.

"Yes, I can see."

There were a number of drawings in colored pencil on the same foolscap.

"Her artwork is very good, too," said Sister Marie.

"Yes, very good," Roman said. What the hell else could he say?

Catrina spread some of the drawings on the table before him. They were indeed very good. Only there was something he could not pinpoint at first, something out of focus, a little crooked maybe.

And then he realized what it was, or rather what it was not.

A drawing of a horse, but the horse had no eyes. Another of a great, sprawling house, but without a single window or door. There was a tree with tiny leaves springing out directly from the trunk, but there were no limbs. And in each of these were children, or at least very tiny people, in the background. Every one of them was truncated at the waist. They had no lower bodies, no legs, as though they were all standing in quicksand already reaching to their chests.

"This is all wonderful," Roman said, rising and hoping his voice did not reveal that he had become physically ill. But from the expression on Sister Marie's face, he knew she was aware of his feeling.

Quickly, then, all that damned stuff still spread across the small table, he said good-bye, made his excuse for leaving so soon, Catrina rising dutifully for her kiss on the forehead once more, eyes downcast, her skin icy cold. Still smiling that dainty little smile, and her eyes bottomless black above the tiny teeth.

"I hope you can visit next Christmas," she said. "It's nice here at Christmas, and all of us sing after the High Mass."

"Yes, of course, we'll see."

"Good-bye."

"Good-bye, Catrina."

Sister Marie escorted him back into the outer vestibule and to the great double doors. She too was smiling. Roman stood for a moment, hat in hand, anguish in his eyes. She saw it, and he hoped she understood that he was incapable of saying anything to her in way of explanation.

"Thank you for coming, Mr. Hasford," she said.

"Be sure to inform me if she wants anything," he said, and felt a complete fool for saying it.

"Of course, Mr. Hasford."

His cab was still at the door, and he got into it before the driver could come down from his seat and assist.

"Back to the hotel, Colonel?" the driver called down.

"Yes, but I'm not a colonel."

The driver whipped his old horse, and the sound of the steel-shod hooves on the driveway stones was like tiny anvils being struck. Roman sank back into the badly frayed leather upholstery and watched the amber light of afternoon flickering past between the trees bordering the streets of Jefferson City. There was some feeling of defeat that day, as though he were a general riding away from a battlefield where his best troops had been decimated. He knew it had only partly to do with Catrina, being able to reason that it was best for her to be in that place, cloistered and cared for and taught. The major part of it was Diana Chesney, gone now. And that left him knowing he was a cup only half-full, cut off somewhere as surely as those little people Catrina had drawn.

Driving through the golden afternoon to his hotel in Jefferson City that day, he recalled past times, when his sentiments could overwhelm him, could make him explode with wrath or else cry. He could cry when a Morgan mare dropped a fine foal. Cry about losing Elmer Scaggs and then Mama. Cry, late at night in his bed, because the course of his life had taken directions he had somehow ordained but couldn't control.

But now he was past crying. Not because it was unmanly, because he didn't believe it was, but because some hard cynicism had crept in to raise a barrier to crying, and now it was all devil-take-the-hindmost.

Besides, he thought, if I cried now, I don't know who I'd be crying for, Catrina or Diana or myself.

Maybe it was on that trip to Jefferson City, the last he would ever make, that he thought for the first time, Who's left that cares? Or that I care a damn about? Four colored people. And a papa who most usually doesn't even know who I am.

And he thought once more, Devil take the hindmost, Mama. Everybody pays, one way or the other.

21

For the folk of Gourdville and those in the surrounding county, it was good when May arrived. It was time for an awakening from long winter doldrums, a time to get out into fresh air and take stock of the situation. And there was plenty to take stock of, because of the railroad.

The Frisco had cut a tunnel through the mountain at Weedy Rough, about forty miles to the south, and now had level track all the way past Fort Smith and into Texas.

"Why, a man can get a car right down here on First Street," Raymond Ort of the bakery said, "and ride all the way to Paris, Texas, without gettin' off. Only who the hell wants to go to Paris, Texas?"

Business was booming. The railroad was buying staves and crossties and fenceposts at the tie yard. Tobacco prices were up, and bales of the brown leaf were going off on freight cars. There was enough winter wheat to keep all the county's mills grinding six days a week, and a lot of the meal and flour went out from the loading platform just north of the Frisco passenger depot. Benjamin Tark had found markets for his peach brandy in Missouri, and therefore became an asset to the community, bringing in money instead of just being a dyed-in-the-wool atheist half-blood Indian savage, living in sin. Omer Sample was hiring boys to work in the apple vinegar plant, and his gallon glass jars were dispatched in wooden crates marked "Fort Worth." Newton Black, at the feed store, was shipping in the latest formula bran for milk cows and beef cattle, and his loading platform at back of the store overlooking the baseball diamond was creaking under the weight of one-hundred-pound burlap sacks filled with the best bone-meal fertilizer.

There was another sure sign of spring, besides the white blossoms of black locust trees. Glen Torten and his wife, Thelma, had resumed their evening confrontations in the section house for the entertainment and enlightenment of citizens who had come to the depot platform to watch the northbound passenger train go through. The entertainment part was obvious, and the enlightenment part mostly concerned the new words children heard, whereupon their mothers said things like "I ever hear you usin' that word, I'll wash your mouth out with soap!"

And all over the county, the boys were courting the girls, bringing boxes of candy from the drugstore to present as gifts, or sometimes even two packages of spearmint chewing gum, and most of them were wearing black bow ties that just clipped onto the collar, which everybody said was a sure sign of rising sap or some such thing. Hell, they said, those clip ties cost thirty-five cents apiece.

Corliss Buckmaten continued to grind out the news about births and deaths and marriages, and he still attacked the czar of Catrina Hills Farm and asked why Roman Hasford was always slipping off to Yankeeland, where he surely must hatch wicked plans to fleece the honest citizen. And that spring he asked the question in the columns: "Why is Roman Hasford so seldom seen now in his emporium of autocracy, the Farmer's and Merchant's Bank, that shrine to Republican Reconstruction?"

"Poor Corliss," said Harley Stone, mayor and hotel owner. "Still talking about Reconstruction, and Reconstruction has been gone so long nobody even remembers what it means anymore."

"Lookee here," said Anson Greedy, the barber. "Ole Corliss may have a point. Roman Hasford is well overdue for a haircut; he ain't come in a long time."

Roman Hasford still did not come as spring ran into summer. Nor did he attend the spring and summer running of the fox by the Northwest Arkansas Fox Racing Association, although his father did, in company of Isaac Maddox. In fact, Roman's only contact with anybody during all that time was with Owen Caulder, who came to Catrina Hills each week with his dog Trixie, to borrow more books and to bring back those he had borrowed the week before.

In mid-May, Doc Hazlet Cronin was summoned to the farm of

James Chesney in the middle of the night, and there, before dawn, he and Molina Chesney assisted Diana Chesney Tage in delivering a seven-pound-three-ounce baby girl, whom James named Berdeen. Doc Cronin reported that Ausbin Tage, the husband, was nowhere in evidence, but that the new arrival appeared to be as strong as a Frisco station hand and right good-looking, if such a thing could be said about any minutes-old babe.

Only a few citizens knew that on this particular night Ausbin Tage had been at Brown's Tavern doing the thing at which he was most proficient, getting drunk, passing out, and sleeping in front of the smoky fireplace.

There was a lot of talk in the county about Diana's baby. Shotgun weddings were not unheard of, nor were babies born too soon after marriage vows to have been conceived in wedlock. But it didn't happen often, and when it did there was considerable shame and disgrace associated with it. It wasn't as bad as having an outright bastard in the family, but almost. The stigma of a morally loose young woman in a clan drove families into isolation or else into wagons, bag and baggage, to search out some distant place where life could start from scratch again with neighbors who were unaware of the mortal sin that had been committed.

James Chesney did neither. He stood pat and played out his hand defiantly, as Anson Greedy put it. Ausbin Tage, who had provided the child with a name, increased his intake of booze, if that were possible. He spent more time hanging out at his daddy's farm than he did at the Chesney place, where he and Diana were supposed to be maintaining a household within a household.

It remained a marriage all right, at least in name, maybe because James Chesney carried Ausbin Tage on his payroll at the Frisco tie yard. Everybody could see that Ausbin didn't lift a hand to earn his wage. There wasn't much money involved, but even what little there was exceeded anything that had been in Tage pockets since the time the old man had been a fairly good farmer and the old woman had been alive to watch the pennies.

"By God," said Isaac Maddox, "James Chesney's settin' a bad example, payin' a man a salary to be his daughter's husband."

Nobody could understand why James Chesney would particularly like Ausbin Tage. Nobody else did. But when James Chesney needed somebody in a hurry to avoid bastardy in his family, maybe Ausbin had been the only one he could think of, maybe even the only eligible bachelor James Chesney knew.

Well, looky here, they said, James Chesney and Ausbin Tage's daddy were thick as a wolf pack, always spending a lot of time jawing together after services at the Presbyterian church every Sunday, so who knows what kind of deal they might have struck? Two strange men, they said.

What Diana thought of her husband was anybody's guess. And there were a lot of guesses. But just about every last soul in the county who was old enough to know how babies were started figured Ausbin Tage wasn't that baby's daddy.

Anson Greedy was cutting Judge Terrence Shadbolt's hair one rainy afternoon in early June, and the subject came up because it was the kind of subject made to order for a barbershop. Nobody else was there at the moment, so the tone was of course conspiratorial.

"Your Honor," Anson Greedy said, "who you reckon is the daddy of that little Berdeen?"

"It doesn't make any difference," Judge Shadbolt said. "In the eyes of the law, Ausbin Tage is the father."

"Maybe in the eyes of the law," Anson said, clicking his scissors against his comb, "but back in September when that baby got her start, I'd bet this barbershop against a dollar that Diana Chesney didn't even know Ausbin Tage."

"Anson," said the judge, "I doubt you'd find anybody around here who'd take that bet."

So everybody was guessing. It wasn't an easy task, because nobody knew much about Diana Chesney. She was like her mother, a stay-at-home. She wasn't out running around the county on picnics and hayrides like that Lucerne Delmonico, they said. A lot of people in the county had never even seen her. Just a few who had been on the square at those infrequent occasions when James brought her to town with him.

The Chesney clan wasn't much for socializing. No one was ever invited to their house for Sunday dinner. They didn't visit anybody else. Sometimes James Chesney and his two boys went to one of those fox races that Isaac Maddox promoted, but even then, James didn't talk much to anybody except Martin Hasford.

"It's like old James feels close to anybody who's got an affliction," said Criten Lapp, who, because of his and his brother's vocations as undertaker and county coroner, considered himself an expert on affliction. "Him with that clubfoot and all. Feelin' like maybe he's got something in common with other invalids but not with anybody else. And Eph Tage, he's as close to an invalid that I ever seen who's still movin' and talkin', mean-tempered as he's been since his old woman died."

And nobody knew any more about Molina Chesney than they did about her daughter. They had long been a puzzle, those two Chesney women, because in any other family, when a man went to church his woman and daughter were supposed to trail after him, and pray like he did, and sing like he did, and put a nickel in the plate like he did.

But with the Chesney bunch, it didn't work that way.

"I reckon Molina's got her own religion right at home," said Anson Greedy, lathering faces in his barbershop.

"You ever seen her, Anson?" asked Ennis Lugi, waiting his turn for a haircut.

"Yes, I did. When they first come. Seen her oncet. Best-lookin' woman I ever seen in my whole life. Bar none."

"Well, Anson, what's that Greek religion you talkin' about she does at home?"

"How the hell do I know?"

So all that summer the people throughout the county had a new little stranger to talk about, because no matter what Judge Shadbolt said about that kid having a legal daddy, she sure as hell, they said, started her journey without benefit of marriage license. All the women said it was a shame, the child having to grow up with such a stain of sin, like a purple birthmark across her face. Most of the men said it never failed; the least likely female you could think of to be passing her favors around suddenly pops out with a brat.

And of course there was all kinds of speculation and fantasizing about some slick county stallion climbing into a window at the Chesney farm in the dead of night—maybe when there was lightning and thunder—and having a little romp on the mattress. And all kinds of guesses and giggles about who the stallion might be. In Glen Torten's Billiard Parlor it became a standing joke among the pool shooters and moon players.

"Aw, come on, J.D.," one would say to another. "Tell us about how you snuck into that Chesney gal's bloomers!"

When old Eph or Ausbin Tage was around, such banter was suspended. But the general perception of the Tage part in the whole business was reflected in how pool-hall hangers-on referred to the new baby. It was never "Berdeen Tage," but always "that Chesney bastard."

And so everyone remembered it as the summer James Chesney got himself a granddaughter by accident. Also the summer the Gourdville baseball team beat Fayetteville twice, which a lot of citizens said was as unexpected as what had happened to Diana Chesney.

22

Maybe because winter was the grim time of year, the things that happened then were always remembered in stark gray and white tones. Without bouquet.

Through spring and summer and fall, all the trees came on lettuce yellow and turned through June to waxy green and then in October blazed in red and golden blankets across the hills. There were flowers and flashing birds and Prussian blue skies and sparkling emerald water in the running streams.

These were the colors of optimism and hope.

In spring and summer and fall, there was the odor of honeysuckle or mown wheat or black locust blossoms or fresh rain in the dust or cucumber pickles being canned.

These were the good smells of earth bountiful.

But in winter the colors died and the smells dried up. The only place such things were sustained was inside snug walls. The orange flame of fireplace, the aroma of roasting chicken or frying ham creating a sense of well-being, sheltered from the great world beyond the frosty windows. Outside, it was bleak, making the inside feel all the more safe and comfortable.

So things that happened in the outside world, beyond those sheltering walls, were always remembered as harsher and more bitter than they would have if they'd happened in spring, summer, or fall.

And the Trouble came back in winter.

During the Brown boys' absence, new people had arrived in the county. Having no sense of personal involvement in the Trouble, they could view it almost as though it were one of those ancient myths to which old residents were attached, like that of the ghost of a Cherokee maiden who had died during the Trail of Tears near Indian Springs, and came back each year in the month of November to walk along the limestone ledges where the bright water ran out of the mountainside to form a pool and then a whispering brook that wound through the woods and emptied into Sugar Creek.

There were still a few ancient citizens who claimed they had seen the maiden and heard her wailing. Maybe, they said, she was cursing Andrew Jackson, who had been President when the Removals started.

Other, less ancient, yet still longtime residents had the same kind of memory for the Trouble. They had seen it, or at least parts of it.

Well, there were a lot of things about the Trouble to have seen. An election bought, and rumors of impotency and a young man maimed and another man murdered and the Brown boys going off to the Territory, away from hearth and home and civilization. And it was also widely held that the county's only whore had disappeared because of the Trouble. Which had delighted some and disappointed others.

A lot of things were laid to the Trouble. Like the plague of grasshoppers in the summer after that election. Or the lack of rain during the spring after the murder. A farmer's horse got into the feed shed and foundered because, as everybody knew, a horse was too stupid to stop eating when it had had enough. A farmer's fox dog died of distemper. There was an outbreak of measles. And constipation. All because of the Trouble, some said. It was a visitation of God's wrath, they said, because of the Sodom-and-Gomorrah evils that permeated the whole county when the Trouble came.

There had even been some mention of it from certain pulpits.

But among those who had seen the Trouble and personally knew the taste of it, time had faded its cruelty, much as sunlight fades the colors in a calico dress left too long on the clothesline.

So, finally, the Trouble became much like the Cherokee maiden at Indian Springs. Something to be remembered without dread, something to mention casually without looking nervously over one's shoulder.

And now, although the Trouble had amounted to many things and had spread itself over a number of years, it seemed in recollection that it had been a single, instant disaster come and gone like a tornado. And like the times following a tornado, with so much to do and so much happening and so many seasons speeding past, the Trouble mellowed into that hazy blur of unreality buried in the community. Just another one of the bricks that made up the whole structure. Just another one of the stories old men could someday tell to unbelieving grandchildren. Just another one of those chapters found in every community's book that created hatreds that would last longer than the reasons for them could be remembered.

So, like all other communities, whether or not they had something like the Trouble, everything marched along as surely as the cycle of spring and summer and fall and winter. And as surely, too, today would not be as yesterday had been, nor either one a forecast of tomorrow.

Nothing had changed the citizens of the county like the railroad. The railroad meant more than shipping apples and barley and tobacco and brandy to markets beyond the reach of horsedrawn vehicles. It meant bringing the outside world into town each day, and with amazing speed.

It meant the arrival of *Harper's Weekly*, very popular because of all the pictures. It meant the *Chicago Inter-Ocean* and the *St. Louis Globe*, newspapers that people could read to reinforce their political views, but that, at the same time, opened all the world to them.

"Do you know," Harley Stone said while bickering with dairyman Brian Felcher about butter prices, "this new bridge in Brooklyn would reach from Ephraim Tage's farmhouse right into the Frisco depot!"

"Hell, who'd want to build a bridge between Ephraim Tage's farmhouse and the depot?"

"I mean, it's that long. I figured it out. It cost fifteen million dollars. You wouldn't think there's that much money in the whole world."

"There ain't."

Citizens read that most of the wild Indians were on reservations now. Well, the neighboring Cherokees were not wild. They had their own schools and policemen and laws, they had their own country. And everybody hoped to hell they'd stay in it.

Jesse James was shot in St. Joseph, Missouri, and then there were a lot of verses published in the St. Louis newspaper about it and a traveling minstrel show that gave one performance on the front porch of the Stone Hotel while the audience stood or sat in the grassy plot at the center of the square. The best part of the whole thing was this fat lady in a purple dress who sang a sad song about Mr. Howard being killed by a dirty little coward to lay Jesse James in his grave. Accompanied by a banjo picker. She sang it three times.

Why, people said, there was some of the craziest goings-on, unheard of, with a man in New Jersey, wherever that was, making a light that burned without any coal oil. Or the one in Boston who said he could make voices come over a wire. Not the click-clack of Western Union like they had down at the Frisco depot, but actual voices talking.

Crazy as hell, they said, these Yankees.

Some things were better understood. John L. Sullivan had whipped Paddy Ryan and wore his belt with a buckle bigger than a cast-iron skillet, all gold and diamonds. Heavyweight Boxing Champion of the World. And Deputy Colin Hamp, who knew a lot about William Cody, was beside himself when he read that Buffalo Bill had started a Wild West Show.

"No, Colin," said Sheriff Hamlin Bidd, "you ain't goin' to Chicago or anywhere else to see this Buffalo Bill. Remember, you're gonna be the next sheriff around here, and there's some dignity involved."

The railroad brought in the latest books, to be sold or loaned from the Caulder Mercantile. The readers in the county, which may have constituted about 10 percent of the population, liked Joel Chandler Harris and Robert Louis Stevenson. But the favorite was General Lew Wallace's *Ben Hur*.

Other things, too. They could remember when a catalog from Montgomery Ward was the size of a playing card, easily carried in a man's shirt pocket. Now it was as big as the gray-covered book at the post office listing every town and city in the whole country, and a person could order anything out of it from a truss for a rupture to a three-bladed plow.

Big events, too. President Garfield shot almost before the Bible had cooled off from his hand being on it at the swearing-in ceremony, and all the details of the hanging afterward. Which details interested a lot of folks more than the assassination. Chester A. Arthur, from Vermont, becoming the President and, with his wife having died the year before, his sister soon running his White House.

"Seems like a President ought to have a wife," said Raymond Ort.

"What's the difference?" asked Ennis Lugi. "None of 'em gonna buy any of your doughnuts anyway."

There were also plenty of changes right in the county for everyone to contemplate, too. Like a drugstore opening on the square across from the hotel. The proprietor was one Dr. Thorman Gooch, from Ohio, who sold soap and talcum powder and glass jewelry in the front and performed minor surgery in back. And pulled teeth besides.

Dr. Gooch's shelves reflected the amazing medical advances made since the Civil War: Hostetter's Stomach Bitters, which was about fifty proof; Dr. Bull's worm medicine, laxative, and remedy for female periodic discomfort, all sold in bottles with colorful labels. A very popular item was Dr. Epson's Teething Compound, a thick, oily liquid to be rubbed on the gums of tots cutting molars. It worked wonders because in addition to mineral water it contained grain alcohol, tincture of morphine, and cocaine. On the first application, kids stopped fussing and whining, stupefied with joy over the glorious colors flashing through their little heads.

Now there was an ice plant on the banks of Oak Creek where the stream ran through the south part of town. Also a meat market across the tracks from the Frisco depot, carcasses of beef and pork hanging in the window, with an occasional quarter of venison or a pair of rabbits. Also an ice cream parlor and confection emporium, where French perfume was even available. Also a millinery shop on the square, a shoe shop, and three new saloons, the best of them just off the square behind the courthouse. There one could have free sliced roast beef and pickled pig's feet and hard-boiled eggs with the purchase of a five-cent schooner of beer.

Otto Smecker, the owner, claimed he had the longest real mahogany bar in the county, which wasn't saying much because it was the *only* mahogany bar in the county. Otto had arrived from Kentucky with his grown son, Alex, both of whom had tattoos on their arms. These tattoos, hearts and daggers and eagles, were popular, and there were editorial comments that the artists seemed to encourage, like "Mother," or "True Love Endures," or "Bold Republic."

And there was now a buggy and carpentry shop next to Ennis Lugi's livery, where a man could have anything made, from a fancy carriage to an outdoor toilet.

"This town is gettin' too big," Anson Greedy complained. "A man can't step out into the street without danger of being run over by some crazy son of a bitch driving his wagon like his house was on fire."

Anson Greedy himself was part of the progress. He'd installed a cup cabinet where he kept regular customers' personalized shaving mugs. White porcelain, with names inscribed in india ink: Stone, Lugi, Shadbolt, Lapp. When a customer walked into the shop, Anson would be standing before his cups, brushing his ample mustache with the knuckles of an index finger, a towel folded over his arm, admiring himself in the new mirror on the wall opposite the barber chair.

"That damned barber," Isaac Maddox said. "He's beginnin' to act like a Methodist bishop out of St. Louis or someplace. Uppity as hell!"

Isaac Maddox was of course always the good Presbyterian, not holding with bishops. Besides, he never went into Anson's shop to sit under the razor because he shaved himself, and his old wife Lucine had cut his hair since the first day they were married, back in James Polk's administration.

A city police force had been established. The chief of police was Criten Lapp, who was also still coroner and justice of the peace, and the patrolman was his nephew, Alvis Lapp, son of the undertaker, who patrolled the square wearing a beehive hat and carrying a black billy club the size of the baseball team's bat. The patrolman's major task was breaking up fights between schoolkids and escorting willing drunks to the county jail in the basement of the courthouse.

That baseball bat became a big issue. It had been broken and nailed and taped back together so often that the team's manager, attorney Hershel Bactrum, claimed it looked like a buggy whip when one of his hitters started waving it around at home plate— home plate and the rest of the diamond being in the vacant lot behind Newton Black's feed store, where Gourdville played Fayetteville every year. After a great deal of public debate, the sponsors of the team, the Gourdville Volunteer Fire Department, finally agreed to order a new one from Sears, Roebuck and Company in Chicago. But they refused to go any further, so the three baseballs, used since the team's inception, had to be repaired for the coming season, the cowhide covers sewn back together by Judge Terrance Shadbolt's wife, reputed to be the best seamstress in the county.

But not even Constance Shadbolt could return the balls to perfect spheres, so when, with the new season, they were thrown with great velocity, they appeared to do very strange things. Which suited everybody just fine because it always confused those Fayetteville batters.

Everything was going fine, thank you, the people said. And all of it was wrapped up in a neat package at the county fair, the first one they'd ever had. People showed off their apples and canned peaches and prize hogs and pecan pies and golden ears of popcorn. An outfit out of Springfield, Missouri, brought in a steam-operated carousel, complete with a calliope that played various unrecognizable tunes. They also brought in a machine to make cotton candy, and a tent show where a midget and a bearded lady were featured along with cages in which were many of the world's most poisonous snakes, even a king cobra, which disappointed hell out of everybody because the thing wouldn't raise up and spread its hood. It just lay there like a sleeping copperhead.

Danton Rich, who was old Judge Rich's grandson and who had opened a little six-table restaurant on the square, had a tent fly where he sold fried ham on light bread, and slabs of apple pie. He made a lot of money, because nothing seemed to make the citizens as hungry as trudging through the dust to observe mules and cows and sheep. Harley Stone was furious because he hadn't thought of it, which was actually just a part of his irritation with Danton Rich, the rest being his opening the restaurant in the first place. It was taking a lot of business away from his hotel dining room, because Danton Rich's wife made wonderful baked chicken and fried okra.

The fair left a lot of good memories. And a lot of empty peanut bags and livestock droppings on the baseball field, where it had been held. Hershel Bactrum knew there would have to be a major clean-up before his baseball team could start practice in the spring.

Winter came on mild and stayed that way throughout. There was considerable gray sky and rain, but not a flake of snow. It was good contemplating spring's arrival and more money coming into the county. And it was good watching the young people courting. And churches bulging with worshipers. And the saloons doing land-rush business.

It was the winter they took up a subscription and made enough money to hire another teacher for the school—a young man named Noble Carnes, from Neosho, Missouri—to pitch in with the Reverend Claudis Kirkendall and his wife on the monumental task of pounding some education into the kids. There was enough money left over to build a second outdoor privy, so that now everybody didn't have to use the same one. That single school crapper had caused all kinds of trouble. It seemed the girls always got to it first and stayed locked inside until recess was over, so the boys had to go to the line of sassafras trees that separated Gourdville school property from the Frisco station foreman's backyard. The new johnny meant the boys had one of their own now, so they immediately decorated the interior walls with drawings of what they supposed were female genitals and various clever inscriptions above the two holes. "Kirkendall is a Republican asshole." Or "Democrats shovel shit with their fingers."

If nothing else, the faculty had at least taught these lads that in Gourdville there was a two-party system.

Toward the end of February, Courtland Brown was seen riding horseback off toward the Nations. And three days later Sheriff Hamlin Bidd and publisher Corliss Buckmaten and lawyer Timothy Burton took a train to Fort Smith. It wasn't just a normal train ride, because it happened at three o'clock in the morning, after the night telegrapher, Lamar Peevy, got a message over the wire and ran to roust the sheriff out of bed so he could get the other two, with all of them arriving at the depot just in time for Lamar Peevy to flag the regular southbound freight. They boarded the caboose.

Before he climbed onto the train, Sheriff Bidd took the telegraph message, folded it, placed it carefully in a pocket of his denim jumper, and enjoined Lamar Peevy to say nothing about it to anybody else or he would find his ears cut off and nailed to the depot door.

Of course, Melissa Buckmaten and Judith Burton knew their husbands had gone off in the middle of the night, but they didn't know why. And before anybody else was aware that the three men were gone, they were back. Coming as they went, in the dark of night.

But they didn't come back on the train. They came back on horses, from the west, and with them was the Cherokee Poco Jimmy. Once each man was deposited at his door, Poco Jimmy turned back toward the Territory, leading the other horses. He paused only a few moments at Brown's Tavern, then rode off into the night without anybody knowing he'd been in the county. Except for the three men and Sarah and Drake Brown.

Two days after that, just at dark, Courtland Brown returned from Indian Territory, and it wasn't long before everybody knew about that, because Corliss Buckmaten published it in his newspaper. Corliss didn't include many details, but the older citizens of the county didn't need many details to realize the Trouble was back, and soon everybody was looking over his shoulder again.

Courtland had gone to the Cherokee Nation on horseback but had returned in a wagon, the saddle horse hitched behind to the tailgate. Poco Jimmy was driving the two mules that drew the wagon, or at least holding the reins as the mules made their own way and set their own pace along the rocky, frosted mud of the Nations Road.

Sunset was well past when they came in sight of the light from the Brown's Tavern windows, two pale yellow holes in the gloom of a young night promising rain with low clouds coming in from the west. The wagon was a good hundred paces from the tavern when the door opened, letting out a long patch of lamplight.

Drake Brown came out, hatless and holding a smoky-globed lantern. Behind him was his mother with a shawl over her head. And at their feet, four of Sarah's cats.

Poco Jimmy pulled the mules in at the light from the tavern door and looked down at Sarah Brown as she approached the wagon, Drake alongside her, holding the lantern shoulder-high. The kerosene light emphasized the strange curve of shadows on Drake's disfigured face. Courtland Brown didn't look at his wife or son, but sat hunched in the wagon seat, hands clasped between his knees.

Sarah Brown stopped at the wagon and looked into the bed. There, side by side, were two rough-cut pine boxes six feet six inches long, two feet wide, and sixteen inches deep, with lids nailed down on top. On one of the boxes was Courtland Brown's saddle.

"Go on," Courtland said softly, and Poco Jimmy jumped down from the wagon, pulled the saddle out of the bed, cinched it onto the horse, untied the reins from the tailgate, mounted, and rode off into the darkness, toward Gourdville.

Sarah Brown moved to the rear of the wagon, let down the

tailgate, lifted herself onto the wagon bed, and sat facing the west, her back to her husband, her feet hanging down over the lowered tailgate and the elbows of her arms resting atop the boxes on either side of her. She would stay there all night.

Finally, Courtland sighed and climbed down from the wagon with great effort and went into the tavern. After a few moments he was back, carrying a shovel, a pick, a length of rope, and two hickory boards. He kicked the door shut behind him and said, "Come on, Drake, I'll need that light."

Courtland and his son crossed the road, the cats following, leaving Sarah in the dark probably because Courtland figured that's the way she wanted it. They went up the little cedar knoll where Courtland's father was buried under a marker that was nothing more than a limestone rock long since overgrown with gray-green moss.

By the time Poco Jimmy returned, it was almost dawn and misting rain. With him were Sheriff Hamlin Bidd, Coroner Criten Lapp, Corliss Buckmaten, Timothy Burton, and Colin Hamp.

They made quick work of it, then, driving the wagon onto the cedar knoll, the sheriff and coroner getting into the wagon bed to pry open the lids for just a moment, holding the lantern so they could see. Then everyone but Sarah and Drake clumsily got the boxes in place over the hole and down into the earth, using the boards and the rope, then stood back, hats in hand. Drake Brown had begun to cry.

Sarah Brown didn't cry. At last, after what seemed a long time to the others, she broke the silence and said a prayer. It was strong on vengeance and short on the salvation of departed souls. Then she turned and walked down off the knoll in the rain, Drake behind her, wiping his nose with his sleeve, and the cats behind Drake.

One of the others started to pick up the shovel, but Courtland Brown said, "No. I done it so far. I'll do all the rest of it."

For a while, Courtland stood with the shovel, looking down into the grave. Enough light had developed in the east so that the tops of the boxes could be seen, dark gray in the rain. Then he began, and at first the dirt falling on the boxes made a hollow, rattling noise. But soon there was only the thump of wet earth on wet earth, and the sound of his heavy breathing, and from the east, far off, the sound of a locomotive whistle.

It didn't take long. And when it was finished, Courtland Brown said nothing, but took his tools and the rope and the two lengths of board and walked down the knoll to the tavern and inside. The others didn't speak, either, as they went to their horses, head down in the rain, mounted, and started back to town.

The Brown boys had come home.

PART FIVE

PANDORA'S BOX

23

Sheriff Hamlin Bidd sat in his courthouse office, booted feet on the desk before him, and held four papers in his hand. Three were Western Union telegraph message forms and the fourth was a raggedly torn out item from the latest edition of the *Democrat Advertiser*. He held them but did not read them because he already had. A number of times. He knew every word without having to look at them.

He found it impossible at this moment to place them aside. So he held them, as a farmer holds his dried-out ears of corn after a summer drought, as though the heat of his hands could change them, could put green into the lifeless brown husks.

Hamlin Bidd's lips moved slightly as he thought about the words on the papers and what they meant and what he would say to Roman Hasford.

"Damn!" he said aloud. Then thought, Why couldn't it have waited for another year? At least past next November, when there would be a new sheriff elected? Better still, past next February, because by then he would be out of here and on a new farm, a Missouri border farm, and by then looking forward to the explosion of white blossoms along the rows of his apple trees.

"Damn!"

It was a little past three in the morning. He knew that not because he had been watching the moon-faced pendulum clock ticking on the wall, but because the hour had just tolled from the newly constructed belfry on the roof of the very building in which he sat.

When Hamlin Bidd thought about that belfry and its clock, which was every hour when the great gong struck, he shook his head and spat. It had been installed by some son of a bitch from Carthage who went around the country convincing city councils and county judges that their town needed one of these contraptions because all the other towns were installing one. Playing on the itch that made people want to scratch every time their neighbors did.

Can't let the next man get ahead of you, Hamlin Bidd thought.

Anyway, it was past three in the morning. Without any office clock or belfry gong, Hamlin Bidd would have known that because the scheduled northbound freight had just gone through, its whistle blowing and its trucks rattling across the rail sections, shaking windows all over the east side of town and waking everyone the whistle didn't.

He thought for a moment about how things had changed since he first took office. Not just the physical things, like the town's growth alongside the railroad, but the people things as well. Most especially, the people things.

Old Terrance Shadbolt. Yes, getting old now, and Hamlin Bidd remembered the day Roman Hasford had said in his Big House, to Terrance and to Hamlin, you will be the next prosecutor and sheriff. And now Terrance was the circuit judge, in his black robe. And holding himself above politics because he was a judge. Even though he had to get reelected every two years.

And now that fuzz-cheeked Pemberton Grady from Tennessee, who somehow had come in and got Roman Hasford's support and become prosecuting attorney. He always acted like the headmaster of some Goddamned seminary, looking over his pince-nez glasses whenever a felon was brought before him for arraignment.

Owl-eyed little bastard, Sheriff Bidd thought.

Or worse, that damned Alvis Lapp, the city policeman. Bringing in drunks every Saturday night to fill up the jail when the cells were already loaded with serious people, people charged with theft and assault and battery, and when every one of those drunks ought to have been sent home with a kick in the ass.

But no, he thought. Good little Alvis with his police hat brings 'em in and expects me to feed 'em breakfast grub, then work all day on the paperwork vouchers I have to send to the city to get reimbursement, and that damned prissy Harley Stone might get the county the money in the next fiscal year. Just maybe. When the hell is Harley Stone going to decide he don't want to be mayor anymore?

God, where are the old times? Hamlin Bidd thought.

Well, it was too late for a refreshing shave in his bachelor rooms behind the Lapp Undertaking Parlor. There was always hot water there, kept just in case. So now he shaved with cold water at the dry sink in his office, using a large china bowl and pitcher, and a straight razor he kept in his desk. He cut himself only once, and it was a minor cut.

Staring into the mirror above the dry sink, Hamlin Bidd was no more pleased with what he saw than he had been for many years. His mustache was gone completely to gray, as was the sparse hair above each ear. No worry about that on top, because he was bald.

His baldness didn't bother him too much. Nonetheless, he always wore a hat, a gray felt Stetson, narrow brim, indoors and out, winter and summer. He uncovered from time to time, as when some family invited him to Sunday dinner. This didn't happen too often, usually only before elections. He ate pretty well before elections.

Over the years of his tenure, Hamlin Bidd had become perhaps the most powerful man in the county next only to his mentor, Roman Hasford. And if Hamlin Bidd was unhappy with his appearance, he was at least most proud of his record. He had been a good sheriff. He had known from the start that the best peace officers needed to be keen on all that was happening.

"If somebody's ox is being gored," he had said to Roman Hasford, "I ought to know why. And be well acquainted with the ox in question!"

As that morning four days after the Brown boys were buried came on cold but clear and shining, a harbinger of spring, Hamlin Bidd was not the only one around the Gourdville square thinking about his own situation. Corliss Buckmaten had spent only sleepless nights since that gray morning on the cedar knoll at Brown's Tavern. And major among the reasons for his insomnia was the fear that somebody else, particularly a representative of the law, might suspect his involvement in the Brown affair.

Sheriff Bidd had made sure Corliss was aware of the whole mess. Baiting Republicans was one thing, being a possible accessory before the fact of homicide was another.

On that morning, about the time the southbound passenger train came to its screeching, smoky stop at the Frisco depot just at dawn, Corliss rose from his rumpled bed and went to the window of his print shop facing onto the square, in time to see Sheriff Hamlin Bidd leave the courthouse, go to Ennis Lugi's livery stable, reappear on horseback, and ride slowly out the Elkhorn Tavern Road. Corliss Buckmaten knew as surely as he was standing there facing the rising sun that the sheriff was going to Catrina Hills Farm, which did little to calm his nervous stomach.

Corliss was still uncertain about the obituary he'd written. Perhaps, he thought, I should have ignored Sheriff Bidd's comments and enlarged on it.

During their ride back into town after they'd seen the Brown boys put in the ground, the sheriff and Corliss Buckmaten had fallen behind the others, not from any spoken indication that they should, but because Corliss had the sense that Hamlin Bidd wanted to say something for his ears alone.

Which was the case.

"Corliss," Sheriff Bidd had said, "I know you've got to write this in your newspaper. But for the sake of peace and tranquility around here, I'd strongly advise that you keep it toned down."

"Are you trying to control what appears in my newspaper?" Corliss had asked.

"I'm just asking you to use some calm judgment in what you write about all this. It ain't no secret in this county how you feel about Roman Hasford, so I don't think I'm out of line telling you it'd be a mistake to whip that aspect of this mess into a frenzy right at this time."

"Oh. We have to protect the czar of Catrina Hills, is that it?" It irritated Corliss that he had to look up at the much taller Hamlin Bidd when they spoke together.

"No, God damnit, Corliss, I'd think you'd be as interested as me in protecting any of our citizens against wild accusations implied. There's been too much of that in the past. So if you try to make this into something it doesn't appear to be, you'd better be able to prove your words."

They'd ridden a moment in silence, and then the sheriff added, "Just think about the consequences of what you write before you set it in print."

"Consequences to me or to someone else?"

"It slices both ways, don't it, Corliss?"

"Then I can take this as a warning? A threat?"

"I can't judge how you take it. All's I'm saying is, if you go too damned wild on this, it's a pure, solid fact that it's gonna get uncomfortable as hell in this county for a lot of people. Including you."

Well, Corliss Buckmaten thought that morning as he watched the sheriff ride out the Elkhorn Tavern Road, I'm already more uncomfortable than I care to be on account of a bunch of riffraff white trash like the Browns. As I'm always telling Melissa, politics makes strange bedfellows. The only trouble is I'm not sure the Browns are smart enough to understand that politics has everything to do with my opposition to Roman Hasford and all he does.

Once more he ran over in his mind what he had published, wondering if it was enough, wondering if he had buckled under to an unfounded fear.

Funeral services were conducted for Essex and Becket Brown on family property west of Gourdville last Wednesday. The remains were returned from Indian Territory where both men had been engaged in various business enterprises. They were the victims of lethal gunshot wounds suffered at Laughing Road Market near Tahlequah, Cherokee Nation.

Deputy United States marshals from Fort Smith have indicated that they have no clues as to the identity of the person or persons who perpetrated this foul deed.

Mr. and Mrs. Courtland Brown and their sole surviving son, Drake, respected members of this community for years, remain in seclusion at their home.

Melissa came into the printing office wearing a heavy dressing gown, her face puffy with sleep and her hair done up in cotton curlers.

"Corliss, what on earth are you doin' up so early?" she asked.

He didn't answer. She came to his side, placed a hand tentatively on his shoulder. Any time she touched him, it was tentatively. She saw a small trickle of red from one corner of his mouth.

"Honey. What's the matter? You're bleedin'!"

Corliss jerked away from her and wiped the back of his hand across his mouth, looked at the smear of red, and scowled. In talking to himself, as he found himself doing more and more of late, he had bitten his lip without even knowing it.

"Go back to bed," he said.

After she was gone to their living quarters behind the shop, Corliss Buckmaten turned to a tray of type and began to set a page layout, fingers going expertly to the little lead slugs, arranging them in the form line after line. He worked for only a short time, muttering to himself as he set the copy, fury mounting inside him. But unlike most of his rages, this one was directed against himself.

When he was done, he read what he had placed in the page form, swiftly, even though the typefaces spelled out all the words backward.

It has never been our intention at the *Democrat Advertiser* to be party to bloodletting. Distasteful as we find Republicans and Reconstruction, difficult as it is to abide big-money Yankee business practice, much as we abhor certain scoundrels, there has never been in our hearts or minds the lust for maiming and killing except in the just prosecution of honorable warfare.

I, Corliss Buckmaten, swear on the tender soul of my mother that any component we have contributed to the violence visited on citizens of this county was unintentional. But did we play a part? Does some of the responsibility for releasing this storm of political hostility and Old Testament retribution rest on our shoulders?

In keeping with the truth as we always do, it must be admitted. Yes, we do share responsibility.

At this point, Corliss Buckmaten paused, panting with wrath over the unfairness of it all, then continued, his lips moving as he read:

But we cannot retrace our steps, even though it is devoutly to be wished. We cannot recall shafts already let fly. The die is cast, no matter now our disaffection with many of the results, no matter now the horror of it.

We look into the face of a father who has just buried two of his sons and we are ashamed for any involvement we might have had in that event. No matter how innocent the motivation. No matter how blind to future consequences.

There is no innocence. And now it is too late.

Corliss Buckmaten stood before the tray of type, eyes clouded with blinding anger at himself and what he would have called Fate and felt no better for having made his confession, like the confessions he had made as a boy, the priest's low voice from the other side of the dark screen.

For he knew that any such item as he had just set in type would never be published in the *Democrat Advertiser*, or anywhere else except on the pages of his own soul, simply because while he might have been contrite, he would never admit it to anyone but himself.

He heard Melissa moving about in the kitchen in the rear of the shop, and then her footsteps coming near. Quickly, violently, he overturned the tray of set type, scattering the lead slugs across the surface of the makeup table.

24

Roman Hasford and his father were at the breakfast table, and Orvile Tucker was making a great clatter of pans at the huge kitchen stove. On a butcher block were eggs and pork sausage and a jar of hominy and sliced Irish potatoes. Biscuits were in the oven. Coffee simmered in a great cast-iron pot.

"What's the matter with you?" Roman asked.

"We got a mare comin' to foal early, and them hands down at the barns don't know nuthin'."

"Why, hell, you go on down there, then. I can do that grub."

"Mr. Roman, I ain't fixin' to let you ruin a lot of good victuals. The only thing you know about victuals is how to eat 'em."

When Sheriff Hamlin Bidd rode into the yard, all the victuals were prepared and being slapped on the table with considerable abandon. But even in his frenzied activity, Orvile Tucker did not miss the approach of company. He warned Roman, who went out onto the west porch to meet Bidd and invite him in for breakfast, and by the time the two of them arrived at the table, an extra plate and silver and a cup of coffee had already been set down. Orvile had disappeared, on his way to the barns.

"Mornin', Mr. Hasford," the sheriff said, draping his heavy mackinaw over the back of a kitchen chair and dropping his hat on the floor.

"Lark Crozier makes the best honey I ever ate," Martin said, turning a pint mason jar in his hand, the honeycomb inside glistening golden and moist in its sea of liquid.

"I think the bees make the honey, Papa," Roman said. "Sit down, Hamlin. Tie into it."

"Much obliged," the sheriff said.

"You never know where the next mouthful will come from when you're on campaign against the Yankees," Martin said. "And now that damned Grant won't let the sutlers' wagons come across the river. You capture one of those Yankee sutler wagons, you've got brown sugar and real coffee."

"Why, hell, Papa, that's real coffee in your cup," Roman said.

They ate with little conversation, and that about the weather. Each seemed more concerned with the taste of his food, though Roman had little appetite. He'd had little appetite since the news that Ausbin Tage had married Diana Chesney. But now that day was far from his mind, because he knew that Hamlin Bidd had come for something other than a large breakfast, and he had the distinct feeling that it might have something to do with that obituary Corliss Buckmaten had printed in the *Democrat Advertiser*. When they had finished, which took an amazingly short time considering all the food on the table, Roman suggested to his father that he go down to the barns and help Orvile Tucker with that mare.

"I think I will, Doctor," Martin said, and rose with a little bow, then went to a wall peg near the back door, took down a long duck coat, and was gone.

Roman went to the stove and brought back the coffeepot, refilled their cups, and placed the pot on the table. He sat down and leaned back in his chair, then looked at Hamlin Bidd for a long time. Finally he said, "Well?"

"Roman," Hamlin Bidd said, now long past the time when he called him Mr. Hasford, "I reckoned you deserved to know as much about things as I do."

"All that secret running around you've been doing?"

Hamlin Bidd looked a little startled, then smiled slightly, realizing that in various ways Roman Hasford came by as much information concerning the happenings in the county as he did.

"Yes." He produced from his shirt pocket a wad of yellow telegraph messages and took some time smoothing them flat on the table under his blunt fingers.

"You want a cigar?" Roman asked.

"No. I've got to where they upset my stomach." He took up one of the yellow telegraph messages. "I got this over a year ago," he said. "It's from the Federal marshal in Fort Smith. Judge Parker down there had issued a bench warrant for the arrest of Yancy

Crane and the two Brown boys, on suspicion of stealing a lot of horses and cattle in the Nations and sellin' 'em to the railroad. Plus they was in the Territory without authority."

Hamlin Bidd passed the flimsy yellow sheet across the table, and Roman Hasford read it and passed it back. The telegraph message indicated that Sheriff Bidd was being notified because the men in question had been identified as citizens within his jurisdiction, and should they reappear there he was requested to notify the marshal's office at the Federal court in Fort Smith so that someone could be sent to apprehend them.

By now, Roman Hasford had lit a cigar, and the blue smoke curled upward into the cluster of hanging brass lamps above the table. Hamlin Bidd took up the second telegraph message.

"Just recently," he said, "I got this one from the marshal's office at Fort Smith."

He gave it to Roman, and Roman read that Essex and Becket Brown had been killed and that their father had come into the Territory to claim their bodies.

"How did Courtland know they'd been killed?"

"Poco Jimmy," Hamlin said. "He's in and out of here all the time."

Roman grunted and ground out his cigar in a saucer with some honey in the bottom, which made a dreadfully pungent odor in the room.

"It's not all that easy to get a body across a state line if there's been violence," Hamlin Bidd said. "So Courtland couldn't just go over there and bring 'em back. When I got this one, I took a lawyer and Buckmaten to Fort Smith."

"Why Buckmaten?" Roman asked. A sharp edge had come into his voice.

Like his mother, the sheriff thought, when she was coming onto a big temper. "Because, Roman, I didn't want nobody to say later I wasn't doin' fair. And besides, I reckoned Corliss needed to know some of the things those Fort Smith marshals knew about what Yancy and the Browns had been up to over there in the Territory all this time."

Roman Hasford didn't say anything, but his mouth was fixed in a hard line and his eyes did nothing to ease Sheriff Hamlin Bidd's little recitation.

"Anyway, it didn't amount to much. We had to fill out some

papers for the court and then we went up to Tahlequah, where they had the bodies, to make a positive identification. Courtland was there, and once we'd done all the things the law says we needed to do, he brought his boys home. We'd come on ahead, me and the two I'd took with me."

There was a long silence. Then Roman Hasford rose and went into another room and returned with a crock jug.

"This is sour mash," he said. "You want some?"

"No, that upsets my stomach worse than cigars."

Roman poured a small amount into his coffee cup. Thank God he's cooled down a little, Hamlin Bidd thought. After Roman had taken a sip, he looked at Hamlin Bidd and said, "Well?"

"I talked to the deputy marshals," Hamlin Bidd said. "They told me all they knew. After Judge Parker issued those bench warrants for livestock theft, there was some other stuff. There was a lot of talk in the Territory about Yancy Crane and the Brown boys dumping a body in the Verdigris River. Somebody got drunk and bragged about it, they suspected. But they never found a body. Even so, it kicked up a lot of interest in those boys, so when all this happened, the law was close onto it and tryin' to locate 'em."

Roman took a sip of his laced coffee.

"When all *what* happened?" he asked.

"I'm gettin' to that," said Hamlin Bidd. "There's this place just west of Tahlequah called Laughing Trail Market. A little store where you can buy a few things. Not very big. Got a counter with one of those coffee grinders on one end, shelves for various goods, and bins for dried beans and Irish potatoes, like that. Couple of little tables along a back wall where folks can come in and sit down and have some cheese and maybe a can of peaches. And some whiskey. Hard as they always try, the marshals can't keep whiskey out of the Territory."

Hamlin Bidd paused, drawing a deep breath. He took a sip of his coffee, which was cold by now, then wiped his mustache with the ends of his fingers.

"Anyway, the man that runs this little store on Laughing Trail fought with Stan Waite during the War Between the States. He lost an eye somewhere. The Fort Smith marshals call him Squinch. All's that happened in that place, so far as he knew, he told the Fort Smith people, and they told me. Everybody said they trusted him, and he was a good Cherokee and was an informer for the

Cherokee police for a long time, and for the marshals out of Fort Smith, too. He knew the Browns and Yancy. So what I know, the marshals told me they heard from Squinch. Hell, I don't know what his real name is. I never met him."

"It's a long route to what happened, isn't it?"

"It's all the route we got, Roman," said Hamlin Bidd.

"Tell it, then."

"Well, it was one of them cold nights, rainy, dismal. The two Brown boys and Yancy come into this Laughing Trail Market and Poco Jimmy was with 'em. They all went back there to one of them little tables and bought some cheese and a fruit jar of peaches and set down to eat. They all had rifles and leaned 'em against the wall just behind where they was sittin'.

"Poco Jimmy, he didn't stay very long. There was a family of Cherokees on the porch, cold weather or not, sittin' out there talkin', and Poco Jimmy went out to talk with those folks because there were a couple of young women there, I guess that's why he went out."

Hamlin Bidd poured himself another full cup of coffee from the pot on the table and took a long swallow, wiped his mouth, and went on, not looking directly into Roman Hasford's face.

"It was just a usual evening there," Hamlin Bidd said. "Just people sittin' and havin' cheese and peaches. And talkin' on the porch. Then these two white men rode up. Both on good horses and split-tail overcoats with fur collars. They got off their horses and one come up on the porch and started talkin' with Poco Jimmy and the other Cherokees, just normal talk.

"The other one went on inside. Squinch said he came in and stood at the end of the counter where the coffee grinder was, and Squinch was in the middle of makin' another pot of coffee, so he said he'd be there in just a minute, pourin' water into the pot and all.

"But right then Becket Brown got up from the table where the boys was sittin', and come up to the counter to get some more peaches, or maybe some more cheese, and when he was about to say what he wanted, he seen this man behind the coffee grinder. Squinch said Becket Brown just stopped and his eyes popped out and he opened his mouth to say something, he thought, and reached inside his coat. That's when the shootin' started.

"Well, Squinch, like any sane man would do, fell flat on the floor behind his counter to keep from gettin' hit with stray shots, and he said it didn't last very long. Maybe three heartbeats, he said.

"By the time he stood up and looked, Squinch said, the white man who'd done all the shootin' was gone. And outside, him and the other white man just got on their horses and rode away without too much hurry-up. Like they'd just been havin' a glass of lemonade at a church social."

Hamlin Bidd licked his lips. Roman Hasford had begun to make a little drumming sound on the tabletop with his fingertips.

"Squinch kept everybody out of there. He sent Poco Jimmy into Tahlequah for the Federal marshal who's stationed there. Happened to be another one, too, workin' on a case. They were out there within twenty minutes. They said they could still smell the powdersmoke when they went in. What they found was a slaughter pen.

"The Indians who'd been on the porch was still there, tryin' to see inside. A couple of Cherokee policemen had showed up. But they were all stayin' out of it because this was white man's business.

"The marshals asked Squinch why somebody hadn't tried to stop the two men from ridin' away, and he said they didn't look like the kinda fellas it would be easy to stop."

Roman kept drumming, staring straight into Hamlin Bidd's eyes. Hamlin Bidd licked his lips again, took a quick sip of cold coffee, and went on with it.

"Anyway, Becket was in the middle of the floor. Hit twice. Liver and heart. Wasn't any weapon on him. He died a little while after the marshal got there, a few minutes after. Over against the wall behind the table where the boys had been eatin' cheese and whatnot was Essex. They'd brought in these Winchesters and leaned 'em again the wall, and Essex tried to get one in action. It was in his hands. The lever was down where he was tryin' to get a round into the chamber. He was shot once, in the face, just in the left eyebrow. They said there wasn't much left of the back of his head. He was dead when the marshals got there.

"There was blood all over the place, and they figured Yancy Crane had been hit while he was tryin' to get out the back door. But they didn't know for sure. Most of the blood could have been from Essex. You know how head wounds bleed.

"So what happened then was that Poco Jimmy rode right over here and told Courtland, and Courtland went to the Nations. And the marshals took the remains into Tahlequah to an undertaker they got there."

Now Hamlin Bidd brought forth the last of the telegraph messages and passed it across the table to Roman Hasford. And as Roman read it, the sheriff poured fresh coffee into his cup.

What Roman read made the skin along the back of his neck tighten.

IN YOUR INTEREST STOP YANCY CRANE TREATED FOR NON-LETHAL GUNSHOT WOUNDS MUSKOGEE VETERINARIAN DAY AFTER AFFAIR LAUGHING ROAD STOP LAST SEEN MOVING HORSEBACK NW POSSIBLY NOWATA STOP BE ALERT HIS RETURN YOUR AREA STOP ARREST AND HOLD STOP USE CAUTION STOP HEAVILY ARMED AND DANGEROUS STOP UNITED STATES MARSHAL, WESTERN DISTRICT OF ARKANSAS, FT. SMITH.

Roman read it again. Then dropped it on the tabletop. It meant, of course, that Yancy Crane was still out there.

Hamlin Bidd took all his little yellow papers and folded them and put them in his shirt pocket.

"I think those Fort Smith people are a little more interested now in getting Yancy," he said. "I think they figure if there wasn't something more serious than livestock theft on his ledger, Yancy wouldn't have run so hard."

"Do they know about Elmer Scaggs?" Roman asked.

"Sure. But it's not in their jurisdiction, and they know I haven't got anything to hold Yancy on with Elmer. All's we got is suspicion. Maybe someday we'll have more. Who knows? Remember, there ain't no statute of limitations on murder in this state."

Sheriff Hamlin Bidd leaned back in his chair and sighed, happy he had it all out. He'd been rehearsing his words for two days, ever since he had that last telegraph message from Fort Smith.

"Those two men who came to Laughing Road Market that night," Hamlin said, "nobody could give much of a description. The one outside never got into the light. Nobody inside got much look at the other one, the shooter. Except maybe Becket Brown, and it was the last look he ever had, I guess. Squinch told the marshals he was just makin' another pot of coffee, and when this man came in, he just said to him he'd be right with him, just glanced at him, you know. Said he had on a good long coat with a fur collar and a hat down low over his head. Man never said a single word, just stood there behind the coffee grinder. Then all hell broke out."

Hamlin Bidd took a sip of coffee and realized he hadn't added any sugar to it. He did now, stirred, and sipped again. At least Roman Hasford's cold eye wasn't on his face anymore, which the sheriff took as a blessing. Roman was staring instead at one of the bright windows, fingers still drumming, but more lightly.

"I can't say it surprises me much," Hamlin Bidd said. "Lot of hard people come and go in the Territory. And the kinda business the boys were in will make you a lot of enemies and a lot of friends you can't trust. I always figured the Fort Smith law would have to hurry or somebody else over there would beat 'em to it. Maybe it was more than just a rumor about Yancy Crane and the boys dropping a body into the Verdigris. Maybe a couple of this person's friends or family finally caught up to 'em. Well, good coffee. Think I'll have some more."

"Help yourself," Roman said.

"One other thing, Roman," Hamlin Bidd said. "No matter how this happened, you know as well as I do that Courtland Brown and God knows how many other people in this county are gonna hold it against you."

"I know that."

Sheriff Bidd stirred his coffee, waiting for Roman to say more, to provide some clue to things maybe the sheriff didn't know. But Roman said nothing.

"I'd like to think the whole thing would stop now," Hamlin said. "I'd hoped it had stopped already, with the boys being gone so long. Now, who knows? You just be watchful and don't go ridin' around after dark. You got anybody here you can trust?"

"Orvile."

"Anybody else? Those hands you got workin' for you?"

"They shovel shit. That's about the size of it."

"Well, me or Colin Hamp'll be ridin' out now and again, just to keep an eye on things. I'll be watchin' the Browns pretty close, too."

"Aw, hell, Hamlin," Roman said, "the Browns aren't gonna do anything. It's their old friend that bothers me."

"Me too. I'll keep a watchful eye."

"I appreciate it. Now finish your coffee and let's go down to the barns and watch Orvile work that mare."

"I'd like to, but I better get back to town. I got all these God-damned vouchers to write and give the city on drunks the county's fed on Saturday nights. Alvis Lapp is drivin' me crazy."

Roman Hasford laughed, and it amazed Hamlin Bidd that he would laugh now, about anything. Sure, it wasn't a happy laugh, but it was a laugh anyway.

"Watch out for yourself, Roman," the sheriff said as he rose from the table.

"I'll try my best."

Roman spent the rest of the morning walking around his wide front yard, touching his crabapple trees, caressing the cold, smooth bark, looking at the twigs on the far end of branches where soon there would be the buds, then the blossoms, then the fruit. But he wasn't thinking about crabapple trees.

He was thinking about Diana. Her golden hair. Her face as he saw it so many times across Oak Creek when she came and smiled at him. And what he now considered her imprisonment at the Chesney farm. And he wondered why, in this modern age, there were no longer knights in shining armor, such as he had read of in *Ivanhoe* and the King Arthur tales. Knights in shining armor to rescue maidens in distress.

But always with the thoughts of Diana came those of Catrina as well. His own imprisonment. And the haunting depth of her black eyes. And her fragile beauty, like a woodland flower, delicate yet somehow enduring.

He thought of his mother, too. That rock-hard jaw. That determination. That softness of her fingers on his face when he came to her for answers to questions she could never understand.

And finally he thought of Jared Dane.

This whole business made him a little sick. Because he was just beginning to realize that some things set loose can never be put back in the cage. He was just beginning to appreciate the old Greek myth he had read so often, the myth of Pandora's box. He had begun to feel with all his senses the texture of agony with only one possibility of hope. But so far he had not discovered the features of hope's face.

And so, that morning, came the thoughts of Jared Dane.

Roman Hasford didn't fool himself that he'd developed some humanitarian compassion for the Brown boys and Yancy Crane. He'd suspected all along that they were responsible for the murder of Elmer Scaggs. And he was sure that Jared Dane had proven it to his own satisfaction before he went looking for them in the first place.

Even so, this killing left a foul taste in his mouth, and part of its flavor was the fact that he, Roman Hasford, had set events on their inexorable course by reaching out to the Kansas enforcer.

From his years in Leavenworth, Roman knew the kind of man Jared Dane was, and no matter Roman's helplessness and apprehension over the forces at work when Elmer Scaggs was killed, he'd known also that asking Dane's help was like turning a wolf loose in the lamb's fold.

The Browns and Yancy Crane and all the rest of that type around here are just country-bumpkin toughs, Roman thought, and Jared Dane's a professional killer. And I knew that.

Roman had never held much with guilt. What's done is done, his mother always said, and no need getting a long lip over it. But now that was part of the flavor, too.

He'd gone over in his mind the details of that meeting in Topeka. Word for word, as best he could recall it. He'd been doing it for a long time. At least since he'd received the cryptic letter from Dane after the Browns and Yancy Crane had dumped him in an Indian Territory river.

Why hell, he rationalized, I just told him all I wanted was justice. I didn't pay him any money to go around the countryside shooting people.

Now, after Sheriff Bidd's little visit, he had to face a truth he'd really known all along but refused to accept. Justice to Jared Dane didn't mean collecting evidence and turning criminals over to the law. Justice to Jared Dane meant giving the other man half a chance, if that much, then executing him. And Roman knew no payment was required for such a service where he was concerned.

Why, hell, he thought, Jared Dane always looked on me like I might be a member of the family he never had, maybe a little brother that he would watch over. And even knowing the kind of man he was, it was a comfort to me. A comfort to know all I need do was ask him, and he'd be there for me.

Maybe Jared Dane didn't have anything to do with this, he thought. Maybe Hamlin Bidd was right when he hinted that some other hardcase in the Nations had done it. Somebody would have said something about the killer having one arm, wouldn't they?

Now that the Civil War veterans are dying out, one-armed men aren't all that common anymore.

But nobody had said a word about one-armed men in that bloody Cherokee store. So it couldn't have been Jared Dane, Roman thought.

But this attempt to wriggle out from under his discomfort was as hollow as all the other rationalizations. He knew that he, Roman Hasford, had done this thing, even though indirectly, through Jared Dane. Whether Dane had pulled the trigger or had hired it, he, Roman Hasford, president of the Farmer's and Merchant's Bank of Gourdville, had done this thing. It made the cold chills climb his back as nothing had since that day he'd lain in the dry bed of Arikaree Creek, on Beecher's Island, and seen the Cheyenne coming. Except that then he'd been victim of circumstance. Now, he couldn't shake the feeling that he *was* the circumstance.

As he came back to the Big House at noon, his father was waiting on the porch. In Martin Hasford's hand was Roman's shoulder-holster harness and the Colt pistol. As his son approached, Martin held it up.

"You forgot this," Martin said. "Need to wear this, you know."

Despite everything, Roman laughed. And went up the steps and took the gun from his father and squeezed his father's shoulder. They looked into one another's eyes, Roman knowing that in some things and in some moments, his father was not so lost in the pathways of his mind as he might appear. Martin had heard not one word Sheriff Bidd said that morning, yet he sensed that the visit had not been for friendly breakfast alone.

"Thank you, Papa," Roman said. "I'll try to remember."

Martin turned away then, but his gaze was still sharply defined as he looked along the treeline east of the house.

"I took that heavy Winchester out of the rack," he said. "I thought at night I'd keep it in my room. When I was with old John Bell Hood in Virginia, I could shoot pretty good."

Roman laughed again. "Papa, you could shoot pretty good a long time before you ever heard of John Bell Hood. Let's go inside where it's warm and have a sip of brandy."

"All right, Doctor," Martin said, and his eyes had gone vacant again.

25

Roman Hasford rose each morning from his bed in the west room, where he'd slept each night since he'd first brought his bride here, the master bedroom remaining empty, with Martin Hasford now in the east room. As soon as he'd made his toilet and dressed, the shoulder holster with the pistol went on and stayed until he undressed for bed that night. And there were always two Colt revolvers on the table beside his bed.

Martin Hasford had begun to make a circuit of the porches each evening at sundown, carrying the Winchester rifle he kept in his room now, looking like a sentry on duty. Orvile Tucker kept a Savage heavy-bore rifle in one corner of the kitchen, and when he left the house he always carried a single-barrel shotgun and a pocketful of double-ought shells.

Neither of these men, Martin or Orvile, was privy to what Hamlin Bidd had said, which amounted to the fact that Yancy Crane was still out there somewhere and very dangerous. But seeing Roman constantly armed, they guessed something was in peril and made their own arrangements.

Despite what they all obviously assumed were hazardous times, Roman chuckled watching his father, grim as one of Lee's soldiers at Cold Harbor just before the Yankee attack, and seeing the intense, hostile, bloodshot glare in Orvile Tucker's eyes each time he left the Big House with that old ten-gauge cannon.

Why, hell, Roman thought, if some poor pilgrim happened along the road looking for directions, he'd likely get his ass shot off!

The barn hands were all terrified, of course. One of them quit without asking for his pay, simply fading away one night. Nobody knew he was gone until the next morning, when Orvile had everybody out as usual, exercising the mares that were about to foal. The other three hands might have gone as well, except that they probably figured Orvile would come after them with that old shotgun.

Andy Gimshaw, one of the hired hands in question, was on his evening off in Torten's Billiard Parlor, complaining about the dictatorial methods of his foreman. Ausbin Tage, from his usual place at the six-pocket pool table, asked why he put up with such foolishness from a blue-gum nigger.

"I don't know about the blue-gum," Andy said. "But listen, that ain't no ordinary nigger."

"Why the hell you stay on out there?" Glen Torten asked.

"I like them horses," Andy said. "Besides, it pays better than anything else I could get around here. Gimme another glass of beer and one of them pickled eggs you got in the glass jar, Glen."

"Yeah," said Torten, "you can drink all the beer and eat all the eggs you want, but the way you get run around out there at Hasford's, you ain't gonna get fat. You gonna stay as skinny as you are now."

"What the hell," said Andy, brushing a spray of straw-colored hair out of his eyes. "It's a good job. Better'n what most got around here." And he looked at Ausbin Tage.

"What's that supposed to mean?" Ausbin Tage asked.

"You take whatever taste you want from it, Ausbin, but if you start at me with that pool cue, I'll hafta shove it right up your butt."

"Now now, boys, now now," Glen Torten said.

Once each week, Renée Crozier drove a wagon to Catrina Hills Farm from Wolf Cove to pick up laundry and deliver a bundle of washed and ironed clothes and to clean the Big House. Recently, she had begun to bring little Hasford Crozier with her, knowing that the child would be well entertained and delighted with the company of Roman's father, no matter how long it took her to do her chores. Orvile Tucker, knowing the days Renée and her son would be there, always had a plate of oatmeal cookies or gingersnaps waiting on a large plate on the kitchen table.

A little more than a week after Hamlin Bidd came with that

handful of telegraph messages, Renée and the boy arrived with Lark Crozier, who promptly presented himself to Roman, bearing Ora Hasford's shotgun.

"Mr. Roman," he said, "iffen you need, I can lay in awhile here."

"You don't need to do that, Lark," Roman said. "But I thank you." And he thought, Renée's told him about me going armed. Why, hell, everybody must be expecting me to board up the windows and lay in grub for a siege.

Then Judah Meyer, the bank cashier, drove out from town in a buggy, looking frightened at the prospect of trying to control the wild and vicious animal in the stays, actually one of Ennis Lugi's more docile mare drays.

Judah offered his support in whatever way it was needed, and that of Gallatin Delmonico, who naturally could not come himself, involved as he was in the banking business. But mostly what Judah Meyer said was that everybody at the bank looked forward each day to Roman Hasford coming back, and that when he did he would be surrounded by friends who would see to his safety.

See to my safety, Roman thought, as he lay in bed that night. Judah Meyer and Gallatin Delmonico would likely shoot themselves in the foot if they ever picked up a firearm.

Well, Roman thought, Hamlin Bidd has been talking around town about Yancy Crane, I expect. The snarling mad dog. And I'm beginning to suspect it's all a big wave in a teacup, as Mama used to say, and likely Yancy Crane has long ago passed Colorado and gone on to Oregon or some such place. How long can a man seek vengeance?

And here with the supposed renewal of old troubles, he thought, my protectors are a senile old man, some colored people, a fussy little Swiss whose idea of violence is a two-penny discrepancy in the day's ledger, and a Yankee calculating machine called Judah Meyer. Any one of whom would appear ludicrous to any of my enemies.

Mama might be turning in her grave, he thought, but it is more and more difficult for me to take this seriously.

And although he would never do anything to disparage his friends' good intentions, he had to laugh to himself. Cynically, sourly, but laugh nonetheless.

All of which had something to do with his decision to start back to work, if that's what it was, each day. A show of defiance and disregard for stories about danger. Past time to sulk like an old possum.

He dreaded only one thing: James Chesney coming into the bank to visit. As might become frequent, now that James Chesney's affection for Martin had seemed to make it easy for the dour Scot to converse with Martin's son.

But, he thought, a man has to face up to unpleasant possibilities sometimes. Like being face-to-face with a person whose affection would turn to hatred if he knew my part in his family's shame.

Well, maybe the biggest reason for Roman's decision was his certainty that if Ora Hasford were still alive, she'd be furious with him for staying holed up like a timid rabbit in a dark, hollow log.

The day came on warm for March, and Orvile Tucker saddled what he called the best stallion he had bred since leaving Kansas, a three-year-old blue roan he called Sparky because of the way sunlight glistened on his coat. It was a good time for that part of it, because the sun was dazzlingly bright and Sparky was ready to show off his splendor.

Roman knew the horse would be a bull-bitch to handle, borrowing a phrase from Anson Greedy.

"We're gonna have to get that Sparky with a few more mares and then geld him," Roman had said. "He's a fine saddle horse, but he's ill-tempered as a crocodile and he's got a mouth harder than a cast-iron skillet."

"You ain't geldin' that horse, Mr. Roman," Orvile had said, his great eyes bulging. "He's a straight line from old Excalibur you rode in Kansas and that blood Morgan mare. And he gonna sire a whole string for us."

"All right. But when somebody rides him, they better have a length of two-by-four lumber to bust him between the ears when he takes a notion he's the boss."

On the morning of Roman's first departure for town in weeks, he walked onto the north porch and looked at the horse standing at the foot of the steps, Orvile Tucker beside him holding the reins. Both horse and man were glaring at Roman, daring him to say something, and Roman took the dare.

"Well, I see you've got it all planned that I break a couple of legs and rupture myself trying to control that son of a bitch."

"You be good to him, he be good to you."

Roman went down the steps and checked the cinch just to irritate

Orvile, who he knew had likely checked the cinch four times already. Sparky snorted and quivered, and his nostrils flared and his eyes rolled.

"My God, why didn't you just go out in the woods and saddle up a panther for me to ride?" Roman asked.

"They ain't no more panthers in these woods around here."

"Good thing, too. This beast would go out there and stomp 'em all to death."

Roman was hardly firm in the saddle when Sparky broke around the house and down through the crabapple trees and onto the road at a dead run. Then past Ephraim Tage's house in a shower of gravel, and when Tage's old dog ran out to bark the horse very nearly ran him down. The dog went back into the yard to stand in the weeds looking after the cloud of dust and likely wondering what the hell had just passed by.

"Go on, horse," Roman yelled, leaning his face into the whipping mane.

Just inside the town, they scattered a flock of chickens feeding on the grain in horse droppings along the road. Sally Agnes Quint, whose chickens they were, was hanging clothes in her yard and promptly screamed, shook her fists, dropped two of Lorton Quint's just-washed shirts into the dust, and almost choked on a pair of clothespins she held in her mouth.

Into the square, then, and Roman managed to get the horse turned toward Ennis Lugi's stable after sending a mule-drawn buggy onto the sidewalk in front of the mortuary.

Puffing and laughing, Roman dismounted at the open barn door at the livery. And when Ennis Lugi appeared he said, "Give him a nice rubdown."

It was a wonderful ride, one that Roman had enjoyed almost as much as the horse.

In fact, the whole day had started well, with that crazy con-frontation at his own breakfast table, Orville Tucker and his father insisting they were coming with him into town, their rifles already leaning against the wall. He'd convinced them they needed to re-main at Catrina Hills to protect property.

He recognized the pitiful nature of the whole thing. Had Orvile and his father come in, heavily armed, citizens would have taken cover behind the fire barrels around the sidewalks of the square, seeing this pair waving big-bore weapons, one of whom they considered a half-wild African and the other a half-demented old man.

As for the rest of the day, it went so wonderfully that Roman couldn't understand why he'd stayed away so long. Everybody in the bank spent the day bowing and scraping and telling him how wonderful he looked. When he'd first walked in, he saw rifles behind a few desks and filing cabinets and told Gallatin Delmonico to get rid of them at once, and so right away they were carried back to Caulder's Mercantile from whence they'd been borrowed, along with a number of boxes of ammunition. Enough ammunition to conduct a major campaign against the Comanches, Roman figured.

He went into his office and closed the door and laughed at all these poor civilized moneylenders trying so hard to look like barbarian bodyguards. Then he was ashamed, and opened his door and went out and patted everyone on the shoulder and asked about their families and exclaimed on the beauty of March in northwest Arkansas, and sent the bank boy, a mentally deficient forty-year-old named Arno Cleevis who kept the place clean, out for three dozen doughnuts from Raymond Ort's bakery.

During the day, he had visitors. Sheriff Hamlin Bidd came in to give greetings. As did Isaac Maddox, with information on fox-racing plans. Also Alvis Lapp, the policeman, and Pemberton Grady, the prosecuting attorney.

You'd think I had just risen from the dead, Roman thought. Which is pretty close to what I have done.

He went to Anson Greedy's barbershop for a haircut and a shave and a mustache trim. And there he heard the story about Brian Felcher's dairy bull getting loose the week before and charging across the square, scaring hell out of all the horses, then on down Elkhorn Street, scaring hell out of a drunk just staggering out of Glen Torten's place, then across the railroad tracks and into the schoolyard, where they were having recess, and all the kids squealing and running, and the bull going right into the front door of the schoolhouse itself. And as the bull came in the front door, Anson Greedy said, the Reverend Kirkendall and that other teacher, Noble Carnes, went out the back door, and by the time Brian Felcher got there the Mrs. Reverend Kirkendall was leading the bull out of the schoolhouse by the ring in his nose. Which was no great surprise because the Mrs. Reverend Kirkendall was Glamorgan Caulder, and no bull, especially a dairy bull, had ever issued from cow that could not be handled by any one of the Caulder women.

Anson Greedy took almost an hour to tell this story, in little bits and pieces between sessions of razor-and-scissors work. And through all of it, Anson was tactful enough not to mention the shoulder holster and heavy pistol under Roman's left arm that stayed in place from start to finish.

The end of the day was good, too, when Roman went to Lugi's livery to get his horse, and Ennis Lugi said, "Mr. Hasford, I'd as soon you didn't ride this stud hard when you come into town so he needs a rub after you drop him off here. The son of a bitch bit me three times and kicked me twice, and tried more than that. I like to never got the saddle back on him. Mr. Hasford, you oughta geld this damned horse."

"Geld this horse?" Roman asked. "Why, hell, Ennis, if you're good to him, he'll be good to you."

"Damned if that's so."

The Big House looked like home that evening as Roman rode in, the setting sun putting a fringe of gold on the weathervane atop the roof, the kitchen windows glowing with orange light. It looked more like home to him than it ever had before. Orvile Tucker had fried chicken, and the whole house smelled of the white-flour gravy. And best of all, Roman thought, this one day of breaking out again into old routines had eaten up the tension, seeped it away like the air from a child's balloon. Martin Hasford, for the first time in two weeks, did not patrol the porch that evening.

But Martin still had that big Winchester in his room. And Roman, when he went to bed, still had the two Colt pistols on his night table.

And he had something else, too. A habit he couldn't break. Lying awake for an hour, sometimes two, his mind racing in all directions. Unpleasant directions.

There was always Catrina, hovering just below the level of consciousness and popping up at unexpected intervals. She in that Missouri convent school, and he not knowing where it was leading. He'd lost all initiative in Catrina's regard. Like a man watching the weather and having no control over its dimensions. It was a helpless, infuriating situation, and he had no notion of how to deal with it. Courtland Brown with a shotgun, which he would know how to handle. But the relationship between himself and his legal wife was like a delirium cloud of shifting color, impossible to grasp.

And now he had begun to dream about Catrina. Not as she had been in his mother's house, nor as she had been in the Big House, and certainly not as she had been after he discovered he himself could not amend the extent of her abuse. But as she had been in Kansas when his heart ached with sympathy for a beautiful, battered child living like an animal in an old mule barn with an unspeakable monster for a father.

Well, he thought, pity sure got me in one hell of a mess, didn't it?

Sometimes he became so bitter with such thinking that he vowed silently never again to allow himself an instant of compassion for anyone, never again the weakness of a soft heart.

There had been tenderness. With Diana on those afternoons last summer along Oak Creek. A tenderness he had never known before. During all his younger years he had been thwarted in his response to being in love. And when at last he'd overcome his ineptness, it was too late. He'd had to take the happiness of reciprocated love covertly, like a weasel slipping into the henhouse. And now, all turned to disaster—the child and a distasteful marriage to avoid bastardy.

He struggled to keep it out of his mind. But sometimes, late at night, with or without his dreams of Catrina, the memory of Diana came equally uninvited, strong as the odor of honeysuckle, the sun in her hair as it blew against his face, the softness of her lips and fingertips caressing his mouth, the warmth and willingness of her body. And these memories, which should have been as sweet as Diana's kisses, were agony now. When they came, he allowed them only a short run, then swore and threw off his blankets and sat on the edge of the bed. And reached under his night table for the jug of sour-mash whiskey, in lieu of the Kentucky bourbon, he had begun to keep there as a matter of course.

He'd kept a diary when he was in Kansas. It seemed a good way to record all the wonderful and terrible things that were happening to him on the path to manhood. He'd always planned to show it to his mother and father, but never had. Because it had gotten out of hand. He'd written things he didn't want anyone to see, things that embarrassed him or revealed too much of his secret self that he was unwilling to share with anyone.

He had stopped writing when he came home to stay. He'd been busy with getting the bank and the horse farm started, and other things, of course, but he'd stopped mostly because he had come to feel that grown men did not keep diaries. He'd never known of a man in his family, or any other man in northwest Arkansas for that matter, who did. Sometimes a woman might keep what she'd call a journal, but never a man.

A man, thought Roman, doesn't slice up his soul in little pieces and pass them around for somebody else to giggle about. There's just a lot of things a man keeps to himself.

Yet, even though he may not have realized it, writing in that diary had been a release, allowing tension and confusion to flow away in the brown ink on the pages, so that each night he could do his scribbling and then lie down to restful sleep.

But now there was no diary. Instead, there were the sleepless nights of trying to spell out the words on the pages of his mind. But they wouldn't stay put, they darted around, out of his control, no ink to make them legible in the morning.

Now, in the morning, there was the mossy aftertaste of sour-mash whiskey, only the names lingering, all loose, without foundation or structure or moorings, floating free of his will like the white particles of ash that rise and dance crazily in heat waves from a dry-leaf fire.

Jared Dane. Catrina. Mama. Yancy Crane. Diana.

And Berdeen, a name that had no face in his mind because he had never seen her.

The second morning of his coming out, Roman rode a more docile Sparky. Instead of turning west to town, he reined the horse to the east and rode to the old Hasford homestead.

After a short, bareheaded visit to his mother's and grandfather's graves, he went to the old house. All the windows had been broken out by passing boys testing their rock-throwing skills. There was a thick coating of dust on the floors and on the cookstove, the only thing Lark Crozier had left behind. And gray bird droppings across the cast-iron lids where Roman had seen his mother prepare so many meals.

There were charred logs in the fireplace, and ashes scattered across the parlor floor, and a stained feather tick where some passing tramp had slept. There was a scatter of tin cans and, in one corner, where Ora Hasford had kept her china closet, a dried pile of human feces.

It seemed so terribly small. Roman stood in the front doorframe, the door itself long since burned in the fireplace by someone, and in the wall near his face were the bullet holes, reminders of the Battle of Pea Ridge that had been fought here, in his mother's yard and garden.

He remembered Christmas here, the smell of cooking food, the texture of cedar needles fallen from the tree onto the floor under bare feet when he and his sister, Calpurnia, came down with the dawn to see if there were any presents left by Old Kris. He remembered the sound of his father's voice, strong and sure, telling the stories of Christmas in the old country, stories his own father had told him. He remembered the richness of his mother's laughter. And the bright and shining smile of his sister when she teased him about the volume of cornbread dressing he managed to stuff down his gullet. He remembered the sound of the owl in the hollow where the spring water bubbled from the limestone, and the gentle chuckles of his mother's guinea hens as they consumed the worms and bugs and spiders in the yard.

Roman stood in the doorway, leaning against the walls of his boyhood home, looking down the slope through the grove of black locust trees, where he had been when the first partisans rode into the valley and he had seen their columns and the frosty breathing of their horses in the cold air. And he recalled the night he and his mother had stood on this porch and watched the light of Elkhorn Tavern burning.

As he had done a great deal recently, he wondered at his inability to cry. Sometimes he had been ashamed that tears came, but now he was ashamed that they didn't.

That night he drank a great deal after supper, trying to ease a constant, nagging little pain in his lower gut, but once in bed he slept immediately. And had disturbing dreams about his sister, Calpurnia, when they had both been young, with her constantly teasing him and him thinking she was surely the most wonderful and beautiful creature he would ever know.

26

It was a blistering summer. But those who cared to notice saw a change in other weather. The *Democrat Advertiser* spoke in dulcet tones, and the president of the Farmer's and Merchant's Bank seemed to go out of his way to smile and glad-hand everybody, once even greeting Corliss Buckmaten as the newspaper publisher was going into Harley Stone's hotel dining room for his noon repast and Roman Hasford was coming out.

"I seen it," Raymond Ort told Anson Greedy. "Just a normal 'howdy,' I'd call it. But I never seen such good cheer on Mr. Hasford's face."

"Well, at least Roman didn't take in to shootin' at him," said Anson Greedy. "I wonder what it was Harley Stone fed him that day."

"Roman Hasford had sliced tomatoes, vinegar cucumbers, and night before's fried chicken livers. Harley said Corliss Buckmaten was so upset all's he had was rice puddin'."

"You can take them ole-line rebel aristocrats out of the cotton patch," said Anson. "But you'd play hell takin' the rice off their menu. For me, I'd as soon leave all the rice to the Chinamen."

The next issue of the *Advertiser* carried one of the summer's few old-fashioned attacks on banks, Republicans, and railroad lovers. Although Corliss Buckmaten mentioned no names, everybody knew whom he was gouging.

No one gave it much serious thought. Too many good things were happening, even if it was hot and dry and dusty and ticks and chiggers were worse than anybody could recall. For two days in

July it rained and cooled down, but then the clouds all departed for Tennessee, and summer started all over again.

There were some good fox races that summer, although hot weather was not the best time for such things. But as Isaac Maddox said, "You got to keep the dog and the fox thinkin' about what's comin' up in the fall."

The worst part of summer races was that no fire was built for spitting into or warming butts nearby. Rather, the men stood around their lanterns on the ground and hoped that none of their dogs would die from heat prostration before they grew tired of running some old gray that didn't have enough sense to stay denned in such temperatures.

The peach crop was good, but prices were down on the cotton and tobacco markets. Apples were coming red ripe by mid-September, and south of Gourdville, around Tadmor, they were growing grapes that made juicy nibbles and excellent wine. Stone Mountain watermelons were the best in memory, and every Monday morning Alvis Lapp, the policeman, had to borrow a cart from his daddy's undertaking parlor and go around the square picking up rinds that lined the outer edge of sidewalks where the kids on Saturday night had sat to eat what had seldom been bought but often stolen from the fields near town.

Said John Vain, "If I catch those little bastards in one of my patches, I'll give 'em a dose of rock salt in the butt with my old shotgun."

Although John Vain spent many nights slinking along his fence-rows, he never managed to catch a single towheaded thief. But each Monday morning the rinds from his melons decorated the square, attracting swarms of flies and flocks of chickens before Alvis Lapp could get them carted away.

There was only one serious crime committed that summer, when a Madison County man came through, got drunk at Brown's Tavern, and with a knife made several incisions along the ribs of Harold Sample. Harold was eighteen, and feeling it was time to start sowing his wild oats began by going to Brown's and drinking more popskull whiskey than he could possibly handle, then remarking to the stranger that he was such a backwoods hick he didn't know the difference between distilled vinegar and apple wine, Harold considering himself an expert on such matters in view of the fact that his father was Omer Sample, who owned the vinegar works beside the railroad track. It was at this point that the stranger produced a fourteen-inch blade and began his work.

The Madison County man was arrested just short of the Indian Territory line by Deputy Colin Hamp, brought back, tried, and on conviction told by Circuit Judge Terrance Shadbolt to leave and never come back or he would be released on the public square to be dealt with by enraged citizens.

Harold Sample decided that Brown's Tavern, once visited, was visited once too often, and never returned. He did begin to establish a reputation of note, becoming a favorite of many young ladies to whom he promised to show the artistic pattern of Doc Cronin's stitches in his superficial but numerous wounds. All of this educational revelation in return for a few kisses.

"The Goddamned younger generation is goin' plumb to hell," said Harold's daddy Omer.

So the summer wound down. At Catrina Hills Farm, Orvile Tucker was looking closely at bone and muscle and head structure of all the foals dropped in the spring. Martin Hasford had forgotten the purpose of the heavy rifle in his room. He spent most of his days in the shade of the east porch, drinking lemonade and eating gingersnaps and staring across the treetops toward his old homestead.

Sometimes now, at the supper table, Martin would confide that he had been talking to Ora that day and that she was keeping their farm in proper shape and making crocks of sauerkraut and waiting for her husband to return as soon as he recovered from his bad cold. He no longer spoke of General John Bell Hood.

Then it was October. One of those wonderful falls. And the evening Roman would always remember. Darkness came on by suppertime, the brilliant rust and yellow and orange leaves of the hardwood timber on the west ridge looked black against the faint red sky left by departed sun. There was the sharp snap of frost in the air, and somewhere toward the east hounds were running, their voices coming clear and vibrant through the crisp, calm twilight. It was a time when Orvile Tucker's kitchen felt warm and secure and full of all the good smells of kitchens in autumn.

After the meal was finished, Orvile began his usual clattering clean-up. Martin Hasford went upstairs to sit on the edge of his bed in the dark for a short conversation with himself before he slept. Roman moved to the parlor, lit a lamp, and sat in his favorite chair with a new book Owen Caulder had brought to the bank, having decided it was something Roman might enjoy.

Before opening the book, Roman poured a pint-sized brandy snifter half-full of sour-mash whiskey. The Kentucky bourbon had begun to burn his gut down low, so he'd switched to the sour mash, which was distilled locally and came in crock jugs. These jugs, like the Kentucky bourbon bottles before them, were located at strategic positions in the house, and each day Orvile Tucker made the rounds, picking up the empties and replacing them with full jugs.

It was part of that supply system Orvile had devised a long time ago so that Roman Hasford would have no need to worry about it. When he reached, there it was, Orvile Tucker operating like a good staff officer in an army, although he'd never been close to an army. Yet he understood what a lot of famous generals never learned, that procurement was more than half the battle.

Each week, barn hand Andy Gimshaw had the duty of hitching two mules to a wagon and running errands. His first stop was Benjamin Tark's distillery, where he bought whiskey and exchanged a great deal of gossip and observed the interesting things that happen around a distillery. Then he drove to town and stopped at Caulder's for groceries, then on to Felcher's dairy for milk and cheese, then Chesney's slaughterhouse for meats. Andy always went to Ben Tark's first so that he might have something to sip during the rest of his rounds. This routine took the better part of a day. Andy left Catrina Hills just after breakfast and returned just before supper, usually by then more than a little drunk. Orvile Tucker always threatened to maul him with a singletree if he ever got into Mr. Roman's whiskey again. But never did.

So when Roman reached for a jug, he knew there would be whiskey in it. He had never said anything to Orvile. He didn't have to. The whole thing was taken care of as routinely as pumping water into the tank that sat under the roof of the Big House and supplied the needs of all faucets and toilet seat.

With the new book in his lap, Roman had taken a cigar from a decanter on the small library table beside his chair and was about to light it when the bullet arrived. It came with the sudden, stunning rush of all unexpected bullets. It burst through the west-side stained-glass door window, crossed the dark dining room and the foyer at the foot of the staircase, and shot into the parlor where it smashed the hand-painted china globe of Roman's reading lamp, sending a sunburst of shards and flaming kerosene onto the rug.

It had been a long time since Roman Hasford had heard the sound of a bullet at the target end of its flight. But, once heard, it is a sound hard to forget: a sharp, snapping crack, and an instant later the faint pop of the weapon itself, the sound following relatively slowly behind the high-velocity passage of the projectile.

There was no thinking involved for Roman, only instant response. He was out of the chair and into the far corner of the room, away from the line of fire, vaguely aware of his father shouting upstairs, of Orvile Tucker shouting from the kitchen, and then all the lights there being extinguished. But the flaming kerosene on the floor in front of the bookcase sent a wavering yellow light through the room, and Roman bent and yanked up his edge of the rug and folded it over onto the flames, kicking the chair and the library table aside as he went. The room was suddenly dark, like the rest of the house, and the harsh odor of smothered fire stuck in his nostrils as he backed away again, away from the straight line from west door to dining room to foyer to parlor, and now he was in one corner, pulling the Colt pistol from the shoulder holster and cocking it.

"Mr. Roman!" From the kitchen.

"I'm all right. Stay away from the windows."

He waited for the next shot, and thought how absurd it was, standing with that cocked pistol, which wouldn't do him any good at all because the bullet had come from a long way off, out of range of any pistol. He slid the Colt back into the shoulder holster, then heard the beat of his father's footsteps from above. Then a strangled cry and a loud thumping. A lot of thumping.

"Papa?"

There was no answer.

"Orvile?"

"I'm here," from the dark kitchen. "I'm goin' out to look."

"Stay in the house," Roman shouted. "Papa?"

Still no answer.

"Orvile?"

"Right here, Mr. Roman."

"I'm going up the steps."

He felt his way in the dark, but quickly, because he knew this house well from all the time he had negotiated it in darkness when he'd had too much whiskey. Halfway up the steps, his feet found something soft, bulky. Roman bent to feel in the dark and it was his father, sprawled on the stairway, head down. In his hands was the large-bore Winchester rifle.

"Orvile! Come here!" Roman bellowed.

He could mark Orvile's passage to the foot of the steps and then upward, fast, because Orvile knew this house in the dark as well as Roman did. Then Orvile was beside him, his hands on Martin Hasford.

"I don't feel blood."

"He's not hit. He fell. Strike a match."

"Not here, Mr. Roman. No light here."

"God damnit . . . "

But Orvile was already lifting Martin in his great blacksmith's arms, going up the stairs and into Martin's room, and, swearing softly, Roman followed, carrying the heavy rifle.

Orvile had Martin Hasford on the bed, and now he struck a match and it made a foul sulfur odor and only a dim, quivering light.

Martin's mouth hung open and his skin was the color of old pancake dough. His eyes were open and the pupils were so enlarged they seemed to eat the whole of the blue iris. The flickering light did not make the pupils dilate.

The match flickered out and Orvile Tucker had his head on Martin Hasford's chest, ear down, listening.

"Heart like a little biddy gallop," he said. "Little biddy gallop."

Roman touched his father's face with both hands, and the skin was cold. Orvile was pulling a blanket up over Martin Hasford's form.

"Papa," Roman said. "Can you hear me?"

"I think he's got a stroke, Mr. Roman," Orvile said.

"Orvile," Roman said, his hand still caressing his father's face, "get a horse. Ride for Doc Cronin. Then Hamlin Bidd. Get those people out here."

"You gonna be all right?" Orvile asked. "What if them folks done the shootin' come in here?"

"I wish to hell they'd try," Roman said, and his teeth ground together. "Orvile, take that long shotgun."

"I will."

"Don't ride the road. Go the backwoods. Anybody tries to stop you, don't talk. Shoot."

"I will."

Martin Hasford made a gurgling sound and heaved upward on the bed.

"It's all right, Papa," Roman said. He held the blanket up beneath his father's chin.

"You got that big rifle?" Orvile asked.

"Yes, right here. Go on now, go on."

"I will."

Roman had only the sense of Orvile moving, because he heard nothing. He remained on his knees at the bedside, his hands on Martin Hasford's face. The labored breathing made Martin's neck expand and collapse.

Roman began to speak, softly, wanting to reassure with his voice. He found himself recounting aloud the times when he had been a boy and the two of them went into the woods and Martin showed him how to find bee trees and how to trace the movement of deer from their browsing or how to drop a line in the right pool of White River to catch a smallmouth bass. And maybe, most important of all, how to sit in a warm house in winter and read the words of Mr. Gibbon or the Bible or any of the other books that sent the mind far beyond this valley. Roman spoke the words softly, hoping his father could hear. His hands under the blanket on his father's chest could feel the heartbeat, uncertain but undeniable.

Why, hell, Roman thought, this man made me and then taught me and then was a hero in Lee's army, and now he's dying under my hands without even knowing who I am!

Roman came to a pause in his recitation of the past, and Martin Hasford made a gentle coughing sound. Then from the darkness came Martin's voice, weak but somehow with the tone that Roman could remember as a boy.

"Roman?"

"Yes, Papa."

"Somebody took a shot at us, I think."

"Yes, Papa."

"They missed, didn't they?"

"Yes. And they won't get another chance."

There was something like the old gurgling chuckle from better days.

"Roman?"

"Yes, Papa."

"I'm a little bit cold. Could you have your mama bring a comforter?"

"Yes, Papa."

Roman moved in the dark to the closet in this room, found a fat feather tick, and brought it back and lay it across the blanket on his father.

"How's that, Papa?" he asked. But now Martin Hasford had gone back into heavy breathing, his chest quivering under Roman's hands. Roman knelt at the bedside again, silent. And waited for Orvile Tucker, feeling furiously helpless.

It took two hours, but it seemed much longer. Twice during that time Martin Hasford seemed to stop breathing but struggled up mightily, his chest surging. The breath rasped in and out, sounding like a bottle held under water and the air bubbling up.

Roman heard the hack drive into the yard and then Doc Cronin's step across the porch, the west door flung open, the same door with the bullet-shattered window.

"Mr. Hasford!" Cronin yelled into the dark house.

Roman lit a lamp and went down to guide the doctor up to his father's bedside. In the light once more, Roman could see his father's face, and now as before the pupils were dilated, deep, inky pits without any sign of light.

Orvile Tucker arrived as Doc Cronin began his examination, pulling down the blanket and moving his stethoscope along Martin Hasford's chest, where the hair was like thin bristles of white silk in the opening of the unbuttoned shirt.

"Orvile," Doc Cronin said without looking up, "get a fire started in that stove over there, and one in the kitchen, and some water on the stove. I want to bathe his face and chest."

"Sheriff's downstairs, Mr. Roman," Doc Cronin said. "Nothin' you can do here. He's not gonna know you for a while anyway."

In the kitchen, without speaking to Hamlin Bidd, Roman stoked the still-hot coals in the kitchen stove grate, put a pot of water on, and only then went into the parlor and lit a lamp and another in the foyer and yet another in the dining room. After all the hours of darkness, the house was now aflame with light.

Finding no one wounded by gunfire, Hamlin Bidd became almost pensive as he moved about the parlor. There were cigars scattered across the floor and bits of broken glass and Roman's brandy snifter, intact and on its side and still with a tiny pool of whiskey in the bowl.

Hamlin found the bullet embedded in a copy of *Around the World in Eighty Days* on the bookshelf. It was a copper-jacketed slug, mushroomed at the nose from its contact with the pages of Jules Verne's prose, but the base was intact. Hamlin Bidd turned it in his great, blunt fingers, frowning, and finally said, "Looks like about a .30-caliber, maybe. One of these new military loads, from the length of it. I never seen one like it before."

Roman didn't really care what the damned thing was; his thoughts were only on the room upstairs. He kept remembering Doc Cronin saying that Martin Hasford would not know him. But by God, Roman thought, he knew me for a few minutes and spoke to me. He knew me. He *knew* me.

Deputy Colin Hamp arrived and tried to have secret words with the sheriff, but Hamlin Bidd said it was all right to talk right out, and Colin said he'd done all the checking around like he was supposed to. Courtland Brown had been at the tavern all day and all night, and the usual bunch had been at Torten's pool hall until closing time, and everything was calm at all the saloons. It had been quiet, like nobody was aware that a shooting was planned, and nobody strange had come in on the evening train. There was the meeting at the Odd Fellows' Hall, with no excitement either, so it looked like maybe the shooter had just come in without anybody knowing it and blasted away.

"You're gonna make a damned fine sheriff, Colin," Hamlin Bidd said.

They were all in the kitchen, a new pot of coffee on the stove, which Hamlin Bidd had put there, and Roman Hasford at the table, clutching his hands before him and gritting his teeth.

"God damnit," Roman said.

"Doc's doin' all he can," said the sheriff.

It was about three in the morning when Andy Gimshaw came to the kitchen door to report that the other two hired hands had departed on foot, bag and baggage, and that he felt a little defenseless out there in the night with nothing in his hand but a pitchfork. Orvile Tucker, in the kitchen at the moment to fetch a cup of coffee upstairs to Doc Cronin, made no reference to Roman at the table but went into the smoke-smelling parlor and came back with a sixteen-gauge double-barrel shotgun and some shells.

On the back porch, he handed all this to Andy and asked, "You know how to use this?"

"Hell, yes, it ain't nothin' but a shotgun."

Orvile spent the rest of the night going up and down, taking up towels and water and coffee for Doc Cronin.

"God damnit," Roman said again, holding a cup of coffee between his hands, well laced with sour-mash whiskey.

"Doc's doin' all he can."

It was coming on gray dawn when Orvile Tucker came down, went onto the porch and whistled, and Andy Gimshaw came running.

"Get a saddle on somethin' and ride to Wolf Cove Mill and get the Croziers over here," he said. "We need somebody to lay out the dead."

"Oh, my dear sweet Jesus," said Andy. "You think so?"

"I know so. Do it now, boy."

It wasn't long after that when Doc Cronin himself came down, with his little black bag. He sat at the table and sighed, took off his spectacles, and looked at Roman and shook his head.

"Wasn't anything anybody could do, Roman. He's left us."

The new day came on bright and shining, a blazing sun in a cloudless October sky. Andy Gimshaw returned with the Croziers, and Renée went up to Martin Hasford's room to prepare the body. It would be carried in to Tilman Lapp's mortuary and thence back to the old Hasford homestead to be buried beside Ora Hasford. All these details were arranged and handled by Sheriff Hamlin Bidd.

"We'll put him down tomorrow," Bidd said. "I'll send Colin in with the body when Tilman gets here with his wagon, and I'll have Colin get Reverend Kirkendall to come out for a service. About noon, is that all right?"

Roman sat at the table, still staring into the cup of coffee held between his hands, and he nodded. But said nothing.

"I'll stay here with you until we get it all done, Roman," Hamlin Bidd said.

Roman made no response.

But after a little while, Roman rose and went up to the room where Renée had just finished wrapping Martin Hasford's body in a blanket, securing it with safety pins. For a moment, Roman stood beside the bed.

"I want to see his face," he said.

With her long, sepia fingers, Renée undid the pins at one end of the cocoon and pulled down the blanket. Roman knew this was his father but could not recognize him. Renée had closed Martin Hasford's eyes and placed pennies on each.

"Where'd you get the money?" Roman asked.

"It's only mine own, Mr. Roman," Renée said. "You want me take the money off?"

"No. Cover him."

Downstairs, Roman saw Hasford Crozier for the first time, standing in one corner, knowing something terribly bad had happened, his great black eyes wide in his little face. Roman had started toward him when Orvile Tucker came in from the back door, his face set in black, stony fury.

"You better come," he said to Roman.

Afterward, everyone said it was as though Roman Hasford were sleepwalking, saying nothing, doing as he was instructed. He walked that way to the stables, Andy Gimshaw leading all the others there, Hamlin Bidd and Orvile and Lark and Hasford Crozier. When Andy Gimshaw showed them what he'd found at the far end of the horse barn most distant from the house, little Hasford Crozier began to cry, Hamlin Bidd swore a furious, obscene oath, and Roman simply stood staring, as though it were another cup of cold coffee between his hands.

On the floor of the stall were three of the foals from last spring's birthing. They lay with their spider-thin legs crumpled beneath long, slender bodies. In the straw of the stall was a short-handled, ten-pound sledge hammer. Obviously the instrument had been used to crack each skull.

From the far end of the barn they could hear the mares gently nickering, calling to their children.

There was in Roman Hasford's mind a truth as sure as any religious zealot's faith that his father had died because of the attack on Catrina Hills Farm and on himself. As though the bullet intended for him had found the brain of his father. He could not shake the thought that Martin Hasford had gone through a savage war and then returned home to end up the victim of his son's enemies. It was therefore most catastrophic for a particular enemy of Roman Hasford that the letter came only three days after Martin had been buried beside his wife at the old Hasford homestead.

It was a short message, sent through the mail in an envelope showing no return address and a stamp cancellation from a Missouri Pacific railroad train somewhere in eastern Kansas. Just one page, without salutation or signature. A plain sheet of foolscap with no letterhead. But Roman Hasford would have known who sent it, even had he not recognized the handwriting.

During recent convivial bordello visit in company of a Topeka journalist, was informed that previous to my initial adventure in Indian Territory when my intentions became known regarding certain parties of interest to you, a small man appeared claiming himself to be a publisher and showing an uncommon interest in our past associations. This occurred after your visit to Topeka but before my unscheduled swim in the Verdigris River. Now, after all these years, as one of your favorite authors would say, the truth will out.

Roman Hasford immediately burned the letter. There was no need to read it a second time. He sat for a long while at his library table, staring at the rows of books, then took a sheet of paper and a pencil from the table drawer and designed a simple little diagram with three words and arrows pointing from one to the next.

COURTLAND → YANCY → VERDIGRIS

After a while, he added two more words at the front end.

CORLISS BUCKMATEN

Immediately he burned that paper as well, and was amazed at how evenly his heart beat, at how calm he had become. Almost detached, as though recognizing a problem the solution to which would require even-tempered thought.

Why, hell, he thought, reaching for the sour-mash jug, I'm not even flying off the handle. Maybe this is what maturity means.

And from the kitchen, Orvile Tucker could hear that caustic laughter he'd heard so often in past months.

27

After the Catrina Hills horse massacre, as everyone called it, the citizens of the county braced for new trouble. They weren't sure what kind of trouble or from where it might come or how, but a lot of these people who had migrated from the mountains of Kentucky or Tennessee or West Virginia understood the flavor of feuds and how such things fed on themselves. So they watched Roman Hasford with considerable apprehension, and they waited for Yancy Crane to reappear because they were as sure as a jury ready to hand down a verdict that Yancy Crane had taken that shot at Roman Hasford and killed those horses. And likely caused Martin Hasford's stroke. At least that's what Doc Cronin said.

They watched Courtland Brown as well, except there wasn't much for anybody to watch who didn't frequent the tavern on the Nations Road, because old Courtland never left the place, dispatching Sarah and their son Drake into town when required for sugar or coffee or winter underwear.

"All the way 'round," Anson Greedy said, "it's breath-holdin' time."

But nothing happened.

"Calm before the storm," they said.

But the calm stretched out into fall, past election day, when Judge Shadbolt won two more years on the circuit bench, Colin Hamp became the new sheriff, and Newton Black was elected county judge, a nonjudicial position as the county's chief administrator. All with Hasford backing. Maybe not much visible backing this time around, but with plenty of money, the source of which was no mystery to anybody.

All successful candidates had been opposed by the *Democrat Advertiser.*

But people noted that editorials from the hand of Corliss Buckmaten had become almost as calm as everything else. Not so much raving and ranting, they said. Well, old Corliss being old Corliss, a *little* raving and ranting. But nothing like some of those earlier elections, when you'd think the paper would catch fire from all those words printed on it.

Anson Greedy summed it up for everybody. "Old Corliss must be sick."

"Maybe Roman Hasford's sick, too," replied Isaac Maddox. "He didn't do any electioneering this year, but he's been at that bank ever' day. I don't think he missed but four days right after Martin died, comin' in town to that bank."

"You got a suspicious bent to you, Isaac."

"Yeah, well, I just simply don't trust all this peaceful shit around here. I've seen too much of this kind of thing."

Roman Hasford made a conscious effort to remain highly visible, even with the certain knowledge that someone out there would enjoy putting an end to him. It was more than defiance. It had to do with his not wanting any hint given that he was planning for what would happen next. He wanted everybody to believe that nothing would happen next, so far as the Trouble was concerned.

It made Orvile Tucker very nervous, watching Roman ride away toward Gourdville each day, alone. But trying to change a Hasford decision was harder than turning off the wind, as he knew from long experience. So he had to satisfy himself with recitations of impending doom each night at the supper table.

"You hangin' yourself out there like one of them tin cans you used to shoot."

"Whoever it is," Roman said, "hasn't got the guts to come at me head-on."

"You ain't got no eyes in the back of you head. An' you come home after dark lots of times. An' why don't you show more respect for your dead papa and stay home awhile."

"I'm not some old maid who's gonna mope for a year with a veil over my face."

"Then get somebody to ride with you, Mr. Roman."

"I guess you want the job. So you can get into town every day."

"Mr. Roman, I got more jobs now than I can handle. 'Sides, that ain't my kinda work anyway. I ain't Elmer Scaggs. Maybe you never noticed. I ain't even the same color as Elmer Scaggs."

"Why, hell, Orvile, I'm too old a man to get into a blue funk when luck runs a little bad. Pass me down that bottle of stomach medicine Doc Cronin brought. My belly aches."

"It ache all the time 'cause you in a blue funk whether you know it or not, ridin' around the county by yourself."

He made a concession to Orvile's concern. Maybe to placate him. Or maybe just as a change of mind, something different. Or maybe he decided he did need another Elmer Scaggs.

Roman Hasford informed Hamlin Bidd of his intention to hire a man. It was right after the election, and with the sheriff soon to step down from office, Roman offered the job to Bidd. But the offer was declined.

"When I get to be a private citizen again, I don't want to carry no firearm around all the time. I want to grow apples. You probably don't even need such a man, civilized as we're gettin', and everybody talkin' about bringin' in this telephone thing."

"Civilized?" Roman echoed, and laughed. "A man sits in his own home and somebody shoots at him? Civilized?"

"Just a one-whack thing, I'd bet. He ain't been back, has he? Probably long away from this part of the country. Whatever, Roman, I'm gettin' too old to be tryin' to scare off hardcases."

Even though he refused the job, Hamlin Bidd found a man who seemed to fill Roman Hasford's requirements. His name was Bishop Eckor, and he'd been a roustabout for railroads building through the Indian Nations and a horse wrangler for a rich Cherokee family at Tinkiller and God only knew what else. He was a young man, maybe twenty-eight or so, Roman guessed, hard as an oak crosstie and with about the same complexion, dark hair and brown eyes, and a knowledge of firearms that made Roman a little apprehensive when he started wondering where and how it had been acquired.

Nonetheless, Roman hired him, so now citizens of the county observed the president of the Farmer's and Merchant's Bank going and coming with this Bishop Eckor just behind on a big bay gelding and with a large-bore Winchester rifle in the saddle boot under his left knee, and who could guess how many sidearms under his coat.

Having set this situation in motion, Roman Hasford began to have second thoughts, not only because it might destroy his attempt at an appearance of tranquility but also because somebody taking

Elmer Scaggs's place, more or less, made him recall vividly a loyalty that had led to a run of atrocities. So Roman determined to keep his distance from this new man, never allowing him in the Big House, never having close personal conversation with him.

"Mr. Roman, you treat that Bishop Eckor like he was a mangy dog," Orvile Tucker said.

"Orvile, you're getting to be a cranky old man," Roman replied.

"The 'old' part I can't do nothin' about, and the 'cranky' part is 'cause you do thangs make me wonder."

"Well, wonder no more. I want this new man to love the money, not me. You think he needs pattin' on the head, you do it."

"Mr. Roman, it ain't in me to pat him. I don't even *like* him. He cold as a woodyard wedge. But you done hired him."

"Orvile," Roman said, "just so he's got good eyesight and remembers which side he's on."

"You see? Everybody got to be on a side, don't they?"

"I didn't build it. I'm just tryin' to live in it."

A lot of folk around the county thought Roman Hasford *had* built it, this thing they called the Trouble. And sometimes, after a few too many drinks of whiskey or a few too many steins of beer, a few of those who were just on the edge of it tried to keep the Trouble going, being ignorant of its consequences for themselves, or else thinking there could be no consequences, or else having run out of any other gossip.

And like a lot of men who got a vicarious jolt from imagining somebody else's bloody nose, when they were a little drunk it was a lot of fun to put strangers in their cubbyholes. And so it was with Roman Hasford's man Bishop Eckor. Most especially in Glen Torten's Billiard Parlor in the late Friday afternoons of growing cold weather.

"Another bird dog," said John Vain. "Just like Elmer Scaggs. Anybody remember him?"

"I do," Cato Fulton said. "But at least this one ain't as ugly or loudmouth as Elmer Scaggs always was."

"Loudmouth?" Glen Torten said, leaning on his bar and watching two pool shooters in back who had racked balls three times but only paid for one game. "Hell, I don't know nobody's heard this peckerwood say a word. I don't know if he even knows how to talk."

"Well, I'll tell you somethin', boys," said John Vain, "I ain't gonna go up and gouge him in the ribs to find out."

The Trouble receded farther and farther into memory as winter marched along, maybe because there were no manifestations of it, or maybe because there were so many other things to think about.

Mother Caulder died and was laid down beside old Jeff in the growing Methodist cemetery. At the funeral service, preached very well, everybody said, by Reverend Claudis Kirkendall, son-in-law of the deceased, Roman Hasford sat in the front pew with the family. Everybody was a little stunned to see a Hasford in church after all these many years, and some wondered if, as he sat in the house of God, he still had that single-action pistol under his coat. As a matter of fact, he did.

Only a few people who attended that burial had even been in the county when Lizbeth and Jefferson Caulder drove into town with their bulging wagon and forever changed the structure of the retail mercantile business in that part of the state.

So now the Caulder store was in the hands of Gwendolyn, the only daughter not married to a schoolhouse somewhere, and in good hands, everybody said, because it was a dyed-in-the-wool fact that Gwen was tougher and smarter than all the other Caulders put together.

Hell, some of the Old Settlers could recall that when the Caulder wagon first came into this county, it was Gwen using the bullwhip on those oxen. Or was it Glamorgan? Well, no matter. It was hard to keep those girls separated in memory. But if you thought now you could go in that store and talk somebody into a better price for something, they said, you were in for a rude surprise, because Gwen Caulder could sell fourteen dollars worth of pinto beans and put sixteen dollars in the till and put a pound and a half of beans back in the bin.

Owen Caulder had already announced his intentions before his mother died, and those included marriage to the daughter of a man in Tadmor who was minister of the Shiloh Primitive Baptist Church there. Her name was Callie and she was the granddaughter of the founder of Shiloh Church back in 1842. That intention was rock-solid, the people said, once Owen bought a gold wedding band in Dr. Thorman Gooch's drugstore and paid the staggering sum of forty-eight dollars for it.

More important was Owen's plan to migrate south, even south of Tadmore, to a little mountain community called Weedy Rough, where he would buy into a mercantile store using money he'd saved through the years plus whatever additional funds he might need in the form of a loan from the Farmer's and Merchant's Bank of Gourdville.

Owen made his good-byes in early spring. They included going to Catrina Hills Farm and spending the better part of an afternoon there, not walking but riding a Catrina Hills mare, and where old Trixie once trotted behind him, there was now a whole pack of the best fox dogs in the county, about half of them Trixie's brood.

Owen confided to Roman Hasford that the real reason he was going to Weedy Rough was more than the old Caulder itch to move on, more than the prospect of starting a good business in a new community. The real reason was that Weedy Rough nestled in some of the wildest hill and timber country in the state and boasted more gray foxes per square inch than any other place in the whole universe.

Gourdville was changing, and a large part of it seemed to be its young breaking out from old forms, to the consternation of their elders.

Why, there was young Adam Matt, son of the Democrat postmaster, standing on the porch of Republican Anson Greedy, waiting to pay court to Anson and Barbara Greedy's daughter, Iva Lee.

Why, there was Denny Felcher, a good Baptist famous for having broken his arm the day the railroad came, paying thirty-five cents at a pie supper for a coconut pie prepared by Dodi Lugi, daughter of the stablemaster and Presbyterian to the hilt.

Why, there was Lucerne Delmonico coming home at Christmas from the young ladies' college she was attending in Akron, Ohio, and scandalizing the town by showing striped red and white stockings above her high-top, pearl-button shoes, which could only be done when Lucerne lifted her skirt above the ankles, as she found many occasions to do.

The younger kids had stopped stealing John Vain's watermelons, mostly because there were no watermelons to steal. Now they took John Vain's pumpkins, for what reason nobody knew, because unlike the watermelons, the kids certainly couldn't eat raw pumpkin. The Reverend Zechariah Smith held a Baptist revival, assisted by visiting clergy from Monet, and claimed that many souls had been saved from among the county's sinners. However, the volume of business in the town's saloons was not affected.

Judah Meyer, the cashier at the Farmer's and Merchant's Bank, was making regular trips on the Frisco to Fort Smith, where there was a synagogue, and now daily wore a little black and gold skullcap on the back of his head, which many of the women in the country said was very attractive but that everyone knew Judah wore to hide his bald spot.

Then there were longer-standing residents who departed, not like Mother Caulder into the grave, but to Texas, as they said— away from it, whatever "it" was—and in the night sometimes, not even known about until certain yard dogs or cats that belonged to these departed folk began to appear at other doors for some kind of provender.

Sometimes these displacements had a certain odor of shame about them. As in the case of James Chesney.

This dour Ulster Scot had heard the remarks being passed about his little baby granddaughter, the Chesney bastard. And while he knew he could himself stand against such things, he came to know as well that when this beautiful child, her hands and fingers magic along his cheeks, got to school age, she would face those same taunts. And not knowing whether she'd be tough enough to stand them, James Chesney finally decided he would not put the child to such a brutal test.

So James and Molina packed a wagon and left, mule-drawn, at least as far as Van Buren, where they would board a train for Texas. And carried with them Diana and the baby.

The Chesney Meat Packing Company, as it had come to be called, would be operated by James's son Campbell, established in the old Chesney homestead with his new wife, Hazel, daughter of Doc and Rolanda Cronin. And thus-far-bachelor Hiram Chesney would run the tie yard and live in the house behind it just now being built with Farmer's and Merchant's money.

Roman Hasford heard of the move well after it had been accomplished, when Hiram Chesney casually mentioned it to Judah Meyer in the bank lobby. It was only midafternoon, but Roman left the bank, went to Lugi's stable for his horse, and rode to Catrina Hills, establishing himself in his parlor, where a new rug had been laid, but where there was still the smell of burnt wool, and thereupon launched a five-day drunk.

Mostly because when James and Molina Chesney and Diana and her baby, Berdeen, had slipped out of the county, Ausbin Tage had gone with them. Roman took his first drink of sour mash thinking about that scaly necked peckerwood raising little Berdeen as his own daughter, and the thing got worse with each succeeding sip. And there were a lot of sips.

Roman Hasford had never been short on imagination—which he'd always taken as a good thing, entertaining, an exercise of painting pictures on the canvas of his brain—but now it became a brutal, sickening thing. Yet somehow it was fascinating, to be encouraged. Another drink, and another more vivid picture. Seeing in his head the lovely Diana with Ausbin Tage. Giving for him as she had for Roman. Whispering in Ausbin's ear, as she had in Roman's, "You make me so happy."

Were they together intimately only in darkness, or did Diana open herself to him in full light of day, as she had to Roman?

During those five days, with all the images in his head, all the questions he could not stop asking himself, he broke each and every one of his fine brandy snifters by throwing them against the bookcase. He also loaded one of the rifles in the rack and went out in the darkness and fired a full magazine toward the surrounding night, cursing at the top of his voice. He also, just at dawn one day, raged into the dining room and shattered the hand-painted bone china he had bought for Catrina as a wedding gift, piece by piece, until the floor was deep in jagged shards like knife-edged snowflakes.

And when he collapsed at the end of each orgy, no matter where he was, no matter the time of day, Orvile Tucker came and lifted him and carried him to his bed and covered him and waited. And then, when Roman came around, Orvile brought milktoast and poached eggs and spooned them into Roman Hasford's mouth like a mother feeding an ailing child.

I gotta get out of this place, Orvile thought. But knew he never would.

It was during the recuperation from his five-day binge that Roman Hasford stood for the first time before his shaving mirror and saw the gray in his hair at the temples and a fringe of it, like frost, along the lower edges of his mustache.

PART SIX

THE BABYLONIANS

28

Frisco had been a name admired, a name next only in glory to that of King David, who had pulled it all together in another wilderness and made things work. But in that time after Mother Caulder was laid down and James Chesney took off for Texas with his bastard granddaughter, it looked as if the Babylonians were coming.

"And you know what *they* did," said John Vain, although he wasn't really clear in his mind what they had done, or how long after King David was dead that they'd done it.

Nor was anybody else.

But it didn't matter about Holy Scripture. You could fit Holy Scripture to anything that came along. That's why it was holy, maybe.

What was happening now with Frisco, and a lot of other things, made some people in the county understand that, King David or not, there was a second edge to the blade of Progress. An edge they were feeling. An edge that hurt. Some men, who had been ready to wave banners for the railroad at the start, now spoke the word *Frisco* and spat.

People began paying attention to Corliss Buckmaten's editorial comments once more. After all, Corliss had been attacking the railroad from the start, and now there was reason to appreciate his words. A monster, he wrote, controlled by a Yankee, Republican government.

For some time a few citizens had been reading in the newspapers available once a week in the lobby of the hotel and in Doc Gooch's drugstore, newspapers from the North, about railroads rebating a lot of freight charges to preferred customers. And about disparate charges for long and short hauls. And about stagecoach lines being squeezed out by loss of mail contracts. But what the hell, everybody in the county said, that's all happening up in Pennsylvania or some such far-off place.

Well, now it was happening right there in the county. Those wild words Corliss Buckmaten had been writing for so long became more than little symbols on newsprint. Nor did he have to mention the czar of Catrina Hills Farm anymore, because he'd been doing it so long that everybody by now associated Roman Hasford with the railroads automatically. So a great many folk whose sympathy had been with Roman after three of his foals were murdered forgot about the foals and started thinking instead about their going deeper in debt at his bank because their profits were drying up.

The copy in the *Democrat Advertiser* became searing and vicious about the railroad situation. The Old South, Corliss wrote, destroyed once by overwhelming Yankee armies, was being destroyed again by overwhelming Yankee money. People got the point. Money, in this county, meant the Farmer's and Merchant's Bank of Gourdville.

"Corliss ought to be happy as a sow in slop," said Isaac Maddox. "But he ain't. He acts like his best dog just died."

"Corliss is sick, I tell you," Anson Greedy said. "He ain't actin' natural."

Natural or not, all of the *Advertiser*'s portents seemed justified when the United States Supreme Court passed down a decision that the various states could not enforce any local law that interfered with interstate commerce, so that even if a citizen could throw some heavy weight with a Little Rock legislator, or maybe the governor or even a senator, it didn't matter for anything. The railroads were protected by the Yankee Republican government and its court, just as Corliss Buckmaten had said all along.

Benjamin Tark, the biggest distiller in north Arkansas, said, "It costs me more to send my good brandy and sour mash to Monet than it does if I was shipping it to St. Louis. But Monet is my market. I can't compete with them big distiller people in St. Louis."

Which was true.

Omer Sample had the identical problem with his vinegar and apple cider.

As for apples by the bushel, John Vain said it cost him more to ship a hundredweight to Tennessee's western border than it did for New York apple growers to freight theirs to Little Rock, and it was more than five times as far from Albany to central Arkansas as it was from the Vain orchards to Memphis.

There was more. All attributable to the Roman Hasford stripe of hardhearted money man, according to the *Advertiser* and without Corliss Buckmaten having to mention Roman Hasford by name. When you mention a money man, everybody said, who else is there?

Like tobacco.

"My God," said Cato Fulton one night at the Odd Fellows hall. "All my wholesale customers has stopped buyin' my plug and pipe and cigar leaf. Because if they buy anything from somebody besides them Duke's Mixture people in Carolina, then them Duke's Mixture people won't sell 'em any of these new tailor-made cigarettes."

"You gotta start growin' tailor-made cigarettes," Glen Torten said.

"You know what, Glen, you're a real funny man!"

Melissa Buckmaten watched her husband through all this, and although she had never spoken a word to Anson Greedy in her entire life, she found herself holding the same opinion as the barber: her husband was sick. He had become withdrawn and irritable. His stomach was always upset.

"You looked so much better all last winter, honey," she said, "when you didn't get so mad setting these terrible things you say about rich men and everything."

"What would you have me do?" Corliss asked. "Report the births of calves and the results of spelling bees?"

"You just don't act like you have any joy in life anymore."

"I'm sorry, my dear," Corliss said, wiping his face with a handkerchief, as he did almost constantly now. "I don't have any choice, do I? It is my duty to point out things these ignorant hill farmers could never understand otherwise."

"Well, it looks to me like anybody can understand going to the poorhouse."

"Yes," Corliss muttered. "Yes. But perhaps I can help them know why, distasteful as it might be."

"Well, sometimes I wish we'd never left cotton country."

"Yes, I know."

* * *

Corliss Buckmaten's renewed diatribes in the *Democrat Advertiser* were not lost on those at Catrina Hills Farm.

"Mr. Roman," Orvile Tucker said, "you ain't done none of that railroad stuff. It's beginning to get on my nerves."

"It's been getting on my nerves for a long time," Roman said, sipping his sour mash as he sat in the library, looking at Orvile standing in the doorway wearing a half-apron just like Roman's mother always wore.

"You orta let me go down there some night and burn that newspaper place down," Orvile said.

Roman laughed. "Orvile, you're gettin' mean in your old age."

"Mean is mean and right is right," Orvile said.

Roman Hasford was no longer laughing, or even smiling. His face had clouded over with some quick, twisting movement, and his eyes became hooded.

"I will destroy Corliss Buckmaten," he said softly. "And all the others with him."

Although Orvile Tucker, in his loyalty, had developed an intense hatred for the little ex-Confederate major who published the Gourdville newspaper, when Roman Hasford said this, there was a chill along Orvile's back. Because it was said with a completely cold detachment, like somebody speaking of stepping on a bug.

So Orvile turned back to his kitchen, thinking about destruction and the forms it could take, and while he was there with lips moving, talking silently to himself, Roman Hasford came up beside him and laid a hand on his shoulder.

"No more killing, Orvile. I promise you that, too," Roman said. And sighed and looked at the meat laid on the chopping block ready for the pan. "Orvile, just fix me a little oatmeal mush. My stomach hurts."

That night in his bed, Roman Hasford lay awake as he so often did, thinking about all the people he had known who were now gone. And of other things as well.

It had been many months since he'd had that last letter from Jared Dane and had drawn his little diagram. But now, at last, he knew what he would do.

I can't get my hands on Yancy Crane, he thought. Oh, he'll be back someday, unless he dies somewhere, somehow. He came back before and failed, and he's the kind of son of a bitch who won't stop. He'll be back. For Yancy I have to wait. The others I can reach now.

On the day Roman Hasford went to the depot to buy a round-trip ticket to St. Louis, Bishop Eckor was there, staying back in the growing evening shadows with the horses while Roman spoke with Isaac Maddox on the platform, both of them waiting for Number Six to arrive. Isaac's youngest son was coming home, bringing his wife and five kids, on the same train that would take Roman north. So Isaac was bubbling as only an old man can when a son and his family are returning to put down their toes in clan soil.

Roman remembered Otis Maddox from the two or three years they'd spent together in the Leetown school, before the war. He recalled that it had been Otis who'd bloodied his nose when Roman paid too much attention to Carlotta Sims, giving her a pecan praline cookie for lunch one day and pulling her braids at recess besides. Roman couldn't even remember Carlotta's face, but he remembered his bloody nose.

That evening on the Frisco platform, Roman asked Isaac Maddox whatever had happened to the Sims family.

"Good Lord," Isaac said, chuckling, "I ain't thought about them in years. Viola run off with this man from a travelin' circus, come through here during the war. They taken all the young'uns with 'em. Right after, Lester, he went off an' joined some army or other, I don't know which. Then, when you was in Kansas I guess it was, Viola come back lookin' fer Lester, but he never got back from wherever it was he went. They'd sold the Sims farm at public auction, delinquent taxes.

"I never seen Viola when she come back. Them that did said she smelled like coal oil from livin' with that fire-eater from the circus." Isaac laughed. "Never heerd what happened to Viola or her young'uns. She went on down south, Texas or someplace. Love's a funny thing, ain't it? An' bein' horny."

Anyway, reunion with Otis would have to wait because on that blustery evening in Gourdville, Roman mounted one end of a coach while Otis and his herd descended from the other.

Roman rode to St. Louis on one of Mr. George Pullman's new

sleepers, Pullman's Palace Car Company having a contract to join their coaches to Frisco trains, the kind of contract that was current with every major railroad in the country.

Roman recalled Pullman's name being mentioned by some of his railroad friends in Kansas, and it was nice to ride on one of his cars. But he found it rather embarrassing and awkward to dress and undress in a lower berth with nothing but a green drape separating him from the aisle, while strangers were passing and he was in contortions trying to get his pants on, and nothing covering his manhood but flannel underwear.

St. Louis had changed since Roman Hasford last saw it, just a year after the war was over. Now there were brick and marble buildings that seemed so tall as to be in danger of tipping over into the busy streets below. Trolley cars were new, along the river streets, electric ones with cables overhead where blue sparks flew out like small lightning. Corners were crowded with poles. Gaslight poles and telephone poles. The latticework of telephone lines over the streets provided perches for blackbirds, at mathematically measured intervals, from which they could drop an occasional grainy, white deposit on the pedestrians below. Except in wild huckleberry time, Roman assumed, when the deposits would be purple.

The river had changed, too. There were big paddle wheelers that made the Mississippi their highroad, but no more the little traders that went to the headwaters of streams in the West, looking for Indians with buffalo hides. Because now there wasn't any Indian country, and if there were, it would be reached and breached by a railroad.

Before going to the home of Calpurnia and her husband, Allan Pay, Roman went to the Commercial Bank of Missouri, an institution with which he had done much business and where some of his reserve funds were deposited. He talked with a number of executives, all glad to see him, as though he was some sort of wild animal out of the wilderness, and gained their help and support in what he needed to do.

Late in the afternoon, somehow reluctant to find his sister's house once more, he searched for a certain Irish bar where he had been served his first drink of whiskey in Missouri so many years before. But he couldn't find it and had to settle for another. For three more, in fact.

The first thing his sister said to him when she saw him was, "Roman! You're getting gray. Did you ever think we'd be old?"

And then she hugged and kissed him. She was gigantic, it seemed, and smelled like curry.

No, he never thought they'd grow old, in those days when he and Cal had played along Wire Road, making little nests in the red sumac, all of it at her direction, with him doing as she said except in occasional flashes of rebellious temper.

Her house was as he remembered it, particularly those damned needlepoint chair bottoms that seemed too nice for resting one's ass. Allan Pay was so old, and Cal herself fat and slack-jawed, old beyond her years with swelling joints so bad that sometimes Allan had to carry her around the house. She was no longer the sparkling-eyed beauty he had adored. Only once, when she mentioned the maid they'd had on his first visit who had tried to rub against him, did she laugh, and suddenly the old shine was there. An elderly woman, with a son older now than Roman himself had been when he first came here.

"Eben will be so disappointed that he missed you," Cal said.

"He's finished his law degree at Urbana and he's in Chicago doing bar examinations," said Allan. "Have another slice of this rhubarb pie, Roman."

"I haven't seen him since he was a baby," Roman said. "Who does he favor?"

"His father," said Calpurnia.

"No, I think his mother," Allan said. "He's a very handsome man."

"Of course," said Cal.

"Of course," said Roman.

There was a long, painful evening, Roman detailing the deaths of Ora and Martin Hasford but careful not to mention shootings or frustrations or still-present dangers. Allan Pay apologizing for not coming to funerals, Roman waving it off because they could not have gotten there in time, anyway. Then they discussed the long-overdue business of headstones, and the next day Allan Pay escorted Roman to a place where the marble monuments, gray and pink and black, stood like a forest of stone, blank, waiting for graven names. They selected rather modest ones, to be properly inscribed and shipped to Gourdville.

It was enough. It was too much. Roman explained that he must return home due to business pressures, and spent another night in his sister's house but went to a hotel and contracted for a room, because there was much more business that needed doing in St. Louis. It was the usual sort of hotel for that time, and Roman was served by a man dressed like a boy in a red, waist-length jacket and pillbox hat, who offered good whiskey and women in later hours. Roman opted only for the whiskey.

He sat for a long time that night, in the dark, sipping but not drinking heavily. Looking out his open window toward the river. And wondering whatever had happened to the glorious, vibrant, beautiful Calpurnia he had known thirty years before.

Somehow, then, he began to perceive for the first time the odors of this place where his sister now lived. The coal-smoke sulfur. The hint of dead fish from the river. Black roofing tar. Sour shock of uncollected garbage or a leak in sewer lines.

And with that, he began to recall the smells of his boyhood home. The black locust trees blooming. The chopped cabbage in his mother's kitchen. The fresh, clean sharpness of new horse droppings in the summer dust of Wire Road. The throat-contracting jolt of walking into a kitchen in cold weather when spiced apple cider was brewing on the stove.

And most of all, the smell of his sister's hair when they were young.

The stay in St. Louis extended to a week, much longer than Roman Hasford had planned. He became apprehensive about an accidental meeting on the streets with Allan Pay, in which case there would be embarrassing explanations to be made. But the meeting never happened.

He finished all his business and, along the line, managed to do some shopping. He bought two summer suits, both seersucker, a new derby hat to replace the rather weathered fedora that he wore, some cotton shirts, and on frivolous impulse some silk underwear. He laughed to himself about what his mother would say if she knew he was wearing silk underwear.

Actually, he never wore it. He soon threw it away, the very idea of it against his skin somehow seeming degenerate.

He bought one of the new Kodak cameras and rolls of film in boxes, with the address where they could be mailed once exposed.

"We guarantee you'll have your pictures back in only three weeks," the clerk said.

He bought Orvile Tucker a large pocketknife with mother-of-pearl handles, three blades, and a corkscrew.

He looked at some of the new revolvers on the market but decided none were as good as the Colt single-action he had carried for so long.

Finally, then, to the depot and the first leg of his journey home. There had been a letter from St. Scholastica more than a month before, asking him to come at his own convenience. So now, riding a smoker car to Jefferson City, he had time to wonder what it meant. He was a little terrified at the prospect of coming face-to-face with Catrina once again.

The façade of the school looked particularly forbidding because it was raining and the stones were gray like the sky. The trees had not yet leafed out and stood like black skeletons.

At the entrance, the hack driver asked, "Cap'n, you want me to wait for you?"

"Yes," said Roman, and drew a deep breath.

He was ushered along a narrow hallway by a nun not much bigger than Hasford Crozier, swishing in her flowing black habit, and into what he assumed was an office, austere in the extreme, with whitewashed walls, a bookshelf with volumes Roman figured were used in the lessons here, a wooden cross behind a small desk, a number of ladderback chairs. There were two narrow windows, high in the room, and a system of yellow wires on white porcelain insulators culminating in a suspended bare lightbulb that gave off a faint glare of illumination.

It was a very uncomfortable place. He suspected it was much like the rooms where they kept condemned murderers just before taking them out to the hangman.

When the Mother Superior came in, he knew immediately that he had never seen her before, although she gave the impression that she had seen him. She was small, not so small as the nun who had escorted him here, but small nonetheless, and her pale face was encircled in white and black. There were beads and a metal crucifix, all of which were designed, he suspected, to render him speechless. Which they did, design or no.

Yet with her first words, he sensed straightforward honesty, and the sweat in his palms became of no account.

"Mr. Hasford. I'm so glad that you could come," she said. "Catrina is on retreat, so she will not be here."

"I see," Roman said, although he wasn't sure he did.

"It is you and I who need to talk," the Mother Superior said.

"I see," Roman said, and felt some vast, overwhelming relief that the only person he'd have to deal with here was this little woman, and not Catrina.

"May I come directly to the point?"

"Please."

"I know you're a busy man."

"It isn't that. I'll give you all the time you want. It's just that there seems to be some important reason that you asked me here, and I'd like to get to it."

"Yes, it concerns the life and soul of a young woman who has become very dear to us," she said. "May I impress you with the seriousness of what I say?"

Roman clasped his hands and nodded and looked around this bare room and said, "Yes, Sister, if you'd tell me now."

She stared at him for a moment, and the eyes in her alabaster face were like agate marbles. Then her mouth softened. When she spoke, it was with a rush of words, but softly and each well chosen, as though given great thought beforehand. She said that Catrina had become a member of the school, assisting in the instruction of Latin, for which she had an obvious talent, and that she had expressed a desire to make teaching her lifework. But more than that.

"Mr. Hasford, Catrina has told us that she would most surely desire to become a Catholic."

Roman almost shrugged, but didn't. And he saw what he thought was a smile playing at the corner of the Mother Superior's lips.

"In that event," she said, "I need to know certain things. If I may be frank. There are personal things here. Will you help me?"

"Of course," Roman said, and felt suddenly as though he were on a witness stand, sworn. And perhaps he was.

"Has she ever been baptized in some other faith?"

"No. She has had no other faith."

"So she has said. Good."

"You didn't believe her?" There was an edge of belligerence in his voice, and the Mother Superior smiled truly now and shook her head.

"Of course we did. But we must confirm with other witnesses what she has said."

"All right. She has never been baptized."

"Good. Then she will be with us. Now, Mr. Hasford, there is a greater request. She would have her marriage annulled."

Well, Roman thought, this woman knows how to hit you with a sledgehammer, don't she? He said nothing.

"This is very important. She has said that your marriage was never consummated. If this is true, then under certain circumstances an annulment is almost a matter of course through a dispensation from Rome, but in practical terms it is done by the bishop in St. Louis. But only if it was never consummated, and only if you do not object on the basis of your living with her as husband and wife."

Roman became conscious of crows cawing somewhere outside in those leafless trees. And of the smell of chalk dust. And most obviously of the Mother Superior's eyes on his face.

"The marriage was never consummated," he said. "And it would be impossible for me to live with her as husband. What else do you need?"

"The church would appreciate your making arrangements for a civil divorce. It isn't necessary, but it would be most appropriate. It would be confirmation of your approval, among other things."

"I can manage that."

"Yes, I had understood that in your community you might be able to do that, or almost anything else you wanted."

Now the smile was there again, in that confined, restricted face, and suddenly Roman thought her very beautiful.

"I can do that."

"Good. I'm sure that next time, Catrina will be happy to see you. Will want to see you. She has said that you were always very kind to her, Mr. Hasford. Now, you understand, she is in a very emotional state and cannot see anyone."

"I understand."

"Then we are agreed, you and I?"

"Yes. And I'll provide money for her still."

"It isn't necessary, Mr. Hasford. If you'd like, you may contribute to our general fund. But we cannot take contributions for specific young ladies after they have finished their schooling and tuition is no longer required."

"Whatever. I'll send some money. Do whatever you want with it."

"Thank you. Mr. Hasford, would you like some tea?"

"No. It's time I left."

"Very well. Once more, Mr. Hasford, Catrina has great affection for you and your father."

"My father is dead."

There was a quick, wide-eyed pause, and somehow Roman felt viciously happy that he'd said it so abruptly.

"I'm sorry," she said.

"He was an old man. You can tell Catrina or not, whatever you feel's right."

Then she led him to the front portal, chatting as she went about the length of the spring thaw in Missouri. At the door, she held out her hand and Roman took it and, still holding it, looked down at her and said, "Sister, you come at things the way I like it. It's too bad you can't be an officer in my bank."

The Mother Superior laughed, her head back.

"Ah no, Mr. Hasford. It's too bad you can't be an officer in mine."

The rain continued all the rest of the day in Jefferson City, and into the night, and the next morning, too, when Roman Hasford went to his train. Still laughing. If not apparent on his face. A bitter, self-deprecating mirth. Annulment. Now, after these many years, the end of a marriage that had been ultimate proof of concern for a little girl's abuse. Now, after the summer of Diana, after the arrival of Berdeen, after Ausbin Tage and Texas for the Chesneys.

It was a hard, brittle, sharp-edged hilarity, feeding on its own irony, increasing with each reconsideration. Funny as hell. Lost opportunities. Gone dreams. Mama, Papa, Calpurnia, Mother Superior. Trinity and the metal cross. Annulment! Too late! And so Roman laughed.

On the coach south to Monet, Roman thought with some satisfaction that the night before he'd had only one drink and slept soundly. And now he was calm, confident in what he had planned. He watched the passing landscape of southern Missouri, the rolling land and the cattle grazing, then finally took from his inside coat pocket a small notebook and opened to the pages where he had written, and saw the name of the man who would soon arrive in northwest Arkansas. Then tore out that page, the page with the name on it, and crumpling it in his hand, he went to the toilet at the end of the car and burned it and dropped the ash into the pot and flushed it onto the tracks.

Back in his seat, Roman Hasford lay back and closed his eyes and recalled the conversations. Just to be sure. Not the conversations with Calpurnia, not those with the Mother Superior, but others. Just to be sure.

"This is your fox race," Roman had said in his hotel room the last night of his stay in St. Louis. "But remember, the money comes from me. Not direct, but through a fund my friends have set up in the Cattleman's Bank of Kansas City. My name won't appear anywhere beyond the vaults of that bank. Nobody but you and me and the trustees of that fund will know my part in it."

"I understand," the visitor to Roman's hotel room had said.

"I want to be sure you do. A lot of people know I do business in St. Louis. I wanted to move this out of there. So, the Cattleman's Bank of Kansas City."

"The reason is perfectly clear."

"Also, remember that one-half of your net will be deposited in that same Kansas City bank, to another trust fund. In the name of Berdeen Chesney Tage. But your drafts to the fund will never use that name. Only a number. I don't want anybody seeing that name lying around. You forget that name. Just remember the number."

"I understand, Mr. Hasford. No one will ever know from me the beneficiary of that trust fund."

"All right. It may not matter. There may not ever be any net profit."

"I can assure you there will be considerable."

"We'll see. So much the better if there is, but you know my object in this is something besides building up a lot of trust money somewhere."

"I understand."

"You'll have a free hand. You do something I don't like, you'll hear about it. Not from me, but you'll hear."

"I understand."

"Even in politics, once my own people have passed out of office of their own accord, support anybody you think is best. Party doesn't matter."

"I understand."

"You've come with considerable recommendation."

"I hope so."

"Use everything you know."

"Rest assured."

"I'm looking forward to watching you work."

"I'll try not to disappoint you."

"We'll see. All right. I guess we're clear on all of it now."

"All of it."

"I wanted this one last meeting," Roman Hasford had said, "because tomorrow, when I leave St. Louis, you'll be a complete stranger to me. So good-bye."

"Goodbye, Mr. Hasford."

Now, on the Frisco, rattling into Monet with dawn, Roman Hasford felt vibrant, free. Hell, he thought, I didn't even take a sleeping car down here, and I liked it better just sitting in the seat than all that berth business. It's almost home now, almost home. I wonder if the gravestones for Mama and Papa got there already.

Almost home. Where the only family left was an aging, graying black man. Roman Hasford was suddenly very anxious to get there and see bulging bloodshot eyes and the glistening cheeks and hear the lovely, loving growl of disapproval that had become his only conscience.

29

When Patrick Macky stepped down from Number Five, the early morning southbound passenger train, it was full, bursting spring in the Ozarks. The black locust trees along the fences of the stationmaster's house and the section foreman's house were a fluffy green like the layered lace of some ancient monarch of Erin, a simile Patrick Macky liked. And the crabapple tree in the schoolyard across Elkhorn Street was in bloom, a detonation of pink and white. Almost as brilliant as the flower on Patrick Macky's coat lapel.

Patrick Macky looked about him, sniffed the air with considerable approval, and rubbed an ample belly gloriously concealed beneath a red and purple silk figured vest with a watch chain looped across it. Suspended from the chain was a great fob that he would say was a pure, genuine gold nugget from the California rush, brought back to him by his uncle, Thaddeus Elander. What he would not say was that no such uncle had ever existed in the California gold rush or anywhere else. Nor that the fob was really a teardrop-shaped glob of brass coated with slightly less than fourteen-karat gold. The kind of thing that, if worn about his throat instead of hanging against the flowered vest, would eventually have turned his neck green.

Of such things are great stories made, and, as it turned out, Patrick Macky knew as much about turning out great stories as anyone who ever set foot in the state of Arkansas.

It seemed to the citizens of the county that Patrick Macky was always smiling. And at the same time clamping a large cigar at one corner of his mouth with a set of fine, strong teeth. These cigars were as much a part of him as the florid face and the booming voice. They were not normal cigars, but gigantic Havanas. He left a trail of them behind, discarding each as it approached midpoint, then whipping out another from shirt or vest or coat pocket. It appeared that all of Patrick Macky's pockets were filled with these cigars.

"I ain't ever seen cigars like them," said Ennis Lugi at the stable. "You could take one and whip a reluctant mule and never knock off the ash!"

In a town where all the men wore hats and most were bearded, Macky was always bare-headed and clean-shaven. People figured him at about forty-five years old, but it was hard to tell. His plump, red face had its share of wrinkles, they observed, but maybe that was the result of all the smiling and laughing. And although there might have been some trace of gray at the temples, that was hard to tell, too, because Patrick Macky kept his hair clipped skin-short except on top, where there was a coal-black spray as stiff and unmanageable as the hog bristles in a good clothes brush.

He tended toward white shirts with orange sleeve garters. No coat, but always a vest. Button shoes with high heels. And even with those he stood only five feet two inches tall, people figured, which were about his dimensions from side to side as well. No one really measured it, because although Patrick Macky was always smiling or laughing, there was a steel-brittle glint in his Irish eyes that discouraged close inspection.

He was one of those men who exuded good humor and fond fellowship at long range. But closer, he created uncomfortable rumblings in the stomach and the urge to back off. The kind of man who could be telling a joke and at the same time calculating the best blow to use against the listener's jaw.

Mr. Macky, as everyone instinctively called him from the start, took a room at the hotel, a permanent room, to Harley Stone's great delight, explaining as he did so that he'd taken three wives and found them all miserably inadequate in ways impossible to describe in polite conversation. And none could cook worth a damn, either. So he was just an old bachelor businessman, destitute and here on this last frontier, shunned by his natural church because of all those divorces.

"And what might your business be, Mr. Macky?" asked Harley Stone, smiling across the register.

"The business of staying alive," Mr. Macky said with an explosion of gray-blue cigar smoke from the center of his face.

A lot of citizens in the county wished they were as destitute as he because Patrick Macky started spending money as it had never been spent since those first days, years ago, when Roman Hasford came back from Kansas. He had a letter of credit from the Cattleman's Bank of Kansas City, Missouri, and a folder full of cashier's checks from the same place.

The first thing Patrick Macky did was visit the Gourdville bank and buy a property next to the post office on First Street, facing the railroad tracks. A large stone building once a grain warehouse but foreclosed two years before on a defaulted mortgage. Then to the circuit clerk's office in the courthouse to file the deed. In his own name. The property having been purchased with one of those Kansas City cashier's checks in the amount of $1,500.

Then carpenters began to appear on First Street, and there was a lot of hammering and sawing in the old stone warehouse. And two Western Union workmen arrived and installed a wire in the place, running right off the main line, a telegraph key set up in a small metal cage at the front of the building. Stonemasons laid down a solid foundation in the center of the building. Large holes were knocked from the north wall, the one away from the post office and facing a vacant lot, and windows installed. Large windows. In the rear of the place, they built rollers and racks. And a loading platform.

Everyone wondered what the hell was going on.

They wondered even more when a steam engine was shipped in on a Frisco flatcar. It was a small steam engine, but obviously brand new, right out of Cincinnati, Ohio. It was hauled and jerked and yanked into place at the rear of the old stone warehouse.

Then, in early July, they got their answer. It also came on a flatcar. It was something most of them had never seen. It was a Hoe-type revolving press. And with it came half a dozen rolls of paper, each as big as the water tank on the rear roof of Harley Stone's hotel. These were installed on those roller racks that everybody had been wondering about. And the press was placed down on that solid stone floor in the center of the building and directly before those big windows, where all the town's kids could stand on a bench provided outside and look inside and see the marvels of Progress.

On the day the press was installed, a huge sign was installed as well, across the front of the building, facing First Street. It stretched the entire breadth of the building. In black Gothic letters a foot high, on a peach-colored background, it proclaimed: THE ARKANSAS DISPATCH. And in smaller letters, A NEWSPAPER FOR ALL THE PEOPLE. And in smaller letters still, P. MACKY, EDITOR AND PUBLISHER.

"Well, I'll be damned," said Isaac Maddox.

On that same day, with Corliss Buckmaten taking to his bed, seven young men arrived from St. Louis on Number Five. They had a determined set to their jaws. They wore bowler hats and single-breasted suits and shoes with very pointy toes. They were met at the depot by Patrick Macky and escorted like a squad of infantry to Harley Stone's hotel, the owner of which was beside himself with joy because it appeared that these young men would be in town a long time, maybe indefinitely. And all bachelors. All unattached. All taking their sustenance from Harley's very own kitchen, their warmth from his very own blankets in his very own beds.

Had Corliss Buckmaten known Patrick Macky's qualifications for running a newspaper, he would have stayed in bed a lot longer than he did. Macky was out of the St. Louis School of New Journalism, having worked there for a man named Joseph Pulitzer on the *Post-Dispatch* before Pulitzer went to New York. Macky had learned his game from one of the best teachers and was delighted to have a go at running a twice-weekly newspaper that would be competing only against a thing called the *Democrat Advertiser*, a pre–Civil War kind of paper moribund by the late nineteenth century.

Macky was a Republican, too, like his mentor. But to Roman Hasford, the politics didn't matter. What mattered was that Patrick Macky was completely ruthless. And Roman had thought, in those times he'd talked to Macky in St. Louis, Why, hell, he's just like Jared Dane. Except he doesn't have to use a gun!

It was during this same season that Asa Lorch arrived with his wife, Temperance, and went to work in the Farmer's and Merchant's Bank. Asa was as different from Patrick Macky as sour from sweet. Patrick Macky could be found every night in various establishments, telling his stories and having a few drinks with locals. Asa Lorch was never seen on the streets except in early morning and in late evening, going to and from his house on North Third Street to the bank and back, tall and stooped, intent, with a hollow-cheeked face and a large nose. There was another difference. Nobody in the county was aware of any connection between Patrick Macky and Roman Hasford, but Asa Lorch was the Farmer's and Merchant's Bank's new loan officer.

In what had been until then an empty second floor at the bank, used only for storage, an office was established for Asa in a bay-window room overlooking the square. Because of his nose and the job and the bay-window nest above people going about their everyday business, he was immediately dubbed the Hawk. At first, there were those who called him Hasford's Hawk. But that didn't last long because of fear. With the arrival of Asa Lorch it became increasingly apparent that there was grave danger in speaking ill of the Farmer's and Merchant's Bank and its president. Not physical fear, but monetary. Those who continued to speak thus soon found money pinches coming from all kinds of new directions.

Roman Hasford had hired Asa with only one instruction, having already determined from St. Louis bankers the capabilities of this man.

"There are preferred customers in my bank," Roman had said. "There are those who aren't. I'll tell you which are which. For the preferred, I'll make the terms of loans. For the others, you make it as tight as you can. I want to be able to call in a loan anytime I decide."

"What about local law backing foreclosures?"

"Let me worry about that."

Gallatin Delmonico was appalled.

"Why, hell, Gallatin," Roman said, "in the long run, you'll make a lot more money."

"It's not the money that concerns me."

"Well, what do you want me to do? Make you a deputy sheriff?"

Gallatin walked away, looking sick.

But not so sick as some. Benjamin Tark, whose distillery business was in trouble because of the economy and more surely because he was trying to swim in a big pond with larger fish along the route of the Frisco track markets, came in for his annual loan. Now desperate not to enlarge but just to stay afloat. Asa Lorch, who was seeing Ben Tark for the first time and had his name in a small book provided by the president of the bank, said it was no concern of his and that as a matter of fact nobody in the bank gave a good shit whether he survived or not, because he was no longer the kind of risk the bank wanted to assume.

Furious, terrified, and almost incoherent, Ben Tark rushed downstairs to see the president himself, who had been expecting him.

"Ben," Roman said from behind his big desk, "it's hard times. For all of us. I can understand you trying to reach better times breaking the law, but the bank can't help you do that kind of thing."

"Breakin' the law?"

"Yes. It's against the law to sell whiskey in the Indian Territory. It's against Federal law."

Benjamin Tark sat with his mouth hanging open. He made three attempts at speech before any sound came.

"I ain't even set foot in the Nations for years," he said.

"Doesn't matter. You provide the whiskey. You sell it to Court-land Brown. Or maybe you've got a percentage arrangement with him. Doesn't matter which, it's breaking the law when a certain young Cherokee loads that whiskey on horses or mules and takes it over to Going Snake or Tahlequah or Vinita and sells it."

"Mr. Hasford—" Benjamin Tark started, but Roman raised one hand to interrupt him.

"Now, Ben, it's happened too often. A lot of people have seen it happen. I know about it, and most of the people in this county know about it."

Benjamin Tark was panting, squeezing his hands together be-tween his knees.

"You know all about Poco Jimmy, Ben. The one who carries the whiskey to the Territory. You know all about him, don't you? Just like everybody else knows about him."

Benjamin Tark twisted his hands, his mouth hanging open still but not trying to talk now.

"We might reconsider your loan application if you went to Colin Hamp and told him all about it. Then he could send that information to the Federal authorities in Judge Parker's court in Fort Smith. That's right, Ben, we could reconsider, I'm sure, if you made a deposition, sworn testimony about what happens to that whiskey you take to Brown's Tavern. Why, hell, Ben, you know there's not enough people in this whole county to swill down all the stuff you take out there. We'd help you with what you say."

"Mr. Hasford," Ben said, then paused, the sweat running along his dark cheeks, his hands working like great brown snakes with each other between his knees. "Mr. Hasford, if I done something like that, Courtland Brown would have my ass."

"Ben," Roman Hasford said, slowly reaching out and dropping his cigar into a tortoise shell ashtray on his desk, and smiling, "Courtland Brown's time is up. He's going to the penitentiary. People are sick and tired of his way of doing things. And if you don't cooperate, you'll be going right along with him."

For a moment, Benjamin Tark was speechless. He shook his head.

"I can't do it, Mr. Hasford, I can't do it."

Roman rose and came around the desk and escorted Benjamin Tark out of the office and across the lobby of the bank, one hand on Ben's shoulder. At the door, Roman took Ben's hand and shook it.

"Ben, think about it," he said. "If you don't help us finish that whiskey trade in the Nations, then *you're* finished. If you do, then maybe I can help you."

He let the distiller get to the edge of the sidewalk where his horse was tethered, then called to him. "I'll be sending my man Andy Gimshaw around as usual tomorrow for a few jugs of that fine sour mash you make," said Roman. "You've got a good business right here, Ben, if you know how to keep it. Sleep well tonight, Ben."

In Benjamin Tark's eyes was a blazing pure hatred that Roman Hasford somehow enjoyed.

As Roman walked back across the lobby of the bank, he was aware of Gallatin Delmonico watching him as though he knew exactly what had been happening.

"Is something the matter with you?" Roman asked.

Gallatin Delmonico said nothing but turned and moved behind the tellers' counter, and Roman went into his office and slammed the door behind him.

The cigar was still smoldering in the tortoiseshell ashtray as Roman picked it up and began to puff it. He knew that he should feel like a dyed-in-the-wool son of a bitch, as the locals would phrase it, but in fact he felt fine. With a glowing excitement that ran all the way down to his fingertips.

That night at the supper table, as he and Orville Tucker spooned up a rabbit stew thanks to Andy Gimshaw's ability with a twenty-gauge shotgun in the woods east of the Big House that afternoon, it didn't even bother him when Orville looked at him with those huge, bloodshot eyes and said, "Mr. Roman, how come you mouth turn down when it used to turn up?"

"What?"

"How come you don't laugh no more like you done in Kansas when we was breedin' them good horses and gettin' drunk together on beer when a fine foal dropped?"

"Why, hell, Orville, that was a long time ago."

"How come you mouth turn down at the corners now?" Orville asked, and Roman laughed because he knew Orville had been into his supply of sour mash during the afternoon.

"It's just the mustache, that's all."

"No, it ain't all."

And that night in his room in his moments of recall before sleep, Roman Hasford thought, why, hell, it's just the mustache. That's all.

On the first day of school that fall, every Gourdville child found on his or her desk Volume One, Number One of the *Arkansas Dispatch*. It consisted of four standard-sized pages, each filled with a teacher's delight of entertaining stories from American history and geography. It was ideal for reading aloud to the class on that first hectic day of the semester, when little bottoms were trying, after a summer of freedom, to accommodate themselves to hard seats for the first six hours of what was generally viewed as the beginning of a dismal, winter-long torture.

In that first issue of the *Dispatch* were retold in the flamboyant language of Patrick Macky the sagas of George Washington and the cherry tree, throwing the dollar across the Potomac, the winter at Valley Forge, the treason of Benedict Arnold, the victory at Yorktown (without any mention of the French), all culminating in the Father of Our Country.

There were rather romantic translations of other stories: a newspaper called the *Boston Gazette*, which really started the American Revolution; the dastard Burr shooting the gentleman Hamilton in a duel; Dolley Madison saving the White House silver from the British; the terrible ordeal of the heroes at the Alamo; the savage Sioux killing poor General Custer and his brave troopers at the Little Bighorn.

Patrick Macky, with his soon-to-be-recognized tact and foresight, ignored any mention of the War Between the States in this still-divided county.

There was a list of the Presidents, a list of states in the Union, with the dates they were admitted (Arkansas displayed in boldface type), a list of the major rivers in the United States.

Best of all was the complete story of the Statue of Liberty, which covered half of the front page, and was dominated there by a steel engraving of Lady Liberty standing in New York Harbor, holding up her lamp for those huddled masses. Appropriate poetry by Emma Lazarus followed, and when the Reverend Kirkendall read it, it was reported, there was a tear in his eye.

Naturally, his old connections in St. Louis being what they were, Patrick Macky spent a lot of prose on the part his old mentor played in raising funds to have the statue erected, Joseph Pulitzer using his *New York World* to coax pennies from some of those same huddled masses.

Of all the heroes lionized, leading the list were two newspapers. Which should have indicated to anyone who cared to stop and think about it that Patrick Macky may have avoided grinding any controversial axes from the Civil War, but he sure as hell knew how to sharpen his own.

It was stunning. For a lot of reasons, not the least of which was that nobody had ever seen a small-town newspaper in that part of the country displaying a high-quality illustration. The teachers, led by Glamorgan Caulder Kirkendall, thought it a most wonderful teaching device. Patrick Macky knew what it really was: one hell of a promotion for his newspaper. Because each kid in school that day carried home a copy for the old folks to see. And at the bottom of the back page was a notice. For the first fifty people subscribing to the *Dispatch* there would be a free frame, complete with glass, in which all patriotic families could display that steel engraving of Miss Liberty on their living room wall. What's more, for those first lucky fifty plus the next fifty would be a reprint, on parchment paper, of the Declaration of Independence *already* framed under glass, available for only seven cents.

Corliss Buckmaten was violently ill. Melissa couldn't understand it.

"Why, Corliss, I thought it was a nice newspaper," she said, holding a cool, damp cloth to his forehead.

"Oh God."

30

Everybody knew that Roman Hasford read more than anybody else in Gourdville or, for that matter, the whole county. Not only all those books that he and Owen Caulder had been exchanging for years before Owen went off to Weedy Rough to run a store and enjoy fox races, but Eastern and Northern newspapers and magazines through subscription. These newspapers and magazines came by mail, and Walter Matt, the postmaster, being a talkative person, often expressed his amazement to various friends that anybody in the Arkansas hills would have an interest in the things happening in places like Chicago or London, which was in England, Walter always explained.

But what Walter Matt did not explain, because he did not know, was that all this reading qualified Roman Hasford to have some appreciation of what was happening or about to happen in the county. And what was about to happen was something called the New Journalism. And only two people in the whole state, maybe, understood one of the foundation blocks of the New Journalism.

Why, hell, Roman thought, it's better than a gun. Monopoly. Get everything the other man can't, and keep it!

Roman Hasford knew a great deal about monopoly. He'd seen it operating in Kansas, but that had been from afar. Here, having established the only lending institution in the county, even though there was no monopolistic intent, perhaps, he had observed it first-hand.

Now the citizens of Gourdville and the county were about to see it operating in their own community, through the New Journalism, even though they could probably put no name to it, nor even comprehend how it worked. But Roman Hasford knew, and now once more he observed it from afar.

Well, he thought, not too afar. Hell, it's my money and it's my man. And I picked a good one.

Patrick Macky joined two press associations, one of which sent news by Western Union telegraph. Western Union had an agreement with the press association that it would send no news by anybody else. And the press association agreed that it would use only the wires of Western Union. The second association sent feature and entertainment material, express mail, usually on paper-thin stereotype plates that could be reprinted in whole or in part. It was from here that the illustration of Miss Liberty had come.

What Patrick Macky knew and Corliss Buckmaten was about to find out was that both these press associations would not take another client in any area where they already had one. Unless the original client agreed. Naturally, not many publishers, least of all Patrick Macky, were willing to have their national news and entertainment source available to competitors.

Hence, monopoly. Monopoly on what the citizens would know about things going on in Chicago or St. Louis or New York or Washington. Stock-market quotations. Election returns. Freight rate fluctuations. Sex and murder sensations or results of prize-fights and horse races. The development of new harvesters or fertilizers.

Not to mention views held on important issues by somebody other than a next-door neighbor. Editorials, political cartoons, and speeches made hundreds of miles away now appeared on the magazine rack of Doc Gooch's drugstore.

Not to mention entertainment. During the first month of publication, Macky ran a full page on astrology. With a headline that read in bold face:

OLD AS THE EGYPTIANS
ZODIAC GUIDES WORLD
SEERS AND LEADERS

Following which was the announcement that the *Dispatch* would run a weekly horoscope for people of northwest Arkansas, so that they might manage their own lives with the assistance of the stars in heaven. All these horoscopes, of course, coming from the press associations.

Within the first month, the *Dispatch* had a circulation of over two hundred. Not counting drugstore and street sales and all those issues sold to candy butchers on every Frisco passenger train that stopped at the depot. Advertisers began lining up. Advertisers, the lifeblood of newspapers.

Except for extras, which Patrick Macky enjoyed, the *Dispatch* published every Tuesday and Friday evening. Two pennies a copy. Even cheaper on subscription. It was delivered by boys, three of them, in town. By horseback rider, also three of those, into the countryside. And once the postal service initiated rural free delivery, which Patrick Macky seemed to know was coming soon, the *Dispatch* would arrive in mailboxes outside Gourdville, sent under the new, low rates for newspapers.

But until people in the countryside began receiving mail from the post office, Patrick Macky gave them the *Dispatch* from the very hand of his own people, unaccustomed as most of them were to horseback riding. There was many a blistered and sore butt and thigh among them as a result. But Patrick Macky would have no excuse. On Tuesday and Friday, the *Dispatch* would be on the kitchen table at suppertime.

Competition to be one of the three newsboys in town was fierce. In that first edition left at the school was a small insert offering the jobs to qualified applicants, whatever that meant, with promises of earnings of up to three dollars a month. Plus a prize before Christmas going to who ever among the newsboys brought in the most new subscribers. Like a new bicycle right out of Chicago. There were three serious fistfights in the schoolyard. One resulted in nine-year-old Carl Ort, the baker's son, having his new lace-up shoes torn off and thrown into the boy's privy.

It was obvious from the start that Patrick Macky intended to sell newspapers. And that he knew how.

Advertisers were rushing to the *Dispatch* office before the end of the second month, by which time the circulation was already a thousand.

A classified section was added to each Friday edition, so that if a farmer had a calf to sell or some widow had decided to take in washing, for a few pennies the information could be broadcast across the county.

Circulation increased.

Patrick Macky knew about contests. So he ran contests. Guess how many beans are in the glass jar in the *Dispatch* front window and win a Sears, Roebuck cookstove with warming oven. Be the first to work out the word puzzle in this issue and win a set of bone china dishes from Montgomery Ward.

Naturally, on such transactions Patrick Macky paid Sears, Roebuck or Montgomery Ward or whoever only a fraction of retail price on merchandise, because it was good advertising for them as well as for the *Dispatch*.

Circulation increased.

When it came time for the county to award a new contract for legal printing, County Judge Newton Black naturally awarded it to the *Dispatch*.

"Hell," said Newton, "nobody reads that thing Corliss puts out anymore. Is he still printing it?"

What Newton Black did not mention to anyone was that in a casual conversation with the man most responsible for his holding the office he did, the subject had come up and Newton Black's mentor had remarked that legal notices should certainly be printed in the newspaper of greatest circulation.

"It just seems to me," Roman Hasford had said, "that such a thing makes sense."

It made sense to the county judge as well, and hence Corliss Buckmaten's *Democrat Advertiser* lost its one greatest source of income. All those tax notices and delinquencies and sheriff's sales and other information ordered from the circuit clerk or the county judge started appearing in the *Dispatch*.

There was a lot more. Patrick Macky scandalized county ladies when he began to publish some of the love-nest-homicide stories off his wire service out of those dens of sin, Chicago and New York and London, England. Or wherever. Downright nasty, the ladies said. And kept reading. To help them feel better about such enjoyment, there were also church schedules and a Bible verse on the back page of Friday's issue, another thing they'd never seen in Corliss Buckmaten's newspaper.

The *Dispatch* began to serialize books, without too much concern for copyrights. As a matter of fact, with complete disregard for copyrights. Like Charles Dickens's *A Christmas Carol.* It took a full year to run it, even editing out a lot of passages. And the last installment fell on Christmas Eve, a tribute to Patrick Macky's planning.

And still more. For Patrick Macky knew how to take advantage of that great outside world.

The Army Signal Corps had set up a number of weather stations across the nation. Some of these were immediately west of Arkansas, the direction from whence most of their weather came. The Signal Corps reports were available to the press associations and to their clients. So now, from the pages of the *Dispatch,* county residents for the first time could have hints of what might be coming, plus quick information on how much hail had fallen in Guthrie, Oklahoma Territory, or the velocity of winds in Topeka, Kansas. And advance notice of meteor showers and eclipses.

Circulation increased. So did the number of pages, from four to six (with a single-sheet insert) to a full eight. Tuesday and Friday, delivered to the door without fail—rain or shine, hot or cold.

There were little fillers at the ends of columns. Like the weekly geography puzzle, with the question in Tuesday's issue, the answer in Friday's. The device was applauded by the teachers in the school.

One week, the question was "Where is Madagascar?" and it almost caused a serious adult fistfight in Glen Torten's Billiard Parlor when Glen and John Vain, both well into the celebration of Halloween after consuming a dozen steins of beer each, got into an argument over it.

"It's in northern Missouri," said John Vain. "I been there."

"Like hell it is," Glen Torten said. "It's a river in Canada. Everybody with a lick of sense knows that."

"You're a liar!"

"You're a suck-egg mule!" So loyalty to the *Advertiser* crumbled, even among Democrats. The *Dispatch* didn't appear to have any politics. But it had just about everything else.

Like advertising. "My God," Corliss Buckmaten wailed to Melissa, "he's got a man over there who doesn't do anything but transact business. What kind of a newspaper is that anyway?"

Most of Patrick Macky's determined young men did things other than transact business. They went out and found local stories, a very large factor in circulation increases. Gossip became set in factual print. Interesting guests at Harley Stone's hotel were re-

ported. Babies delivered by Doctors Cronin and Gooch were reported. A Frisco worker's foot being crushed when a rail fell on it
was reported. The theft of half a dozen Methodist church hymnals
was reported. Norma Felcher's prolonged illness was reported.
It was even reported that Alvis Lapp, the new chief of city police,
had a four-leaf-clover-shaped birthmark on his left shoulder.

"There ain't nothin' private anymore," Anson Greedy said.
"Next, ole Pat'll be telling us who got the longest tallywhacker in
the county."

Not just local stories, either, but stories about local people in
other places. Like the time Patrick Macky sent the best of his
determined young men to Fort Smith, there to stay and report on
the entire trial of Courtland Brown, Benjamin Tark, Poco Jimmy,
and Drake Brown in the Federal court on charges of selling whiskey
in the Indian Territory.

Why, people could sit in the barbershop or the lobby of the hotel
or the domino parlor and talk about that trial just as though they'd
been sitting in Judge Parker's court.

And a big plus for Patrick Macky's enterprise was that while he
had a correspondent in Fort Smith, there were three hangings on
the huge gallows that stood on the lawn of the Federal court there.
These were reported by the *Dispatch's* man in minute and grisly
detail, each word sent and received on the days written, the very
days the great trap dropped. With every syllable coming along the
Western Union wire Macky had contracted for at the start, its key
in his newspaper office.

But the big news from Fort Smith in that time was the Courtland
Brown trial. The United States attorney had hauled Courtland and
Poco Jimmy and Benjamin Tark before a grand jury—Drake
Brown, too, for good measure—and the grand jury returned a true
bill against them. They went to trial in Parker's court.

There were a dozen Cherokee witnesses who said that Poco
Jimmy was a known bootlegger for white man's whiskey in the
Nations. Poco Jimmy had already seen a long stretch in the peni-
tentiary opening out before him and had decided to turn state's
evidence against old Courtland. Then, in the course of the trial,
Benjamin Tark made the same decision.

So Courtland Brown was convicted and sentenced to six years
in the Federal pen in Detroit. Poco Jimmy got the same, but five
of those years were suspended due to his cooperation. Ben Tark

got off with two years' probation, also because he'd testified on the prosecution side, and because he was only an accessory before the fact. Drake Brown was acquitted.

"Ole Courtland ain't ever gonna come out of that penitentiary," said Ansel Kimes, the section foreman. "I been in one of them places back in my stud days, and he's too old to pull six in Detroit. They'll be plantin' him in Federal soil."

"I never knowed you was a convict," Otto Smecker said from behind his bar. "What'd they get you on?"

"It was in Ohio. Assault and battery. I spent two in a state pen. Case of mistaken identity."

"Well, of course, I knew it was something like that. You want another jolt of that rye?"

Poco Jimmy didn't go to the Federal pen because he'd already spent a year in the Fort Smith jail before the trial. Sheriff Colin Hamp had arrested him outside Brown's Tavern one night, on certain information provided by parties unknown, including the fact that Poco Jimmy had a lot of whiskey on two pack mules. Colin Hamp brought him in to Gourdville's jail and the next morning escorted Poco Jimmy and the whiskey onto the Number Five to Fort Smith, then took the young Cherokee to the Federal magistrate there, who arraigned him on suspicion of traffic in liquor in the Indian Territory.

Every word printed in the *Dispatch.*

Well, almost every word.

"Yes sir," said Anson Greedy, leaning back in his barber chair. "Right after Colin taken that Cherokee back to Fort Smith and then them two Federal marshals come up here and arrested ole Courtland and Drake and Ben Tark, you knew something was coming unraveled."

"I didn't see it," Harley Stone said, "but I heard the night Colin brought Poco Jimmy in and put him in jail before he took him to Parker's court, Roman Hasford rode in after dark and went down to the jail cell where Poco Jimmy was and talked to him a long time. You suppose Roman Hasford had anything to do with all this?"

Anson Greedy exchanged glances with Isaac Maddox, and both tried to suppress smiles.

"Well now, I don't know," said Anson Greedy. "Roman used to buy pigeons from Poco a long time ago. So maybe he was just expressin' sympathy."

"Yeah, sympathy," Isaac Maddox said, and laughed outright.

Patrick Macky knew how to squeeze a story to its bitter end. Thus, when Sarah and Drake Brown came back from Fort Smith, that same young man who had reported the trial was there at Brown's Tavern almost before Sarah and Drake had time to comb the cinders out of their hair. He did not come alone. Asa Lorch was with him, representing the Farmer's and Merchant's Bank, and Sheriff Colin Hamp.

"It was a good thing somebody who was armed went out there that day," Anson Greedy said. "Else Sarah might have blowed the Hawk's head off."

Anson Greedy understood that even though Harley Stone might be uncertain about Roman Hasford's part in all this, Sarah Brown was not.

The *Dispatch* reported that Asa Lorch had been on this visit merely to observe, in order to make a sizable loan available to the newspaper. In order for the newspaper, in turn, to assist this jail widow, as they had begun to call Sarah Brown.

"We must help this poor, hapless woman," the *Dispatch* editorialized, "and we are destitute of money. But the Farmer's and Merchant's Bank has come to our rescue."

The *Dispatch* reported that Patrick Macky was buying out Brown's Tavern with the bank's loan so that Sarah and her crippled son could go to Yankeeland to be near her old husband in that penitentiary in Detroit. All of which made a hell of a long-running story that people in the county wanted to read.

In fact, when Patrick Macky personally edited stories about this poor woman and her impaired son, ladies all across the county wiped a tear from their eyes, even though each of them had considered Brown's Tavern and everything associated with it a den of Satan's pit, beckoning husbands and sons and brothers and lovers to perdition.

Whatever, Sarah Brown sold the tavern. And on the evening Sarah and Drake stood on the Frisco platform waiting for the northbound, that same determined young reporter from Patrick Macky's stable was there, notebook in hand, leaning down, smiling, asking questions.

After the train left with Sarah and Drake on it, and the young man returned to the *Dispatch* office where Patrick Macky was waiting, there was some shouting. In the next Friday issue of the newspaper, there was a long story about the "jail widow" leaving town. In which it was reported that she said, "I have enjoyed all my friendships here and will always remember them."

What she actually said on that railroad platform was, "Roman Hasford is a blood-red son of a bitch, and before my death I will find a way to fry his ass in his own juice!"

There were other local stories reported in the *Dispatch*. Not so well read, perhaps. Nor so much discussed in the barbershop and hotel lobby.

Gallatin Delmonico departed, having sold his interest in the Farmer's and Merchant's Bank to Roman Hasford. It was reported that the bank paid Gallatin his original investment plus four percent interest on the money for all the years since the bank had been established. Compounded annually.

What Patrick Macky did not report was that on the winter evening when Gallatin and Missy boarded the northbound train, no one came to see them off except Judah Meyer. Nor was it reported that Gallatin Delmonico had said to Roman Hasford that same afternoon, "My conscience will not allow me to stay here now, the way you've begun running this bank."

"Maybe it'll make you feel better if I tell you I'm going to pay you a little bonus for your work here," Roman had said. "Just for old times' sake."

"Old times' sake? I wish we could go back to old times."

"Oh? What old times? The times before they butchered my friend? Before they circulated foul stories about me and my poor wife? Before they dragged my good family name through the dirt, and my old mother still alive to see it? And listen, Gallatin, all of that when a lot of what's made *better* times in this county I paid for. So go someplace else to find those old times."

"Mr. Hasford, you've become a vicious man."

"Mr. Delmonico, I hope you fare well."

"God help you, Mr. Hasford."

"There's not been much help from that quarter so far, as I see it. Until it happens, I'll help myself."

Gallatin Delmonico was not the only citizen of the county who had seen or sensed a change in the operation of the Farmer's and Merchant's Bank of Gourdville.

Criten Lapp, who was still coroner even though his eyesight was failing him, and his brother, Tilman, the undertaker, spoke of such things on the night they stood in the mortuary, leaning on the coffin in which reposed the remains of old man Tage.

"You know who'll buy his farm, now it's up for sheriff's sale because of delinquent taxes," said Tilman.

"The bank'll get it cheap. Nobody wants to buck against Roman Hasford. And with old Tage's farm right cheek-by-jowl with Catrina Hills, Roman'll bid on it. I guess Ausbin, down in Texas, couldn't send enough money to keep his daddy's farm, and hell, maybe he don't want it. So why not Roman?"

"You reckon Roman's got a list?" asked Tilman.

"What kinda list?" asked Criten.

"List of people on one side or the other over the past years. And not just politics, or the Trouble. Like them that done some snickerin' about that girl wife he had out there for a while, and things like that. Seems like those people have a hard time gettin' loans, anyway. Ones who had loans, seems like they get foreclosed a lot, don't it?"

"Well, all's I can say is I'm glad I never done any of the snickerin'. I don't owe the bank a lot. Maybe you and me and Isaac Maddox and Gwen Caulder and folks like that don't have much to worry about."

"Looks like a list to me."

"Glen Torten's ass is all squinched up. That damned Asa Lorch may call in his loan."

"Yeah, wrong side, wasn't he? And look at Ben Tark. They foreclosed him right after the trial."

"Yeah. And he went around sayin' some pretty harsh things about bein' double-crossed. I don't know what that means, but I'd hate to have Ben Tark sayin' I'd double-crossed him."

"It sure looked strange, didn't it? Two days after the bank got the distillery, that Samuel Dickie was here from Missouri, buyin' the property. Now making whiskey just like Ben did."

"Yeah, but I'd bet a pretty penny he ain't tryin' to sell any over in the Nations."

They laughed.

"Where'd Ben go, you ever hear?"

"No, but he lit out of here, didn't he?"

"Cato Fulton's pinchin' money and livin' on snow belly, I hear."

"Yeah. John Vain's out there on his farm about to starve, I hear. Frisco freight rates makin' it hard to make a dime sendin' his produce somewhere, and people around here a little leery about buying his stuff. Because he was on the wrong side, you see?"

"Looks like a list to me. A black list."

"And Brown's Tavern, settin' out there on the Nations Road, empty. Some of the kids say it's haunted by the souls of them two boys buried on the hill across the road."

"Yeah, and Corliss Buckmaten."

"Yeah, old Corliss, he ain't hard on nobody now. Can't tell everybody what a dyed-in-the-wool son of a bitch Roman Hasford is because he ain't got no newspaper no more."

"He musta swallowed bitter puke to go over and ask for work with Patrick Macky."

"Man's gotta put beans on the table."

"Sure, but I tell you, what Patrick Macky pays him, they may be beans on the table but Melissa ain't wearin' any more of them expensive hats she always liked to parade around the square."

"Pat Macky's got old Corliss writin' obituaries."

"And that weather stuff. Pat lookin' over his shoulder ever' minute with a blue pencil to change what Corliss writes if he don't like it."

"Has him sweep up the place, too. Corliss Buckmaten sweepin' up the place."

"Well, hell, can you imagine Corliss tryin' to make a livin' growin' anything? Or runnin' a sawmill?"

"Bitter puke."

"Corliss and Melissa all hangdog, stayin' in back of that old newspaper shop. Don't even go to church no more. But maybe it was all right for Corliss to ask for a job with Macky. At least old Pat Macky don't take sides, I mean."

"I wonder," said Criten Lapp.

Tilman straightened and slapped the coffin of old man Tage.

"Well, into the ground tomorrow."

"I guess Ausbin ain't comin' back for his daddy's funeral."

"Not's I know of."

"He used to have that mangy ole yard dog, and Roman Hasford hated that dog. I was always a little surprised the dog died a natural old-age death. I figured Roman'd shoot him one day. But he never. Shoot the dog, I mean."

"Well, into the ground tomorrow."

"It ain't a bad-lookin' casket. Ausbin didn't send enough money from Texas for taxes, but he bought a nice casket."

For a moment Tilman Lapp stared at his brother across the coffin. Then snorted.

"Hell, Ausbin Tage never paid for it."

"Oh?" said his brother. "Who did?"

"Roman Hasford."

Over the seasons now at Catrina Hills Farm, Roman Hasford spent more and more time on his porches and less and less going into town. For haircuts and sometimes shaves he still went to Anson Greedy's shop, but mostly he stayed at the Big House, watching the landscape changing through green spring to rust-dusty summer to frost-scented fall. And even into white-ground winter, there he sat in a rocking chair with a lap robe over his legs. He didn't go fox hunting anymore, even though Otis Maddox and his daddy, Isaac, always rode by with their hounds on the way to White River country, shouting an invitation. With Roman's father and Owen Caulder gone, it wouldn't be the same anymore. But sometimes, in autumn, with the brisk wind from the west and the leaves gone burnished-brass and crackling in the flow of air, Roman sat well into the darkness, clutching the lap robe about his legs and a blanket about his shoulders, and listened. And sometimes he could hear the dogs, far to the east, a faint, quavering wilderness symphony, brutal and pristine, that always made the hair on the back of his neck stand stiff.

Roman Hasford enjoyed reading Patrick Macky's *Dispatch*. Every issue of which was delivered to Catrina Hills Farm, even after rural free delivery, by horseback rider. And perhaps of all its readers in the county, he best understood the stories from the outside world.

Like the Congress of the United States making a half-hearted attempt to control monopolies with such things as the Sherman Antitrust Act. Or a global influenza epidemic that didn't affect northwest Arkansas. Or an earthquake in Japan that killed more people than lived in the whole county. Or Jim Corbett whipping John L. Sullivan. Or details of the World Exhibition in Chicago. Or the growing furor and indignation with the Spaniards over their treatment of people on an island called Cuba.

Orvile Tucker, who was not in any sense an avid reader but who had made himself literate down through the years, was aware of the *Dispatch* and what it had done to Corliss Buckmaten. And one late-autumn evening after he and Roman Hasford had eaten and a harsh wind was blowing dead leaves against the windows, making little pecking sounds like night birds, Orvile Tucker looked at Roman across the table and said, "You put him up to it, didn't you?"

"What?"

"That newspaperman. You put him up to it, didn't you?"

"That newspaperman? I read his newspaper. It's a good newspaper."

But lying in his bed that night, Orvile Tucker knew it was true. And it left an imprint on his mind half admiration and half abhorrence.

He remembered Roman Hasford's words: *I will destroy Corliss Buckmaten.*

Orvile Tucker knew it was true. And so he took up the silent dialogue with himself that made it possible for him to reconcile anything that Roman Hasford did.

I gotta get outta here. He don't pay no attention no more to the horses. He just sits out there and sips and reads them books. I gotta get outta here. Maybe next spring. Maybe.

But where? Too old to even want a woman anymore. Ain't had no woman since Kansas. Well, twice, when I went to Sedalia to talk horses. Then some women. A woman then ever' night.

Mr. Roman, he go to Fort Smith and brang back a woman for Lark Crozier. He never brought back none for me. Too old in the head, he says. Me no older than Lark Crozier, but maybe that's right. Maybe that's right. No thought for a woman, and no itch for the worry woman brangs.

Like slave days, in Tennessee, wife pretty as Renée, maybe more pretty. Long time past. Wonder where-at's that woman now. Wonder where-at's my two boys. All lef' behind when I run off from Tennessee to Kansas. All gone a long time, all old now or et up by the war or maybe starve to death in the cold somewheres.

Maybe go from here now. Old man. Even Roman old now. Go from here.

But where to?

31

The main lobby of the Farmer's and Merchant's Bank was approximately square, bisected by a wall-to-wall counter facing the door and the plate-glass window. This counter was interrupted by an opening at the center, with a swinging gate. As a customer entered the bank, there were the tellers' windows to the right, the cashier's cage to the left. This entire counter was topped by an iron grille-work, like heavy chicken wire, with appropriate openings through which the business of money could be transacted.

The lobby was bright and cheerful because the window faced south, so the sun always shone in on the black-and-white mosaic tile floor. When it was cloudy, everyone remembered that soon the sun would return, not only shining on the floor but reflecting from all the polished walnut woodwork.

At either end of the customer side of the lobby were stand-up desks with sunken inkwells and trays for pens. And beside each, a highly polished brass cuspidor. Above one of these stand-up desks was a large calendar, always with some scene involving a steam locomotive coming head-on, below a word in praise of the Frisco railroad. On the opposite wall above the stand-up desk there was a framed print of Currier and Ives stylized horses pulling a sleigh through the snow.

The calendar changed every year, except that each one came from Frisco. The picture of the horses whose heads were too small was never changed. It had been there since the bank opened years before, and its reds were beginning to fade.

Behind the counter was a partition extending the length of the room. Centered here was the door marked ROMAN HASFORD, PRES-

IDENT in gold leaf. If the door was open, the president was not there. If it was closed, he was. Not everybody knew this.

Toward the cashier side of the president's office was a dead-end hall used for the storage of blank forms and paper and all the other things banks needed to conduct business. Judah Meyer had dubbed it the Paper Passage. It contained file cabinets, but mostly open shelves stacked with office supplies.

Directly behind the cashier's cage was another door opening into an office for the cashier and loan officer. But Asa Lorch was seldom seen there. Almost always he was in his "Hawk's Nest" on the second floor, reached by a spiral metal staircase located in the corner behind the cashier's cage.

On the other side of the president's office was a second hallway. This one led to the alley, having a door at the far end, and from that door one could look to the left, or west, and see the loading platform at the hotel kitchen next door, and beyond that the front of Caulder's Mercantile on Fourth Street. Across the alley was the slab-sided double toilet, one door marked Ladies, the other Gentlemen.

Because this hallway gave access to such a facility, Judah Meyer called it the Privy Passage. Of course, he never used this term within hearing of the two women tellers, Lucinda Black, daughter of the county judge, and Maybella Gooch, wife of the doctor who also owned the drugstore.

Next to the Privy Passage and directly behind the tellers' counter the wall was uninterrupted except for the vault door with all its dials and handles and turn-screw wheels. Set in the wall above the vault door was a large, circular clock, its hinged glass front allowing Judah Meyer to open it each morning, insert the key, and tighten the mainspring.

This was the device that opened the safe. For, as in many banks in large cities, this was a time-lock vault. If the round massive, door was closed at any time, and the dials and handles and turn-screw wheels properly manipulated, the safe would close and not open until 9:30 A.M. the following day. Except on Saturdays and Sundays. And Christmas and Independence Day. Or any other specific day for which Judah Meyer set the clock to keep the vault closed.

There was a small metal lockbox kept in the cashier's office desk overnight, always with about a thousand dollars inside. This was for distribution to the tellers so that business might go forward between 9:00 A.M., when the bank opened, and 9:30 A.M., when the vault did.

As in the case of all banks since modern banking began—probably in Venice at about the time various artists were daubing paint on the ceilings of holy places—each day saw a regular routine. A fact well noted by those who expected to make withdrawals of money. It was a routine as predictable, they said, as mules passing wind after ingesting a large bait of sweet potatoes.

At 7:30 A.M., Asa Lorch arrived, unlocked the door, entered, locked the door, and went to his perch in the Hawk's Nest. At 7:45, Judah Meyer arrived, giving his usual cheery greeting to Arno Cleevis, who was always waiting on the sidewalk.

Arno Cleevis. He had wandered into this town many years before, without any means of explaining who he was or where he had been. Roman Hasford, despite the violent objections of Gallatin Delmonico, had hired Arno to clean the bank and do little odd jobs, which Arno performed very well.

Since then, Arno had slept in an empty stall at Ennis Lugi's stable, for which Roman Hasford paid Ennis four dollars a month. Arno ate in the kitchen of the Stone Hotel, for which Roman Hasford paid Harley Stone ten dollars a month. Arno had his clothing from Caulder's, for which Roman Hasford paid the wholesale rate.

To say that Arno Cleevis wasn't very smart, Roman Hasford always said, missed the point. He had nothing inside his skull with which to be smart. He functioned somewhat like a salamander whose responses to life's problems were generated in some gray ganglia perhaps in the vicinity of his colon.

It took Roman Hasford ten years to convince Arno that he need not beg dimes on the streets of Gourdville when he wanted an ice cream cone. If he wanted an ice cream cone, the Farmer's and Merchant's Bank would stand good on the purchase.

Certain citizens, mostly those who had snickered about the old stories of Roman Hasford and his child bride, called Arno "Hasford's Dummy."

Arno was not spectacularly handsome. In fact, he looked like a mangy old hound, even to the sad, brown eyes. Ennis Lugi had provided a place for bathing and shaving, but then everybody was afraid to give Arno a razor. So about once a week Roman Hasford told Arno to get his hair cut at Anson Greedy's, and a shave as well, and Arno always went. Because Roman Hasford was Arno's god, and whatever Roman said, Arno did.

So each morning when Judah Meyer arrived, there was Arno. Judah unlocked the front door, he and Arno went in, Judah to wind the vault clock and distribute money from the small metal lockbox to the teller trays, Arno to stoke fires in the stoves if it was winter and then sweep the floors and polish the cuspidors, always having forgotten that he had swept the floors and polished the cuspidors the day before, after closing.

At 8:15 A.M. the tellers arrived, usually in tandem, and Judah Meyer unlocked the front door to let them in. And almost immediately inside, Mrs. Maybella Gooch would call Arno Cleevis into the Paper Passage and comb Ennis Lugi's stable straw from his hair. The conversation was always the same.

"My gracious, Arno, what are we going to do with you?" Mrs. Maybella would say. "You're always losing your comb."

"It's such a little bitty thang, Miz Maybella."

At 8:30 A.M., Albert Smith would arrive, also let in by Judah Meyer. He was the son of Baptist minister Zechariah Smith. Town wags said he'd backslid considerably since the day his daddy baptized him in Oak Creek and in a fit of religious passion almost drowned the boy. He was assistant cashier.

Albert always wore an off-white celluloid collar and a bow tie. And his recent attempts to grow a beard and mustache gave him the appearance of having just tried to eat a bowl of coal cinders. The lady tellers enjoyed small giggles at Albert's expense, but of course he never knew it.

Asa Lorch had attached a large map to the back wall of the president's office. There, over a three-county area, he had stuck varicolored pins showing mortgages and deeds and other bank interests. Roman found it distasteful and never looked at it. But in the early mornings, before Roman arrived, if indeed he ever did on certain days, Arno Cleevis had a love affair with that map and the colored pins.

Arno was the only employee who dared sit in the president's chair. And each morning, once he had done his chores and Maybella Gooch had combed the straw out of his hair, he dashed into the office where the great chair waited. And sat, sprawled, swallowed by the chair, swiveled around with his back to the door, his head cradled in soft leather, his eyes, those hound-dog brown eyes, bright as they ever were while he contemplated the wondrous Thing. He didn't know what a map was, or what the colored pins meant, but he knew, just sitting there in the president's chair, that the whole of it was a panting delight unknown to any other mortal.

He never stayed too long. By the time Roman Hasford arrived, if he came at all, Arno would be away in Harley Stone's hotel kitchen, eating buckwheat cakes and pork sausage. But for the first few moments of the day, say about thirty minutes, Arno enjoyed the ecstasy of discovery, each day anew, the images of color and space and time whirling unrestrained inside his head.

At 9:00 A.M., Judah Meyer would go to the front door and unlock it, and another day of business began. Asa Lorch in his perch upstairs. Maybella Gooch and Lucinda Black smiling at their posts. Albert Smith in the cashier's cage. Arno Cleevis in the president's chair.

Thus it was on Wednesday, January 17, 1894.

There was nothing to distinguish this as an unusual day except that it was very cold and snowing outside. Everything was as ordered when the courthouse clock struck nine. Roman Hasford had arrived in town with his "bird dog," Bishop Eckor, having ridden direct to the west side of the square where Anson Greedy was waiting to give him the biweekly hair-and-mustache trim and shave.

Bishop Eckor led the horses to Ennis Lugi's stable, then hurried back across the square, having left the big rifle in the saddle boot because he figured that on this frigid day Roman Hasford was as safe as safe could be. And hurried on through the falling snow to the alley behind the hotel and along that to the toilets in back of the bank. And just in time, breathing a sigh of relief, sitting there with pants down, having been afflicted with a bout of diarrhea since midnight and now ready to subject his naked ass to the cold in order to rid his bowels of the demons therein—without, he hoped, squirting his intestines into the crapper hole in the process.

Sheriff Colin Hamp was hurrying along North Third Street from the widow Frazby's house, where he had gone the night before without taking an overcoat. And now, his stocky figure shivering, he dogtrotted along toward the square in a short jacket, Stetson pulled low against the snow, cheeks icy as the backstrap of the Bisley model Colt pistol at his belt.

Cold, cold, cold, Sheriff Colin Hamp thought, then concentrated on his route. Get to the alley just short of the square, turn right and along behind the bank and to the kitchen of the hotel and into Harley's dining room and a large pot of coffee and a plate of those fresh doughnuts Raymond Ort always brings over from the bakery for breakfast guests. God, it's cold, cold, cold!

Beginning to apply the warm lather to Roman Hasford, reclining in his barber chair, Anson Greedy could look from his window and see Corliss Buckmaten going along Elkhorn Street toward the railroad and his job at the *Dispatch*, his head down, his long coat seeming to sweep the snow behind him as he went.

Brian Felcher's dairy cart was parked in front of Danton Rich's café across the square, the old horse in the stays frosted white with snow. Anson Greedy knew that Brian would be inside enjoying a cup of Danton's hot chocolate.

Other than that, the square was empty. There were two gray squirrels down from their leaf nest in one of the oaks at the center of the square, jousting in the snow. Charging, retreating, scampering. Anson Greedy smiled as he watched them, fingering the hot lather along Roman Hasford's jaw.

It was 9:10 A.M. when Harley Stone, watering a potted palm in one of his lobby's front windows, looked out and saw the five horsemen come into the square from the west. They wore wide-brimmed hats pulled low and split-tailed riding coats, all crusted with white. Under the fender of each saddle was a rifle.

They drew rein in front of the bank, paused for a moment, then one of them turned his horse back and rode to Fifth Street and into the alley behind the hotel and the bank. The other four, still in front of the Farmer's and Merchant's, dismounted, and one stood with the horses as the rest moved to the door of the bank.

Gwen Caulder, ready to open her store, saw the rider go into the alley and stop at the rear door of the bank, then dismount. It seemed strange to her so she took down from her retail rack a Springfield .45–70 rifle and inserted a round and continued to watch through one of her frosted windows.

Across the square, on the south side, Tilman Lapp stood at the window of his mortuary, eyes muddy with sleep. He saw the squirrels playing in the snow. He saw the horsemen. And watched as three of them went into the bank. One remained outside. And then, as Tilman Lapp continued to watch, the one at the hitch rail with the horses pulled a rifle from a saddle boot.

"Oh shit," said Tilman Lapp, and turned back into his undertaking parlor to try to find an old Marlin rifle that he hadn't fired in thirty years.

Lucinda Black looked up from her counter tray and smiled as the blast of cold air came in with the three men.

"Well, heavens to Betsy," she said, "Mr. Tark, we haven't seen you in such a long time—"

She stopped abruptly as Benjamin Tark came through the swinging gate and pulled a large pistol from beneath his coat and shoved the gaping muzzle almost into Miss Lucinda's mouth.

"Get right over yonder, Miz Lucinda," Ben Tark said, waving the pistol. "You too, Miz Gooch, right back over yonder agin the wall. Now! Now!"

Directly behind Ben Tark was a small man, his weasel face red from the cold under the wide, spreading brim of a slouch hat. He pushed past Ben Tark as Ben began scooping money from the teller trays and stuffing it into his coat pockets.

"You can't come back here," Judah shouted, unable to accept what was happening, even though he knew from all he had heard that this was Yancy Crane. "You can't come back here."

But Yancy Crane was already at the door to the president's office. He slid a long, slender rifle from beneath his coat, lifted it, and fired.

The explosion made everything in the room jump—the hanging kerosene lamps, the cuspidors, the pen staffs in the stand-up desks. The high-velocity bullet smashed through the high back of the president's chair and through Arno Cleevis's head, taking Arno's forehead and most of his face with it, and splattering the map with a gray-red smudge. Arno made one great, convulsive jerk, then sprawled motionless in the arms of the chair as though he were still contemplating the colored pins.

Albert Smith collapsed to the floor on hands and knees, wailing. "Oh God, oh God, oh God!" Somehow, as he went down, his celluloid collar had become loose and was now thrust out below his left ear like a forgotten bed slat.

The third man was at the cashier's cage, giggling, dancing, kicking at Albert Smith. It was Poco Jimmy, almost hysterical with excitement.

"Where's the money, get out the money!" he screamed. He was waving a burlap sack in one hand, a pistol in the other. Then the pistol was back in his waistband as he began to take bills from the cashier's drawer and push them in wads into the sack.

Yancy Crane turned the rifle toward Judah Meyer.

"Open the safe," he said in a calm, level voice. But Ben Tark had begun to shout now.

"Why'd you shoot so soon?" he yelled. "Why'd you shoot, everybody in town gonna know now."

"Shut up. You, Meyer, open the safe!"

"I can't open the safe. It's a time lock."

Yancy Crane's face twisted in a spasm of fury and indecision. He turned toward Ben Tark.

"Damn you, why didn't you tell me it was a time safe?"

"Why'd you shoot so damned soon? Everybody gonna know now." Ben Tark was still trying to clean out the teller trays, but many of the greenbacks were falling to the floor.

"Where's the money?" Poco Jimmy was screaming.

"Our Father who art in Heaven, hallowed be Thy name," Albert Smith said to the floor.

Gwen Caulder heard the shot from inside the bank. And she saw the man behind the bank dismount and stand beside the bank's back door, look around quickly, then pull a revolver from beneath his coat, still holding the reins as his horse became nervous and started to stamp and snort.

Gwen Caulder stepped out onto her windswept porch and took what she knew was the most devastating shot she could take. Deer hunters called it the butt shot, right between the hip joints and up through the whole body without any bone to deflect the slug. The old rifle kicked like a steam engine and the cloud of white smoke was whipped away by the wind, and in the alley the horse collapsed, folding up on himself like a closing book.

Coming near the east end of the alley, Sheriff Colin Hamp heard the shot inside the bank, too. A muffled thump. Then the cannon racket of the Springfield from the Caulder Mercantile. He ran, turning into the alley, and saw the horse down and the man trying to pull the horse up by the reins, pistol still in hand. And as Colin Hamp ran, yanking out his Bisley model Colt, the door at the Gentlemen side of the privy came open and there was Bishop Eckor, trying to hold his pants up and cock a belly gun at the same time. Colin Hamp saw Bishop Eckor fire both barrels of the .41-caliber derringer, saw the man trying to hold the horse jerk and fall against the back wall of the bank, cursing, still trying to pull the horse up. And then the second shot came from Caulder's Mercantile. The big 500-grain lead bullet caught the man at the knee and cut him down like a stalk of corn. He screamed, not in pain, but in utter astonishment, and his hat flew in one direction, his handgun in the other, and Bishop Eckor, with finally at least one suspender strap over his shoulder, ran across the alley, throwing his empty derringer aside and grabbing up the big revolver the man had lost in the snow. The man was down, thrashing and yelling, blood on his boots, blood on his coat, blood on his shirt collar.

Inside the bank, they could hear the shooting from the rear.

"God of our fathers," wailed Albert Smith, still on hands and knees.

"Where-at's the money?" Poco Jimmy was screaming, dancing, laughing.

"You Goddamned dumb heathen," Yancy Crane shouted, "a time-lock safe, a time-lock safe."

He was backing out, toward the front door, panic now on his pinched features, and Ben Tark whirling, scattering money, wild-eyed, losing his bearings.

"Wait a minute!" Ben Tark shouted. "Wait a minute!"

He looked at Maybella Gooch and Lucinda Black, clinging together in each other's arms against the east wall.

"I never done it, I never wanted to do it."

Then, seeing Yancy Crane leaving through the front and Poco Jimmy gone crazy and disappearing in the Paper Passage still screaming about money, money, money, Benjamin Tark lost all sense of direction and ran back along the Privy Passage to the door that led to the alley.

When Benjamin Tark burst through the door into the alley, Sheriff Colin Hamp, rushing up close by then, saw only the heavy revolver in Ben Tark's hand. Colin Hamp fired and Ben Tark's knees buckled and he dropped his gun and greenbacks were spilling from his coat pockets into the wind and he fell sideways, over the man already against the bloody wall.

"Wait a minute!" he screamed, and Colin Hamp shot him again. Ben Tark sprawled facedown over the head of the dead horse, and suddenly Bishop Eckor was there, scooping up Ben Tark's pistol from the snow, and with Ben Tark still moaning, Colin Hamp and

Bishop Eckor ran into the Privy Passage, going toward the bank lobby.

Deputy Sheriff Nathan Bridger came to the front steps of the courthouse.

"What the hell goin' on?" he said aloud.

Carrying a heavy Winchester rifle from the gun rack in the sheriff's office, he saw the four horses in front of the bank, one man trying to hold them, then another small, stooped figure rushing from the bank and clutching at the reins of one of the horses, then mounting, and the first man, still trying to hold the remaining horses, yelling something. It was then that Nathan Bridger started shooting.

The first shot hit one of the horses in the neck just behind the ear and the horse went down, squealing, legs thrashing. The second shot hit the man, whose hands slipped loose from the reins he was still trying to hold, and he fell, throwing up a cloud of powdery snow, then was up and in a burst of speed rushed into the center of the square, sending the playing squirrels wildly up into the oaks, then fell again, his coat spreading like the wings of a bat.

The mounted man was whipping his horse toward the west, along the Nations Road, and the remaining two horses at the rail broke free and ran after him, their empty stirrups flapping.

Nathan Bridger reloaded, thumbing fresh rounds into the Winchester.

Danton Rich heard the shooting. He ran from his café with a little .22-caliber rifle his son used for rabbit hunting, and seeing the man riding off the square, coattails flying, Danton Rich rested the rifle against the dairy cart and fired, missing everything except one of the windows in the front of Harley Stone's hotel, the bullet leaving there a neat spiderweb hole in the glass beside one of Harley's potted plants.

Tilman Lapp, who had been the first to know, was on the sidewalk in the snow, hearing all the shots, then seeing Yancy Crane dashing west. He lifted his old rifle and fired, and it exploded in his face, showering his cheeks with bits of metal and black-powder residue.

"God, I've shot my ownself."

In the bank, Yancy Crane gone, Ben Tark gone, Poco Jimmy was doing his dance of madness down the Paper Passage, still shouting "Where's the money, where's the money?" and pulling blank forms and sheets of paper off the shelves, going back to the very rear wall of the building, where, in this hallway, there was no exit. Then he turned, just as Colin Hamp and Bishop Eckor appeared at the lobby end. Poco Jimmy, screaming with laughter, tried to disentangle his old Remington revolver from his waistband. Colin Hamp fired and Bishop Eckor fired, with both hands, and Poco Jimmy's arms flailed upward as though trying to leave his body and he was smashed back against the rear wall in a snowstorm of white paper and paper clips and pen staffs and ink bottles and greenbacks. In that narrow space there was a sudden burst of red, like flying drops of grease from the surface of white-hot skillet, and as Poco Jimmy was slammed back and then seemed to trickle down into the mass of paper debris, he left a great, wide swath of scarlet on the wall at his back.

Hamp and Eckor turned, without words, because no words were necessary, and ran for the swinging gate in the counter and on to the front door. On toward the street, where there was nothing now but a dead horse and the facedown form of a man in the snow at the center of the square.

Both women in the bank had found their voices now, but there was nothing from their lips except little mewings. Albert Smith, still on hands and knees, continued praying. Judah Meyer stared, in a trance, as the sheriff and Bishop Eckor dove through the front door, breaking the glass. There were more shots, and both men dove back inside again. And the sound of a whining ricochet through the snowy square.

Nathan Bridger, at the courthouse steps still, was shooting at anything that moved.

"Nathan," Colin Hamp shouted from the safety of the bank doorway, "it's me! Stop shootin', for Christ's sake!"

Then Colin remembered the two men in the alley and turned to Bishop Eckor, making his voice heard above the ringing in their ears, the ringing brought on by gunfire.

"Alley. Alley. Don't let them two get away."

Bishop Eckor turned and ran back through the bank, aware now for the first time that he had seriously soiled his underwear and pants and smelled even worse than the sulfur-and-gunpowder odor so heavy in the dense swirl of smoke in the lobby. Therefore he was happy to be out into the cold and away from all these other people.

Sheriff Colin Hamp, peeking around the corner of the bank doorway to be sure his deputy was not still spraying the square with large-caliber bullets, ran onto the sidewalk. And stood there, looking around as though he had never seen it before.

From across the square, Tilman Lapp was limping toward the bank, his face spotted with red and black powder pocks. Roman Hasford and Anson Greedy were running from the barbershop, Roman with a Colt in one hand and half his face still white with shaving lather.

Asa Lorch came down the metal stairway from the Hawk's Nest, looking as he always did but carrying a white chamber pot into which he had just puked. He set the pot beside the crouching, still-praying Albert Smith, then turned without a single word and mounted the staircase again to his bay-window perch above the square.

Across the lobby, Lucinda Black and Maybella Gooch had begun to disengage from each other, Lucinda crying now, Maybella beginning to work up to furious indignation. And Judah Meyer, pushing himself away from the west wall where he had felt himself glued for an eternity, thought, That was the most exhilarating experience I've ever had.

Then Judah Meyer came abreast of the narrow hallway and looked and saw the red-speckled blank forms and foolscap and, faceup, staring at him with open eyes, what was left of Poco Jimmy. And Judah Meyer turned, and bent, and threw up in the chamber pot that Asa Lorch had already put to the same use.

At that moment, as though on cue, there was the rattling click that indicated the time lock had opened the vault. And from the east side of the square, the single stroke of the courthouse bell clock marking 9:30 A.M.

And the two squirrels in the square came back down from their oak trees to play in the snow.

32

By the time Sheriff Colin Hamp and his two-man posse, consisting of Deputy Nathan Bridger and Hiram Chesney from the tie yard, rode pell-mell into the snow toward the Nations in search of Yancy Crane, most of the gunfire delirium had burned itself out. Roman Hasford was in the bank, along with what seemed half the town's population, he grimly to assess, they to satisfy morbid curiosity, little of which could be done from the front side of the counter because little of the bloodletting was visible from there.

Everyone stood back, crowding the stand-up desks and the front windows, out of respect maybe, or more likely fear. Not from fear of the sight of gore and spilled brains but from fear of Roman Hasford. Because those who knew him well, and those who knew him slightly, and those who knew him only by reputation had all heard of his violent temper and vindictiveness. And so they stood wide-eyed, waiting for the explosion.

But no explosion came.

Shaving-soap lather still on his face, the president of the Farmer's and Merchant's Bank moved about this scene of carnage, Anson Greedy the only person with courage enough to move beside him. But even Anson Greedy was preoccupied with Roman's reactions. Still in Anson's right hand was a straight razor, but he was completely unaware that it was there.

Roman went into his office and stood for a long time looking down at the pitiful form of Arno Cleevis, his face mangled beyond recognition, his slight frame slouched in the great leather chair.

Even then, Lucinda Black was still weakly shouting the name

of Yancy Crane, whom she had known in her childhood as sheriff of this county.

"With the back of the chair to the door," Roman said, "Yancy couldn't see who it was. He thought it was me."

"I reckon," said Anson Greedy.

Later, Anson Greedy reported the situation as he saw it, as all good barbers do. There was no noticeable change in Roman Hasford's expression. Except for a little tightening of the lips. A little glitter in the eyes. But no explosion.

What Anson Greedy did not report, because he did not know it, was that even had no one mentioned Yancy Crane's name, Roman would have known who fired the shot through the back of the president's chair.

Roman walked to the head of the Paper Passage but allowed himself only a brief glance at the tangle of Poco Jimmy's madness. Then, turning away, he reseated the Colt six-shooter in the holster under his left arm, wiped the soap off his face with the barber's cloth that was still pinned around his neck, and ripped off the cloth and threw it on the floor. That violent, wordless movement was the beginning and end of his suppressed rage. And so all those watching, the ones who knew him well, the ones who knew him slightly, and the ones who knew him only by reputation, sighed with relief because all of them knew that here was a man whose single whim could change the life of anyone in this county. Not one of those watchers understood the controlled anger. Had Orvile Tucker been there, he might have. But he wasn't there.

"What the hell are all these people doing in here?" Roman asked. And, turning to Chief of Police Alvis Lapp, "Get everybody out of here. Now!"

And Alvis Lapp, responding as all public servants responded to the man who has made them public servants in the first place, did.

Later, Anson Greedy shook his head and laughed. "Well, remember, Roman Hasford don't set in any church pews around here, but he's the one who buys 'em."

It seemed that the townspeople were galvanized into clearing away the debris of the robbery almost as if, were it done fast enough, they could pretend it never happened.

Benjamin Tark and the other bandit wounded in the alley were carried to Gooch's drugstore and there, on improvised operating tables, Doc Gooch and Doc Cronin gouged lead out of flesh and sutured still-bleeding wounds. Standing by was one of Alvis Lapp's policemen with a shotgun. But these two bank robbers were not going anywhere, guard or not, and the younger man would probably never walk again, even if Doc Cronin could save his left leg.

This young man was Kingsnake, the Cherokee who as a lad had come to Gourdville years before with Poco Jimmy to sell birds. Roman Hasford had seen him as they carried him, dripping, through the bank lobby on the way to Gooch's drugstore.

"You'd been better off staying over in the Nations, boy," Roman had said, but Kingsnake had made no sign that he heard, gritting his teeth with the pain that was coming strong, now that nerves shocked by crashing bullets were coming alive once more.

Patrick Macky and a platoon of his men were everywhere, notebooks and pencils in hand. Patrick himself was one of the first into the bank after Roman arrived there, and after assuring himself that the only loss was a flurry of loose bills gone in the alley wind as they blew out of Benjamin Tark's coat pockets, he rushed back to the *Dispatch* office. And that late evening there would be an extra, complete with a crude sketch on the front page, a sketch of the bank and environs, with an X marking each spot where the dead and wounded had fallen.

Tilman Lapp, still wiping specks of blood from his face, organized a carrying party to get the dead to his mortuary. First Poco Jimmy and Arno Cleevis. Then, before moving the man at the center of the square, he asked Roman to come take a look. Tilman had turned the body over in the snow so it was faceup when Roman came.

"Clarence Vain," said Tilman Lapp. "He can't be over sixteen years old."

"How in the hell did he get involved in all this?" Roman asked.

"The Vains never been a hotbed of good feelin' for the Hasfords, Roman."

"Will you let his folks know?"

"Criten will. He'll want one or both of 'em to come in and make an identification. It's gotta go on the coroner's report."

"At least his face didn't get chewed up like the other two."

Inside the bank, Asa Lorch finally came down, pale, his hands shaking, but ready to do his part of the clean-up. Judah Meyer had been so shaken that Roman sent him home, as well as the two women and Albert Smith—Albert speechless and hollow-eyed, his celluloid collar sticking out, Lucinda Black still crying, Maybella Gooch in a growling rage.

"Lock the front door and the vault," Roman said to Asa Lorch, "then get this place scrubbed out."

Roman turned to Alvis Lapp, one of the few left, and said, "How many prisoners are there over in the jail?"

"Four. Two of mine, two of Colin's."

"See Pemberton Grady," Roman said. "See if we can't get them over here to clean it up. I'll pay two bits an hour to them. I reckon our prosecuting attorney ought to be glad enough to let some of our unruly citizens see where it can lead."

Waiting for the prisoners to arrive, as he knew they surely would, Roman Hasford stood at the bank's front door and looked out through the shattered glass. It was snowing so hard he could not see the Lapp mortuary, across the square. Only he and Asa Lorch and Anson Greedy and Gwen Caulder were still in the bank, Gwen Caulder having come in from the bank as soon as they carried off the alley wounded, in her hand the great long rifle.

"Asa," Roman said, "get somebody to nail something over this door window."

"There's lumber and tools upstairs," Asa said. "I'll do it myself." The color had come back to his face. At least as much color as was ever there.

After Asa had gone, Roman placed a hand on Gwen Caulder's shoulder. "Lady," he said, "I am grateful that you're on my side."

"I made a mistake. That last shot, I should have aimed higher. I might have saved the county a lot of money. It's cheaper to bury 'em than to try 'em."

Anson Greedy giggled. By now his straight razor was back in a vest pocket.

"Roman, your man Bishop what's-his-name. He's over at the store getting some new underwear and pants. Somehow or other, he messed the ones he had on."

"Well now, there's a real gunfighter for you," Anson Greedy said. "First time he gets in a shoot, he dirties his britches."

Roman Hasford couldn't suppress the laughter. It came uncontrolled, convulsively, and even as he laughed he was thinking, That damned Yancy Crane, I should have written Jared Dane after the Brown boys were taken care of and told him to keep at it until it was finished!

By the time Colin Hamp returned, Roman was in Harley Stone's hotel dining room drinking coffee and listening for the tenth time about the sound of Danton Rich's .22-caliber bullet coming through the front window of the hotel lobby.

"It almost hit one of my palms," said Harley Stone.

Colin Hamp and Nathan Bridger, caked with snow, came directly to Roman Hasford, and Colin showed him a long, skinny rifle. Roman took it and worked the bolt, and a bottleneck round leaped out. A military load. Then he remembered Hamlin Bidd saying on the night somebody had taken a shot at the Big House that it was likely one of those new military rifles.

"Why'd he drop it?"

"Who knows?" said Colin Hamp.

"I may have got one into him when he was ridin' off," said Nathan Bridger.

"Yeah, well, we never found no blood," said Colin Hamp. "We lost him a couple of miles west of old Brown's Tavern."

"Damned snow," said Bridger.

"Gotta go send some telegraphs," said Colin Hamp. "Let other peace officers know."

"Yes, you do that, but keep this rifle," said Roman.

Harley was talking about the rash of bank robberies, one in Harrison, one in Eureka Springs, one in Gravit.

"Why, it's just an epidemic of bank robberies."

But Roman knew this was no part of some epidemic. This was Yancy Crane. Now gone in the snow. And there was a lot more of the snow coming down outside.

Bandaged and sewn back together, Benjamin Tark and King-snake were hauled to the Frisco depot and loaded on a southbound freight caboose for transport to a hospital in Fayetteville. One of Alvis Lapp's policemen was with them. The one with the shotgun. His name was Legget Reed and he was twenty years old and this was the most wonderful thing that had ever happened to him because he had never been outside Benton County in his entire life.

"What have they got in Fayetteville?" Legget Reed asked the brakeman.

"Oh, about ever'thing they got ever'where else, I reckon."

Before full dark, when Roman Hasford and Bishop Eckor in his new underwear and britches were about to ride back to Catrina

Hills Farm, three telegraph messages came for the president of the Farmer's and Merchant's Bank of Gourdville, from other banks in Fayetteville and Eureka Springs, offering money at low interest so he would have operating cash until everything came back to normal.

It was a nice touch. Roman instructed Lamar Peevy, the night telegrapher at the depot, to respond with a standard telegram of appreciation and an assurance that no loss had been sustained.

Orvile Tucker had a chicken pie browning in the oven at Catrina Hills Farms, and for the first time Bishop Eckor was asked into the kitchen of the Big House to eat. Between mouthfuls, Roman told Orvile what had happened in town, and Orvile sat, shaking his head and clucking his tongue. Thinking, Lordy, bad thangs happen an' finally he don't act like it even faze him no more, like he build a hard shell aroun' him that he lives in, like a old turtle, with nothin' showin' but what sticks out on the end of a long neck. That hard mouth. Them beady eyes. But that hair, not even goin' white no more. Just stop goin' white like it jus' come to a certain place an' decides it ain't goin' no whiter. No matter what. Hardheaded, stubborn. Look at him poke that pie down his throat. Like there ain't no sorrow no more for anything. Like all the sorrow been used up. A man could cry when a new foal drop, I tole him. But can't cry no more for nothin'.

Well, Orvile Tucker was right, as far as it went. But there were some things he didn't know. That morning, when Roman Hasford had first seen the bespattered walls and floor of his office and the Paper Passage, he had made the decision. He was going to sell the bank. Or at least a large interest in it, keeping a few securities and a few mortgages, maybe. But get rid of banking. And worry only about which porch of the Big House would be bathed in sunshine. And spend some time at Wolf Cove Mill with Lark and his family. And think about horses again. And maybe even hire some people to start working the old Hasford farmstead and refurbish the old Hasford house above Wire Road.

It wouldn't be difficult. There were a lot of people in St. Louis and Kansas City who would jump at the chance to buy out a fine bank like this one.

So maybe Yancy Crane and the Browns had won after all. Because they'd finally succeeded in getting Roman Hasford out of the banking business. When he thought about that, it didn't bother him too much. Small advantage those bastards would get from it, he thought. Why, hell, he thought, I've never been a banker anyway.

Back in Gourdville that night, not a single issue of the *Dispatch* bank-robbery extra was sold on the streets, because in the increasing intensity of the storm, nobody was on the street. The whole press run sold to Gooch's drugstore, where the blood from the quick-surgery had been mopped up, and in Harley Stone's hotel, and to the candy butchers on Frisco's Number Six passenger northbound.

So Patrick Macky kept his type-rotating press running into the night, getting more newspapers ready for local consumption the next day. Citizens of Gourdville who lived near the *Dispatch* office could hear the little steam engine huffing and puffing until almost midnight.

One of the *Dispatch* people stoking the boiler on that engine was Corliss Buckmaten. And now, knowing all the details of the attempted robbery through the good work of Patrick Macky's reporters, he tried not to think about it because he was ashamed of what he thought: So long as somebody had to die in this thing, it's too bad Arno Cleevis was sitting in that chair instead of Roman Hasford!

PART SEVEN

COME WINTER

33

It was only the second time there had been what could be called a social gathering at Catrina Hills Farm since the Big House was built. The first had been nearly a quarter-century before and had been designed to launch Roman Hasford into machine politics in the county. This one, called in the waning months of Grover Cleveland's second term, was designed to launch Roman Hasford out of county politics and just about everything else except minding his own business.

Most of the same people were invited. At least the ones who were still alive. There were a few new faces, like Patrick Macky and Otis Maddox and Gwen Caulder, the only woman asked to attend. Each of the old bunch who had somehow survived to this day were a lot longer in the tooth, as Isaac Maddox put it.

The purpose of this gathering was to introduce what Roman Hasford considered to be the power structure in the county to the new owner of the Farmer's and Merchant's Bank, a Mr. Leland Commanger from St. Louis, who had made it known that he would change the name to The Commanger Commerce Bank and Trust Company. Which everyone agreed he had every right to do, having bought a controlling interest for what was rumored to be in the neighborhood of twenty thousand dollars, a very exclusive neighborhood indeed, they said.

Most of this crowd knew that Roman Hasford would retain considerable assets, including their own outstanding mortgages. To ensure, they assumed, that new management would not run roughshod over old preferred customers. In fact, most everyone who attended Roman Hasford's second social affair reckoned they could continue to come to him as private citizens when they needed loans and venture capital because they'd been doing it for so long that it was uncomfortable to change.

Asa Lorch and Judah Meyer were conspicuous by their absence, Mr. Leland Commanger having allowed that he wanted to bring in his own people. Roman had already paid Asa and Judah handsome bonuses and given both men glowing letters of recommendation to carry with them as they began the search for new positions elsewhere.

It was one of those wonderful Ozark autumn days when the foliage was blazing yellow and red in the sunlight. The jays were warning harshly that winter was not far away. And there were the scents of ripe persimmons, apples crushed for cider, and old geraniums exhausted with blooming all summer and ready for a rest.

In addition to Orvile Tucker serving the guests, Lark Crozier and his family had come, Lark having brought about thirty pounds of his barbecued goat. Renée operated the kitchen while her husband and Orvile kept glasses of sour-mash whiskey in everyone's hand. Hasford Crozier, now a tall, strapping, chocolate-colored young man, tended the porch tables where the platters of fried chicken and potato salad and baked beans and crisp corn bread were laid out. A major part of his job was to shoo the flies away from the food.

But after a few snorts of sour mash, cooled down with beer drawn from the kegs iced in one of the yard horse troughs, nobody worried too much about flies.

Throughout all this, it was observed that Gwen Caulder had taken as many sips of sour mash and beer as any of the men but remained the most clear-eyed of the whole crew.

"I'll tell you something," former sheriff Hamlin Bidd said. "That's an admirable woman. Any man who could take her to wife would have to be a lion tamer."

Roman Hasford, after introducing Mr. Leland Commanger to his guests, transacted only one item of business all day. In his parlor, alone with Patrick Macky, he dissolved their handshake partnership in the newspaper, for a consideration of three thousand dollars.

"Send the money to the trust fund in Kansas City," Roman said. "And then we're closed out. You're your own man."

The little Irishman laughed.

"I've always felt myself to be that anyway, Mr. Hasford. It has been a charming experience. Not to mention profitable. I hope the *Dispatch* has accomplished what you intended."

"It has, Mr. Macky. You've done a great service to me and to the community along the way."

"Would you like me now to explain to Corliss how this all began?"

"No."

"Very well. Let me say that any suggestions you may have henceforth, I will be glad to consider."

Roman pursed his lips and rubbed his chin.

"Well, I have been thinking. Isn't it about time you went to three, maybe four, maybe even five issues a week? And put in more of that stuff from faraway places. For the benefit of the Reverend Kirkendall's schoolchildren."

"And for their papas and mamas," said Patrick Macky. They both laughed, and Patrick Macky presented Roman Hasford with one of his foot-long Havana cigars.

More and more, Roman Hasford read that "stuff from faraway places," as though he were deliberately turning his back on the local scene, as though he had had enough of it. More and more, he sat on his porches, reading and watching the birds. As for those good intentions in his old age, he procrastinated.

He talked about it. But he didn't do anything to improve his horse herd. He didn't do anything about putting the old Hasford farmstead and fields into shape. He didn't visit Wolf Cove Mill. What he did was sit and rock and read and worry about all the ailments that seemed to come with inactivity. An increasingly sensitive digestion. A constant discomfort in the lower belly. The return of vicious headaches each time the weather changed. Even the old snakebite on his leg ached when it rained.

He thought a lot about that snakebite. It had happened when Roman took his first and only adventure with the army. A campaign against the Cheyenne in '68. Or was it '69? He couldn't remember. But he could recall vividly that rattlesnake striking him. And the face of the man who had likely saved his life afterward. The same man Jared Dane and his men had shot dead during the attempt to rob an express office.

As she had been doing all these years, Renée Crozier came each week to clean the Big House. Always bringing freshly ground corn-meal or a mason jar of honey. And sometimes with her in the little wagon was her son Hasford Crozier, who helped her about the house when furniture had to be moved, but who usually sat on the porch with Roman Hasford, on the floor beside Roman's chair, and asked questions about the time in this valley when Lark, his daddy, had been a slave.

Roman had repeated many times the story of Lark guiding him from Elkhorn Tavern to the Hasford farm on the first night of the Battle of Pea Ridge. And the stories about Lark's mentor, Tulip Crozier, the old Jew who had started Wolf Cove Mill, and who would get so drunk he'd fall off his horse, all the while singing ribald songs about red-arsed apes and other members of the animal king-dom. And the story about the day when partisans hanged Tulip Crozier with baling wire from a rafter in his own mill.

Down through these seasons, Orvile Tucker watched Roman Hasford for signs of aging. But could see little more than a slight shrinking of the face, making it more gaunt, and a slight contraction of the lips over teeth that Orvile knew were aching. Roman Hasford even complained of the aching after eating sweets. And so sugar almost disappeared from Orvile Tucker's larder. When Roman com-plained about it, Orvile would glare at him with those same blood-shot eyes, now crowned with the wool on his head going white.

"Ever' tooth in your head gonna fall out. You eat sweets, they gonna fall out. Then what? You don't like soup. But then soup all you can eat. And you too hardheaded to go in there to town and see that new tooth man they got."

"I never been to a dentist in my life and I'm not gonna start now. Besides, I don't like going into town."

"Why not? Most of the people don't like you, you done run off. An' Yancy Crane, he so old now, he likely in a grave somewheres. Ain't nothin' to be afeerd of."

"I've never been afraid to go into town, Orvile. I just don't like the damned town."

"Well, you made most of it. But if you don't like it, then take a nice trip. Go see your sister in St. Louis. Go see that nephew in Fort Smith who worked for old Judge Parker till he died last year."

"Why, hell, Orvile, I don't want to go off to any of those places. But I guess you wouldn't be happy unless you could get on me about something."

"Well, I ain't fixin' you no chocolate pie!"

So Roman sat on his porches, in his rocking chairs. Even in winter. Reading, looking, thinking. Passersby said, The Old Man don't move inside the house unless there's a damned blizzard.

A lot of people called him the Old Man now.

He was becoming a stranger to his own county. To the young ones growing up. To the newcomers. Even those who thought they had known him before saw him seldom now.

There were a lot of new people replacing old people. Somebody new on John Vain's farm. Somebody new warehousing apples in Cato Fulton's tobacco sheds. Somebody new setting up a law practice in Timothy Burton's old shop. Because all those old people were gone. Moved on. Victims of the times.

But the old residents who remained knew that the ones who'd left were not victims of the times. They were victims of the Trouble, and of having been on the wrong side. Oh yes, moving on was a matter of choice, but the Old Settlers knew it was not choice, knew there was a lot more than just choice, and that something was sitting out there at Catrina Hills Farm in a rocking chair that had taken all choice away.

Not that they disapproved. Most of them reckoned it had turned out pretty well. But they still didn't know how the hell it had happened. And the very idea of that man in his rocker out there at Catrina Hills frightened them. So they tried not to think about him. And he tried not to think about them.

And so Roman Hasford sat and read the new daily newspaper. Well, at least daily Monday through Friday. About the Cuban insurrection beginning. About General Kitchener in Sudan, going to avenge the murder of Gordon. About Queen Victoria's Diamond Jubilee.

Why, hell, he thought, maybe I ought to go over to London for that. It'd sure shut old Orvile's mouth for a while.

About the Royal Automobile Club in England.

I've got to have one of those things, Roman thought. But certainly didn't mention it to Orvile because had he done so, with Orvile's love of horses, any mention of these new gasoline contraptions would create all kinds of new opportunities to bitch and carp and complain about the white man heading straight for hell and taking everybody of good, healthy color along with him, like it or not.

*   *   *

It had been more than a year since Roman Hasford was in Gourdville when the telegraph message came from Jefferson City. From
St. Scholastica. Hand-delivered by Lamar Peevy, the Frisco night
telegrapher.

Roman read it with amazement and confusion.

WILL BE PASSING THROUGH GOURDVILLE ON RAILROAD TRAIN
APRIL 17 STOP LOOK FORWARD SEEING YOU STOP SISTER MARIA.

Who the hell is Sister Maria? Roman thought.

But on the day, he rose at 5:30 A.M., cut himself twice while
shaving, and went down to Orvile Tucker and Bishop Eckor, waiting on the back porch in a warm rain, and there mounted Little
Blue, a mare sired by Sparky, and rode to town. With Bishop Eckor
just behind on another of Sparky's children and with the large
Winchester under the saddle fender.

By 7:00 A.M., ten minutes before the southbound arrived, Roman
Hasford was on the depot platform, standing dry in the overhang
of the station roof while Bishop Eckor stayed with the horses in
the rain. On the platform with Roman was Lorton Quint, stationmaster, leaning against a baggage truck loaded with milk cans and
a bulging gray bag of mail.

"Little rainy, ain't it?" Lorton Quint said, looking sideways at
Roman Hasford.

"It's April," said Roman Hasford, and that was the end of the
conversation.

When the engine rumbled past and screeched to a stop, and the
coaches came abreast of the platform, and Lorton Quint pushed his
baggage truck to the open door of the mail car, Roman looked along
the line of coaches. There was the usual discharge of passengers,
mostly drummers carrying woven straw suitcases and wearing
cheap derby hats. But then he saw her, in flowing black, except
for the stark white linen tight about her face.

It had to be Sister Maria. Catholic nuns didn't alight from this
train in northwest Arkansas on any kind of regular basis. So Roman
started for her, striding, thinking how small she looked. Then
stopped dead and started, because this was not one of the nuns he
had met at St. Scholastica. This was Catrina!

She came directly toward him along the platform, boldly, and Roman had the wild thought that *boldly* was no word for a nun. But she was certainly determined, and smiling, and holding out her hand from the folds of that endless black habit.

"It's such a pleasure seeing you once more," she said, and her voice was not the faint whisper he'd always known. It was confident and full.

Roman took her hand, warm and so small in his that he felt as though he were holding nothing but a tiny bit of heat, and no real flesh at all.

"I didn't know who Sister Maria was," he said.

"I apologize. I should have written. It's been my name since vows."

"Well," he said, releasing her hand.

"I'm going to San Antonio. We have a school there. I'll be teaching Latin and Spanish."

"Well. Spanish, too, then." And couldn't help thinking that when he'd found her, she couldn't write her name.

"Yes. And I wanted to tell you how much it has meant to me, the help you've given."

"Well," Roman said, having trouble with his hands now, what to do with them. She was looking at him steadily, and it was impossible to believe that this small woman, swathed in that flowing black habit, was the same little girl he had brought to Catrina Hills Farm as his bride so long ago.

"I still call the place Catrina Hills," he blurted.

"Thank you. You have always been so kind over the years."

"Well."

"I wanted to see you and tell you how grateful I have always been that you made a new life possible for me."

"I'm glad for you."

And having said that, he gave only a passing thought to the fact that this wasn't exactly what he'd had in mind when he brought her out of Kansas. But the sight of her, and her radiance, dissolved any possible bitterness over the innocent part she had played in making Catrina Hills Farm a childless bachelor's den.

The conductor appeared and touched a finger to his billed cap. "Sister," he said, "time to board now. We're going."

She reached out her small hand again and Roman took it, and then she was gone, turning and swirling along the platform and then helped by the conductor up and into the coach. Roman stood and heard the locomotive whistle and the bell ring, and the spin of the drivers to take the slack from the couplings. And then the train was moving past him. And as her coach went by in the rain, he could see her, face framed in white, in one of the windows, waving. And suddenly he wondered why she had never said his name.

Smelling the cinders wet in the rain, he remembered how he'd found her, with a strange timidity as she stood in her father's old discarded brogans on small feet, brogans that seemed to swallow her feet all the way to the knees.

Afterward, he would tell Orvile Tucker that he'd gone on to the dentist because of Orvile's constant harping. But when he walked off that station platform into the rain, going along Elkhorn Street toward the square, dentists were not in his mind. Nothing of the moment was in his mind, not even the direction in which he was walking, not the rain soaking through his hat, the water finally making little rivulets down his cheeks.

Bishop Eckor followed behind, leading the horses.

As the news passed through town that Roman Hasford was there, stalking through the rain with a hard, sour look on his face, everyone started assessing the possibilities of personal disaster, as though the Prince of Darkness had just passed by, thumbing through his flame-red book of names.

At the square, Roman paused. Realizing where he was, looking about in some dismay, he turned quickly into the staircase beside Danton Rich's café and mounted to the offices of Doctor Newlin York. Still hardly with any notion of why he was there or what he was doing, like a sleepwalker. But coming face to face with the man, barely ready for business, whose advertisements in the *Dispatch* had caused citizens of the county to call him Completely Painless Newlin, Roman said, "What the hell."

And so found himself in a horribly uncomfortable chair, where he submitted himself to the most physically agonizing two hours of his life as Completely Painless Newlin extracted and filled, the extractions being done with something that looked like a tool for pulling horseshoe nails and the fillings only after furious grinding with a drillbit attached somehow to various lengths of pulley and spindle and cable and activated by the doctor pumping vigorously on a floor pedal like the one that operated the organ at the Methodist church.

After it was done, the shock of it harsh enough to deaden the surprise of having seen Catrina in that nun's habit, Roman Hasford stood before Doctor York, his cheeks puffed from the wads of cotton packing on gums, and trickles of blood running from each corner of his mouth.

"In my youth," Roman said, "had you subjected me or any member of my family or my livestock to such pain, I would have shot you in the head."

But because of all the cotton, it came out in a mumble that the good doctor was completely incapable of understanding, so he bowed and smiled and asked for thirty-eight dollars, cash. And heaved a sigh of relief once paid and Roman Hasford gone from his chamber, because it had been rather trying on his nerves to probe about inside the mouth of a man who sat in his chair with a .45 single-action Colt pistol under his left arm.

Bishop Eckor was waiting with the horses. Seeing the swollen jaws and the bloody chin he said nothing as Roman took Little Blue's reins and mounted. And hence, still without a word, they rode back to Catrina Hills Farm.

When Orvile Tucker saw Roman, he blinked. "Well, how many did you kill?"

"What are you talking about?" Roman said, pulling bloody wads of cotton out of his mouth and throwing them into the wood box.

"I figured somebody beat you up that bad, you was gonna sure kill somebody."

"Dentist."

A slow, large, toothy grin spread across Orvile's face. It irritated Roman, but he reckoned he knew how to take the air out of that balloon.

"I saw Catrina at the train station. Passing through. She's with the Catholic church now." And, a well-meaning lie, "She said to say hello."

Orvile Tucker stopped smiling and started to move away, then turned back to Roman, who stood there in his kitchen, jaw swollen and chin bloody, and without really looking at him, Orvile reached out with one of those massive black hands and laid it on Roman's shoulder for just an instant.

"Can I have some chocolate pie now?" Roman asked.
"Not tonight. Maybe tomorrow."

In his bed, the various hurts in his mouth only partially soothed by the large quantities of sour-mash whiskey he had consumed during the day, Roman Hasford tried to think of Catrina. He tried to manufacture some monumental self-pity.

But it didn't work. He was already having trouble remembering how she looked on that rainy depot platform.

Rather, the image that kept repeating itself in his mind was the beaming face of Orvile Tucker when Roman had mentioned the dentist, and the pressure of the hand on his shoulder after he'd mentioned Catrina. The thought of Orvile Tucker was protective, like being in the warm bed, dry and secure with the sound of rain still falling outside.

Even had he suspected it, he would not have admitted it to himself, but this black man, former slave, blacksmith, horse breeder, companion, had become more than all those things. He had become what Roman Hasford needed most in these new childhood years of advancing age. The authoritative critic, ever watchful. But with a deep tenderness and empathy. Even for Roman's most absurd flights of mood. Orvile had in fact become the one standing in the footprints of Ora Hasford.

34

During the summer after Roman Hasford saw Sister Maria, he became more irascible. Temper always ready to fall off the deep end.

Orvile Tucker flirted with the idea of putting locks on the rifle rack and the dining room sideboard cupboards where he kept the chinaware he'd bought at Caulder's Mercantile after Roman's fury had destroyed the old wedding set years before. But he didn't because he reckoned if another of those monumental tantrums came, no lock yet devised by man would be able to withstand Roman's rage, and likely would only make it worse.

There was no need for locks, as it turned out. Roman's disposition did not turn vicious now but seemed only to slide into what Orvile called Old Maid Sour. Just a whining and carping. Just an irritable dissatisfaction with everything. So maybe, Orvile Tucker reckoned, it was just the result of Roman's bad digestion and gut ache.

Or maybe seein' that cat-face girl again, he thought. All this Old Maid Sour comin' on. Seein' her, an' now eatin' his soul out about it.

Actually, Roman Hasford had almost no conscious thought of Catrina after that rainy-day meeting on the Frisco depot platform. As though his entire experience with her needed to be washed from the slate.

But maybe Catrina stayed buried somewhere in his mind so deep that he wasn't aware of it. And maybe it was because of that he took to going back to Oak Creek, to walk there in summer, as he had during what he'd come to think of as the season of Diana. To reassure himself of his manhood and, even more, the certainty of a woman loving him.

In his thinking, it had become the bitter hallmark of his life that women found nothing about him to love. Except for Diana. And perhaps that thought, not at all subconscious, was beginning to take its toll in his advancing years, when he became more and more resigned to the fact that now it was too late for any such thing to happen. As though he had used all his chances and none other would ever come.

Like a diamond, he thought, that season of Diana. A diamond almost lost in all the glass baubles of every other season. So finally he clung to it, outrageously tried to bring it back.

Orvile Tucker watched Roman Hasford trudging off into the trees south of the road that ran before the Big House and always wondered if he should follow. Not because there was any of that Yancy Crane kind of danger, but because Orvile reckoned that in Roman's present state of mind he might just keep walking and never come home.

Such a thing never happened. And each day, when Roman was back well before sundown, Orvile Tucker would work in the kitchen, chuckling to himself about his own foolishness, and reckoning he was not the only foolish one here, because although everyone knew that the perils of former days were past, Roman still carried the old single-action Colt pistol with him wherever he went. Even to Oak Creek.

It was during that summer when Dr. Hazlet Cronin came to visit Catrina Hills Farm on a regular basis, after Andy Gimshaw, as one of his last acts as an employee of Roman Hasford, went into Gourd-ville with the message to Doc Cronin that Roman wanted to see him. Two days later Andy Gimshaw was gone, for whatever reasons he might have had, but gone nonetheless.

"You so sour lately, nobody wants to work for you," Orvile Tucker said.

"Small loss," Roman said.

Doc Cronin came out that first time driving his hack and carrying his black bag. Orvile Tucker didn't hear anything that was said, although he tried. Roman and the doctor sat in the parlor before the bookcase, and when Orvile went in to take glasses for the sour mash, conversation ceased. A little later, Roman and the doctor went upstairs, and from the sounds of their footsteps Orvile knew they had gone into Roman's bedroom. They were there for a long time. Then, finally, Doc Cronin came down, carrying his little bag, took a sack of Orvile's gingersnaps for his wife, Rolanda, and drove away. And that night Roman ate his supper without a word. And for the next weeks, Doc Cronin came regularly and when he did, Orvile Tucker went down to the horse barns because he recognized that whatever it was that went on between Roman and Hazlet Cronin, he was not supposed to be included.

And still each day, Roman walked to Oak Creek and sat on a large rock alongside the stream, feeling the sun that came in speckled patterns through the leaves of the sycamores and willows. He always took his hat off and let the breeze play with his hair. It was long hair now. He had stopped going to Anson Greedy's barbershop. Sometimes Orvile Tucker's complaints became so insistent that Roman allowed him to trim it back at least an inch or two.

"You lookin' like one of them no-account hobos come off the railroad trains," Orvile would say.

"What do you know about hobos coming off railroad trains?"

"You don't remember nothin', do you? 'Fore I ever seen you the first time, I seen white-trash hobos on railroad trains. That's what you look like."

"All right. If it'll make you shut up, get the damned shears."

"I already got 'em right here."

"All right. Don't cut off my ears."

"I might, 'cause right now, with all that hair, I can't even see where your ears is at."

It was a good summer. There was more than the usual August rain, and Oak Creek was running almost bank-full and clear, rippling with blue-black minnows swimming in schools in the eddies. Then September came. On that day he sat on his rock and the sky was cobalt blue, a perfect stage for the spectacle of a hawk being pestered by crows. Roman watched and chuckled, having seen it so many times before, the hawk flying on majestically, the crows diving at it. A big red-tail. And the crows finally either growing tired of the game or fearful of its consequences, flying off with their raucous cries toward the woodlands to the east.

Perhaps because he had been so intent on watching the hawk and the crows, when he finally realized someone was on the Chesney side of the stream it startled him, and he leaped up, his hand going automatically under the light summer jacket to where the pistol waited. Then he saw it was a girl, and he had the impression that she had been there a long time. And when he saw her fully, the sun dappling her hair and her face, his heart gave a thump and he caught his breath.

It was Diana!

In exactly the same spot where he had first seen her almost twenty years before, and looking as she had then, with great billows of honey-colored hair, creamlike, porcelain skin, disturbing eyes rimmed with the black lashes and brows. The same full lips. But they were not smiling now, as she looked across the stream with a gaze so intent that it seemed to radiate heat more felt than the late summer sun.

He took a few steps toward the bank before he realized this could not be Diana, the young, vibrant Diana. As he came abreast of her across Oak Creek, she was frowning slightly, her eyes never leaving his face. Roman had the horrible thought that this was all illusion and that the girl would vanish before his eyes, evaporate like windblown dust and leave him standing there like a fool, with his mouth open, nothing around him but the bright sun and the sparkling water and the fluttering green of sycamore and willow leaves.

Then he knew who this was. It was Berdeen, as surely as if she had her name branded across her forehead.

So he spoke, astonished that he could find a voice in a throat that felt tighter than woodscrews in green hickory.

"Hello. I see you've found my favorite place."

She did not evaporate. She stared at him with those great eyes, but she did not smile. She seemed as immobile as marble, yet clothed in a calico dress that fell straight from a simple collar to her ankles, and beneath which Roman could see her bare toes.

"My name's Roman Hasford," he said, still astonished that he could talk at all. His heart was thumping hard against his ribs.

"I know who you are," she said, and it *was* the voice of Diana. "Uncle Campbell says everyone knows who you are."

"Your Uncle Campbell's a fine man."

"Am I still on his land?"

"Yes, of course, but it doesn't matter, you can go anywhere."

"I've come to live with Uncle Campbell for a while," she said, still looking squarely into Roman's eyes. "Mother wanted me to come here because she said it was a good place."

"I knew your . . . I knew your granddaddy." By now, Roman had moved closer to her.

"He died last winter, so mother said I could come now. Granddaddy didn't want me to leave Longview. Grandmother didn't, either. But she's gone, too."

"I'm sorry. They were friends of mine. Did you say Longview? Longview, Texas?" Roman couldn't bring himself to ask, Where is your mother? Where is Diana?

"Yes. Granddaddy's tannery is there. Now Daddy runs it by himself."

Daddy. That's Ausbin Tage, Roman thought, and the bile came up his throat. He swallowed it and concentrated on the features of this girl's face, still half expecting her to vanish suddenly and leave him there beside Oak Creek, talking to phantoms of his own imagination.

"Well," he said. "So you've come to live with your Uncle Campbell?"

"For a little while."

There was still the frown, and for the first time she looked away from Roman's face, turning her head from side to side with almost furtive glances up and down the creekbed, as though afraid someone might find her there.

"I've got to go now."

Berdeen turned and started into the willows on the Chesney side of Oak Creek, and Roman, almost in a panic to keep her there, called out.

"You need a horse."

She stopped, but turned only her head, looking across one shoulder. "What?"

"A horse. To see our countryside. Tell your Uncle Campbell I've got some gentle horses."

"Oh." She started off again, and again he called.

"Berdeen. I'm glad you came back."

She didn't pause, but her head turned ever so slightly aside and he could see it—a smile, full and broad, that made her look even more like her mother. Roman Hasford felt the hard, choking knot in his throat and this time was glad it had come, because had it not, he would have called again.

His feet were wet. As he had spoken to her he had walked into the shallows of Oak Creek, and only now did he realize it.

* * *

When Orvile Tucker saw Roman coming back to the Big House that day, he knew something had happened. Maybe just in Roman's mind, but something had happened. Roman was walking as he'd always walked in his youth, when Orvile first knew him, striding out. Almost a trot. Headlong. Intent.

By the time Roman started up through the yard where the crabapple trees grew, Orvile was waiting on the south porch, watching the treeline across the road, expecting to see someone following.

"What's the matter?" Orvile called.

"Where's Bishop?" Roman asked, bounding up onto the porch.

"Horse barns. I got him walkin' them two foals we got las' spring."

"Get him. Send him in town. Tell Terrance Shadbolt I need to see him."

"Terrance Shadbolt?"

"Yes, Terrance Shadbolt."

Roman was at the door, then stopped, paused, turned, and Orvile was amazed to see him grinning.

"No. Invite Terrance and Constance here to Sunday dinner. You can cook fried chicken."

"Sunday dinner?"

"For God's sake, Orvile. Don't you understand anything anymore?"

"Well, I . . ."

"Wait. Not just the judge and his wife. But Doc Cronin. Yes. Them too. Hazlet Cronin and Rolanda. Sunday dinner. Fried chicken."

"Well . . ."

Roman was into the house. Bursting in, striding to the parlor, pacing back and forth. Throwing his hat aside. Pausing. Looking at his books. Pacing again. Pausing long enough to take a long drink from the jug of sour mash always present beside his reading chair.

Why, hell, he thought, that gives a man something to think about, don't it?

James Chesney had to die before that girl came back. Tough old James Chesney, still not willing to let his granddaughter face the stigma of bastardy. But not Diana. Tougher than her papa. Tougher than hell. Defiant. Rub the gossips' and the busybodies' noses in the beauty of that girl. And the girl?

Roman had to take another long drink of the sour mash. How much did she know? How much did Diana's brothers know?

Anyway, he thought, it's finally time for reckoning. It's time for a lawyer. No matter the consequences. It's time for the truth.

And Terrance Shadbolt was the best lawyer around. Out of politics now, getting a little old, but in private practice, with a mind still blade-sharp. And of course, Terrance Shadbolt owed Roman Hasford a lot. He owed Roman Hasford his jobs as prosecuting attorney and as circuit judge.

Time to call in that account, Roman thought.

And Hazlet Cronin? And his wife, Rolanda?

Why, hell, Roman thought, their daughter Hazel is Campbell Chesney's wife, mother of Campbell Chesney's four children. And as of right now, this moment, Berdeen is living in that home.

Besides, Roman thought, lifting the sour-mash jug again, if it's time for squaring all accounts, Doc Cronin already knows some things nobody else does.

For the rest of the week, Orvile Tucker complained and griped about having to prepare a sit-down dinner for guests. No such thing had happened at Catrina Hills Farm since the few family gatherings immediately after Roman's marriage, when Ora and Martin Hasford were still alive and Catrina was living in the Big House.

"Why don't you stop bellyaching?" Roman asked. "Get Renée and Lark over here to help. We've had guests before."

"All them men outside smokin' and spittin' tobacco juice an' drinkin' down whiskey and beer an eatin' with their hands, that ain't the same thing as havin' high-tone ladies sittin' at the dining table."

"It's a chance for you to use the chinaware you bought."

"Linen tablecloth been in the closet so long it smell like a mouse nest."

"Hang it on the clothesline in the sun."

"I already did."

Orvile's grumbling had become so much a part of their relationship that without it this whole business would have been unnatural.

Actually, he was delighted that Roman was showing some interest in something other than sitting on the porch with a book in one hand, a glass of sour mash in the other.

Old Maid Sour turn a little sweet now, he thought.

So Orvile, Renée, and Lark began on Saturday to prepare the meal. Roast hen with corn bread dressing, Orvile emphasizing his independence by ignoring Roman's specific request for fried chicken. There were half a dozen vegetables to go with the hen and scalded lettuce and one of Renée's deep-dish apple pies. And Lark made a rice pudding like the one they'd served at Elkhorn Tavern before the war, when he'd been a slave there.

Orvile sent Hasford Crozier to Caulder's Mercantile to buy a white cotton shirt with collar, a pair of corduroy trousers, and black lace-up shoes.

"Why I gotta put on all this bib an' tucker?" the boy asked.

" 'Cause I say so. Listen, boy, you hush and do what you tole. You gonna serve out the grub to the table, an' you ain't servin' out no grub to a table in this house lookin' like you just crawl outta some goat pen."

"Do what the man saze, baby," Renée said. "Don't you know he de big majordomo roun' here?"

At which she laughed and goosed Orvile, and he glowered and stalked out to wring the necks of two hens.

Roman didn't realize he was getting something besides fried chicken until he was seated with his guests and Hasford Crozier carried in the roast hen. A frown crossed Roman's face, but it didn't last long because the smell of the bird and the sage-and-corn-bread dressing was enough to make any irritation momentary.

After the cobbler and the coffee, Roman led them into the parlor and everyone found a soft chair while Hasford Crozier brought in bowls of mint candy and glazed pecan halves.

"Well, Roman," said Rolanda Cronin, "I can't remember a better dinner."

"Maybe it was like a little bribe," Roman said. "I wanted to have you all here because you're old friends. And I'm going to ask you a favor."

"Ask away," said Judge Shadbolt.

"What I'm going to say is something I'd like to keep among us, at least for a while. But it's important that I say it with witnesses I can trust."

Everybody exchanged quick little glances, and for the moment the mint candy and glazed pecan halves were forgotten. Roman went out into the kitchen, for two reasons. First, to be sure Orvile and the others had gone outside as he'd told them to do, once the candy and nuts were served. And second, to allow his guests to digest what he'd just said. When he returned, all eyes were on him, with tense expectancy in the old, familiar faces.

Roman felt better than he had in years. Not physically, because his belly ached, but in spirit. Because now, after all the time of self-reproach, he was about to do what Ora Hasford had said needed doing. She'd said it when Roman had been a little boy and had been found with a penny in his overalls pocket that Tulip Crozier had given his sister, Calpurnia. And now Roman could hear his mother's voice with complete recall. From decades past. Even though at the moment he might not have been able to remember each of the platters of food placed before him less than an hour before.

"Family's your rock," Ora Hasford said. "If you treat it right, it's always there. So if you do a bad thing that hurts family, don't hide it. Because if you do, it will rot your soul. Own up to it. Not just for the sake of somebody you hurt. But for your own sake."

There was more than that. Because now, after having taken himself out of county politics, after having taken himself out of revenge sought for wrongs real or imagined, after having taken himself away from arranging the terms of other people's lives, he was into it again. Conspiring and cashing in favors and manipulating. It had always been exhilarating, though it was something for which he could never be proud. But this time the pride was there.

Why, hell, he thought before addressing his guests, it's time I paid up, too.

It was like a confessional, maybe. That parlor at Catrina Hills Farm. The four respected people waiting expectantly. Like priests. And priests, he hoped, had no choice but to give him absolution.

Well, a dinner party at Catrina Hills was unique in the history of that place. And so, of course, it was marked by the people of the county. It could not but attract attention. And it did.

Because although Roman Hasford had pretty much cut himself free of their lives, the citizens in and around Gourdville were still sensitive to the movements of the Old Man who lived at the Folly.

And when two of the county's leading elder citizens and their wives went there on that September Sunday, their going became known. But not what happened. At least not for a while.

Likely it was something that had tough hide on it, they said. Because the Old Man, they said, didn't lay out grub for special guests just for the pure joy of social intercourse.

Hell, they said, it never happened before, did it?

So, as with everything else down through the years that had transpired at Catrina Hills, and as with everything else down through the years that concerned Roman Hasford, they gave it a name. The Dinner.

The Folly. The Child Bride. The Trouble. The Old Man. And now, the Dinner.

And they all waited to see what the hell it meant.

35

Thunderation! Orvile Tucker thought. Here me and this man together since Kansas. Since before old Custer dead. Since before
railroads all over the place. Since before he had anything in his
pocket 'cept a few jinglin' coins. So now I gotta creep aroun' listenin'
like some old woman at the keyhole, tryin' to know what he's doin'.
And not managin' to hear anything, at that.

Because Orvile Tucker had known the Dinner was not just laying
out grub for high-toned folks. The Dinner was something that made
Roman Hasford forsake Old Maid Sour. At least for the present.

So what was it? Orvile Tucker wondered afterward. Nobody
'round here knows 'cept him, and he don't tell me nothin', play me
like a fish on the line, like a cat with a mouse, let me guess.

Everything went on into autumn, Orvile waiting each day of it
for something to change, something to happen. But nothing did.
Except that Roman Hasford was different.

Rockin' and grinnin', Orvile thought. Sittin' on one of them porch
chairs, sippin' whiskey and rockin' and grinnin'.

Then Campbell Chesney came. Orvile thought Campbell Chesney acted real uppity, real snotty. No smiling or fine talk. But
Roman took him down to the horse barns. And sold him Baby Bess,
a little blue roan mare that had dropped fine foals twice and was
only six years old. Orvile Tucker was outraged that Roman sold
her; that mare, from a good line of quality dames and sires, maybe could go a long time producing. And he sold her for forty-five
dollars.

He's paid more'n that for a pistol, Orvile thought, and pistols can't even birth no more pistols, like a good mare can foals. Forty-five dollars!

Thunderation!

So Orvile put on the silence. He wouldn't talk. He'd throw down the grub on the kitchen table and not say a word, not sit down to eat, just throw down the grub and then walk out the kitchen door and stomp around the porch, kicking at the pillars.

It didn't matter. Roman just talked and talked and talked. Like he was talking to his ownself. Talked his damned head off. About old things. Like when he was introduced to General Hancock at Fort Leavenworth, or when he watched gentlemen shooting buffalo from the windows of a railway car, or when he started his fortune with a garbage-collection outfit. Everything calling back old days. Everything about Kansas, or maybe about here in this Arkansas county when he had been a boy. But never anything after he'd returned from Kansas to settle here. Like Courtland Brown, or Elmer Scaggs dead in the mud, or somebody trying to shoot him, twice. Just old-time things.

Then Orvile saw Baby Bess again. On the road in front of the Big House, a young white girl riding her sidesaddle. Just meandering along, the girl looking up to where Roman was sitting in his rocker on the porch. And Orvile saw the girl and the horse again and again, even when the weather was bad, with Roman sitting out there in the weather as though he was just waiting for them to come along. Watching the road.

The girl rode Baby Bess sidesaddle. A little roan that likely could outrun any stud in the county with just a whisper of spur, and here's this girl riding her sidesaddle. Always with a big hat tied down on her head, and out from under that hat a billowing flare of hair like spilled honey, even on cloudy days when there was no sunshine on it. Just meandering along, looking up toward the Big House. Not doing anything but looking, and Roman on the porch not doing anything either. Just bent forward in his rocker, waiting for her to wave so he could wave back. But she never did.

Thunderation, Orvile always thought, and he sold her uncle that horse for less money than it would cost a man to ride all the way to St. Louis and back on the Frisco.

End of September and through October and right into November it went on, until the new man came. And when the new man came, Orvile had a lot more to think about than Baby Bess.

The new man, Dylan Price, had a dove tattooed on his left forearm. Later, when Orvile Tucker saw him taking a bath in the kitchen in a galvanized tub brought from the pantry for just such occasions, Orvile saw another tattoo. All in the color of deep blue, of a hound chasing a rabbit, and the rabbit headed right into the hole of Dylan Price's backside.

I wonder how drunk a man gotta be, Orvile thought, to have such a picture put on his ass.

The new man talked in a strange way that Orvile Tucker had never heard. And Orvile Tucker knew all the words. Well, most of them. But the new man strung them together in an alien patter. Acted as much a gentleman as Judge Shadbolt or Roman Hasford, when Roman was on his best behavior.

He'd been in armies, this new man. All kinds of armies. And this Dylan Price had a crystal hardness like glass in his manner, even in his face and his eyes, a shining toughness that was difficult to define. So Orvile Tucker was a little afraid of him and, of course, resented his intrusion. But he couldn't make the resentment last because this man, with a scar or two on his face and a pair of hands battered and knobby from too much use as balled fists, was somehow charming and friendly.

When this new man, Dylan Price, first arrived with a letter from Roman Hasford's nephew, Eben Pay, and Roman hired him and said that for the first night he could sleep in the Big House, but thereafter would take a bed at the horse-barn bunkhouse, where only Bishop Eckor now slept, Orvile reckoned the stay would be a lot longer than that. And it was true. When November ran its course and December came, Dylan Price was still there, in the room where Catrina had been.

Thunderation!

They sat in the parlor before all the books, Roman Hasford and Dylan Price, and this new man would sit drinking sour-mash whiskey with Roman and *sing*. Sing the kinds of songs that made the hair on the back of Orvile Tucker's neck go stiff. In a deep and resonant voice, haunting, as though it came from some secret place like the sounds of foxhounds running.

How could a man resent somebody who sang like that?

Orvile Tucker would sit on the last step of the staircase, in the dark, listening. Until Roman discovered him there and said Orvile should come into the parlor. No, didn't say it, ordered it. So, after that, Orvile sat in one corner in a ladder-back chair, in the shadows, and listened and watched the play of lamplight across the features of this new man.

"I like those Welsh hymns and carols," Roman said. And Orvile liked them too.

That year, for the first time, there was a Christmas tree in the Big House. Dylan Price went into the hills behind the horse barns and cut a small cedar. Then rode one of the Catrina Hills horses in to Caulder's Mercantile and brought back a box of shiny little stars and balls and made popcorn and strung the puffed white kernels on thread, using a needle with his strong soldier's fingers as though he had used a needle and thread many times before. And put up the tree in the parlor and decorated it with the shiny things and the strings of popcorn. And when it was done Roman laughed and said it was beautiful.

Then this new man, Dylan Price, told tales of Africa, where he'd been a soldier. And looked at Orvile when he said that part of the greatest courage he'd ever seen was black men coming against rifle fire at a place called Rorke's Drift in Natal. And asked if perhaps Orvile Tucker was down the generations from the Zulus. Hell, Orvile didn't know.

"West coast of Africa, likely, your people," said Dylan Price. "Ivory Coast. Gold Coast. The bloody English called it that. But they took most of their riches not from bone or metal but from slaves. And not only the English. But anyone who could."

Orvile Tucker might have been only vaguely aware of what he spoke about, and Roman Hasford asked, "What do you mean, only a part of the greatest courage?" and Dylan Price said the other part had been the ones standing against those charges.

Thunderation! When this man sing *or* talk, Orvile thought, the hair stand stiff along my ole neck!

The lilt of his voice was like music, even with the burr of rough edges on it. The smile bright, but with that steel glint in the eyes, hard as the jacket on a high-powered rifle bullet.

Like he think the best jokes are how foolish we all be, Orvile Tucker thought. An' he know all the jokes.

It was as contagious as measles. Humor and compassion. Experience of jagged shards. But time-tempered against sharp edges, and saying with a song, "Brutal it is, but to hell with long faces!"

There had been so many times when Orvile Tucker had sensed Roman Hasford riding adversity and saying to hell with it. Only now this Dylan Price did the same thing but in a different way. With a laugh and an easy grace, not with that drawn-down mouth and bitterness written from ear to ear.

How you help likin' a man like that scoundrel, Orvile thought.

Roman Hasford was drawn mightily toward this man, and Orvile Tucker could see that. And understood it, because he was drawn as well. And in just a few short weeks, as though this Dylan Price had been a trusted, longtime friend.

Still, each morning before he rolled out Roman's breakfast biscuits, Orvile Tucker counted the sterling silver. And the guns in the rack. And slipped upstairs to listen at Dylan Price's door to hear the breathing inside. And finally began feeling guilty about this checking and he stopped.

Dylan Price told stories of the recent war in Cuba, and Roman laughed at some of the crazy things that had happened there, as did Orvile Tucker.

This Dylan Price, at the horse barns, laughing with Bishop Eckor, and Bishop laughing, too. A man Orvile had never seen even smile before. Price and Eckor together, pitching hay, shoveling shit, exercising horses, mending fences even in sleet and snow, and Dylan Price would kick Bishop Eckor in the butt and both would laugh and keep doing the work. Orvile had always thought that anyone kicking Bishop Eckor in the butt was buying a quick ticket to bloody hell.

Or teaching Orvile in the kitchen how to make Yorkshire pudding. Just a little meat drippings in a biscuit and a hot oven, Orvile thought, and anybody could have thought of it.

Wales, he said he came from.

Where the hell's Wales? Orvile thought. Way beyond Illinois, surely. Way beyond Tennessee, maybe.

Sometimes this Dylan Price told stories of Roman's nephew, Eben Pay, and how they'd been in Cuba together. And at those times, Roman would lean forward in his chair and his eyes would be bright and he would clap his hands. And turn to Orvile and say, "That's Cal's boy, that's Cal's boy, off there in Cuba with Dylan Price and Teddy Roosevelt!"

It was good when Dylan Price talked of Cuba. Because he spoke of the black soldiers there. Fine soldiers, he said, Ninth and Tenth Cavalry they were, blacker than Orvile Tucker, Dylan Price would say, looking at Orvile, and good soldiers. And although he knew nothing of soldiers, Orvile Tucker understood that of all the things Dylan Price knew, the things he knew best were about soldiers.

"I have known soldiers of every color," Dylan Price would say. "Some I have fought with. Some I have fought against. From India to Africa to Cuba. Men is men is men. No matter the color when it comes to bayonet."

What the hell do that mean? Orvile Tucker wondered. But the hair still stood up stiff when it was said.

Dylan Price made Orvile Tucker feel young. And maybe more important, he made Roman feel young as well. With him, now, no ticking clocks, no sand running down in the glass.

Yet, the more he was near Dylan Price, the more he was afraid of him. Not with the screaming voodoo fright that Renée Crozier could bring on with her tales and twitching fingers and images of blood-sucking bats and dark things that come in the still of night with fangs and claws. But just a respectful, overwhelming awe. A warm quicksand. A snakebite without fangs.

Thunderation!

"He's family," Roman Hasford said to Orvile one morning in the kitchen after Dylan Price went to the barns. "Why, hell, he was down there in Cuba with my nephew, wasn't he? And Eben Pay sent him to me, didn't he? He's family."

As though Roman Hasford was eagerly reaching out for someone to replace all the family who were gone.

Orvile could not help but notice that as time went by, Roman and Dylan Price often had long, low-voiced conversations that suddenly ceased when Orvile walked into the room.

What they talkin' about? he wondered. They stop drinkin' sourmash whiskey and start talkin' low. They just talkin'. About what? And why don't he tell me?

So in that time it came to Orvile Tucker, as it had not before, that maybe there was never total confidence shared between a white man and a black man. Love could be shared. But maybe not confidence.

Somehow it didn't matter, that revelation. Because maybe there were others who knew about the love. As on the day Dylan Price came into the kitchen, placed his hard hand on Orvile Tucker's shoulder, and said, "A good man that, and you watching over him down these many years. A fine soldier you'd be, Orvile."

Now Roman Hasford was calm. Sitting into winter on the porch. In a rocker, lap robe over his legs, blanket over his shoulders. Watching the seasons change from cool to brisk to cold. With a smile on his face. Not a large one, but there nonetheless.

Except sometimes when he bent suddenly and held his stomach, then staggered back into the house and upstairs. And Orvile Tucker would hear a small cry, like a pup-dog kicked, a whimper, but with echoes of agony. Roman's face was growing gaunt, and his shoulders, once square and hard, seemed to be shriveling like a leaf at the edge of fire, and his eyes more hollow each day. Endlessly hollow, so there was no color to them. And his hands losing flesh so that each knuckle showed like a hickory-nut hull under stretched parchment.

Roman was eating less and drinking more, but the sour-mash whiskey seemed to have little effect on him. And Orvile Tucker groused and bitched and complained and cajoled, saying Roman was going to dry up and blow away with the wind if he didn't take on more grub like he once had.

Then one morning Orvile Tucker went upstairs to see why Roman was still in bed and the sun already an hour high, and this in early February. That was when Orvile saw it. Saw it lying on the night table beside the .45 single-action pistol that was always there. On a tray with a towel beneath it, and a vial or bottle or something with a liquid in it. He knew what the object was, because he'd been around horses all his life. Long and shining, a tube the size of a twelve-gauge shotgun shell, with three rings at one end. For two fingers and the thumb. And at the other end a long, thread-thin shaft. The needle.

Roman lay faceup, his eyes half open and clouded, his mouth open, his breath coming harsh, and Orvile knew that Roman was unaware of anything around him.

Orvile turned in a panic and ran out, and in the hall came face-to-face with Dylan Price. They looked at each other for a long time, Orvile panting.

"What is it?" Orvile asked.

"Morphine."

"What's that?"

"A medicine. A very strong medicine discovered a long time ago by a man in Germany. Strong medicine it is."

"What for?"

"To stop the pain," Dylan Price said.

"What kinda pain?"

"Deep belly pain."

"I thought them doctors give laudanum for that."

"Not strong enough for this pain, Orvile. Only morphine is strong enough."

"Who stick that needle into him?"

"He does it himself. When it gets so bad he has to."

Then Orvile went down the stairs, headlong, into the kitchen and onto a chair. Roman's chair, where he always sat for his breakfast. And Orvile Tucker lay his face on the hardwood tabletop, his hands hanging limp between his legs, and smelling the bacon burning in the cast-iron skillet on the stove, the bacon for Roman's breakfast that Orvile had known even when he put it in the pan that Roman would not eat. And his great blacksmith's shoulders shook and the breath rasped in his throat and his teeth bit at the tabletop.

36

For Orvile Tucker, everything grew more confusing as February went along. Roman's pain was like an anvil on his heart. He didn't know what to do.

"Treat him as you always have," said Dylan Price. "There's nothing else any of us can do."

So he tried. But not entirely as he always had. He stopped badgering and arguing. And he lay awake at night waiting to hear those little cries of anguish from Roman's bedroom.

It didn't help that he was feeling his age. His joints ached. He worried about that morphine, that strong medicine. He became so clumsy in the kitchen that his hands were always showing raw burns and knife cuts. He hired Hasford Crozier to come and help him, to live in the Big House and sleep on a bunk in the pantry just off the kitchen, where Orvile could find him in a hurry even in the middle of the night.

"You stay away from them horse barns," he said to Hasford Crozier. "That Bishop Eckor nothin' but white trash. You treat him nice he come around, but you stay in the Big House."

"I like them horses," said Hasford Crozier. "I don't like makin' out no biscuits an' stirrin' sauce. Women does them thangs."

"Now you do it. You stay in the Big House 'cept I send you out or 'cept when you go to the toilet. You use one of them outside toilets. You don't use that toilet upstairs with the water in it. That for Mr. Roman and Mr. Price."

"Look like effen I make the biscuits and stir the gravy, I could use that toilet. I ain't ever used no toilet with water in it."

"An' you ain't gonna use this one. I make the biscuits and stirs the gravy, too, an' I don't use it. An' you ain't either."

Same as trainin' a young colt, Orvile thought. Smart-aleck boy. What they been doin' with him over there at Wolf Cove Mill, that Lark and Renée lettin' him run wild like a deer-woods dog! But it was nice to have the extra pair of strong hands in the kitchen.

It was after Hasford Crozier became a part of the household that all the people who had attended the Dinner returned. Orvile was furious. Nobody had told him anything about it. They arrived on one of those bright, blistering cold days when the sun was in a cloudless sky, giving off no heat at all, and the hard frost was still on the ground where the Big House shaded it. They came in a surrey driven by Ennis Lugi's son-in-law Hargen Meeks, who'd married Dodi Lugi just last summer and since then had operated the Lugi taxi service, which was mostly seen in Gourdville, going between the Frisco depot and the Stone Hotel after the arrival of passenger trains, but which was also available for special occasions.

The surrey was black with yellow wheels, and as it came up into the Big House yard, the two horses pulling it were exhaling huge clouds of white vapor. Under the canopy were Judge Shadbolt and his wife, Constance, and Doc Cronin and his wife, Rolanda, and they were giving off almost as much vapor as were the horses. They were bundled and wrapped in robes and blankets and Russian-style fur caps like the ones the frontier army had been using for years, maybe this last because Judge Shadbolt's son Wilbur had been serving as a cavalry lieutenant in the Dakotas for the past four years.

But more than the Dinner guests came this time. Riding behind on saddle horses were the Chesney brothers, Hiram and Campbell, like a small escort, except, as far as Orvile could tell, they were not armed.

What the hell are them folks doin' out on this kinda day?

He should have known something was about to happen, because that morning Roman had come down dressed in his best suit and a necktie. He looked like a scarecrow, the clothes hanging on his bony frame in horrible drapes and the shirt collar, which always before had made his neck bulge over it, as loose as the loop on an ox yoke. His boots were polished. And he'd shaved. Well, probably

Dylan Price had shaved him. Orvile knew only that except for the drooping mustache, Roman's face was minus whiskers. And it had a blue, wrinkled look.

"Start a pot of spiced sassafras tea," Orvile said to Hasford Crozier when he saw that surrey turn into the yard from the road.

Dylan Price had Roman well established in the parlor, sitting behind the big library table, and had built a fire in the fireplace and, a long time before the surrey arrived, had been pouring sour-mash whiskey and had said, "Have a little tidbit of cookie ready."

Orvile Tucker only caught bits and pieces of the conversation, once all those people had been escorted into the parlor by Hasford Crozier. He heard Roman introducing Dylan Price to everyone. Then Orvile carried in a tray with cups of spiced tea for the ladies, and a bottle of brandy for the men. Rolanda Cronin said she was so chilled from the ride that she reckoned she needed to have her tea bolstered with a jolt of the brandy, and Constance Shadbolt reckoned the same thing.

Orvile Tucker served Cornish cakes that Dylan Price had instructed him about. They'd ordered the orange-colored saffron flavoring by mail some weeks before, all the way from Cincinnati, but Orvile had had no thought of laying out such things to anyone except Roman.

When it came time for business, after the brandy had evaporated Constance Shadbolt's and Rolanda Cronin's chill, Judge Shadbolt took a fat document from his inside coat pocket and lay it before Roman, then returned to his chair. Everyone was in a chair, except the Chesney brothers, who stood before the fireplace side by side, looking very grim and clutching their glasses in hands that showed white knuckles.

At the library table, Roman opened the document the judge had given him and said that he assumed all present had read it. All had. Except for Dylan Price, Roman said, and he knew what was in it because he had been told. Then Roman read it, page by page, while everyone else in the room sipped brandy and munched the saffron cakes and the oak logs in the fireplace snapped gently, sometimes giving off little spurts of blue flame amid the normal orange.

When he had read it all, Roman looked directly at the Chesney brothers and said, "I'm sorry now that I didn't come forward before."

"Well, you was married then," said Hiram. And his tone was not particularly warm.

"I hope when you read this," Roman said, "it wasn't too much of a shock."

"It wasn't," Campbell Chesney said, and his voice was no warmer than his brother's. "At least now it's set straight."

"I hope so."

Then Roman took a quill pen and an ink bottle that Dylan Price had brought and the pen made a loud scratching sound as he signed each page, slowly, deliberately. When he'd finished, all the others went to the table, one by one, and signed the pages. And resumed their places. At which point Orvile came in with more brandy, but the ladies, at least, allowed that they'd had enough.

"I wanted all of you to witness my signature," Roman said. "I don't want any trouble on probate."

"There will be no trouble there," said Terrance Shadbolt. "I've discussed it with Judge Grady."

"With anybody else?" Roman asked.

"No. According to your instructions."

Once more, Roman looked at the Chesneys, still with their butts to the fireplace, glasses in hand, creases between their eyebrows.

"I guess the judge told you. We've all pledged that any details to be made public will be up to you."

The Chesneys nodded, but said nothing.

Doc Cronin rose. "I think that's all of it now, so let's give Roman some time to rest."

Everyone seemed anxious to be out of the house. Even into the cold. Roman Hasford, moving with halting steps, led them to the door, and Hargen Meeks, wiping crumbs from his mouth, came from the kitchen, where he'd been drinking coffee and eating saffron cakes. Orvile Tucker gave the women small sacks of the cookies to take with them. Hasford Crozier, grinning, held the door, saying, "You all come back, now."

Everyone was across the porch then, going down to the surrey and the two saddle horses, and Orvile was hissing at Hasford Crozier, "Get yo' ass back in the kitchen and stay there till I come talk to you! Who you think you are, invitin' folks to Catrina Hills?"

The judge and the doctor and their ladies were mounting the surrey, and Hiram Chesney was going up into his saddle, all making great clouds of white vapor, but Roman had held Campbell Chesney back with a tentative hand on his sleeve.

"Campbell, you acted like you and Hiram knew," he said.

"We did," Campbell Chesney said, and he looked into Roman Hasford's face with those astonishing Greek eyes so like his mother's. So like Diana's. "Not at first. But later."

Roman was a little flustered. He started to reach out and touch Campbell's arm again, then drew back his hand. Here was a man to whom Roman had loaned money for every venture he desired, yet Roman was flustered and drew back his hand.

"Why, hell, I guess I ought to thank you for not coming over here and shooting me."

"We thought about it," Campbell Chesney said, a harsh note in his voice. "But we reckoned not. It was long past by the time we knew. But it was close, Hasford. It was very close."

Campbell Chesney turned to leave, and Roman followed him to the edge of the porch. The surrey was already turning away, Hargen Meeks whipping his two reluctant horses, and Hiram Chesney was astride, holding the reins of Campbell's horse in his hand. Waiting, watching with hostile eyes.

"How'd you know?" Roman asked.

For a long moment Campbell Chesney stood at the bottom of the steps, as though he hadn't heard. Then he turned his head and stared at Roman Hasford.

"Diana wrote a letter when she sent Berdeen. Told us all about it," he said. "She told us to leave you alone. That's why we never come here with shotguns."

Then he was off quickly to his horse, mounting, and with a last look, defiant, he and his brother reined about and rode after the surrey.

Standing in the cold on that porch, Roman Hasford almost rose to some of his old fury, almost shouted after Campbell Chesney that it was good he hadn't come or he'd have ended in a shallow grave and in a hurry. But he didn't shout, the thought there only for an instant because all his mind was full of one thing. Diana told her brothers about Oak Creek when she'd sent the girl back. And told them to leave him alone!

"Inside now, Mr. Hasford, with you," said Dylan Price, his strong hands on Roman Hasford's shoulders. "Inside now, and a fine new fire I'll make and a hot toddy, me and Orvile, two old soldiers, us. Now come, come, come."

Roman was shivering. With the cold and with something inside. Dylan Price led him into the parlor and to his chair. And no matter the good thought that Diana remembered, the glint in the Chesney brothers' eyes seemed reflected in the dancing flames of the oak logs in the fireplace.

"Oh God," Roman said. "It's miserable to be hated."

"Better it is than not to be thought of at all," said Dylan Price. And after easing Roman Hasford into the chair before the fire, he found the shawl and placed it around Roman Hasford's shoulders.

"No it isn't, no it isn't," Roman Hasford kept saying.

Dylan Price thought once more of that silver-inlaid dresser set and the German porcelain figurine he'd seen the first night he'd spent at the Big House. He knew all about those items because Roman had told him. Well, maybe not all. Dylan Price had the strong feeling that there was a lot more about Catrina Hasford that Roman allowed was none of his business.

"I thought it was all beautiful," Roman had said. "But she didn't even look at any of it when I gave it to her."

Shortly after that confession, Dylan Price, without consulting with Orvile Tucker or Roman either, had boxed the vanity set and the Little Bo-Peep and placed the box in the attic, beside the water tank. Because they were things of a past he figured best forgotten. Leaving no trace in the Big House of something, whatever it was, that bore so obviously bitter a taste.

So, when the time of morphine needles came, Dylan Price thought of those things again. And decided to remove them farther still. He took the box from the attic, and a shovel, and rode north of Catrina Hills Farm into the deep timber, almost to Missouri, and there in a thicket of jack oak buried the whole business. But before consigning the mementos of Roman Hasford's marriage to their grave, he broke the figurine and the glass in the mirrors with the handle of the shovel, thinking as he did so that the locals considered breaking a mirror bad luck for seven years.

"The bad luck is already here," he said aloud. "And will run its course in less than seven years, I'd guess."

And so, shattered porcelain and glass and silver inlays into their hole, and good riddance, he thought. He rode back to Catrina Hills with a strange peace of mind, thinking that maybe he had performed some kind of exorcism, freeing Roman Hasford at last from an evil that he, Dylan Price, could not comprehend. And never would.

37

"What happened to the Christmas tree?"

He was in the parlor, hands motionless on the lap robe that covered his legs, wearing a housecoat that Dylan Price had bought at Caulder's Mercantile a month before, and fleece-lined slippers. He was sitting in one of the porch rockers that had been brought in because he liked it better than any of the overstuffed, expensive parlor chairs.

Besides, he no longer sat on the porch.

"Mr. Roman," Orvile Tucker said, "they ain't no Christmas tree no more. It's the beginning of March."

The deep-sunken eyes seemed to search for the source of Orvile's voice. The parchment hands fluttered momentarily on the lap robe, and Orvile tried not to look at them. They were like a pair of old, discarded leather gloves, wrinkled and empty. And the fingernails. When Orvile could bring himself to clean them, they reminded him of ten tiny tortoiseshells, ridged and hard as glass. Yet brittle as overdone pie dough.

Worst of all was the face. The bones under the eyes and the cartilage under the nose seemed about to split the blue-veined skin, to burst out. He no longer had his mustache. Doc Cronin had ordered it shorn because little ulcers were forming on the lip under the hair. So Dylan Price shaved him while he was in one of his deep morphine stupors, and he never noticed the loss. Or if he did, he said nothing.

Orvile was cutting his hair short now because it had been difficult to keep clean when it was long. Orvile and Dylan Price and Hasford Crozier bathed him in the big kitchen tub, and it took all three for the job, because although his arms looked like chicken wings after the skin had been peeled off, he could develop amazing strength, and he always fought against getting a bath.

On the day when Roman Hasford realized the Christmas tree was gone, Orvile had been trying to feed him milktoast, which he refused to eat, and suddenly he sat straight, his deeply hidden eyes glinted, and he said, "Somebody's coming."

And it was true. Because as everything else had deteriorated, his hearing had become more acute, more foxlike.

It was Sheriff Colin Hamp, met on the west porch by Dylan Price and Hasford Crozier. Colin said he had a telegraph message he reckoned Mr. Hasford ought to see.

"Come down off that horse, then, and inside, and tread gently," said Dylan Price.

Colin Hamp went only as far as the parlor door, then stayed there, hat in hand, as Dylan Price took the yellow flimsy paper and held it for Roman Hasford to see.

"I can't read it, the light in here's so bad. Read it to me."

So Dylan Price stood in the parlor, where the winter sun glared in brilliant morning light through the windows, and read it.

" 'To Sheriff, Benton County, Arkansas, in your interest re Gourdville bank robbery and homicide stop male white man identified Yancy Crane apprehended by Pinkertons this city last day February on outstanding Federal warrant charging sale of liquor Indian Territory held in custody United States detention barracks here pending communications with Fort Smith authorities on possible extradition and trial Benton County on capital charges stop before completion this procedure said detainee found hanged in barracks stop no suicide stop hands tied behind back stop no leads on culpability other inmates stop request information next of kin for disposition of remains stop Clelland Burnett United States Marshal, Eastern District of Kansas, Topeka.' "

Roman Hasford bent forward, blinking his eyes. His fingers moved on the lap robe, then were still. A smile slowly spread across the tight skin of his face and there was a hollow sound from his chest, a chuckle, a dry, rustling chuckle like old leaves in the wind.

"Pinkertons. Pinkertons. Yes, yes, yes. That son of a bitch never stops. I wanted him to stop."

He sat back in the chair and sighed, his fingers moving again, spasmodically.

"Can somebody write a letter for me? Light so damned bad in here."

Dylan Price turned back to Colin Hamp, still standing in the door, hat in hand, and passed the yellow flimsy paper to him and nodded.

"Thank you, Sheriff."

"You can tell him," Colin Hamp said, as though Roman Hasford wasn't sitting there immediately before him but was off in some distant place, "that I already telegraphed them Topeka people and said there wasn't no next of kin here. So I reckon they'll bury old Yancy in their own graveyard."

"Yes, I'll tell him. We're much obliged."

Then, having dismissed the sheriff, Dylan Price went to the library table and took out paper and quill and ink bottle and sat down in what was usually Roman's chair and said, "What should I write?"

"I know. But I've gotta be sure," Roman said. "He always had a bunch of Pinkertons around. I know. But I've gotta be sure. Listen. This letter. On Number Six. Tonight."

Dylan Price turned to Orvile Tucker, who had been standing in one corner through all of this.

"Number Six the northbound passenger train," Orvile said.

"Aw yes, I remember now," said Dylan Price, and, turning his face back to Roman Hasford, asked again. "What should I write?"

It took three train changes before that letter would arrive in Topeka. It would take three for any reply coming back. But the whole process required less than two weeks.

Dylan Price himself had spoken to postmaster Walter Matt, explaining that there might not be much time left, so when the response came, if indeed one did, speed was necessary. The return letter should be sent by special dispatch to Catrina Hills Farm immediately on arrival.

Walter Matt then explained the regulations regarding the postal service, and added that he had never really cared much for Roman Hasford anyway. Whereupon Dylan Price explained that he would himself pay for a special courier, and if Walter Matt was not willing to assist in expediting such a thing for a dying man, then he, Dylan Price, would knock out all of Walter Matt's front teeth with his fists.

Walter Matt, not being a combative man, began to watch the contents of incoming mailbags very carefully after this, and when he saw the envelope with a Kansas Pacific Railroad motif and the stamp canceled in Topeka, Kansas, he personally took the letter to Ennis Lugi's stable. There the envelope was placed in the hands of Hargen Meeks, who, when he wasn't helping his father-in-law shoe horses or driving the surrey taxi about town, was available for quick horseback dashes about the county for a price, which Walter Matt assured him the new roughneck at Catrina Hills Farm would pay.

Throughout this time, Orvile Tucker was appalled because Roman had moved into his bed upstairs and never left it. Orvile took up poached eggs and brought them down again, untouched. Orvile took up pots of tea, then brought them down again, untouched.

And now the morphine was being administered by Dylan Price because Roman was unable any longer to do it himself.

On the day when Hargen Meeks rode up with the envelope from Topeka, it was raining. Dylan Price walked onto the porch to take the letter and to pay Hargen Meeks, then send him back to town, although it was obvious that Hargen Meeks was anxious to be present during the opening of the letter. Dylan Price called Orvile Tucker from the kitchen and they both went up to the room where Roman lay without seeming to breathe, staring at the ceiling.

"It's here," Dylan Price said.

Roman Hasford, even in his present state, needed no explanation. "Read it," he said.

As Dylan Price carefully opened the envelope, Orvile Tucker stood well back, looking at Roman. Roman's hands had suddenly become agitated, moving about on the bedcovers above his belly where the demon ate, hands white and colorless, twitching like bleached spiders lost from their webs.

"Read it."

" 'Topeka, Kansas. March 17, 1899. For Roman Hasford,' " Dylan Price began. " 'One can suppose a kind of poetic justice that our old friend Y.C., who attempted to murder us both, should pause too long and be too drunk in Topeka as he was traveling through to God only knows where.

" 'As to your question. You must surely know by now that I have many close associates in Topeka. Pinkerton detectives, peace officers, judges, turnkeys, and habitual inmates of our jails. The latter of which are most willing to perform many little duties for appropriate remuneration. I fear these are most unsavory men who do not shirk from any opportunity for recompense, no matter how distasteful the task.' "

Roman broke in, raising one skeletal hand.

"That part. Read that part again."

And Dylan Price did.

"Inmates of jails most willing to do . . ."

"Yes, yes, yes. The son of a bitch. He did it. He *did* it. All these years gone by, but still he did it. Go on, go on. Read the rest."

And Dylan Price did.

" 'Through the good offices of my many acquaintances in the Federal marshal's office, I have other information for you. These authorities have been most helpful and have always maintained files on persons who at one time or another have offended the peace and dignity of the United States.

" 'Courtland Brown died in the Detroit penitentiary during the first year of his incarceration. Drake Brown died last year from complications of an old head wound, about which I need not instruct you. Sarah Brown, who seems indestructible, is in eastern Michigan, inmate of an insane asylum for the indigent.

" 'So, a business concluded, long overdue.

" 'On a personal note, I am feeling the ravages of passing years, but living well enough on returns from my railroad stocks. And unconcerned about all those people who would gladly have seen me drawn and quartered because now they have all died of old age or gone blind for the same reason.

" 'The doctors are constantly refitting me with an artificial left arm and hand. My first one was attached to the stump during the time when I was recovering from being shot and dumped in that Indian Territory river. Each time since, they have become more sophisticated. The one I wear now is a medical marvel of cork and wood and wires and porcelain. It is the only part of my anatomy not constantly exhausted.' "

"Wait, wait, wait," Roman broke in again, his voice croaking weakly. "Read that part again, about recovering."

And Dylan Price did. And as he did, Roman almost sat up in bed, a sharp little hacking laugh shaking his chest.

"Yes, yes, yes," he said. "I knew it. Nobody said it was a one-armed man behind the coffee grinder that night. Because he had *two* arms. And those damned gray suede gloves he always wore. On a cork hand. I knew. My God. Read the rest."

And Dylan Price did.

" 'It is unlikely I will see you again. We have effected many things together. Some good. Perhaps some not so good. However, there are many people who remember that we passed by.

" 'And now farewell, Roman Hasford. I am still your friend.' "

That was all. But Roman, even with his head on the pillow, seemed to lean forward for more.

"Did he sign his name?"

"No."

The harsh little laugh came again, then choked off into a weak cough.

"He knew you'd know who he was," said Dylan Price, although Dylan Price had no idea who it was who had sent the letter except for the name he had written on the letter sent from here less than two weeks before. But it didn't matter. Because now something else did. Dylan Price bent close to Roman Hasford's face, then turned to Orvile Tucker.

"Get Bishop Eckor into town now, for Doc Cronin. Quick, man, quick."

"He didn't sign his letter," Roman Hasford whispered.

It rained all day. And into the night. And was still raining at dawn. The sound was like a whisper on the roof. The smell was like April, although it was still only mid-March. The windows were open and the curtains drawn back, and from the barns came the sounds of mares making their voices heard before dropping the foals in a few weeks.

Toward the east, toward the old Hasford farm, there were crows sounding their rasping calls from bare branches, as though making a farewell to winter before the new leaves came. And to the west, the whistle of a locomotive coming into the grade crossing at Gourdville.

Twice, as they stood about the bed, Roman Hasford seemed to laugh. It was a sound unlike any they had ever heard. Then once, after laughing, Roman spoke as clearly as he ever had.

"Orvile?"

Orvile came to the bed, and for just a quick moment Roman's eyes focused on him clear and sure, focused on the great, wet face.

"Stay close to me," Roman said. And Orvile Tucker stayed, on his knees beside the bed, holding one of the parchment hands between his thick black fingers.

"I don't want to be alone," Roman said.

Dylan Price bent over him and said, because Orvile Tucker was incapable of saying it, "You're not alone. We're here."

Hasford Crozier was there. Bishop Eckor was there. And Orvile and Dylan and Doc Cronin. Everyone that could be found in a hurry. But no Judge Shadbolt, executor of this great estate. And not Catrina or Calpurnia or Diana or Berdeen Chesney Tage. Or anybody else that had ever mattered. Or would soon matter.

Once there was an intense convulsion of pain, and Doc Cronin administered a massive dose of morphine, pulling up the comforter to expose a bony foot and calf. Then, in a moment, Roman Hasford was calm.

Once, he said, "Mama."

And at the last, his eyes opened wide in their deep pits and there was an expression of dismay and wonder on his skull-like face.

"What have we done?" he asked weakly. "What have we done?"

Then he muttered his last words.

"Jared Dane."

EPILOGUE

The House on the Knoll

It was November again, and the north wind out of Missouri was giving its annual whispered warning under the eaves of the house that the days of real winter were close behind.

Dylan Price sat in one of the Old Man's beechwood rockers, on the west quadrant of the porch, taking advantage of what little warmth came from a weak afternoon sun. Across his lap was one of the heavy, quilted robes that the Old Man had often used to the same purpose, to keep legs and feet warm. But not now, as then, to conceal a jug of sour-mash whiskey or a cocked single-action pistol.

Now it was past the time for constant whiskey and constant weapon, each of those in plentiful supply but safely locked in cabinets within the house, the one taken out only for occasional sips, the other only for cleaning and oiling, Dylan Price still being enough of the old soldier to keep weapons in proper condition, even if there was no expectation of their use.

On the floor beside him was the daily newspaper, and the wind played with its pages gently. From inside, Dylan Price could hear the muted scoldings and arguments and consultations of the black house servants, all in a dither of excitement in preparation for a large party on this very night in honor of the man having a nap in an upstairs bedroom, under the very same feather tick Dylan Price himself had used on his first night spent in this place. Eben Pay, just appointed United States Attorney for the Western District of Arkansas and now visiting his old comrade of the Spanish war and his cousin Berdeen, the Mistress of Catrina Hills Farm. From time to time Dylan Price could hear Berdeen's voice. Berdeen, his wife, the mother of his children; Berdeen, who always gave the hired help instructions in the same precise, rather harsh yet somehow gentle tone Dylan Price had come to associate with her father, Roman Hasford.

Dylan Price was not unlike most old soldiers. He was an addict of reverie. Now, waiting for Eben Pay to awaken and come down, he allowed his mind to go free, let woolgathering consume his half-asleep thinking, such a pleasant thing for former soldiers, and for the Welsh as well.

Most of the Old Settlers in this county were dead. Dylan Price knew that the few who remained found it impossible to believe there was no longer an Indian Territory just beyond the western horizon. For in the year 1907 the Five Civilized Tribes Nations had combined with Oklahoma Territory to form the forty-sixth state of the Federal Union.

As for the younger generation, he knew as well that they were more concerned with things younger than the Indian Territory. Which younger things were made known to them through the pages of State Senator Patrick Macky's *Daily Dispatch*, a copy of which was on the floor beside him now. The paper that had been fluttering noisily in the wind. Dylan Price smiled. Pat Macky would like that, his newspaper making noise even as it lay unread.

Theodore Roosevelt was much in those pages spun off Pat Macky's new presses. President now, the hero of San Juan Hill. At that thought, Dylan Price muttered an obscenity to the old soldier inside himself. But there were better thoughts. That new canal called T.R.'s Big Ditch. Yellow fever conquered.

Dylan Price had known the tropics back when the Jack was a prime killer, before there was the children's toy called a teddy bear, named for the old commander of the Rough Riders. Rough Riders. That produced another unspoken obscenity.

Well, thought Dylan Price, T.R. has no corner on nationalistic enthusiasm. In Great Britain, Queen Victoria dead and her fat playboy son Edward VII king, the British were launching a magnificent battleship called HMS *Dreadnought*, a ship so powerful that some said it marked the effective end of naval warfare because nothing could stand against it. Dylan Price doubted that.

Other great ships, too. Floating hotels. One was called *Lusitania*. Everybody was going crazy building ships. T.R's Great White Fleet. And in Europe, in addition to all those huge vessels, boats that sailed beneath the surface. Submarines. Especially in Germany.

Flexing muscle, Dylan Price thought, and having served in a red coat during Victoria's time of empire, he knew a great deal about muscle-flexing. All those armies.

And crazy happenings. Not long ago they'd executed a man in Auburn Penitentiary in an electrically charged chair. Imagine, Dylan Price had heard locals say, a crazy thing like that instead of a good, reliable rope. Imagine, they said, replacing old Judge Parker's gallows in Fort Smith with a piece of furniture!

The new gasoline-engine automobile was everywhere now, although when it first came here to northwest Arkansas, all the fuel had to be shipped in cans from Pennsylvania. You can't go out in the woods and chop it down, the people said with considerable disgust. Just when everybody had become accustomed to the railroad train, they bring in that noisy, foul-smelling horseless carriage that can go all kinds of places unexpected and along the way scaring hell out of the livestock and the kids.

The first gasoline-powered automobile had appeared exactly where everyone thought it would. At Catrina Hills Farm. At that time it was only the second internal-combustion device in northwest Arkansas, the first being at Hiram Chesney's sawmill.

Dylan Price had been aware that people of the county had expected to see the mistress of Catrina Hills Farm wherever they saw an automobile back then. And me at the tiller, he thought. Yes, a tiller, just like a damned boat, only it was at the front end and not the rear. At least now, he thought, the one we have is equipped with a steering wheel.

Another thing, people calling the house about automobiles passing and causing their hens to stop laying. Even after there were two dozen such machines in the county, they still called the house on that damned telephone. As though Berdeen had, along with all her other power, the ability to regulate the laying of hens.

Always on the anniversary of the Old Man's funeral, they'd drive to the Hasford farmstead so that Berdeen could lay flowers on the graves of people she had never known but who had started her on her course. And Dylan Price was not unaware that on those trips there was an inordinate number of people out along the Elkhorn Tavern Road or Wire Road, there to watch them pass.

At least, thank God for small favors, nobody called her "the bastard" anymore. Maybe because a lot of the younger group didn't even know it. And maybe because the older group realized how an insistence on calling her that was a good bet that bad things could happen to a person. Not the kind of bad things that could have happened when Roman Hasford was alive, when people went about carrying firearms, but bad enough to result in a broken jaw administered by Dylan Price himself.

But maybe none of that had anything to do with it. Maybe she wasn't called "the bastard" anymore because there was respect that went with being the mistress of Catrina Hills, the richest person in all the county, and beyond too. Even richer than Leland Commanger, who owned the bank. Well, he owned part of it. The mistress owned the rest. And land, a lot of that, and securities and stocks and bonds held in St. Louis and Kansas City banks, and a thriving horse farm, thanks mostly to me, Dylan Price thought.

After the Old Man died, he thought, I have not been exactly inert, nor was I even before he passed on to his glory, or whatever it was he passed on to.

Now there wasn't anybody in the county who didn't know who she was. The Old Man's daughter. However that knowledge was come by, and there had once been a lot of stories about it, most of them far from the mark, they knew who she was.

Dylan Price dozed off, the lap robe keeping him warm, the drone of voices from inside the house a comforting, reassuring sound. But it went on in his dreams, half wakeful, half in sleep.

They said in this county that although Berdeen might own everything, Dylan Price owned her. When he heard that, from his sources of information equally as effective as the Old Man's had been in his time, Dylan Price's mouth grew hard and his eyes became brittle. Because he knew that nobody, nohow, nowhere, owned Berdeen.

Berdeen Chesney Tage Price was her name now. But the few Old Settlers remaining said "Tage" should be scratched out and "Hasford" put in there someplace. Because she was Ora and Martin's granddaughter. But only the few remaining Old Settlers worried about it. Nobody else. They just called her the mistress of Catrina Hills Farm, and most of them weren't even aware of where that name for the horse ranch had come from much less that "mistress" had been coined as a term of derision.

But by God, everybody said, she owned it all. Automobile and stud horses, whitewashed fences and plowed fields. Lock, stock, and barrel. Whole hog and squeal.

The terms of the Old Man's will were never published outright in Patrick Macky's newspaper, although folks figured Macky knew a lot about it. But there were little hints. And as time went on, and not much time at that, some of the things were obvious. And other items slipped out, word of mouth.

As they always do, the people said.

The source of a lot of information was Hazel Chesney. She was the daughter of Doc Cronin, who had attended Roman Hasford as he was dying of cancer and who had died himself just a year later. Hazel had to know a lot, being the aunt of the mistress and Doc's daughter besides, and Hazel had never been famous in the county for keeping her mouth shut.

So everybody knew the entire Hasford fortune had been willed to the bastard Berdeen and her heirs in perpetuity. And part of that perpetuity was twin boys, one named Roman after Berdeen's daddy and the other named Llewellyn after Dylan Price's daddy. Which seemed just fine to everybody, even though they couldn't spell one of the names with any accuracy.

People still watched the Big House. Just as in the old days. But for a different reason. Then it had been to see what might happen next with the Trouble. Now, not many people knew what the Trouble was, but they watched because folks always watch the richest woman in the county.

Then, not many people had been inside that house on the knoll at Catrina Hills Farm. There was a joke among the Old Settlers that the Old Man was so crazy and jealous of that house that once it was completed he'd had all the workers who'd actually seen the inside taken out and shot and buried in the woods.

But now a lot of people had seen it, inside and out. The Price dinners and holiday parties had become the talk of the county, even of the state, maybe. They were social people, the Prices, and they even attended the Methodist church almost every Sunday. And at Christmas the mistress put on a big party for the kids in the Odd Fellows hall and had food and gifts for everyone.

There were those in the county who said she did it to show off her money to those who'd called her a bastard. But then there were a lot of those visitors to the Big House who didn't know she was a bastard. Horse dealers and their wives from Missouri and Illinois, wearing diamonds and pearls and coming on the Frisco. Or Owen Caulder, from Weedy Rough, with his family. He hadn't known the mistress or her husband either, in the old days, but he'd known her daddy. And he knew the house and its books. He always spent as much time there as he did with his sisters Gwen and Glamorgan.

Dylan Price knew all these things, sleeping or awake. His sources of information in Gourdville were so good that he often had reports of conversations from essentially hostile places, an irony that made him smile. As from the very first place he had entered in this town, those many years before. Glen Torten's Billiard Parlor.

Berdeen got it all, they said, and she did. Almost. There were those stipulations in the will. About the Old Man's niggers, as everybody called them. A wad of cash for Lark Crozier at Wolf Cove Mill, for instance.

"You ever think about it?" asked one pool shooter. "The Old Man never acted like a man, havin' a woman."

"Yeah, well, remember, that good-lookin' little swamp nigger woman was over there at the Big House ever' week. That little woman wasn't nothin' to turn up your nose about."

"Maybe so. They tell me he went off down south to brang her up here anyways."

"That's what I'm sayin'. It's your shot."

The will. Orvile Tucker had been provided food and clothing and warmth and bed for as long as he lived, right at Catrina Hills Farm, though you'd have thought he'd be dead by now anyway, they said. And Hasford Crozier was majordomo at the Big House now, for as long as he wanted to be, and acting like a school-educated white man, with the mistress letting him read all those books the Old Man had.

There were some other little things. Some cash money for Bishop Eckor and Colin Hamp, because they'd done so much to stop that bank robbery when the Old Man owned the bank. And the Old Settlers said he'd have given former sheriff Hamlin Bidd a few dollars, too—even though Hamlin hadn't been able to arrest anybody after Roman Hasford's friend Elmer Scaggs was murdered— except by the time the Old Man died, Hamlin Bidd had been dead for two years.

"Dropped dead prunin' apple trees," said the pool shooter.

"That's why I never pruned no trees," said the other. "Nine ball in the side pocket."

"My kin never had no use for the Old Man. But I say now, when that woman come back up here from Texas, before the Old Man died, she never went to see him. First time she ever set foot in his house was at the funeral."

"Well, hell, she went to the funeral, anyways."

"So did ever'body else in the county. But, hell, she mighta done more than just ride her horse past the Old Man's place before he died."

"Maybe she didn't even know the Old Man was her daddy."

"The hell she didn't. She knew. She knew. Eight ball in the corner."

And there was speculation about Eben Pay, too.

"That lawyer from Fort Smith always comin' up here," said one pool shooter.

"Yeah, Eben Pay. Calpurnia Hasford's son. He's the Old Man's nephew."

"They go to Fort Smith all the time, too. On the Frisco."

"Sure, to visit that Eben Pay and other folks down there, I hear. Her husband and Eben Pay, they was together in Cuba."

"Well, that Eben Pay or whatever, he never come up here when the Old Man was alive, did he?"

"Not's I know of."

"Well, she got it all now, and maybe this Eben Pay comin' back to get some for his ownself."

Such thoughts were not new to Dylan Price, even in his own bed, his wife beside him. He had begun, with the Old Man's death, to invite the Fort Smith attorney to the house, and initially it was at considerable irritation from Berdeen, who always opined that here was Eben Pay, only about eighty miles away by Frisco line, yet the man had never come to visit his uncle, her daddy. But Dylan Price, speaking to her as though he were a platoon sergeant instructing a recruit on the function of a magazine rifle, always pointed out that it had been through the good offices of Eben Pay that he himself had shown up in northwest Arkansas in the first place to become friend and confidant of Roman Hasford, and then husband to Roman Hasford's daughter.

After a time, Berdeen saw the justice of this, perhaps all too aware of the fact that she herself had not ever come into this home of her father to say hello before he died, even after she became aware that she was his daughter.

Besides, she soon found that Cousin Eben, as she came to call him, was a very personable and urbane man. Maybe there was flowing in her veins some of that fierce and uncompromising family loyalty that had marked her grandmother Ora Hasford. So now, this party celebrating Eben Pay's advancement in the legal world.

And now, a new-found family curiosity too.

Once, Berdeen said to Dylan Price, "Who is this Jared Dane? I've found his name in some of Father's letters and in the diary. I think we should invite him here."

"No," said Dylan Price. "Even if he were still alive, which I doubt, you want nothing absolutely to do with Jared Dane. From what I know, Jared Dane would scare you completely out of your bloomers."

"But he was Father's friend."

"And more's the pity. Leave that sleeping dog lie, wherever he might be."

"No one who was Father's friend could be that bad."

"I think perhaps he could."

This dreaming and woolgathering ended when Eben Pay touched Dylan Price's shoulder to wake him and announce that now he was refreshed and ready to pay respects to the graves of his grand-parents—and, almost incidentally, that of his uncle Roman.

So Dylan Price rose, throwing off the lap robe, and they walked to the horse barns, where the automobile was housed in what was called a garage. After much coughing and smoke, which terrified the horses, sending them about their pens whistling and kicking fences, Dylan Price and Eben Pay drove out onto the Elkhorn Tavern Road and turned east toward the old Hasford farm.

They left the automobile on Wire Road, below the old Hasford farmhouse, which the mistress had rented to the grandson of Isaac Maddox and his young wife, along with one hundred acres, and walked up to the clearing behind the house, where the three grave-stones stood gray sentinels.

Dylan Price and Eben Pay stood before the graves, hats off, and the breeze moved their hair. After a while, Eben Pay began to read the carved inscriptions on the stones, aloud. With a kind of detached reverence. Maybe because he had never known any of these people, who were his own people.

He read the first two and then paused for a long time. And then read the third.

" 'Roman Hasford. 1846–1899. R.I.P.' "

Then paused.

From beyond Wire Road they could hear somebody working a mule, pulling stumps out of a field that had grown corn and wheat under Hasford hands before the Civil War. And in this very clearing, near the old house, the Price twins had found old bullets and artillery shards.

"Doesn't seem like very much," said Eben Pay. " 'Rest in Peace.' "

"It never is," said Dylan Price.

"It seems there should be more."

"You've seen that little tintype portrait?"

"Yes."

"It's fading. Yes, fading it is, until no features are distinguishable. A sad pity."

"Yes. The only view of him we have, I suppose."

"Not all," Dylan Price said. "She found an old diary he wrote in Kansas."

Eben Pay looked at Dylan Price.

"I'd like to read that."

Dylan Price laughed.

"Little chance you'd do. She won't let me see it. And now she's even taken the tintype and hid it from me. So only she can watch him disappear."

They stood a moment longer. A flight of bully jays flew into the cedars, scattering cardinals like scarlet and orange flower petals before a gale. Dylan Price bent down and found an apple-sized rock and threw it, and the jays flew off, scolding, into the high timber along the eastern ridge, going on toward the White River.

"I'd like to read that diary," said Eben Pay.

"Oh, I don't think she'll do. It's a very private thing between herself and her Da."

Eben Pay pulled his hat down onto his head, looking once more at the gravestones of his people. "Well, he didn't get to see the new century, did he?"

"No," said Dylan Price. "I doubt it worried him. He'd seen more than enough problems in the old."

They turned away then and moved around the house, the Maddox woman peeking at them from the kitchen window. Then down through the grove of old locust trees and to the road where the automobile waited, looking strangely out of place here on this road where Dylan Price knew from all he had learned that Yankee and Rebel soldiers had passed, where the old Butterfield stagecoach had churned up dust, where Ora Hasford and her young son had ridden their wagon, Ora with the mule's reins firmly in her strong hands, going for an afternoon's visit to Elkhorn Tavern.

Jones, Douglas C.
   Come Winter

(1)

DATE DUE			
DEC 3 '89			
FEB 1 2 1990			
MAR 1 4 1990			
JUN 1 9 1990			
AUG − 1 1990			
OCT 1 5 1990			
NOV 1 5 1990			
JUN 2 5 1991			